The thane whirled to se̲͟e̲͟ ╌╌╌╌╌╌╌╌╌╌ another of the Hylar warrio̲r̲s̲.̲ ̲T̲h̲e̲ ̲d̲w̲a̲r̲f̲ ̲m̲oaned in terror as the tendrils of darkness slammed together—and then he was gone, in a shocking instant. Empty armor tumbled to the floor like a useless shell.

Capper Whetstone lunged and swung his axe with crushing force, but the weapon passed right through the vaporous apparition. The captain of the guard stumbled back an instant before a lashing limb of darkness could reach him.

CHAOS WAR SERIES

The Last Thane

by Douglas Niles

The Last Thane
©1998 TSR, Inc.
©2001 Wizards of the Coast, Inc.

Distributed in the United States by Holtzbrinck Publishing. Distributed in Canada by Fenn Ltd.

Distributed to the hobby, toy, and comic trade in the United States and Canada by regional distributors.

Distributed worldwide by Wizards of the Coast, Inc. and regional distributors.

Cover art by Todd Lockwood
First Printing: June 1998
Library of Congress Catalog Card Number: 97-062371

9 8 7 6 5 4 3 2

ISBN: 0-7869-1172-7
620-08393

U.S., CANADA,
ASIA, PACIFIC, & LATIN AMERICA
Wizards of the Coast, Inc.
P.O. Box 707
Renton, WA 98057-0707
+1-800-324-6496

EUROPEAN HEADQUARTERS
Wizards of the Coast, Belgium
P.B. 2031
2600 Berchem
Belgium
+32-70-23-32-77

Visit our web site at **www.wizards.com/dragonlance**

Prologue

A melon swelled at the end of a twisted vine. The moist orb grew rapidly, as emerald darkened to shadowed purple. The sphere distended, bulging oblong, finally bursting into a soft pile of stinking viscera. The fetid stuff was momentarily black on the colorless soil, but the stain faded quickly.

The garden was in bloom, a checkerboard of colored swaths mounding the ghost-white terrain. But this was not the white of purity, of clean linen and bleached paper. Instead this terrain was like colorless death, maggots crawling in vile ordure or blind eyeballs milked by disease. It was a shade lacking in beauty, vibrancy, or any kind of vitality.

Even so, to the lone observer the garden was a place of sublime beauty and marvelous, chaotic perfection. Zarak Thuul's eyes were red, the hot crimson of deep-seated coals fanned by a breath of air, and they now flared brightly as the cycle of corrupt life was enacted again, as hideous fruit once more swelled and writhed upon the land.

Now the garden was also claimed by twisted, flailing trees. Leafless and bleak, the trunks curled through grotesque gyrations until limbs drooped, laden with obscene fruit. Dropping like overripe plums, the growths splatted onto ground that was soon covered in a layer of soft muck. Then the trees turned against each other, reaching with tortured, lashing limbs, branches landing vicious blows. One trunk shrieked as it was splintered by the pull of two neighboring trees. Another, roots breaking free of the yielding turf, toppled into the rot and trembled as the effluent seared the bark and hissed with caustic fury into the fleshy timber.

Zarak Thuul was pleased, for rarely did his garden produce two gratifying harvests in such rapid succession. For moments such as this did he endure the rest of his bleak existence, surviving until his life could once again have meaning. For this he would tolerate the nothingness of the Abyss, the enforced idleness that had already spanned millennia. No matter how great the interval, he reminded himself, his was a confinement that one day must end.

And then fire blazed through the dark sky, and the daemon warrior threw back his head, laughing in pure exultation. The meteoric blaze curled in a wide arc, trailing sparks, embers, and a churning maelstrom of overheated air, spiraling downward in a graceful path, gliding closer and closer to the red-eyed watcher. As the aerial flames descended, broad wings became visible, gossamer foils outlined in shimmers of heat, widespread and uptilted to catch the draft raised by their own infernal presence. The roaring swelled, like a furnace cast open to admit the sudden force of the bellows, and now Zarak Thuul felt the fire on his face, on the perfect black skin of his chest and belly and sexless groin. He raised his hands in greeting, but only as the blaze halted before him did he fully discern the creature within that cloud of fire.

A crocodilian head, with skull and skin outlined in living flame, rose on a serpentine neck. Liquid skin flowed, a surface of oily fire. Vast wings were folded against monstrous flanks as a tail of crackling blaze curled inward, casting sparks onto the daemon's naked feet. Zarak Thuul felt the heat as the kiss of a hungry lover.

"Ah, Primus, my pet. I fear you are too late to enjoy a splendid blooming."

The fire dragon snorted, smoke and embers bursting over the mouldering landscape. "Gardens are too tame for me. Can we not take to the air and cast fire through the Abyss?" The statement began contemptuously but closed on a note of pleading.

Zarak Thuul laid a coal-black hand upon the silky neck. Tendrils of flame curled through his fingers, caressing his wrist and forearm as he allowed his touch to soothe the creature. Yet as he contemplated his answer, his thoughts were far from content.

"You know I must remain . . . that I am bidden," he whispered, the sound a harsh growl.

"Bah! The queen has other things to concern her. She knows not whether you stay in your cage or depart to relish the breadth of our dark domain. Come—come with me, now!" The fire dragon lowered the broad wedge of his head, staring at the daemon warrior's face from the haunted, lightless sockets of its eyes.

"We are a curious pair, you and I," demurred the daemon, his own eyes firing into hot yellow as he met the beseeching gaze. "You, all fire and light, except for those eyes."

"And you the black of lightless death," the fire dragon responded ironically, "except for those eyes."

3

Their gaze held for timeless moments, and in that interval the daemon warrior knew a power of emotion that, surprisingly, was even more gratifying than a rush of pure hatred or the thrill that inevitably followed the spilling of hot, fresh blood. Companions for as many eras as Krynn had ever known, the pair spoke to each other with expressions of fire and shadow, and for a long time they had no need for words.

"But the queen does not forget," Zarak Thuul said finally, knowing that the dragon already understood the anguish in his words. "She remains the mistress of the Abyss, and so long as I am here, to her rule I must submit."

Primus snorted again, his mighty wings partially unfurling with a swath of dry, baking heat. The mulch on the ground steamed, and where it lay beneath the span of those wings it bubbled and burned into a sooty black. Quickly that darkness faded, ashes whisked away by an otherwise unnoticed breeze, until the ground underneath the great serpent was again washed in dead white, slightly rosy here and there from the reflection of seething flame.

"They say the queen has other matters, forces that draw her attention away from the Abyss. They say she makes another campaign upon Krynn, this time with a legion of knights who fight in her name—"

"And they say this time she will win." Zarak Thuul completed the statement with stark bitterness. "Her enemies are reeling before her. Even here in my exile I know that Palanthas has fallen to her armies. And they have taken as well that tower the Solamnics thought they could hold forever."

Zarak Thuul spit, his acidic drool landing with a hiss upon the mouldering rot. Though he felt no affection for the enemies of Takhisis, Queen of Darkness, he knew her ultimate triumph would inevitably leave her bored again. And when she was bored, she took an overly intrusive view into the lives of her minions—and of those, such as the daemon warrior, who were not her minions, but who had the misfortune to exist in the Abyss, the place where above all others the queen's will held sway.

"It may be that she will not be the victor in this war," suggested Primus, with a shadowy squint of his fire-rimmed eyes. "For there is word that the Father of Us All has awakened and will take a role."

The daemon stiffened, forcing his fingers into the hot flesh of the fire dragon's neck. With a grunt of annoyance Primus tried to twist away, but Zarak Thuul pulled the great head downward to stare commandingly into the serpent's eyes.

"It may be that you have heard something, some news you would do well to impart."

Primus snorted softly, taking pleasure in his advantage. Zarak Thuul tightened his grip, and the fire dragon's exhalation sharpened, tinged by annoyance.

"I am not a dog to be hauled about by a master's hand." The serpent's voice was a low growl, like a bonfire roaring in the distance.

His black face expressionless, the daemon warrior released his grip and took a step backward. "Nor am I a pawn to be toyed with, like some court fool. If you have knowledge, speak it to me. Now!"

Primus exhaled enough heat to bubble another swath of the decaying garden. Fumes swirled around his broad nostrils as he drew another breath, stretching his wings to a majestic pose. Only then did he speak.

"The mortals of Krynn are ever foolish, and now they strive to master their own gods. They think Paladine and the queen will be their saviors, one pitted against the other. But I tell you now: the Father of Chaos himself has been awakened, and his wrath is mighty."

"And he will go to war against his children!" Zarak Thuul saw the promise clearly, clenching a rock hard fist into the palm of his other hand. "Perhaps then may all the legions of Chaos fly to his name!"

5

"Too, surely the lesser gods must fail in strife against their own father," Primus suggested. "For he who gave them life is able to take it away."

"You are right, my fiery pet," the daemon concluded, touching the great wyrm again in affection. "The queen will be occupied with matters elsewhere."

"And thus we, my lord, are free to fly where we wish."

Now the decision was easy.

Zarak Thuul swung gracefully onto the back of the great creature. Tendrils of flame swirled to form a depression, and the daemon sank easily into a comfortable recline. He needed neither saddle nor bridle, for the supple back of the monster shifted obligingly to accommodate the rider. The black of Zarak Thuul's obsidian skin reflected eerily in the cradle of flame, and his eyes glowed like twin spots of burning death, steady and focused and bright even against the inferno that was his monstrous mount.

With a sweep of fire and wing, Primus took to the air. Zarak Thuul crowed aloud, shrieking the wild joy he felt, exulting in the power of the fire dragon's flight, in the speed of ascent. Below lay the tortured domain of the Abyss, realm of the Dark Queen and, for countless eons, the daemon warrior's prison.

But now the mists of ether were a tenuous barrier. He would wait only a little longer, and then he knew that the barrier would part and all the planes of existence would lie open and inviting beyond.

A Thane's House

Chapter One

"Where's my helmet?" Baker Whitegranite whispered to himself. Despite his ill temper, a mood that grew darker with each heartbeat, he kept his voice low. He was not so irritated that he was ready to start a fight with Garimeth, who so far as he knew was napping in the next room.

Instead the dwarf stomped around his spacious study, moving scrolls and parchments, pushing a stack of musty tomes aside, looking under his desk, behind his chair, even in the wooden cabinet that stood near the door. All the while he was cognizant of the steady trickle of the water clock, knowing he had to get down to the Thane's Atrium within two hours. Since it would take nearly half that interval just to descend eighteen levels in the lift, his time was limited.

Exhausting all the crannies in his study, he decided he

had no choice but to step through the door to the sitting room, where—predictably—his wife broke from her light slumber and sat bolt upright on the divan beside the cold hearth.

"I'm sorry to bother you, Gari, but I've looked everywhere," he began, watching her carefully but unable to gauge her reaction. He felt the familiar burning in his gut. "Have you seen the Helm of Tongues?"

Garimeth's wide, pale eyes stared at him, and he was once again reminded of the walleyed coldness that was a dark dwarf's gaze. Why it had never bothered him when he was courting her was a question he had long since ceased to ponder. Now he shrugged, nonplussed by her silence.

"I said, I was—"

"I heard you," she snapped, then snorted wryly. "And I wish I had seen the damn thing. I'd enjoy watching you hunt through all the wrong places."

Baker sighed, removing his spectacles to polish them on the hem of his overshirt, letting his watery eyes fasten on his wife's round, pale face, now comfortably blurred.

"It might be in the cedar wardrobe," he declared, ignoring her taunt and moved by a sudden remembrance.

"To the Abyss with your stupid toy!" Garimeth cried, rising to her feet and fixing him with those wide, milky eyes. She stepped closer so that her glare was no longer softened by his astigmatism. "Sometimes I think you would sit there and play with your scrolls and your translations even if the city were falling down around you!"

The words stung, probably because they resonated very close to the truth. Quickly Baker felt the cold, hard shell close around his heart. It was a shield he wore too often, yet even now a trace of the old hurt, the pain that used to wrack his days and torment his nights, broke through the defenses and rose into his voice. He shoved his glasses back onto his face

"I will be treated with respect!" he declared carefully. "I

8

am the acting thane of the Hylar, and I will not allow you to scorn me!"

"Acting thane? Then why do you spend so much time looking into the past, seeking ancient lairs and forgotten legends?" sneered Garimeth. "It's as though you were afraid of your throne!"

"It is a seat of high honor," Baker snapped. "Until my cousin returns I shall treat it with the respect it deserves—as will my wife!"

"For me to honor the chair I would have to honor the dwarf who holds it." Her tone was as cold as her eyes.

"Why then are you here?" demanded the thane bluntly. "What brought you from the home of your own clan to join me in Hybardin?"

"You had a certain style back then, something I admired." Her tone made it clear that the "something" was no longer a consideration. "And even Hybardin had its appeals for me."

"And still does," he goaded, "compared to the lightless hole of Daerforge."

Her laugh was dry and derisive. "Light is overrated. Besides, I have received word from Daerbardin—where my own brother soon will take hold of a real throne!"

He knew she had her spies and didn't ask how she had gained the information. "Your brother is undoubtedly dead, or he will be soon," he retorted instead, feeling a guilty flush of pleasure as the remark brought a momentary twinge of fear to his wife's small, tight mouth. The throne of Clan Daergar could only be won through a series of deadly duels, and they both knew the odds of a candidate's survival were slim.

Her features twisted, and he saw he had provoked her into a rage. Wildly she looked around, and Baker quickly snatched up her decanter of wine, depriving her of the only ready weapon. And at the same time he felt his own rage erupt. He raised the bottle, ready to throw, and then slowly the emotion faded. Though still burning beneath the power of his self-control, it was no longer a lethal force.

"Why don't you go to your brother now?" he growled. "Leave me, leave the city of the Hylar, and return to the darkness!"

"In a heartbeat, 'my lord thane,' " she mocked. "But for the fact that here I have made my life, and here lives my son!"

The last words broke his shell to pieces and left Baker drained and numb, with no spirit for war with his wife. He turned toward his own dressing chamber, anxious for nothing now but to put distance between himself and his enemy.

He decided to go down to the Thane's Atrium even before he had to. The helm was forgotten as he collected his royal stamp, donned his robe, and departed his house.

Partly to avoid his wife and partly because he needed a touch of serenity, he left through the side door into the garden. Here he took time to relish the cool damp air, the mist swirling along the ceiling that domed up to fifteen feet overhead. As always, the soothing presence of his dark-bred ferns and the clumps of round mushrooms cooled his agitation and steadied his nerves.

The centerpiece of his garden was the fountain that surged gently upward, trickling steadily under natural pressure, waters gathering in a bowl to spill through fluted spouts across a variety of small pools. They were not just any waters, for this was a fountain of phosphorescence, clear liquid that possessed a soft, innate brightness. The streams ran from pool to pool like pathways of pale lights, creating a glowing spiderweb on the floor of the wide garden chamber.

By the time he passed through the gate from the garden onto the street he was in fairly high spirits. The lift station was quite a few blocks away, and as he walked he met and greeted many Hylar on the uncrowded streets. Yet he moved without a bodyguard or an escort of any kind; mountain dwarves at peace were an unpretentious people.

But were they in fact at peace? He allowed his worries to intrude into his thoughts, wondering about his cousin Glade Hornfel Kytil. How fared the true thane and his mighty army? Had they encountered the enemy they had marched forth to face? And when would they be back?

These questions bothered him as he rode the smooth mechanism down the shaft bored through the bedrock of the Life-Tree.

As if in answer to his silent fears, at the Level Ten lift station he met a messenger, a young dwarf on his way from the Thane's Atrium to Baker's residence far above.

"My lord! There is a missive, from Thane Hornfel! He sent a courier on dragonback, and he arrived in the Life-Tree but this past hour!"

In a few more minutes Baker had hurried to the Atrium where he learned that a brave Hylar courier had in fact risked many dangers to bring this letter to Thorbardin. After insuring that the weary and travel-stained dwarf was getting a hot meal and a much-needed bath, Baker took his seat on the royal throne. A servant handed him a parchment and then respectfully withdrew.

Baker Whitegranite looked at the parchment and drew a deep breath, certain that he wasn't going to like what he was about to read. He removed his crystal spectacles, polishing them carefully as he stared around the blurred surroundings of the thane's royal receiving room. Puffing on the lenses, he made sure they were meticulously clean before perching them once more on the bridge of his large nose. For a moment he stared at the wall, at the display of weapons and shields that had snapped back into focus.

But he knew there was nothing to be gained by delay.

My Dearest Cousin,

I will be blunt: We arrived too late in Palanthas. Blame it on the storms that hampered our passage around the Cape of Caergoth, or curse the blue dragons that struck our fleet on the approaches to the Bay of Branchala. Or say it was the fault of fractious Thorbardin, if you will, because the mountain dwarves of all the clans cried the danger to the world but in the end allowed the Hylar to march alone to face the legions of the Dark Queen. (I am still aggrieved that even the Daewar, a clan I had come to trust almost as our own kin, could not find a way to think beyond the stone walls that enclose them.)

Or call it bad timing and leave it at that. In any event, we arrived on northern shores to find that the great city, our objective, the capital of Solamnia and leading beacon of light in the modern world, had fallen. Yes, my cousin, Palanthas is in the hands of the Knights of Takhisis. I can guess your distress as you read these words, for it is the same anguish that gripped my heart and chilled my soul as we drew near to those alabaster walls.

To compound our failure, I must admit that we never reached them. Inevitably, the dragons drove us back. They came in numbers such as we have not seen since the War of the Lance, and they splintered the hull of our flagship with their blasts of lightning. My own son, Arman Kharas, was drowned by this onslaught. I would ask that you hold that piece of news close to your heart, as the times are too troubled for us to reveal that my throne now lacks an heir.

Baker lowered the paper; his hand shook too badly for him to continue reading. Arman, his own cousin—the promise of Thorbardin, a dwarf whose destiny had been to raise the Hylar and the rest of the five clans to heights dwarvenkind had not enjoyed since before the Cataclysm—Arman Kharas was slain. And he'd been killed in a manner more horrifying to a dwarf than any other, for he had died at sea, his feet planted upon a frail wooden hull.

Such a death was a dire event in its own right, but Baker saw immediately that it was also rife with grim omens. With the reluctance of the Daewar to serve in their customary role as trustworthy ally, the clan Hylar was terribly vulnerable to its dark dwarf neighbors.

He looked down at the parchment, at the letters inked in Hornfel's thin, precise hand. Baker knew the slender handwriting was paradoxical, for his thane's brawny forearms and well-muscled shoulders were the clear signs of a fighting man.

"Yet you make your letters like a poet, my cousin," he had told Hornfel, more than once.

Baker again regarded the parchment with apprehension. For the space of several heartbeats he almost believed that if he failed to read the news in the letter it would be as though those events had not occurred. But these were the fantasies of a kender or a human child—certainly not fit subjects for the meditations of a dwarf. Especially not one who suddenly felt the burden of unwanted responsibilities weighing upon himself with suffocating force.

> With the rest of the army, as well as the able accompaniment of the Ten, I retired to the north, making landfall in one of the small coves along the coast. From there, we gleaned word of news to the south.
>
> Not only Palanthas had fallen. So, too, had the Knights of Takhisis taken the High Clerist's Keep. It is the grim truth, cousin: The bastion that stood as such as symbol of might during the last war has been forced to lower the Solamnic banner. Now the five-headed dragon of Takhisis flies from the upper battlements, and the Knights of Solamnia face execution, torture, and worse.
>
> But even as you grieve I must tell you that this is not the worst of my news, for it was not long after debarking that we received word of a new threat.
>
> In fact, the entire world seems wrenched by forces beyond my comprehension. There is no other way to say it: The sky has begun to burn, air and cloud consumed by living flame. It began over the ocean to the north, and as of this writing it has not ceased nor shown any sign of waning. During the day crackling heat seethes between the clouds. At night it is

as if half the heavens are ablaze, and we gape with wonder and horror at the terrifying portent. All intelligence, and the prognostications of every wizardly and priestly augury as well, suggest that monstrous horrors are looming.

I send this missive now as a summer of unnatural heat lies heavily upon Krynn. Cousin, I long to feel the cool shade of Thorbardin, to ride the still darkness of the Urkhan Sea. But alas, it is not to be—not now and not in the foreseeable future. For, as you may have guessed, we Hylar are going still farther to the north. We remain on watch against an enemy we cannot imagine. We have as our goal a ridge of islands, hitherto unknown, that have erupted from the sea and stand as barrier isles beyond the northern coast of Ansalon. The Teeth of Chaos these rocky outposts have been called, and the name seems apt.

I know not whether we shall meet with success, or even face a prospect of real survival. But I do know this, O Wise and Thoughtful Cousin: If these Storms of Chaos are allowed to swell unchecked, the future of Krynn will no longer be numbered in ages, nor centuries, nor even years. If we and those who prepare to fight beside us (including knights of both Solamnia and Takhisis—how's that for irony?) cannot hold this wild force at bay, I do not believe our world can survive another winter.

For a long time Baker sat still, unaware of the low hum of Hybardin that penetrated even the stone walls of his study. Not my study, he reminded himself; this is the office of the true thane! His stomach burned, as if these unpalatable truths were eating away at his insides. And with that grim image in his mind he forced himself to read the rest of the letter, knowing—and dreading—what would be revealed.

This last I impart not to fill you with admiration for our boldness nor to place overmuch fear upon your shoulders. It is simply this: I shall be gone from Hybardin until this task is done, be it one year, five, or ten. It may cost me my army and my life. There is quite simply no other alternative.

The result, of course, is that I must ask you to hold the reins of my office—not merely for the summer, as we had originally planned, but for however much time is required until the completion of my mission. I know, Cousin Whitegranite, you would much prefer to continue your studies and your meditations unimpeded. I, too, share your fascination with the mystery of the Grotto, and I look forward to the day when you can devote yourself to the puzzle that has eluded our greatest minds for more than two thousand years. Was the first lair of the good dragons in the place we now call Thorbardin? You have convinced me it is possible. If anyone in the kingdom can unravel the mystery hidden in those lost scrolls of Chisel Loremaster, that scholarly dwarf is you.

But, sadly, the days of research and your ultimate triumph must lie in the future. Duty has a way of calling us all, in one way or another. My work will be done by my strong right arm and my army. Yours has always been through your pen, your mind, and your words.

Just as I know your reluctance, I also perceive your capabilities, perhaps better than you do yourself. You are a wise dwarf, Baker Whitegranite, but do not forget to let yourself be advised. Too, you must not be afraid to lead.

Finally, I am certain that the news in this missive has caused you no little fear. (Reorx knows these events are enough to turn my own beard white!) I must ask that you share the knowledge of what has happened with the rest of the Hylar. It is up to you whether or not to inform the other clans. But if you do so, try to master their understandable fear. We are a proud and capable people, but our nation is prone to fractiousness. It will be up to you to limit that divisiveness, to hold up an example of promise and cooperation.

We must assume, Cousin, that the threat looming over the world of Krynn will not spare our dwarven realm merely because the clans are sheltered beneath the peaks of the High Kharolis. The danger will come to Thorbardin soon enough, and you must insure that we dwarves are ready.

I leave you in trust and confidence to hold my throne and my clan. Baker Whitegranite, Thane of the Hylar. It has a solid echo to it.

Farewell, Cousin, and may the gods allow us to touch our beards together again in this world.

—Glade Hornfel Kytil, Absent Thane of Hybardin
And King of the Mountain Dwarves

Baker read the letter again, and once more, seeking some germ of encouragement, a piece of advice that would help him to face the trials ahead. He felt a rising surge of resentment against Hornfel—irrational, to be sure, for even an uneasy throne in Thorbardin was preferable to a journey across an unknown and treacherous sea.

Indeed Glade's very movement of an army by sea was a stark measure of the urgency that impelled him, that even now drew the Hylar into the little known ocean to the north. For a moment Baker yielded to a wave of awe, stunned his cousin would even attempt such a voyage. He remembered the fallen prince, and shook with grief. How could Glade even carry on in the wake of such a personal tragedy?

Yet Hornfel Kytil was a true thane, made from the stuff of heroes; if anyone could prevail, it would be him. Meanwhile, Baker would have to see that Thorbardin stayed in one piece and remained ready to meet any threats, either internal or external.

But could he do all that?

In truth, he wasn't the least bit sure. Baker had been good at one thing all his life: the craft of scholarship, of diligent and reliable research, and the writing of words with a fluidity pleasing to the listener's ear. None of that had prepared him to rule a kingdom of agitated clans, and yet now he would have to try.

In agitation he got up and paced across the throne room into the adjoining office, where he stopped before his desk. He looked at the stack of parchments and tablets, a mess that covered half of the marble work surface, and felt a rising dismay. Most of them were petitions and claims of one sort or another. For the past mooncycle he had only bothered to read a handful of them. He had acted upon none since he had believed Hornfel would soon be returning.

How could he, Baker Whitegranite, be expected to adjudicate between two disputatious Hylar? He had seen Hornfel's court, of course, and was well aware that angry dwarves tended to be, well, angry. He had no stomach to face them, knowing that his decision must inevitably make at least one of the disputants even angrier.

He wandered the great stone room in a daze, mystified and depressed. His hands idly touched the halberds and axes, the great swords and solid shields that lined the walls. It was a grand legacy of war, two thousand years and more of courage, promise, and steadfast reliability. Each of these martial tools had its place in that history, a blade blessed by Reorx, made of steel sanctified by the best dwarven craftsmen. A long time passed before his thoughts were able to focus, and to return to the missive from Hornfel.

For a moment he thought of his own apartments and was tempted to slink back to Level Twenty-eight before still more emergencies were laid upon this vast desk. But even that gave him no prospect of peace. Indeed, he quickly realized he felt safer here than at home. Garimeth had been so unpleasant recently that it seemed pragmatic to avoid her as much as possible. He sighed, recognizing how pathetic it was that this was one thing he could be grateful for: His new responsibilities would give him ample excuse to remove himself from his wife's presence.

But at the same time new duties of necessity would take him farther from his beloved studies. He longed for the familiar weight of his helmet, the bronze Helm of Tongues that was a treasured artifact of the Whitegranite family—as well as a magical device that allowed him to decipher writings even in the most arcane of languages. It was in the cedar wardrobe, he suddenly remembered. Anger at Garimeth surged anew as he realized how she had distracted him from his search.

Still pacing, Baker stopped before the wide golden doors that opened onto the vast balcony of the thane's hall. He knew the vista that awaited him, the plunging cliff of Hybardin falling to the docks a thousand feet—ten city levels—below. He had a lifetime's familiarity with the vast dark sweep of the Urkhan Sea stretching into the distance of the dwarven kingdom. Sometimes he found solace in that view, but now his hand hesitated on the knob and he decided to let the doors remain shut.

He found his thoughts, without conscious command, returning to his wife. As always, there was the familiar tangle of emotions, memories, and regrets, the whole mix stirred together with a growing measure of distaste.

Garimeth Bellowsmoke had been an unusual bride for a Hylar nobleman. An esteemed daughter of clan Daergar, she had a dark dwarf's ill temper and selfishness. Still, many years ago she had been beautiful. The daughter of a Daergar ambassador to Hybardin, she had known the right words to say to a foolish young Hylar noble. And, though it shamed him to remember this, he had allowed himself to be blinded to the multitude of her faults because she was utterly, fabulously rich.

He tried to recall the beauty that he had once beheld in her shock of pure black hair, in the eyes of a violet so powerful and intense that he had once compared them to the finest opals. Now that hair was streaked with gray and pulled back into a severe bun. Her eyes were constantly clouded by displeasure. Her once-smooth face was scored by lines of age, and a permanent scowl seemed to have settled into the grooves of her chin and forehead.

Baker had memories of her coquettish laugh, of kisses and caresses that had thrilled him, of her daring as a lover. She had excited him in ways that no self-respecting Hylar maid would ever have considered. But those days had been all too brief, lasting only until her pregnancy. Garimeth had blamed him for her discomfort, and following the birth of their son she had withdrawn her affections. He shook his head, casting the thoughts away. He was too old for lust or for love. And even if he wasn't, he doubted the sharp and brittle creature who was his wife, at least in name, could arouse him to even the beginning stages of passion.

The marriage, of course, had made him rich. The union had also served to advance and solidify Garimeth's status, for in Hybardin she had been able to wield influence and prestige in the highest social circles. Despite her dark dwarf ancestry, her intelligence and wit, biting though it often was, had briefly made her popular among the wealthiest and most powerful dwarves in the Hylar capital. In Daerbardin or Daerforge, the two cities native to her clan, Baker knew his outspoken wife would have been relegated to a mere listener, perhaps gossiping about the masculine powers of her realm but unable to exert any real influence.

"Why can't we be more like the Daergar?" he muttered in disgust, suddenly captivated by the notion of a wife who treated him with courtesy and who feared the blow of his clubbed fist should she act improperly.

Immediately he flushed, ashamed by the traitorous thought. Or was he really ashamed by the knowledge that there were times he would like to punch her right in her savagely critical mouth? Such an attack would be most un-Hylar, at least insofar as a Hylar would let his neighbors know his true nature. But who could long conceal from himself the yearning of his own dark thoughts?

Lady of the House

Chapter Two

Garimeth had made up her mind, and now everything she had to do was laid out for her in a neat pattern, like a road carved into bedrock. She made the necessary preparations around the house, then took the lift down to Level Ten, where she expected to find Baker in the Thane's Atrium. Humming absently to herself, she was comfortable with the distance the other passengers, all Hylar, gave to this dark dwarf who uncustomarily lived in their midst.

In the outer rooms of the royal garrison she found a number of young Hylar warriors gathered around an obviously fatigued traveler. The latter had a bloody bandage over one eye, and though he wore no tunic his britches and boots were stained with the mud and dust of the outer world.

"What happened?" she asked.

Despite her Daergar ancestry, she was well known as the wife of the acting thane, and thus the guards answered her willingly enough.

"Redstone here flew all the way from Palanthas on dragonback, with a message from Glade Hornfel for your husband."

"Indeed," she said coolly. "And does our king return to us with similar haste?"

The sergeant bit his tongue, but a nearby youngster had apparently not yet learned the value of discretion. "Not now—not for years, maybe!" he exclaimed.

Concealing her smile, Garimeth nodded somberly as she left the Hylar. Making her way to Baker's office, she knew beyond a doubt that her timing would be perfect.

The acting thane started guiltily as he heard the door open behind him, and then he sighed, no doubt realizing there was only one person who would presume to enter his sanctum without so much as a knock.

"Hello, Gari," he said, his expression neutral behind the graying bristle of his beard.

"There was a message from Hornfel," she said bluntly, accusing him with her eyes. Her suspicious look suggested she thought he was trying to keep a secret from her.

"Yes, I read it just a few minutes ago," he agreed cautiously. "But how did you know?"

"The whole city is talking about that courier. They say he looked like something a cave bear coughed up."

Baker grunted. "The poor fellow had quite a time of it: a shipwreck, attacked by a dragon. We are fortunate he arrived here at all. He told me he was the lone survivor out of a party of twelve Hylar."

"And his news?"

She watched carefully, wondering how much he would tell. The acting thane drew a deep breath. He would reveal portions of the momentous news, but he was not yet prepared to discuss the whole matter with his wife. "It's important, but I need some time to think—"

"Time to think? You could take half a century, and you still wouldn't know what to do," she snapped.

Baker stiffened. "If you came here to belabor me, you might as well leave right now. If you don't, I shall summon my—"

"You don't need to summon anyone. I'm going," she sneered, and now she was exhilarated, ready to make her announcement. She smiled tightly as she sensed his bridled fury, and loathed him for his impotence. "But first I'll say what I came here to say."

He waited.

"I have decided to Break Bond with you," she said, her tone blunt and devoid of any emotion. "My things are packed, and I shall depart on the next lake boat for Daerforge."

"You—you're going home?" Baker stammered.

"That's what I said."

"But why?"

Garimeth relished the shocked tone of his voice, and snorted in dry amusement. "Why not? In truth, you gave me cause to think before. I have decided that you bore me. The Hylar bore me. It's time for me to do something more . . . interesting."

He squinted, adjusting his glasses in his typical and fruitless effort to see more clearly.

"Baker Bad-Eyes," she mocked him. "How can you ever expect to act like a thane of Thorbardin?"

Somehow he forced out the words. "Then go, and good riddance to you," he snapped. "I don't suppose you have told Tarn?"

"Our son has known of my intentions for a long time. He has promised to visit me when I am settled in my old clanhome back in Daerforge."

That, at least, was true. She reflected that her son was the one good thing to come from her overlong dalliance among the Hylar. Without further words she left Baker, and sent a message to her son as soon as she was back in her own house, the house that had been hers for too many decades, now.

Garimeth was thoughtful as she packed her most cherished clothes. She would send later for her full wardrobe, since she wasn't about to stick around here for another day. It would take several such days before the full array of her belongings could be gathered.

She passed into their sitting room, determined to bring a few boots and items of outer wear that she had left in the cedar wardrobe. Upon opening the door she noticed the familiar bronze gleam of the possession she had dubbed her husband's 'toy'.

In truth, she knew better. The Helm of Tongues, an artifact cherished through generations of the Whitegranite family, had uses that she herself had only begun to appreciate. Of course, it was useful for simple purposes: the wearer of the Helm could decipher text written in any language, reading it as though it were printed in precise mountain dwarf. That made it invaluable to a fussy scholar such as Baker Whitegranite.

But Garimeth had discovered something when she had first donned the metal object some three or four decades earlier. It had a benefit far more suited to her tastes. In addition to its powers of translation, the Helm of Tongues allowed its wearer to sense the deepest thoughts and feelings of other dwarves, without the target ever suspecting that he or she was being thus revealed.

Garimeth had learned through discreet questioning that the latter ability seemed to be unique to her, or at least, particular to dark dwarves. Perhaps the Hylar temperament was too naïve for this use.

Now her first impulse was to cast the item aside and continue to gather her jewelry, but with a tight smile she paused, then picked up the metal helmet. Even after all these years it felt surprisingly light in her hands. She looked closely at the intricate scrollwork marking the smooth bronze surface. She couldn't resist placing the object on her head.

As always, it felt marvelously comfortable, as if it had been molded to fit her scalp, though, as far as she knew, it fit Baker's larger head with similar comfort. But the sensations she was feeling went beyond, far beyond, mere comfort. Already there was that familiar tingling in her nerves, like a caress of blissful delight quivering in her belly, tightening the focus of her mind. Her senses felt exceptionally keen. The rusty colors of the tapestry hanging in the room were brightened to a blood-red crimson that shimmered like a living, breathing thing. The deep-paneled oak seemed to have a texture like a dramatic landscape, all valleys and ravines and lofty crests.

These senses extended beyond the natural, and she suddenly felt a presence in the next room, knew that her husband's house-servant Vale was moving about in the dining chamber. Though that loyal dwarf made no sound, the helm allowed her to picture his exact position. A thick wall of solid stone separated them, and still it was like she stood right behind Vale, watching as he went about his cleaning.

The servant reached high with a feather duster, sweeping the top of a cabinet, and Garimeth was seized by a capricious impulse. The power of the helm augmented her thoughts. With her mind she reached out, grasped him by the wrist, and pushed. The feather duster hooked around the base of a delicate candelabra, moved sharply, and the glass object fell to the floor.

The shattering of crystal, and Vale's gasp of dismay, were audible even through the closed door. Under other circumstances the dwarf woman would have hastened into the dining chamber and relished the chance to rebuke the clumsy servant, but now she merely shrugged. Her husband's possessions were no longer any concern of hers.

At least, his mundane possessions. Removing the helmet, she looked at it again, and made a sudden decision. With a barely concealed smile of pleasure, she tossed the object into her traveling trunk and continued to prepare for her departure.

Perhaps Baker wouldn't miss her, but by Reorx he would certainly notice that she was gone.

Long and Short Views

Chapter Three

Amid eggs of gold and bronze, of silver, brass, and copper, there was an orb of purest platinum, a spherical treasure blessed by Paladine himself.

Then the Graygem came to the Grotto as it came to the rest of Krynn, as a harbinger of Chaos that reached into the substance of the world, and planted its wild seed. And the platinum egg was changed by the essence of Chaos, and changed it would remain.

While the other eggs hatched, and the dragons were born, the egg of platinum had been changed, altered by the chaotic force of the Graygem. And so it remained in the nest and so it would stay, until a true ruler of the dwarves would raise it, and release the power from within.

—From the Early Chronicles of Chisel Loremaster

I like those words as much today as I did when I wrote them, more than three thousand years ago. I know Baker Whitegranite gave them careful thought when he translated them just a fortnight past, though it is true that at that time he did not ascribe to them their proper worth.

In another few weeks, of course, he will number them among the most important phrases he has ever read.

But that time lies still in the future, and I think it would be good, now, to consider the Kingdom of Thorbardin as it is, at the height of its glory, shaded from the brutal sky during these hot summer days. The Storms of Chaos loom on the horizon, and over the world, but the bitter winds have yet to commence their sweep across Krynn.

The "house" of Baker Whitegranite and Garimeth Bellowsmoke lay in many ways at the very heart and the ultimate height of this great dwarven kingdom. Situated on Level Twenty-eight of the Life-Tree, its balcony commanded a vista of the great sea nearly three thousand feet below, while the pulse of the kingdom's greatest city measured its beat at the house's doorstep and beyond. And in its garden were the cool, brilliant waters that gave such pleasure to the acting thane of the Hylar.

Hybardin, called the Life-Tree, was a place unique in the world of Krynn, and among all the planes for that matter. It existed in a massive stalactite, a half-mile in height and that same distance in width, at least at its widest diameter, which, naturally, was at the very top. The great shaft of living stone tapered as it plummeted downward, passing through the many levels of the Hylar city, each layer somewhat smaller and more compact than the levels above.

Water flowed everywhere in Hybardin. The dwarves had channeled countless natural springs to form fountains, pools, gardens, canals, and small, trilling brooks. These served a practical function in keeping the city clean, but they were cherished for their beauty, for the cool mists that soothed the lower levels where the forges smoked and roared, and for the splashing vitality they brought to neighborhoods and homes.

As well as water, Hybardin was a city of light, for more than any other clan of mountain dwarves the Hylar loved to behold the world with their eyes. They had keen hearing and acute smell and they could discern some shapes even in nearly complete darkness, but they maintained a network of constantly burning lanterns, torches, and fires so that each of their streets was illuminated, and within every inhabited house could be found the friendly glow of candle, lamp, or coal hearth.

As an observer reached the middle strata of the Life-Tree, he would notice that the streets and byways of the city moved from regions of noble manors to the crowded houses of hard working dwarves. Finally, descending into the lower levels he would find smithies clanging, bellows roaring, and furnaces baking as they flamed and seared the metals dwarven crafters could meld like no other artisans. Yet even here the pragmatic Hylar retained their love of beauty, and thus there were gardens, fountains, and streams even in the midst of their soot-stained work and the fiery heat.

The tapered column of stone did not extend all the way into the lake. Rather, it reached a blunt terminus some distance beneath the floor of the city's Level Three. Through a span of forty feet of space, the bottom of the stalactite was joined to the rocky islet below by a multitude of metal stairways and no less than five transport shafts. Four of the latter provided service only to Level Three, but the greatest of the transports occupied a long, hollow cylinder in the very center of the Life-Tree. This, the Great Lift, was a transport that extended all the way from Level Twenty-eight down through the base of the stalactite to a platform in the center of Level Two, which was a raised plaza above the encircling ring of the city's waterfront docks that formed Level One. Twin cars, one going up while the other descended, could carry more than a hundred dwarves each.

In its extent and beauty and populace, Hybardin was a true wonder of the world, yet it was not the only remarkable place in Thorbardin—which, after all, is a realm boasting no less than seven great cities. Still, the Life-Tree serves the chronicler as a useful center, a focal point and a commencement for any look at the kingdom of the mountain dwarves.

Hybardin was linked to the rest of the underground realm in many ways. Dwarves were ever delving, and through the centuries they had bored tunnels through the rock at the top of the stalactite. Some of these had been pressed forward to such extent that they linked with similar tunnel networks outlying the other dwarven cities. In this way was the whole mountain a honeycomb of passages. It is safe to presume that the total network of such tunnels was too vast for any single dwarf's comprehension.

The bustling docks and wharves of the city's Level One served as the prime location for commerce in the realm, for from these berths goods came and went from across the Urkhan Sea. Four great chain ferries connected the Life-Tree to cities and roads around the shore of the lake. Several teeming cities—Daebardin, Theibardin, and Daerforge—pressed close upon the shoreline. Other cities such as Daerbardin, Theiwarin, and Klarbardin dwelled deeper under the mountain or along a sinuous fjord of the subterranean sea. And all of this great kingdom—cities, sea, tunnels, roads and vast warrens—was an underground domain roofed by the massif of Cloudseeker Peak and the lofty crest of the High Kharolis.

But Thorbardin was more than a kingdom of cities. It was an amalgamation of dwarven clans so different as to make a casual visitor wonder how they could share a common heritage. The mountain dwarves dwelled in five clans, each of which was centered in one or two cities.

Each of these clans was ruled by its thane, and these five dwarves were the most powerful citizens of the kingdom.

In the best of times these thanes were united under the King of the Mountain Dwarves, a post that Glade Hornfel Kytil had held since the War of the Lance. But now the king was gone, and Thorbardin was home to five thanes, each unique to his clan.

Close allies to the Hylar were the Daewar, the other light-loving clan. They dwelled in a large, well-ordered city on the north shore of the lake, but in these days of tension they had been swept into internal crisis. Daewar eyes were turned inward, upon themselves.

At the western end of the Urkhan Sea were the cities of the Theiwar, dark dwarves who cherished the magic that lingered in the lightless alleys and byways of their domain. Spells of seduction and betrayal were worked amid creations of wicked beauty. The Theiwar hated the dwarves of all the clans, but their most passionate loathing was reserved for the Hylar, the dwarves of light and water and solid, honest stone, the antipathy of everything held dear by the Theiwar.

Darker even than the Theiwar was the clan dwelling at the eastern end of the great sea in the twin centers of villainy called Daerforge and Daerbardin. In the cities of the Daergar murder was a form of high art and treachery a skill learned in infancy.

Daerforge rose from the edge of the water like the façade of a grand fortress. The city was arrayed in three vast levels, while turrets, balustrades, and overlooks jutted across the face of the rock in a forbidding display of fortified stone.

The lowest level lay at the water's edge. Here docks extended into the lake, and the links of the great chain ferries clinked steadily between the city of dark dwarves and the brilliant beacon of Hybardin, gleaming ever brightly—hatefully—across several miles of underground lake water. Behind the Daerforge waterfront great ovens and furnaces roared, and despite huge ventilation shafts the air retained a taste of soot and ash.

The second level of the city was rife with the scent of molten metal. Here the great smelters and casting plants capitalized upon the heat generated a hundred feet below.

The upper level of the dark city was a place of living compartments, a teeming den of Daergar houses ranging from splendid manors arrayed along the ramparts above the sea to crowded alleys so low-ceilinged that even dwarves had to hunch downward to walk here. A dozen or more Daergar might live in one small room, and it is to one of the smallest and darkest of these warrens that the chronicler now directs the reader's attention. For it is here, in the crowded and roaring festivity preceding a great celebration, that another branch of our story begins.

* * * * *

The dwarf was as dark as the shadows through which he moved. Cloaked in a robe of supple silk, he crawled through a tunnel that served as a ventilation duct from deepest Daerforge. On his back was a blocky shape marked by the distinctive wooden thwart of a heavy crossbow. The weapon, like the dwarf himself, was fully wrapped in dark shrouding. Upon his feet were moccasins of soft leather, also black, and his hands were concealed by gloves of a rubbery, skintight membrane.

His eyes—pale, luminous, and staring—peered through a narrow slit in the robe that covered his face. He moved with utter silence, testing each handhold and foothold as he crept upward through an angling shaft. For many hours he had passed through the inky darkness, and now as he drew near to his destination, he would make no mistake, nothing that would yield a telltale sound or sign of his presence.

The shaft turned at right angles so that it ran horizontally, but even here the cloaked dwarf moved with painstaking care. Placing one knee after the other, one careful handhold at a time, he crawled forward. Eventually he drew near an iron grate that allowed air, smoke, and sound to waft into the stone-walled duct. He heard sounds of laughter and argument, the boasts, insults, and curses that were the hallmark of any Daergar gathering. Once those noises swelled into angry shouts and the masked intruder stiffened, wondering if he had missed his chance. But the bitter words settled into murmurs again, and apparently no blows were exchanged.

Finally he reached the grate. Ever so slowly he extended the top of his head over the opening, giving himself a view into the chamber below. The room was utterly dark, but the Daergar's eyes were keen enough to penetrate that murk.

About a hundred dark dwarves were crowded into the room. The smells of sweat, ale, and vomit were thick in the air, clear indication that the festivities had been going on for a long time. Most of the crowd was male, though the watcher could see a few females working and playing among the dark dwarf warriors. The observer took his time, scanning the sea of Daergar in the crowded banquet hall until he found the one that he sought.

Khark Huntrack was the strong, sturdy dwarf, seated amid a ring of burly bodyguards. Additional guards stood at the two doors that gave access to this chamber, and these barriers were closed, locked and solidly barred. A sharp rapping came from one of those portals, which was opened a crack by guards holding drawn swords. They left an aperture just wide enough to let a few more dark dwarf wenches slip into the room. Each of these was frisked with some enthusiasm by one or another of the guards, and only when it had been determined that none of them were armed were the bawdy females allowed to enter and mingle with the celebrating Daergar warriors.

Another keg was tapped with a loud hammer blow, and pitchers were filled from the foaming outflow. Khark

Huntrack himself took a big swig from one of the first mugs, wiping the back of his hand across the froth on his beard. He uttered a loud belch that was greeted with applause, but the surreptitious observer knew Khark wouldn't be caught drunk. His bodyguards, too, were sober.

Grinning behind the gauze of his face mask, the watcher wriggled around in the ventilation tunnel until he could reach the frame of his crossbow. He assembled the weapon and tightened the mighty spring with silent, practiced movements, all the while keeping his eyes on the gathering in the room below. At last he removed a steel-shafted dart from his small quiver, laying the missile into the groove atop his small but powerful bow.

Only then did he pull the gauze from his face. He settled the weapon onto the edge of the grate and took his time, drawing a careful bead on his target. When he was absolutely certain that he had a clean field of fire, he removed a tiny vial from a pocket at his shoulder. Uncapping the bottle, he smeared a dark, oily substance on the arrowhead.

He took aim again, exhaling slowly as he felt the sweet tension in the spring and pressed the smooth wood of the stock against his cheek. His finger seemed a piece of the weapon, melding itself to the trigger, slowly applying tension. Never blinking, he studied his target with those luminous eyes.

Khark Huntrack took a long pull from his mug, leaning his head far back to drain the last drops. His eyes, shrewd and slitted, met the stare of the figure perched at the ceiling grate and widened in surprise.

The chunk of the crossbow's release was a sound that cut through the boisterous crowd in the hall. The missile flew downward, missing the mug and Khark's upraised arm, vanishing into the nest of tangled curls that was the Daergar's beard. The dark dwarf tumbled backward, his chair smashing onto the floor, and Khark's lips worked desperately, struggling to make a sound, perhaps to utter a curse or a prayer.

The room had fallen into a stunned, shocked silence.

"Poison!" hissed one bodyguard, leaping to his feet and snatching up his master's drained mug.

But another of the guards was more astute. He knelt beside the stiffening corpse, touching the shaft of the missile that jutted upward from the nest of the messy beard.

"No," said the second dark dwarf, eyes swinging upward to regard the ceiling grate. There was no sign of the assassin, but the Daergar pointed upward with certainty.

"Slickblade," he said.

At the word all the Daergar in the room gasped in horror and, in unison, backed away from Khark Huntrack's lifeless body.

The World of Tarn Bellowgranite

Chapter Four

The young dwarf swaggered along the waterfront of Hybardin, gratified as the thronging Hylar parted before him. Let them stand aside, he thought with private scorn. Let them wonder who I am.

The reaction was welcome and not unfamiliar. As always, it provoked a sense of his own uniqueness, a powerful and arrogant awareness. If a burly Hylar dockman had failed to step out of the way, Tarn Bellowgranite would have been quite ready to move the fellow with his fist. He found himself glaring at the crowd, looking for someone who might give him the satisfaction of a fight. But these Hylar seemed to have other matters on their minds, for no one took the trouble even to return his stare with a similar expression of belligerence. Instead, each dwarf lowered his eyes as Tarn looked his way, or shifted himself to quickly study the dark waters of the lake. Some bent to inspect some particularly tempting bit of mushroom, bread, or meat offered by one of the dockside vendors.

Tarn should have been used to this by now, but on some deep and hidden level the attitude of the Hylar bothered him. Yet he was still one of them, in more ways than he was ready to count. His head was crowned with the golden hair, considered a mark of beauty among the Hylar, and even his beard was a straw yellow, unusually light. But his eyes were his mother's: large whites surrounding pupils of an abiding violet that darkened to purple when his thoughts were grim, as they were now. Those were eyes that could never be found in a Hylar's face, and Tarn knew that his habit of staring frankly at strangers was cause for great unease among the dwarves around him.

Let them be uneasy then.

He reached the chain ferry on time, and his mother arrived soon after, accompanied by several servants and a great cargo of crates, satchels, and bags. She nodded as she saw him, then turned to the business of ordering her luggage stowed. Only when that was arranged to her satisfaction did she turn back to her son.

"You're really going?" he asked her, still somehow surprised despite her message to that effect this morning.

"Of course, and I'll expect to see you soon," she replied. "There's room for you in the house, so plan to stay for a long time."

"Yes, I'll come. I don't know when, just now, but I will."

"Don't let your father bully you into staying away," she warned, scowling so he knew she was serious.

"I won't," Tarn responded, though privately he doubted that Baker Whitegranite could bully anyone—and certainly not his son.

"Good. Remember, you are half Daergar. Don't let this place of lights and gardens drive you mad. It just about did that to me."

Tarn had been to his mother's homeland enough to know what she meant. Where the Hylar preferred flowing water, graceful architecture, and at least the minimal light provided by the sunshafts and their many small, smokeless lamps, Daerforge and its great sister city, Daerbardin were places of unrelieved darkness. Where the Hylar built for beauty, the Daergar built for strength. Great, blocky bulwarks marked the ends of the wharves there, and the buildings were ugly but practical, square of edge and thick of wall. The wide streets of the Daergar city were straight, unadorned by gardens or fountains; such amenities were recognized as a waste of space by the ever practical dark dwarves. Instead, they had avenues along which entire armies could quickly be moved from one side of the city to another.

"I'll be careful," he assured her. "And I'll come as soon as I can."

He helped his mother load her things and watched as she sailed away. Her mood had been brisk and cool, though she sharply chided the boatmen, Hylar and Daergar alike, whom she deemed overly careless in loading her crates on the large craft. No damage was done, and Tarn watched his mother's spirits brighten once she'd had the chance to utter a few choice insults.

Her farewell to her only son had been formal, though her wish that he come to visit was undoubtedly sincere. Still, she clearly had other matters on her mind, so Tarn's presence at her departure seemed a mere afterthought. He doubted that she felt any of the emptiness, the sense of alienation, that now overwhelmed Tarn as the boat lurched away and he turned to amble along the crowded wharf.

Above, the overhang of the Life-Tree swept outward and up, lofting the great city of the Hylar into the cavernous heights of Thorbardin's vast, central chamber. Though he had grown up in this city, Tarn was still able to feel a sense of amazement. Hybardin had been carved over the course of twenty five centuries, one room or passageway at a time, into this great pillar of rock. The island at the base of the pillar was completely encircled by docks, wharves, warehouses, and the machinery buildings anchoring the great pulleys and gears that ran the ferries. He could clearly hear the clanking of steel mechanisms as the chain linking Hybardin to the great manufacturing center of Daerforge lurched in constant motion, pulling the broad ferry over the still waters of the Urkhan Sea. He watched until the flatboat had almost disappeared into the distance.

A great barge had just tied up to the wharf, the cargo vessel having been hauled to Hybardin by the same chain that was now carrying his mother's ferry back to the east. Loud crashes sounded as dockworkers lifted out bars of Daergar steel and stacked them to the side. The raw metal shafts would be sent to Hylar craftsmen, who would form the strong metal into blades and spearheads valued across Krynn. Now the air echoed with harsh curses as the Daergar foreman, no doubt irritated by the light from an overhead lantern, berated his team of workers.

The actual dockside laborers were Klar, Tarn saw, hardy dwarves of the tribe that, according to legend, had been maddened by their experiences during the Cataclysm. The entire clan had been trapped in lightless tunnels with insufficient air, food, and water. Those of the Klar who eventually clawed their way to freedom had proven the strongest of the band, but they—and all their ancestors—had dwelled at the brink of madness ever since. Tarn felt a twinge of sympathy as he saw a Klar worker, towering a head taller than his Daergar overseer, confront his brutal and belligerent superior with a look of dark, glowering hatred. The Daergar raised his whip and shouted an unintelligible insult, and the sullen Klar went quickly back to work.

Now, as he wrestled through the crowds mingling in a narrow lane that encircled a decorative fountain, Tarn found himself scorning the Hylar propensity for frivolous waste. Surely the waterfront would be better served by removing that fountain and widening the road.

Determined not to yield his space, Tarn angrily shouldered aside a plump Hylar merchant. That dwarf, his fingers bright with gem-studded rings and his neck ringed by heavy gold chains, turned to rebuke the insolent youngster, but something in the look of the half-breed's violet eyes caused the merchant to hold his tongue.

Again the roadway widened as Tarn reached the next section of docks, where another heavy chain extended across the water to the south, connecting the Life-Tree to the Sixth Road, one of the main avenues of food supply, not only to Hybardin but to all the dwarven cities on the Urkhan Sea.

Tarn watched a crew of working Daewar, dwarves who preferred bright illumination for their activities, and soon his eyes adjusted to the glare of their lanterns. He reflected that his sight was probably the one advantage he had inherited from the cursed match that had brought his parents together. While he was not bothered by light, and unlike the Daergar and Theiwar he could even walk the surface of Krynn in relative comfort under bright sunlight, his vision in full darkness was as adept as any dark dwarf's.

He thought, as he spit into the waters of the lake, that it was precious little consolation in exhange for the fact that nowhere in Thorbardin could he really feel at home. Turning, he cut across the dock and climbed one of the four broad stairways connecting the waterfront to the city's second level. This was a broad, flat plaza focused around the great lift station in the center where the metal cage descended from the hanging mountain overhead to provide a link to Level Three and all of the Life-Tree above.

He continued on across the plaza, a bustling marketplace where dwarven merchants from all the cities of Thorbardin hawked their wares. Food and drink, clothing and jewelry, and even small tools and minor weapons such as knives and daggers, were all offered by vendors who claimed stalls amid the tangled lanes that twisted among the shops.

Tarn cursed as something tumbled into the back of his legs. Looking down, he saw that a rotund gully dwarf had tripped over something to sprawl headlong, and his momentum had nearly toppled the bigger, sturdier half-breed.

"Be careful, you oaf!" snapped Tarn, aiming a kick of his heavy boot at the clumsy Aghar's head.

"Watch you step!" protested the gully dwarf, nimbly dodging the blow that would have knocked him senseless. Tarn stumbled, barely catching his balance before he fell, while the filthy little dwarf stood firmly and glared up at him. "I here first!"

Knowing better than to waste his time in fruitless argument, Tarn turned his back, only to see the pudgy Aghar, moving very quickly for such an awkward-looking fellow, dart around him and wander over to a stand where a bristly haired Theiwar was selling marinated mushrooms. In spite of himself, Tarn chuckled. The gullies were pathetic and irritating, but it was hard for him not to feel a certain kinship to these, the rudest and lowest of Thorbardin's dwarves. After all, like himself, the Aghar had no true home in the great kingdom. Instead they had to make do with whatever the rest of dwarvenkind was willing to give them.

The gully dwarf made a great show of sniffing disdainfully at the shriveled balls of fungus, then ducked a backhanded blow that the vendor aimed at his head, disappearing below the front of the stall. When a Hylar lady, her reddish-gold hair bound in twin braids, stopped to inspect the wares, the Theiwar turned his attention to a possible paying customer. Still enjoying himself, Tarn watched and waited.

The gully dwarf made his move.

A grubby hand reached over the lip of the table and

snatched a particularly succulent mushroom. Immediately the little fellow streaked away, knocking aside shoppers, diving between the legs of a startled Klar.

"That's it, you little thief!" screamed the Theiwar, his already squinting features screwed into a map of fury. The dark dwarf touched his left hand to a ring that he wore on his right forefinger, and pointed that digit at the fleeing Aghar.

"Stop!" he shrieked, and the word was far more than a statement of command. Standing a few feet away, Tarn felt queasy, and the hackles on his neck rose as they always did in the presence of magic.

The gully dwarf stopped. With a look of dumb amazement, he stared at his feet, which were planted as though anchored to the ground. He twisted around and regarded the Theiwar with stark terror as the vendor came around the side of his stall, drawing a long dagger. Grinning savagely, the dark dwarf ran a finger along the edge of his blade, relishing the Aghar's terror as he walked nonchalantly forward.

"Let's see how nimble-fingered you are when you've lost your hand, you wretched little—*oof!*"

The Theiwar fell backward, the air driven from his lungs by Tarn's sternly planted elbow. Getting up from the ground, the fungus merchant snarled in apoplectic anger, his fury now directed at this new target.

"I'm sorry. Did I bump you?" asked the half-breed innocently, extending a hand and then withdrawing it as the Theiwar's knife whipped past his fingers.

"You bastard, you'll pay for that 'shroom, or I'll take it out of your hide! And maybe I'll take it anyway," the dark dwarf blustered. Once more his left finger touched the ring, though his pointing was made awkward by the fact that he still clutched the dagger in his right hand.

Tarn's own slender short sword was in his hand, swinging upward faster than the squinting Theiwar's eyes could follow. With a single sharp clang the two weapons came together. The dark dwarf's knife spun away and Tarn's blade came to rest at the base of the ring finger.

"Put that ring in your pocket, unless you want me to do it for you." Tarn spoke calmly, but the keen edge of his blade brushed the Theiwar's skin and drew a trickle of blood.

"Who was that? A friend of yours?" sneered the Theiwar, though he slowly complied with Tarn's request.

"No friend," the half-breed said with a dismissive shrug. "But no enemy either."

Apparently deciding that any further bravado would carry untoward risks, the Theiwar sniffed loudly, turned his back, and stomped into his stall. He squawked in outrage when he discovered that his wares had been greatly diminished during the brief altercation; several other gully dwarves, casually ambling through the crowd, were busy licking traces of marinade from their lips and stringy beards. Though he glowered darkly after Tarn, the Theiwar fungus merchant made no further move as the half-breed ambled out of sight.

Tarn felt a little better after the confrontation. Though the Theiwar, like the Daergar of his mother's clan, were dark dwarves, he despised them. Unlike any of the other clans, the Theiwar were fond of magic and quite willing to employ it to further their ends. In the eyes of any self-respecting mountain dwarf this was clear proof of cowardice. For a moment Tarn wondered, idly, if he should have grabbed the vendor's ring and thrown it into the lake. An attempt to do that, he decided, would probably have taken the fight further than he wanted to go.

His bright mood lasted only until he came around another box of crates. He saw what at first looked like a pile of rags at his feet, but quickly realized that the rags were bleeding. Prodding with his foot, he rolled a small corpse over to see the plump gully dwarf, his throat neatly cut. The Aghar's eyes bulged in surprise, and his mouth gaped in silent protest. There was no sign of the mushroom. Undoubtedly he had been killed by someone meaner, stronger, or more treacherous, someone who had simply wanted that particular piece of food.

Tarn sighed heavily, saddened but not surprised by his gruesome discovery. Such was the lot of an Aghar in Thorbardin. Though no Hylar would butcher one of the pathetic creatures for such a trivial prize, there were plenty of dark dwarves around who wouldn't hesitate to draw blood. If someone had seen the killer, there would be little recourse; doubtless even many Hylar would be secretly pleased that one more of the pesky little scavengers had been removed from the city.

Taking care not to get any blood on his boots, Tarn stepped around the corpse and continued on. He soon encountered a trio of Daergar who looked at him suspiciously, then glanced back at the crates. Tarn spat in their direction and continued on, and the Daergar apparently decided to ignore the insult rather than tangle with a lone dwarf who was so easily offended. One of them hacked and spit loudly toward Tarn's back, and then the trio returned to their task of stacking crates.

Tarn felt a twinge of envy for the Daergar, who at least had a task to do, some real work. All of his life he had lived in comfort, well-supported by his mother's money and his father's status, a proud member of one of the finest of the Hylar's old noble houses. He had come to be accepted, though admittedly with reservations, by much of Hybardin society, and his exotic good looks had made him a favorite consort of some of the wilder dwarven wenches of his own age, not to mention the older matriarchs and grand dames who every so often sent a lascivious invitation in his direction.

It was a good life, he tried to tell himself, but by now he realized the truth: It was an easy life, and for many years that had been enough for him. His mother's departure was a reminder that times were changing, and his life was bound to change, too.

Of course, he could have joined Glade Hornfel's expedition to Solamnia. Though he was only half Hylar, Tarn Bellowgranite would certainly have been welcomed in the thane's army. After all, Tarn was Hornfel's cousin's son, and his fighting prowess was well-known. However, in response to the reluctance of the other clans, Hornfel had declared that he wanted only Hylar in his army. "The pure of blood, for only they will have nobility of soul," were his exact words. Tarn had found it easy to feel excluded, a reaction that had greatly pleased his mother. As regarded his father's disappointment, Tarn didn't really care. Baker Whitegranite was, to Tarn's way of thinking, the worst kind of dwarf, a man who would rather spend his days cooped up in a library than doing something, anything, that would bespeak a course of action.

There was one more reason Tarn had wanted to stay behind in Hybardin, and as he came around the wharves to the western side he saw her. He drifted closer, then settled himself onto a small pile of coal where he could get a good view.

Belicia Felixia Slateshoulders was drilling a group of recruits so young that their beards barely covered their cheeks. She stalked up and down before the would-be warriors, her face locked in a frown, a stout staff in her hands. This rank of Hylar was learning the finer points of holding a shield wall, and Belicia Slateshoulders, a veteran female warrior with sturdy legs, solid hips, and the broad shoulders of a true soldier, wasted no effort in pointing up their numerous failings.

"You! Crettipus! Hold that shield lower! Do you want to get your legs cut off?" For emphasis Belicia whacked her staff beneath the protective barrier, drawing a howl from poor Crettipus. That hapless recruit scrambled backward, holding his shin and hopping on one foot.

"And you, Farran!" She barked at the next dwarf. "When your comrade goes down, you have to get your shield over fast or else the next one of you will go down as well."

She thrust the pole past the stumbling Farran to jab the tip into the solar plexus of a third dwarf. That one went down, gasping, and Belicia strode through the shambles she had made of the shield wall, spinning to smack Farran on the backside.

"If this was a real fight, Raggat here would have been killed," she snapped. Raggat, the fellow who had been dropped by the blow to the belly, glowered at Farran, who stammered an apology.

"Remember, your shield protects the dwarf to your left. If he falls, you have to move quickly! If you let an enemy do what I just did, we're all doomed. Now, are there any questions?"

The chagrined young dwarves, some three dozen in number, were too thoroughly cowed to so much as raise a hand.

"Good. You're learning," Belicia barked. "Now, by twos, get yourselves going on the sword and shield drill. And I want to see some sweat!"

Quickly the recruits paired off. Tarn smiled as he noticed that Farran was quick to find a partner other than the still disgruntled Raggat. In moments the dockside rang with the sounds of blades striking shields.

Tarn didn't know that Belicia had ever taken her eyes off the company, but as soon as the mock combats began she sauntered over to Tarn and plopped down on the small mound of coal.

"Come to join up?" she asked him with a wink.

"Do you think you could use me?" he asked, straight-faced.

She sighed. "No offense, but we could use just about anybody with a warm body and at least one eye."

"I'm sure you'll whip them into proper dwarven warriors in no time."

"It's not only here that we need them," she replied, meeting his gaze with a look that was all seriousness. "But it's all over Hybardin. Thane Hornfel took every able-bodied fighter we have."

"Almost," Tarn replied, unable to keep the bitterness out of his voice.

He was looking for pity, but he met with no success as she replied curtly. "It was your choice, no one else's, that kept you behind. You know damned well he could have used you and would have welcomed your enlistment."

Tarn shook his head belligerently. "With all that talk about Hylar purity, he might as well have called me an ill-bred bastard. He can wage the Solamnian war without me." His temper was lousy, and he felt acutely defensive. He had not come to see Belicia so they could discuss the Hybardin military situation—or lack thereof.

"I guess you haven't heard then," the dwarfwoman replied, her tone softening. "There's a rumor that the Hylar are no longer fighting the army of Takhisis. It's said they're sailing north of Ansalon to campaign against some new threat."

"Sailing? By Reorx! You mean away from the continent?"

"That's what I've heard." Belicia tried to be casual, but she couldn't entirely suppress a shudder of discomfort.

"Where did you hear that news?"

"A courier came from the army just a few hours ago. He went directly to your father but then talked a little bit to the staff of the barracks cooking hall. You know how word gets around, even in an untrained army."

Tarn grunted. The topic of his father was another he had little interest in pursuing.

"Have you seen your father at all, recently?" she probed.

He snorted. "Two weeks ago, but all he wanted to talk about was some silly tale of the Graygem and a platinum egg in that cursed Grotto of his! I swear, I hope he finds the place, just so he shuts up about it!"

"Well, go find out for yourself about the latest news, then. I've got to get back to my company," Belicia snapped in exasperation.

"Wait. I'm sorry," the half-breed interjected. "I wanted to talk to you, to see if perhaps we could get away for an interval. Maybe take one of the freeboats across the lake."

She sighed and shook her head. "Timing: that's always the problem with us, isn't it?" she said, not unsympathetically. "I can't right now. These buffoons will kill each other in a minute—by accident, of course; I don't think any one of them could kill something on purpose—if I'm not there to keep an eye on them."

Tarn nodded, trying to conceal his disappointment. He wanted to tell Belicia about his mother's departure but knew that she wouldn't share his distress. Indeed, most of Hybardin was likely to regard Garimeth Bellowsmoke's return to the Daergar as cause for celebration. Instead he lurched to his feet and gave her an awkward pat on the shoulder. "You'll do just fine with them. Maybe, after they finish their first series of drills?"

"Maybe," she said with a smile.

Knowing he would have to be content with that, Tarn was still discontented.

Why did she have to mention his father?

Dark Daerbardin

Chapter Five

"I ask the question in the presence of all the clan: where is the challenger? Produce him, or the thane's chair is rightfully mine!"

Darkend Bellowsmoke was addressing a great gathering of Daergar. He stood upon a dais in the middle of the Arena of Honor, the large, lightless assembly hall that was the grandest chamber in all Daerbardin. Shaking his great, spike-headed mace at the masses of his countrymen, he spun through a circle, his voice a screech that pierced the farthest reaches of the chamber.

Smoke from coal braziers filled the air, the acrid vapors bitter in his nostrils, but the dark dwarf stood in a posture of triumph, feet planted firmly, one hand on his hip while in the other he held his weapon aloft. Even in the pitch darkness he was visible to the gathered throng, for the

Daergar, like their Theiwar cousins, could see very well even in the deepest heart of lightless Thorbardin.

"Is the challenger drunk, sleeping off the revel of his last feast on Krynn? Or perhaps he is afraid?" sneered Darkend.

There was no reply, nor was one expected. Bellowsmoke was tall for a Daergar and a strapping warrior in his own right. Now he wore his battle armor, plates of black steel that covered his chest, belly, and groin. Supple links of chain mail rippled smoothly over his limbs and his back. His head was almost completely concealed beneath a grotesque helm, the faceplate scored by the image of a leering beast. Long fangs, honed on both edges to razor sharpness, jutted forward from beside his jowls. Darkend's pale, bright eyes flashed through the narrow slits of vision holes, and his hand was clenched around the shaft of the wickedly studded mace. Now he raised the weapon, pumping his hand up and down as his voice once again cried his public challenge.

"Khark Huntrack! I say you are the spawn of a gully dwarf, the dribbling bastard of a diseased whore! I say, show your face to me now, and die like a dwarf or else you shall be known as a coward, and your spleen will nourish the soil of the food warrens!"

Soft gasps were barely audible in the chamber. Darkend's insults had stepped even beyond the usual bravado of dueling dark dwarves. Everyone knew that if Khark Huntrack were alive he would have to come forward and face these accusations or never show his face in Daerbardin again.

Thus everyone knew what they had already come to suspect: Khark Huntrack must already be dead.

Darkend waited a decent interval so that his intended opponent would have plenty of time to appear. The great audience hall lapsed into silence, but no one looked toward the doors in anticipation of Huntrack's late arrival. Instead, all eyes remained fixed upon the strutting figure that paced back and forth across the rounded dais.

Finally a dark dwarf from the front row, a sturdy warrior in the black, bat winged helmet that characterized Darkend's personal guards, leaped to his feet and thrust his fist into the air.

"All hail Darkend Bellowsmoke!" he cried. "All hail the new thane of the Daergar and the banner of the Smoking Forge!"

A rumble of assenting cries rose through the chamber, but it was not the thundering acclamation Darkend desired. Instead, there were mutters of resentment from many quarters, and even a few outright hisses of disapproval. One of the latter was interrupted by a scream, and the aspiring thane smiled grimly behind the mask of his helmet, knowing that one of his agents had just knifed another obstacle to his throne.

"Hear me, dwarves of Clan Daergar! Khark Huntrack is dead!"

The voice came from the shadows in the back of the chamber. Darkend whirled to see a robed Daergar advancing in the middle of at least two dozen bodyguards. The dwarf's protectors had blades drawn, and their guarding posture formed steel-barbed walls before, behind, and to either side of the bold speaker. There would be no knife blade to swiftly silence this dissenter, Darkend saw with a grimace of frustration.

"Gludh Kolgard? Is that you?" demanded the lone figure on the dais.

"You know it is—just as you know that your toady Slickblade killed Khark in the last hours before his ceremony."

"If Khark Huntrack has met an untimely death, then I withdraw my unflattering remarks," Darkend replied, with a bow of facetious graciousness. "Though I certainly had no foreknowledge of the manner nor the agent of his demise."

The hisses and clucks from the gallery were very muted

and swiftly faded away. No one believed Darkend, of course, but neither did anyone think it worth a possible knife in the ribs to state a universally held opinion.

"Now to the business of this day." Darkend cleared his throat, wheeling around in a full circle so that his luminous, dark-seeing eyes could pass over the entire crowd. A hush settled again as the Daergar waited, knowing that before long they would have a new thane or the prospect of further public bloodshed. In either case, there was promise of fine entertainment in the air.

"I have stood upon this dais each of the last six days, since the untimely demise of our esteemed leader, the bold and wise Thane Halt Blackmetal. Six times has a challenger named himself, and six times that challenger has failed to leave this dais alive."

Darkend paused, allowing his words to settle over his listeners. Four of those challenges had resulted in spectacular duels on this very platform, ending only when his Daergar opponent lay bleeding his life away at the feet of the triumphant Darkend Bellowsmoke. Indeed, the armored dark dwarf still felt the soreness in his ribs, the bruising of his shoulder, and the poorly healing cut on his thigh that were his own souvenirs of those fights. On the other two occasions—most recently in the case of the unfortunate Khark Huntrack—the challenger had met with an unfortunate accident on the eve of the contest, and Darkend had been spared the grueling necessity of public battle. Of all those challengers, Khark Huntrack had been the most esteemed fighter, so Darkend judged it particularly good fortune that the assassin had done his work so well.

"Now, as is the custom of Daergar law, I proclaim I have faced every challenger who dared to name himself, and I announce my ascension to the throne of our clan." He drew a breath, knowing there was one more part to this ritual, and praying to Reorx that his next words would be greeted by silence.

"I await only the announcement of a challenge, of one more dark dwarf foolish enough to throw his life away before this issue is resolved!"

He waited, allowing the echoes to ring through the huge chamber. For a moment he thought that the matter was finished, that he had won.

"I challenge Darkend Bellowsmoke's right to the throne!"

The mass exhalation, a communal sigh of anticipation, washed from the crowd like the wind that so often coursed across the surface of the world above. The words came from behind Darkend, but he knew the speaker well; indeed, he was not surprised Gludh Kolgard had spoken out. Still, the confirmation fell upon his shoulders like a weight of iron ore, and Darkend almost slumped under the prospect of another battle. It took all of his powerful will, as well as the concealment of his armor, to mask any sign of his weakness from the gathered clan. He spun, the twin tusks gleaming darkly, almost as if they were already stained with blood, and glared at the dark dwarf who had spoken. Gludh stood utterly still. He was surrounded by henchmen. Slowly the simmering tension in the vast room bubbled toward release.

"I accept the challenge." Darkend broke the impasse at last, he thought with just the right tone of bored acknowledgment. "I will stand here after the interval of one day, that Gludh Kolgard shall have the pleasure of tasting my steel."

Now a roar of acclamation went up from the throng, and Darkend held his martial pose, though his sore arm throbbed from the weight of his mace. He wished he could bring the weapon down right now on the insolent challenger's unarmored skull.

It wasn't fair! He was clearly the master of any one, even any two, of his accursed challengers. Yet Daergar custom demanded that at least seven dark dwarves should have the chance to face him for the throne. Gludh's reputation was well known. He would be among the most dangerous, and he had been clever enough to wait until the last day, when Darkend would inevitably be wounded, battered, and fatigued from the long ordeal of challengers. Of course, should Gludh triumph, he himself would have to face up to six more possible challengers, but that would be little consolation to Darkend, moldering in his tomb.

The throng quickly filed out of the four massive gateways leading from the Arena of Honor, itself located in the heart of Daerbardin's great royal palace—the palace that should already be mine, Darkend groused to himself. Gludh Kolgard was protected by his followers as he left for his own quarter of the great subterranean city, one of the two great centers of the Daergar in Thorbardin. There would be another night of feasting and celebration, though no doubt this time some of the bodyguards would be certain to seal off the ventilation shaft.

"Come, my thane. It will be but a short time before you attain your rightful throne."

The voice was whispered by one of the cloaked figures beside him, and he prayed that Thistle was right. She was his favorite mistress and one who dared to speak to him when all others held their tongues. Yet now even she was a bother, and Darkend had to forcibly resist the temptation to bring his mace down hard upon her head.

Turning, he regarded her coldly, hating the confident light that brightened her milky eyes, yet knowing he would take no action against her now, not when he needed the loyalty of all his followers to see him through the next interval.

"Summon my healer, and see that a hot bath is drawn for me," he demanded, taking some satisfaction by giving her orders as though she were a common servant.

Thistle only bowed, then turned to elbow her way through the press of bodyguards to see that her master's wishes were obeyed. Darkend allowed himself to be escorted out, trusting his henchmen to see no ambush awaited him in the shadowed lanes of Daerbardin as the procession made its way through the huge city of the dark dwarves.

Even as he brooded on the coming duel, he couldn't help but admire the galleries, the wide avenues and looming, fortified buildings that made up this, the greatest city in all Thorbardin. The arena lay at the opposite end of the city from his great manor. Both of these locales were on the highest of Daerbardin's three levels, but the roadway they followed curved downward until they walked along an esplanade that was open to the great ceiling, two hundred or more feet overhead. The middle and upper levels of the route formed balconies lined with dark dwarves who gazed down in solemn curiosity at the one who aspired to be their next leader.

Occasionally a single Daergar or a small group let out a cheer as Darkend passed, but for the most part these watchers were silent, uncaring as to which of the noble dark dwarves would win the fight on the next day.

"You should all cheer me, fools!" Bellowsmoke hissed through the mask of his helmet, "For I am the one who can raise our clan to new heights! Look at me now and see the image of your future greatness! See, and be awed!"

These boasts he spoke mainly to himself, though a few of his nearest bodyguards heard his words and exchanged worried glances. The strain of the seven challenges was wearing on him, Bellowsmoke knew. It was a relief to let the great stone gates of House Bellowsmoke crash shut behind him. Once secure behind those barriers, he stalked to his own apartments, waiting only long enough for one of his minions to perform a thorough search.

"The chambers are safe, my lord, and nearly unoccupied," said the sergeant to Darkend as Bellowsmoke waited impatiently in the lofty anteroom. "There is only Thistle there; she tends your bath and awaits your pleasure."

Without a word the noble dark dwarf stalked into his

sumptuous chambers, turning at the portal to address his sergeant: "Send for Slickblade at once."

"Aye, lord," replied the gnarled dwarf, paling at the mention of the name. Darkend's hand was on the door, ready to slam the iron portal, but before he could move he was startled by a voice from within his room.

"My heart palpitates in anticipation of your every command, lord."

The words were hissed from the darkness behind him and Darkend whirled, seeing nothing except the familiar outlines of his couches and tables. Only after he stared for a moment did he see the assassin, still cloaked in his usual robe of utter black, rise from his comfortable position on one of the softest divans.

Immediately Darkend turned back to the anteroom, where his already pale sergeant had sunk to his knees, drooling in pathetic fear. "You told me that only Thistle was here, did you not?"

The man gibbered, unable to articulate a reply.

Darkend snapped his fingers, summoning another lackey from among his bodyguards. He pointed at the groveling sergeant. "You will blind him now, and cut his hamstrings for good measure. At dinner tonight he will be strangled for the entertainment of the house."

The replacement dark dwarf stepped forward, drawing a long dagger. Willing helpers seized the thrashing sergeant, and though Darkend finally closed the door, even that heavy portal could not mask the sounds of the wretched sergeant's screams.

"Why did you make me do that?" Bellowsmoke demanded, addressing Slickblade as he started to remove his cumbersome armor. "The man was useful to me, if only because he was less treacherous than most."

The assassin shrugged, slumping back to his seat. "He owed me money."

Darkend stared. "He owed you money, and he refused to pay? Perhaps he was more stupid than I thought."

"He didn't refuse. The loan doesn't come due for several intervals. But it seemed a good time for a lesson, a reminder to those other Daergar who owe me money. I can assure you my next round of collections will be complete."

"And I've lost a capable sergeant," spat Darkend. "You know I had no choice, once you showed them all that he reported falsely to me."

"He deserved it," declared Slickblade dismissively. "In truth, his search was perfunctory. You deserve better protection, lord."

"Would that I could get it." The aspiring thane limped to a cabinet of polished black marble and withdrew a decanter of thick, syrupy liquid. He took a long swig from the bottle, then set it heavily on the counter as he turned back to his assassin. "You heard about events in the arena, I presume."

There was no question in the words—everyone knew Slickblade's information was always current and always reliable.

"Of course. And you will want me to remove Gludh Kolgard before the interval has passed."

"Yes. It will be difficult, so I will double your previous fee." Darkend winced inwardly at the concession. It had already cost him a hefty fortune to have two of his challengers removed before the duel. He was only heartened by the knowledge that if Slickblade was successful, his final payment could be drawn from the thane's treasury and not the Bellowsmoke family vault.

"Not difficult. Impossible." The assassin's reply was blunt, even though his manner was as relaxed as ever.

"You are refusing this task, a task commanded by your lord and future thane?"

"I am refusing, as I would refuse should you ask me to bring you the three moons in a leather bag. After the last six challenges, Kolgard has surrounded himself with the best protection money can buy, and he has a lot of money. His house will be sealed top, bottom, and sides. What you ask cannot be done."

Darkend considered his response carefully. When confronted by frustration his usual instinct was to order the offender seized, blinded and strangled. But he would have to curb that impetuous impulse, for the assassin was far too useful to cast aside for mere vengeance. "Are your skills slipping?" he asked. "Or perhaps you're afraid. It is a pity, because I have long believed you the most accomplished practitioner of your trade in all Thorbardin."

"On all Krynn, and you know it, so don't insult me with appeals to vanity."

"You say his house is sealed. Yet perhaps he may succumb to accident on his way to the arena in the morning. You know it is a long and dangerous walk."

Slickblade shook his head. "Even there his guards will be certain to take extra precautions. It is possible that an opportunity may arise, and if so I shall take advantage. But I warn you, my lord, you must prepare as if you will have to fight this duel."

Darkend Bellowsmoke growled and glowered. He was confronted with an unusual situation: Someone was thwarting his will, and it wasn't practical to have the offender killed. Instead, Darkend took another long pull at the fermented syrup of his thick mead and then spoke thoughtfully.

"So there is no way to avoid him in the arena?"

"You can take him. I've watched both of you fight."

"I agree—if I wasn't so sore that I can hardly move!" snapped Darkend. "And the wound in my leg is festering. That damned Forsyx used poison on his blade, I swear."

"Of course he did. Just count it as a blessing that you had the more toxic venom on your own weapon."

"Don't patronize me!" Again Bellowsmoke drank and felt the mead soothe a few of the aches from his muscles. The pain lessened slightly in his inflamed thigh. He felt glum and angry, but he knew Slickblade was right.

A tentative knock on the chamber door interrupted his brooding. "What?" he growled, knowing he only cared to be disturbed for something important.

When the door was opened he stared curiously. He did not recognize the female Daergar who stood there. She was attractive, though her best days were behind her, but there was a firm line to her chin that reminded him of no one as much as himself.

"Aren't you going to welcome me back, dear brother?" the female Daergar asked. Her words were spoken in the elegant accent of the Hylar.

"Garimeth?" The recognition came suddenly and was accompanied by a sharp, bitter laugh. "You've returned to your own, eh? Just in time to see my brains get splattered all over the arena."

"I hope not," she said in apparent sincerity. "I had word you were standing for the throne, and I was growing so tired of Hylar pretensions. Can't you win tomorrow? I'd like a good excuse to spend some time here."

Darkend laughed again, though the sound was dry and utterly devoid of humor. "Come in and share a drink. You know—" He turned to acknowledge the assassin's presence, but was startled to see that the couch was empty. As usual, Slickblade had departed as he had entered: unnoticed and unannounced.

"I will take that drink, brother. It may be I can help you win that seat on your throne."

"I'm willing to listen. No doubt you've learned a trick or two from your stay among the Hylar."

"None that will supplant your steel, but yes, it may be that I can help . . . . "

For a long time the two Daergar talked. Darkend sent Thistle away and allowed his bath to grow cold as Garimeth spoke to him of things she had learned, seen, and done in Hybardin. Finally, when the hour was late, she gave to him a small gemstone. They both understood he would use it only as a last resort.

The stone was magic, Bellowstone knew, and if he used it during his duel with Gludh Kolgard it was quite possible that his ascension to the throne would be tainted. Using magic during a challenge was forbidden. Yet use it he would, if it meant the difference between victory and death.

All the Thane's Men

Chapter Six

Baker Whitegranite looked up from his desk to see the familiar form of Axel Slateshoulders, veteran captain of many an epic campaign, standing at the door of the thane's office and workroom.

"Come in, Axel, please."

Trying to conceal the twinge in his aching stomach, Baker rose and crossed to the door to take the hand of the grizzled, sturdy dwarf who limped stiffly into the room. "I take it you got my message?"

"Aye," grunted Slateshoulders. "Though not before the whole city was abuzz with rumors and fairy tales. What's the word from the thane?"

Was there a subtle jibe in the words? Baker wondered. Axel had been one of Hornfel's most stalwart warriors and had made no effort to hide his disappointment when the thane had turned down his venerable lieutenant's request to be allowed to join the expeditionary force. Of course, any logical dwarf could see that Axel's bad foot, swollen and infected with irreversible gout, clearly prevented him from taking the field. Yet on this matter Axel had declined to be logical, and he had not hesitated to let Baker know that he regarded the bookish scholar as a less than ideal replacement as thane.

Still, Baker had need of advice on military matters, and Axel Slateshoulders was undoubtedly the foremost warrior remaining in Hybardin. So Baker had learned to bite his tongue, ignoring the man's little arrogances in order to accept his counsel.

Briefly Baker repeated the news from Hornfel's letter.

"The important thing is to keep this secret from the other clans," Axel said after clumping back and forth across the office.

"Why?" Baker wondered, standing before his desk. "I should think we'd want everyone to be on the alert. If there is an eruption of Chaos, an invasion of Krynn as Hornfel seems to indicate, we must all be ready to meet it."

Axel looked at the acting thane as if he couldn't quite comprehend the extent of Baker's stupidity. "So the Daergar, Theiwar, and Klar should all be told that our army is now gone, perhaps for years—even forever? What do you think they'd do?"

"Well, if they hear about the danger, they'd make ready to defend themselves." The answer seemed obvious to Baker, and he was insulted by the venerable warrior's condescending tone.

"Don't be a fool!" snapped Slateshoulders. "They'd turn their armies against us. Within a week Hybardin would be under siege, and I wouldn't give a thin copper coin for our chances."

"Surely you're exaggerating!"

"Look, Baker." Axel drew a deep breath, and the thane could tell that he was trying, with visible difficulty, to force himself to speak calmly. "The hostile clans have been waiting centuries for a chance like this. What I'm saying is, we can't give them cause to think they'd win if they attacked us now. And we can't afford to give them an excuse to mobilize their own armies."

"What about the Daewar?" Baker argued. "They've always stood beside us against internal threats. And their army is still in the kingdom!"

"Think about that little contradiction. You say they've always stood beside us. But when Thane Hornfel sought their help for this summer's campaign, they were nowhere to be found, right?"

"True."

"And do you think they'd lay down their lives to defend a Hylar city?"

"At least I can ask Gneiss Truesilver," Baker argued, bringing up the name of the thane of the Daewar who had been a friendly acquaintance for many decades. "I'm to meet him today. He's in Hybardin on some trading matters right now."

"As you wish, but don't get your hopes up," replied Axel.

"Why?"

Axel took a breath and spoke bluntly. "I've heard they have a real problem with a new cult that has been growing among their people. They're listening to some prophet who claims that the Daewar have to excise themselves from 'wicked Thorbardin.' "

"Yes, Thane Truesilver told me something about this fellow. 'Stonehand,' he's called. I know he's creating a lot of problems."

"My point, exactly," the veteran declared.

"How many troops do we have in the city now?" the thane asked Axel. He felt slightly embarrassed that he didn't know the answer off the top of his head.

"Troops? Like to none, I'd say. We have a lot of women and boys who'll fight bravely—they're Hylar, after all—

but precious few, if any, who could be called proper soldiers."

"Your daughter, Belicia Felixia. She's been training recruits, hasn't she?"

Axel Slateshoulders's tone softened, and his eyes glowed with momentary pride. "Aye, Belli's an able captain, that one. And, truth told, there's a few more of her sisters-in-arms that give us a veteran cadre—a small cadre, mind you."

"Thank Reorx that Hornfel wanted only the men," Baker said, almost to himself, before turning his attention back to Axel. "I want you to use that cadre and recruit all the able-bodied youngsters that we have. I put you in command of the Hylar Home Army."

Axel's eyes flashed with a trace of his old martial spirit. "Aye, that's a start. Belicia's got a small group almost ready down at the docks. D'you know we don't even have a decent waterfront garrison?"

"Er, yes," Baker lied. "I had heard something about that."

"Well, good. Everyone knows that's the key place to start. It's where any attack from the other clans will have to land. Anyway, she's got a company down there, and they're almost whipped into shape."

"My own son, Tarn Bellowgranite, is still in the city. Perhaps he can be of use as well."

"Of course," Axel replied. "He can swing an axe with the best of them." The veteran squinted, as if trying to read Baker's thoughts. "I always felt you were a little hard on the boy. Maybe this is just the sort of thing he needs."

Baker brushed away the criticism, though not before he'd felt its sting. "You are in command. Use whomever you think will be of use."

"Very well. I'll get right to work." Axel pivoted on his good foot and limped toward the door. Before leaving, he turned back. "You did right, Thane. That's the kind of decisiveness we need in times like this."

"You don't say? Well, thank you," Baker replied. He felt warmed by the unexpected praise. "Keep me posted, won't you?"

"Of course." The door closed behind him, but Axel's voice, bellowing for the quartermaster and several of his loyal sergeants, came through the barrier until the lame dwarf's awkward march took him through the gates of the Thane's Atrium.

Baker tried to direct his attention to some of the documents requiring a decision, but the words blurred into meaningless shapes and he finally set the papers aside in disgust. Fortunately he was saved from further struggles by the arrival of the Daewar thane.

"Gneiss Truesilver, my friend, how are you?" Baker asked, as the solicitous attendants offered light-bearded dwarf ale and a comfortable chair.

"In all truth, I have been much better," said the Daewar, a frown darkening his normally jovial features. "Though it is not my own health that suffers, but that of my clan."

"I am sorry," Baker offered awkwardly, startled by his counterpart's bluntness. He realized things in Daebardin must be very bad indeed, if Gneiss Truesilver admitted this much.

"There have been some rumors," he continued, "but we don't know the extent of your troubles. If there's help we can offer—"

"Thank you. I know you are sincere. But the tragedy is that it's an internal rot—Daewar pitted against Daewar, and blood close to being shed." Gneiss took a long pull at his ale, as Baker waited patiently. "It was started by that damned maniac Severus Stonehand. He's been preaching about doom and disaster; says there's storms of Chaos on the horizon. Now he's got half Daebardin believing him, ready to move right out of here. The other half is just about ready to throw them out."

Baker felt a chill that had nothing to do with the cold hearth. "Storms of Chaos? Did he really say that?"

Gneiss scrutinized the Hylar thane. "Yes, over and over until I'm hearing it in my sleep! Why?"

In a rush Baker explained about the letter from Glade Hornfel. "He used those exact words to describe the strange sky, the portents that seemed terrifying even to him!"

"I have to get back to my city at once," Gneiss declared, rising to leave.

It was with difficulty that Baker brought up the subject he had wanted to discuss with the Daewar thane. "Hornfel took every able-bodied warrior we have. There are some among us who fear that the dark dwarves will take advantage of our weakness to seize the power they have coveted for centuries."

"It is a danger," Gneiss agreed cautiously.

"I need to know about your army if the dark dwarves strike. Can you aid us in the defense of Hybardin?" Baker suspected he already knew the answer.

"I'm afraid my army is as divided as the rest of my clan," said Gneiss sadly. "It grieves me to say it, but you Hylar will have to fend for yourselves."

"I understand."

The two thanes parted as they had greeted each other, friends over the span of a century. Each burdened with problems that were his alone to bear.

As soon as Truesilver was gone, Baker felt a rising surge of melancholy. He longed for nothing more than a chance to light a bright reading lamp and to sit in his favorite chair with the Helm of Tongues over his head. But of course, there was no time.

Unless he made time. Suddenly decisive, Baker made his way out of the Thane's Atrium and through the gate of the King's Wall that divided Level Ten into defensible blocks. He walked steadily to the lift station at the center of the level, where four broad avenues came together, and there the thane stood aside to allow a flock of noble Hylar ladies to enter before him.

These dwarven matrons were dressed in fine gowns of spun flax, and each wore a dazzling array of golden chains and bracelets, as well as rings and brooches that winked brightly with diamonds, emeralds, and rubies. The buzz of their conversation quickly faded as they recognized the thane. From the looks of pity and speculative appraisal he received Baker guessed they had been discussing the recent departure of his wife. Nevertheless, they curtsied in unison as he stepped into the wide cage of the lift, and he managed to bow with proper decorum. They rode in awkward silence to the next level, where the females departed. Baker flushed to the sound of giggling laughter as the lift carried him up and out of sight.

At Level Twenty-eight, Baker got off the lift. The station was a wide gallery, lined with stone columns and alive with the sounds of running water. Two fountains, one at each end of the hall, spumed a constant shower of spray, while a long reflecting pool divided the gallery down the middle. Bright lanterns washed the area in light, and the scent of dark-thriving mossblossoms sweetened the air. Baker had always thought this one of the most beautiful places in Hybardin though now he might as well have been blind for all the notice he took of the splendor.

Wrapped in the cloak of his gloom he crossed the gallery and plodded down the connecting avenues, passing the gates to many other noble manors as he walked the blocks leading to his own house, on the outer fringe of the level. It was equipped with a cherished balcony overlooking the sea. But that balcony was not his destination now. Instead he went to the side door, into the coolness of his garden, and for a short time he walked the pathway among the ferns. He let the glowing waters surround his feet, soothing his spirit as they always did. For a short time even his stomach felt a little better.

The double doors in the outer wall whisked open a fraction of a heartbeat before Baker could reach for the latch. Unsurprised, the thane stepped across the threshold and stood in the entryway of the house.

"Greetings, my lord." Vale stepped out from behind the door and bowed. Blinking his watery eyes, the servant took Baker's woolen cloak.

"Thank you, Vale." There was some comfort in the loyal attendant's familiar alertness. In tunic and boots, Baker moved toward his own office. "And Vale, send for my son."

"Right away, lord." The servant's eyes widened before he nodded in eager acceptance. "I'll send a courier to his apartments and another to the dock. I know he spends a lot of time there."

"Good, yes. Do what needs to be done," the thane replied, feeling a twinge of chagrin at the thought that he himself seemed to know less about the activities of his son then everyone else.

Baker closed the door to his study and let the familiar atmosphere of his own private chamber comfort him. The fire in his belly still seethed, as it always seemed to do, but there was peace in the silence, the cool stillness, of his abode. He was glad to be back on Level Twenty-eight, far above the thane's official quarters. Here at least it was possible for him to imagine he was far away from the thane's problems as well. For the first time he felt the absence of his wife as a relief, and he took some pleasure in walking from room to room without fearing the sound of her harping voice or brittle sarcasm.

The matters of government would rise up again, but for now Baker could comfort himself with a few pleasant hours spent amid his ancient scrolls. He found them on the desk in his study, the frail parchments protected by tubes of ivory. They had come from an ancient cavern recently discovered and excavated between Levels Nineteen and Twenty. The miner who had uncovered them had suggested they might have been there for a thousand years or more.

Baker's first investigations had confirmed these were

indeed the work of Chisel Loremaster, the cherished chronicler of dwarven history. The words were written in the ancient script of the scions. Fortunately, the Helm of Tongues had untangled the arcane language, magically laying it out for Baker in words as clear as modern Hylar. He had learned that the site of the Grotto did in fact lay somewhere within the Life-Tree. Particularly intriguing had been a new piece of information, a suggestion that the ancient dragon lair was not empty. He remembered the text vividly:

> *The Graygem's power of Chaos is caught within the Platinum Egg and such power shall be unleashed when the egg is raised by the true ruler of the dwarves.*

There was more, much more. Now he went to the wardrobe where he had recalled leaving the helm, then frowned as he saw with surprise that the closet was empty. Not only was the helm missing; he realized that Garimeth's cloaks and boots had been removed. Of course, he had not yet become used to her absence.

Returning to the study, Baker wondered if, in spite of his intentions, he had absently taken the helm down to the thane's quarters. But he was certain that it had been here, just a few days ago when he had been reading the scroll that was still flattened on his desk.

And then he understood.

"Garimeth!" He spat her name with the full awareness of this monstrous betrayal, a theft that struck at more than his person—it reached out to wound his family, to threaten his very legacy. She had taken the artifact out of spite, for she knew that her husband treasured it above all things. And doubtless she knew it could be useful to herself as well.

More significant to Baker than Garimeth's reasons for taking the artifact was the simple fact that the Helm of Tongues was gone. He collapsed wearily into his chair, completely unready to face the task of getting it back. Somehow he would possess it again, but for now he didn't see how. All the scrolls, the secrets of the ancients waiting only for his perusal, would have to wait.

He sat in silent misery for some time. His stomach ached badly enough to double him over in the chair.

"My lord?" Vale's deferential voice gently penetrated Baker's pensive gloom. "Young Master Tarn is here."

"Send him in, please." Baker sat up and rubbed his eyes, trying to organize his thoughts.

"Hello, Father." Tarn stood in the doorway, his violet eyes regarding his father with an expression the elder dwarf could not read.

"Come in, Tarn, come in. Have a seat while Vale gets you something to drink."

"Thank you, but I'd rather stand."

Flushing, Baker stood and faced his son, biting back a sharp response with a considerable effort.

"Can I ask you something?" Tarn demanded.

"What is it?"

"I want to know what you're going to do."

"About what?" Baker replied, puzzled.

"About Mother, of course!"

"Do?" Baker glowered, his temper rising. "There's not much I can do, wouldn't you say? She left of her own will, after all."

"You drove her away!"

Baker gaped, stunned by the accusation. "You don't know what you're talking about!" he replied curtly. He pushed his glasses firmly onto his nose, glaring at his son.

"Yes I do. She was never welcomed here, never belonged to your Hylar society. I am one who can understand that, better than the rest of this stuck-up band of would-be nobles!"

"Any lack of welcome was her own doing. Garimeth didn't tolerate fools gladly, nor did she hesitate to call them fools to their faces. Such an attitude made it difficult

69

to make friends with those same fools. Not that it ever seemed to bother her much."

"How do you know what bothered her?"

"Apparently I didn't," Baker said, slumping again in his chair. Ignoring his son, he rubbed his temples, then slammed his fist onto the table and stood up in sudden animation. "She took the Helm of Tongues—did you know that?"

"No, she wouldn't do that!" insisted the younger dwarf. His tone turned scornful. "You probably misplaced it again. Did you have your glasses on when you looked for it?"

Baker sighed, tired of the argument even though he felt certain he was right. "I do know that she did what she wanted when she wanted to do it. And the needs or wants of anyone else never figured into her decisions. Now, I've heard all I will tolerate from you on this topic. There are matters facing Thorbardin that make our quarrel seem less than petty. I would like to talk to you about them, if you will listen. Otherwise, you can take your leave."

Tarn glared wordlessly at his father, and Baker would not have been surprised to see the young dwarf turn and stalk from the chamber. But instead Tarn exhaled slowly, then nodded in mute acquiescence.

Baker told his son about the letter he had received from Thane Hornfel. "It sounds as though these forces of Chaos are a menace unlike anything Krynn has ever faced."

"Are you warning the other clans to be prepared?"

"Axel thinks we should keep the news secret from the dark dwarves, for now. He doesn't want to reveal our weakness to the rest of Thorbardin."

"He wouldn't. He's as purebred a Hylar as you can find."

Baker ignored the implied accusation. "And you—what would you do if the decision was yours?"

"I would tell them, of course. All of them. Daergar, Klar—even the Theiwar should know."

"And suppose they use the news as an excuse to mobilize, and then turn against us?"

"I don't think they will," Tarn asserted stubbornly.

Baker muttered a curse, profane even by dwarven standards. But he had decided, and though it rankled him to rely on Tarn, to ask him for help, he would proceed. "That's why I need you. I want you to go to Daerbardin, to carry my message of good will to the thane. You must warn him of the danger, try to convince him that this is truly a dire threat. And you must return to tell me if the Daergar begin to prepare to move against us."

Tarn's exotic eyes, the purple of a twilight in the evening sky, narrowed. Baker waited impassively, wondering what thoughts were going through the mind of this stranger who was his son.

"Father, I will go."

"Good. Make your preparations to leave at once. I'll appoint another emissary to speak to the Theiwar. The Klar, of course, will do whatever the Daergar say."

"Very well," Tarn agreed. "I can be ready to go in two shifts of the boat docks."

"All right. And Tarn . . ." Baker added as his son turned toward the door.

"Yes?"

"Thank you. And good luck."

Duel for a Throne

Chapter Seven

Surrounded by his phalanx of bodyguards, Darkend Bellowsmoke strode through the north gate of the arena as if the mantle of thane already rested upon his broad shoulders. He heard the acclamation of the throng and chose to take it as praise, though it was just as likely that the gathered Daergar were cheering the prospect of imminent bloodshed. Acutely conscious of the need to make an imperial appearance, Darkend kept a slow and measured progress down the long aisle. He looked neither right nor left, concentrating hard on concealing any outward sign that would give an indication of his wounded leg.

The dark dwarf climbed to the dais, still surrounded by his henchmen. He clutched the mighty mace in his fist, grateful that the pain in his shoulder was bearable. In addition to the tiny stone, Garimeth had brought him some ointments and unguents. This morning Thistle had smeared the oily stuff over all of his hurts. Now Darkend felt that he had nearly regained his full peak of his physical prowess. Most importantly, he was able to walk without a limp. The inflamed wound in his thigh had subsided to a barely tolerable throbbing.

All eyes turned toward the west gates, the route which lead to Gludh Kolgard's house. An expectant hush settled over the vast, domed enclosure as the dark dwarves waited for the last challenger. Darkend stared at that portal as intently as any young hotblood. Although, in his case he hoped fervently that the Daergar were waiting in vain. Slickblade was posted somewhere along that route. If it was at all possible, the assassin would act to keep Kolgard from appearing in the Arena of Honor.

Though the great coliseum had been crowded for each of the previous contests, today it seemed as though every dark dwarf from the two clan cities of Daerforge and Daerbardin had tried to find a way into the room. Jammed shoulder to shoulder, they crowded the ranks of the bleachers and stood in a thick mass around the rim of the huge bowl. Even the four aisles leading to the gates had grown packed in the short time since Darkend's entrance. If Gludh Kolgard did in fact appear, he and his entourage would have to force their way through the crowd to reach the stage.

More time passed and the crowd began to simmer uneasily. Fights broke out and several Daergar were killed—though as often as not the bodies remained in place and upright since there was not enough room to move them. Darkend began to allow his hopes to rise; maybe Slickblade had found a way to do the task that he had deemed impossible.

But when the outer gates were flung open with a triumphant clang, Gludh Kolgard was alive and hearty. With his face mask open to reveal the fierce set of his jaw and his mailed fist raised to brandish his huge, double-bladed battle axe, he stood amid the score of dwarves who made up his personal corps of bodyguards. Again the crowd cheered as they took notice that he had entered the south gate—a route that had required a considerable detour from House Kolgard, but which had insured that the challenger avoided any pitfalls or ambushes that had been laid in his predicted path.

Slickblade had failed.

"I challenge you, Darkend Bellowsmoke, for the Throne of Clan Daergar, the mightiest seat in all Thorbardin. I say you are unworthy, and the blade of my axe will gladly prove it!"

"Come down here, then, if you are so eager to die!" retorted Darkend. "You have kept this august gathering waiting for too long already!"

Kolgard's response was drowned in the roar of approval, and the very bedrock underfoot seemed to tremble and shudder from the force of thousands of deep, cheering voices. Darkend kept his wide, pale eyes on the face of his adversary. He watched Gludh's bodyguards push a wide path through the crowd so that the challenger could swagger easily, free of any interference.

Abruptly one of Darkend's bodyguards leaped in front of him, then tumbled forward, gagging on a crossbow bolt that pierced his throat. The assailant had been one of the anonymous thousands in the crowd, and Darkend could barely suppress a shudder as he saw how close the missile had come to striking him. Somehow the bodyguard had sensed the danger to his master and had made the ultimate sacrifice in his service.

"An arrow from the crowd? A coward's path!" the patriarch of the Bellowsmoke clan cried as he shook his mace toward the approaching challenger. These words were lost on the Daergar as the excitement built to a crescendo. The dark dwarves, having sipped the first bloodshed, now thirsted madly for the main event.

As Gludh started up the steps leading to the dais,

several more silver darts flashed through the crowd. Some were deflected off of bodyguards' raised shields, and a few dwarves of Kolgard's entourage fell writhing, pierced by the lethal weapons. Another of Darkend's men fell before the two main combatants finally came face to face with each other. Each stood in the midst of a semicircle of armored, brawny henchmen.

"Let the matter be decided between us alone," Darkend stated the ritual words.

"And let the will of Reorx be revealed," replied Gludh, clamping shut the smooth steel barrier of his face plate. Even his luminous eyes were lost in the shadows of the narrow vision slits.

With the compact agreed upon, the bodyguards withdrew to just below the ring of the stone dais. There would be no more assassin's arrows for the time being, the time-honored phrases having commenced the formal part of the ritual. The strenth and skill of the two combatants alone would decide the fight.

The roaring of the crowd slowly stilled and was replaced by a soft buzz of anticipation. Here and there the bodyguards around the periphery of the dais jockeyed for position, stabbing and chopping at each other until a solid ring of dwarf warriors enclosed the circular platform. Bleeding and moaning, several hapless losers thrashed on the floor behind the henchmen. But these wretches were left to die unnoticed. All eyes focused on the impending duel.

Gludh Kolgard struck first, bringing his long-hafted axe around in a vicious swipe. Darkend didn't even need to step back for this attack was all show and the keen blade passed several inches in front of his tusked faceplate. Gludh followed this move smoothly, skirting sideways around the edge of the platform to keep his weapon between himself and his opponent.

The music of battle, a familiar emotion that mingled rage, hate, and exultation, swept through Darkend. He used the strength of his feelings to toughen his will and focus his power against his enemy—a tactic that was second nature after a lifetime of battle and killing. Even so, his subconscious remained aware of his weakness, the pain of his wounds and the toll taken by the days of previous fighting that had led him up to this moment. His movements seemed slow, like wading through sticky mud. He almost felt drugged, his senses and reactions thick. The deep gouge in his thigh was particularly worrisome. It periodically sent daggers of agony shooting through his leg and hip. He planted his feet with a show of firmness, careful not to reveal any outward sign that would give his opponent a clear suggestion of his vulnerability.

Darkend lowered his mace, clutching the haft in both of his mailed fists as he waved the spiked head of the weapon gently back and forth in the direction of his challenger. He held the center of the dais, pivoting only enough to continue facing the circling Gludh. The crowd rumbled, the noise swelling, expanding to a roaring thunder. The great arena shook and compelled the combatants into action.

Abruptly Gludh charged, the great axe raised high over his head. Darkend backed up for a step, then darted to his left. This forced Darkend's foe to hack the blade down and across his body, an awkward strike that his steel-hafted mace easily parried. Following through, Darkend waded in with his weapon smashing left, right, then back to the left. Now it was Gludh's turn to parry, using his axe to deflect each blow of Darkend's wickedly spiked weapon.

Darkend swept ahead eagerly, hoping to bring the fight to a rapid conclusion. Already he could feel the throbbing in his muscles. Fatigue would soon add weight to his weapon and sluggishness to his every reaction. But Gludh met his onrush with feet planted firmly, the axe held crossways in both hands so that ultimately the blows of the mace clattered against an immovable barrier. Defending himself, Gludh seemed to meet the attacks with ease, while Darkend felt his strength draining away with each futile blow.

And then Gludh made a surprising move. Ducking low, he jabbed with the head of his axe almost as if he were stabbing with a spear. In the darkness the moving shadow struck true, and the blunt end of the weapon crashed into Darkend's thigh.

His flesh was protected by a sheath of black steel plate mail, but the wound underneath that plate was still painfully sensitive. With a groan of agony, Darkend staggered backward, striving desperately to hold himself upright. Another attack forced him to pivot and plant his full weight on his injured limb, and the maneuver inevitably sent him tumbling to the floor. Only a frantic roll enabled him to escape the crushing swipe of the axe that smashed the surface where he had fallen. Darkend grasped the steel shaft of his mace with both hands, using the weapon as a bar to deflect the next blow of his enemy's heavy weapon. He managed to knock the wicked blade aside mere inches from the tusked protrusions of his faceplate.

Gludh's blade slashed, barely missing the prone Daergar's fingers. Once again a desperate twist sent the axe blade bouncing into the floor. Darkend kicked his opponent in the knee, forcing him backward and buying enough time for the weary warrior to scramble to his knees. With a wild swing of the mace he pushed Gludh even farther back, and was able to use his good leg to push himself back on his feet.

Trying to lunge in pursuit, Darkend felt his injured leg falter. Although he recovered his balance, his foe was easily able to evade his clumsy swing. Darkend imagined Gludh's elation as his weakpoints were revealed to all. Jeers and shouts came from much of the gallery, while others in the bloodthirsty crowd—presumably those with hefty bets on Darkend—groaned in audible dismay. Snarling louder, the injured Darkend drove forward, limping but still moving with surprising agility. He forced his enemy to fall back around the edge of the dais.

But even in his retreat Gludh sneered in expectant triumph. The arrogant sound of his laughter rang in Darkend's ears. Still the mace-wielding dwarf pressed his attack, reaching farther with each swing until a voice of caution whispered in his mind, reminding him of danger. He knew that Kolgard was toying with him, drawing him into an ever faster pursuit, sapping the thin residue of endurance that allowed his injured leg to hold him up at all.

Darkend halted abruptly at the exact moment Gludh made his sudden move. The retreating dwarf feinted a lunge backward, then planted his feet and swung the mighty axe. The blade whistled past Darkend's chest, a mere inch short of carving a deep and gory wound. The followup attack by the mace was feeble, coming nowhere near his opponent. The sounds of the crowd swelled again as the course of battle reversed.

Gludh threw himself into a frenzied attack, bringing the axe downward, then swinging it across from right to left and the reverse. He made a difficult upswing that sent Darkend stumbling to avoid a potentially disemboweling blow. The mace swiped in response, but now Darkend's exhausted shoulders were straining and weariness brought on by a week of duels turned his arms to lead. Again and again he avoided the lethal slashes, but each came a fraction of an inch closer than the previous attack. Inevitably one of the blows would bite deeply into Bellowsmoke's flesh.

Remembering the stone in his pocket, the enchanted item given to him by his sister, Darkend was sorely tempted to draw it forth as a last resort. But some grim vestige of pride held his hand and he found the strength to plant his feet for one last showdown with his attacker. Drawing on his last reserves, he lifted his mace and met his enemy's blows, parrying the deadly axeblade and striking desperately with his own spiked weapon.

The hammering blows echoed in the great chamber. The mace and axe sparked as the two dark dwarves fought like berserkers. Their weapons were a ringing blur of gray steel, whistling in from one side and then the other. Gludh was apparently content to let his foe exhaust himself with a fruitless series of attacks. When one of Darkend's blows finally swung wide, Gludh struck, bringing his axe down on his enemy's forearm with ringing force. Darkend gasped as he felt his arm go numb. Once again he stumbled away, trying to buy precious seconds to recover.

But Gludh Kolgard was clearly ready to end the fight. He stepped forward, swinging again and again, forcing Darkend inexorably across the dais that suddenly seemed terribly small. Soon the back of Darkend's boot had reached the edge, and Gludh's attacks still came without ceasing.

Darkend swung his mace wildly, merely to hold his opponent back for a fraction of a second so that his left hand could reach into his belt pocket. He quickly found the small stone and rubbed it hard between his fingers.

Gludh brought his axe up, holding the weapon in both hands as he readied himself for a skull-crushing blow. Darkend hurled the stone down to the dais, closing his eyes in the split second before impact.

Even through his tightly shut lids Darkend saw the bright flash of light. The shouts and cries of thousands of Daergar assailed his ears. The assembled masses had been painfully shocked by the sudden blast of brilliant illumination.

Gludh blinked stupidly as he brought his axe down in the spot that Darkend had just abandoned. The sharp blade bit into the floor. Drawing back for another blow, Gludh revealed his vulnerability: his face plate swung wildly. It was a simple matter for Darkend to hiss a cry of victory as he masked his mouth with his flattened hand and thereby make the sound seem to originate from a place several paces to his right. Fully blinded, Gludh spun on his heel and faced the area where he thought he had heard his enemy.

He never fully appreciated his mistake. Darkend's mace came down so hard on his head that Gludh Kolgard was dead before he felt the blow that killed him.

For long moments Darkend stood weakly, drawing ragged gasps of breath as he stared down at the corpse of his last challenger. At first he was surprised at the lack of loud reaction from the vast gallery, but it soon dawned on him that the Daergar in the arena had undoubtedly been as stunned and momentarily blinded as Gludh Kolgard himself.

"Foul!" One bold watcher cried. This was soon echoed by hundreds and then thousands, of voices. The cries rose to a wall of sound as the blinking dark dwarves gradually regained their sight and witnessed the unfair result of the duel.

"Magic!" hissed one burly patriarch, a stubborn and lifelong rival whom Darkend recognized as Berest Elfslayer. "The duel is void!"

"The challenger is dead! I am the new thane of the Daergar, and I claim my eminence before you all!"

The bodyguards of the new thane had already scrambled onto the dais, forming a protective ring around their leader. Darkend stood in their midst, hands on hips and bristling chin jutting forward as he pivoted to face the Daergar. These were the crucial moments he knew— moments when the remembrance of his cheating was fresh and glaring in the minds of all. But his power was convincing as he stood with a rank of armored dwarves facing a comparatively unarmed populace.

"Nay! Let the matter be re-opened. The pretender must face another challenger!" cried Berest Elfslayer bravely.

Trying to ignore the voice, Darkend looked around impatiently. Where was Slickblade? Surely he would silence this rude dissent.

"Foul and cheat!" Berest shouted again, trying to whip up the support which was beginning to grow through the crowd.

"Watch your tongue, Elfslayer!" snarled Darkend. "Lest I remove it from your mouth."

"I will not—"

The response was interrupted by a gagging retch as Berest Elfslayer toppled forward, the hilt of a dagger jutting from his back. Garimeth Bellowsmoke calmly reached forward, retrieved her weapon with a sharp tug, and wiped the blood on the dead dwarf's tunic before straightening up and looking around in cool triumph.

The auditorium was deathly silent. Many recognized Darkend's long-absent sister. Darkend counted off ten heartbeats while he savored the imminence of his victory. Finally he spoke. His voice was clear, calm, and forceful enough to quell any lingering sounds of dissent.

"I will begin my audit of the treasury immediately," he announced, claiming his right which was every new thane's most urgent duty. "My victory feast shall be laid for all the Two Cities at the start of the following cycle. The heralds will cry the word as soon as I am ready to entertain your audiences."

He was greeted by silence, though he heard one solitary grumble of disgust. Out of the corner of his eye he saw Steelcut Gutterblood—a young noble with nearly as much influence as Berest Elfslayer—all but spitting on the floor in his outrage. Yet when Darkend confronted the sturdy hothead with a direct look, young Gutterblood merely dipped his head in the proper bow.

With the eerie silence ringing louder than any echoes of clashing steel, the new thane of the Daergar marched to the center of his phalanx and out the gates of the arena into the broad, deserted streets of the city that was now his rightful domain.

A Throne Made Easy

Chapter Eight

"I have two jobs for you: Steelcut Gutterblood, Younger and Elder. Fortunately, Berest Elfslayer has already been dealt with by my sister."

His rage slightly pacified by his triumph, Darkend Bellowsmoke issued these orders to his assassin, known only as Slickblade.

"Your commands are my life, lord," replied Slickblade with a slight inclination of his head.

For this brief interval the two Daergar were alone, though the shouts of the thane's lieutenants could be heard throughout the halls of the great palace. Juding from the sounds, the search of the premises was proceeding smoothly.

"May they be both your life and the death of my enemies!" Darkend replied, chuckling grimly. Now that he was sitting in the thane's throne, surrounded by the opulence of his position, his mood was beginning to brighten. The throbbing in his leg was gone, the wound itself cleansed and further healed by some ointment found in the thane's pharmacologies.

The assassin made his farewells with formal politeness then exited through one of the secret passages that had quickly yielded itself to Darkend's inspection. As time passed in this great palace, he knew that he would undoubtedly discover more such passages. Momentarily he cursed Halt Blackmetal, his predecessor, for not maintaining a blueprint or some other kind of written directions to the maze of this place.

A knock suddenly thudded onto the great steel doors of his vaulted chamber, reminding him of more pragmatic concerns.

Garimeth Bellowsmoke, alone and clad in a cape of shimmering silver foil, was admitted to the throne room by an unseen doorman. She curtsied with great formality before rising to approach the great chair.

"Ah, dear sister, thank you for responding to my invitation with such alacrity."

"You impress me, Lord Thane, with your command of language. Where have you been 'matriculating,' that you should use a word like 'alacrity'?"

"There are many things about me that you do not know, though we are bound by blood. It would do you well to remember that it may be best to keep some matters in the dark."

"Ever I shall, lord—or may I call you 'brother'?"

"As you will. Your return to our city is fortuitous, for it is my intention that you serve me in many ways, in positions of power and influence, at my right hand."

"My brother knows that he has but to speak, and I will obey."

"My first command is this: You are to insure that my coronation feast is the most memorable in the lifetime of our clan's most venerable elders. The menu shall consist of only the finest blindfish from the depths of the Urkhan Sea. There is to be a plentitude, enough to stuff the belly of even the most lowly footman among my armies."

"A wise choice, Lord. A full stomach is the best way to still a complaining tongue."

"Indeed. As for beverage, you are to buy the finest barrels from every brewer in Daerbardin and Daerforge. Every dark dwarf shall be invited to drink and I want none to grow surly from sucking at an empty spigot."

"Naturally, my brother. And may I suggest the pear fungus from the south warren. The crop has just ripened, and I am told that the mushrooms are the largest and most flavorful in recent memory."

"Good. Buy the whole crop. We'll have it fried, baked, and carved—prepared every tasty way known to the clan's chefs."

"May I inquire as to the funding, Lord Brother? Doubtless you realize that the expense will be enormous."

"The coins will come from my own treasury. I don't want it generally known, but Blackmetal was a cursed old miser. It turns out that there's more steel in those vaults than anyone could have imagined. Heed me, sister. You are to spare no expense. I want every Daergar in the Two Cities to recognize my beneficence, and to feel indebted to the new thane."

"It shall be done."

Garimeth curtsied again, but before she could turn to depart her brother spoke again.

"In your long years in Hybardin, it occurs to me that you must have come into contact with dwarves from all the five clans. Is that correct?"

"Indeed, brother."

"The Theiwar and the Klar? Did you have cause to take note, to learn their ways and their customs?"

"Their comings and goings were frequent in Hybardin and their leaders well known to me. Indeed, I made contacts among both clans. I came to know them nearly as well as I learned the ways of the arrogant Hylar themselves."

"Including their secret speech?"

"Ah! Fortuitously, there is something I have brought from Hybardin, a mere toy to my husband, but I guessed it would prove very useful to myself and to those I choose to aid. It seems I was prescient in this regard. It is an artifact that renders all languages an open slate to me."

"Splendid. Know this, my sister: When my feast has been done, there will be great matters before the clan. I shall rely on your counsel for much of this and your ear shall be my proof against treachery."

"As ever, brother, I am yours to command."

Garimeth's curtsy was deep, her words humble, but even these manners could not conceal from Darkend her tight smile of pure, gleeful ambition.

* * * * *

The feast was a grand success. However, as he leaned on the great veranda of his palace and digested his belly full of food, Darkend was still aware of an undercurrent of distrust lurking in the city of his people. Naturally, he had heard no mention of his use of magic during the duel, but he was well aware that the majority of his subjects regarded his tactic as little better than cowardice.

Still, they had seen him win several duels quite fairly and none could dispute his prowess as a warrior. Furthermore, the subtle presence of Slickblade—who had appeared in many guises throughout the three cycles that the feast had lasted—insured that the least loyal Daergar carefully watched their tongues, even when they thought they were among their oldest and most faithful friends.

For now, Darkend would content himself with the grudging acceptance of his people. Soon enough he would show them beyond any doubt that he was the dark dwarf who should rule them, that he was a thane who would bring them to a glory never before attained by the clan Daergar in all the history of Thorbardin.

From his lofty elevation he could see the blocky structures flanking the beginning of the Fifteenth Road. Great warehouses and apartments rose like cliffs from the straight and precise boundary of the road. The numberous crenellated battle platforms along the walls gave the impression of fortified bulwarks overlooking one of the main roads that connected the two cities of the Daergar. Each of the platforms was the stronghold of one or another of the city's warrior-gangs, and was constantly garrisoned by at least a small troop of armed dwarves.

Darkend's eyes rose to inspect the vast blackness of the straight tunnel leading to Daerforge. Daerbardin, the largest of the kingdom's seven cities, lay at the terminus of the long, lightless avenue. Natural illumination was neither sought nor welcomed by this dark-dwelling clan.

For once Darkend found himself wishing that he could see the Life-Tree of the Hylar. That great stalactite-city hanging from the cavern's ceiling like an inverted mountain, occupied so much of his thoughts, plans, and desires. He would have readily tolerated the hateful expanses of lanterns, lights, and flares that clearly marked the Hylar as a separate people from the Daergar and Theiwar. It was beyond his sight now, he reminded himself, but soon enough he would lay his eyes on that dazzling monument to corruption, wealth, and power

Before then other matters required his attention. The first of these commenced as Thistle came out through the balcony doors.

"The thanes of the Theiwar and the Klar are here, my lord."

"Good. I expected them shortly, and I am pleased that they have honored me with promptness. Have my own robe prepared."

"Aye. But, lord . . . I beg leave to speak to you on a matter of delicacy and importance."

Darkend looked at his mistress with interest. She was hesitant, allowing her dark hair to curl over her face, masking her eyes for a moment. But then she flipped her locks out of the way and glared at the thane with an expression of determination.

"It is about the feast, lord. There have been some complaints that have reached my ears. Funding was provided for many kegs that were not delivered, and no one knows where the steel coin has gone."

Darkend kept his face impassive. He well knew what Thistle was implying. After all, Garimeth Bellowsmoke had been in charge of the budget for the entire celebration and only the thane and his sister had complete access to the treasury. But this was not the matter of most concern to Darkend. Indeed, he would have been surprised if Gari had not found some way to amplify her personal fortune during the course of the task.

Rather, the thane found it curious that Thistle had bothered to call this news to his attention. *She's jealous,* he suddenly realized with a grim thrill. *She fears that her status is in jeopardy now that my sister has returned.*

"Thank you for speaking so frankly," he said, his voice as soft as silk. "I know what must be done."

"I am grateful, lord," replied the dwarf woman, who then withdrew to see to the matter of his royal robe.

Darkend took one last look at the stretch of dark road, then turned toward the great doors. Before he could take a step, a figure emerged from the shadows beside the wall, causing the new thane to stiffen with instinctive alarm. His gaze attempted to penetrate the gloom, and he recognized the shrouded nature of the black-clad form.

"Slickblade?" Darkend's fingers tightened around the haft of his dagger until he received confirmation.

"The same, lord. I am here to report success in the matter of your commands."

"Double success?"

"Of course." The assassin's tone was injured.

Darkened nodded, pleased with the news that certain significant rivals had been eliminated.

"But wait." The thane stopped Slickblade before the assassin turned away. "There is an additional matter . . . a thing I would like you to take care of . . . "

Darkend explained the additional task, which the assassin was more than happy to oblige. Finally Slickblade disappeared, though the ruler of the Daergar couldn't say exactly where he went. The dark-shrouded figure had simply vanished into the shadows at the base of the wall.

Immensely pleased, the thane went back into his throne room where he allowed his attendants to drape his black robe over his shoulders. The garment spread to either side of the great chair like the wings of an enormous bat while the black and red banner of the Smoking Forge was grandly displayed behind him. Garimeth took a seat at his side, and he saw with a tight smile that Thistle was nowhere in sight. The Daergar thane reclined with just the right amount of arrogance as two dwarves, each trailed by an entourage fitting to their royal stations, advanced and bowed.

"My lords, I bid you welcome," declared Darkend, rising and stepping forward as the cloak fanned wide behind him. He took each of the two visiting thanes by the hand, exerting gentle pressure as he looked deep into their faces with eyes that saw well in the lightless vault.

Pounce Quickspring, thane of the clan Theiwar, met Darkend's look with frank, luminous orbs that seemed to swell out of his face. He blinked as the milky lenses of his eyes strained for focus. Darkend shivered, certain that the Theiwar had some item of magic concealed upon his person— typical for a member of his race. Fortunately, Pounce seemed more than happy to keep his private possessions to himself. A bristling head of straw-colored hair grew down the thane's forehead, and he muttered a reply to the greeting with a certain sense of contained agitation.

Beside Pounce, Tufa Bloodeye, long-time ruler of the wild Klar dwarves, squinted to penetrate the darkness. His eyes were flushed with spots of watery crimson that gave ample proof of the origin of his surname. Unlike the suspicious and quiet Theiwar, Tufa beamed cheerfully and shook Darkend's hand with unfeigned enthusiasm. The Daergar thane was pleased by the warm greeting, though he knew that the Klar's disposition could alter dramatically at a moment's notice. Like virtually all of his violent clan, Tufa Bloodeye was more than half insane.

"Allow me to present my sister," Darkend offered as Garimeth came forward. He accorded her a courtly introduction and she immediately escorted the visiting thanes to the banquet table that had been laid at the side of the huge room. Soon Daergar, Klar, and Theiwar were mingling easily as they sampled a variety of beverages and milled about the great throne room among a mixture of other nobles and their many bodyguards.

Abruptly a gong sounded and the stilted conversations faded away. "I have arranged for a trifle entertainment," Darkend announced from the platform before his throne. He indicated a stage at the far side of the room, and all saw that a rack had been placed there. "Please, be seated."

The thane indicated benches that his servants had arrayed before the throne, and quickly the guests and hosts were all reclining comfortably with good views of both the rack and the Daergar thane.

"Bring on the subject," declared Darkend with a clap of his hands.

Guards immediately hustled into view, pulling along a prisoner. Thistle.

At the sight of the thane she screamed and began to plead. "Sire, what have I done? You are my master. Punish me as you will, but not—"

"Gag her!" directed the thane, unhappy with her stream of verbage.

The female dwarf's voice was muffled into a series of strangled sobs as the guards hastened to obey. Darkend beamed, watching as she was tightly lashed to the framework of the rack. He was pleased to see that Slickblade had followed his orders with precision. She was not unconscious, nor apparently wounded from her capture.

"This is my favorite mistress, a great treasure of mine," Darkend began. "I intend to offer her life as a bond for the words we are about to exchange, and as a symbol of the bond that shall be formed between our clans."

Thistle moaned in despair at his words, but Darkend continued as if he had heard nothing.

Now he addressed himself specifically to Tufa Bloodeye and Pounce Quickspring. "We gather here in another cause, that of allegiance between our three great tribes, and I thought it only fitting that my own treasure should serve as the seal of that friendship.

To this end he invited each of the visiting thanes to accompany him up to the rack. They were provided with a rope, a golden tassel knotted with silver ends.

"Please, my guests . . . you must each take an end."

"I shall!" said Tufa Bloodeye, enthusiastically eyeing the weeping Thistle as he took up his cord.

"And I, too," Pounce said seriously, squatting to stare with every evidence of detached curiosity into the female dwarf's bulging eyes. Beads of sweat bursting from her brow, Thistle tried to say something, but could only chew frantically on the gag.

"Good," agreed the thane of the Daergar, placing a hand at either end of the cord which dangled just below Thistle's neck.

"Tonight we shall talk of great deeds, of mighty goals and important promises. In the nature of our sacred trust, we shall commence by taking this cord and sealing the throat, the breath, and the life of my cherished mistress."

"And then, my friends," Darkend declared warmly, as he himself hooked the noose over Thistle's head, "we shall commence a celebration that, Reorx willing, shall not cease for a thousand years."

An Emissary

Chapter Nine

Already Tarn could see the improvements that Belicia had made in her ragtag company. First of all, the number of prospective dwarf warriors had more than tripled in a few days. Obviously, Axel and Baker were somehow finding fresh recruits from among the population of Hybardin. And now the dwarf woman had her recruits marching in time and forming their shield wall with a marked sense of speed and precision. From his comfortable seat atop a sack of mulch, Tarn watched the Hylar train, a process that now required a sizeable swath of the dockside.

"Line forward!" Belicia Felixia barked out the command. Her dwarves advanced, shields and swords set, their straight line unwavering.

"Double march! Now, charge!"

The half-breed couldn't help but admire the quick but

coordinated advance made by the line. Now the young dwarves rushed forward with lusty abandon, a hundred voices rising in a fierce, swelling roar. The pounding of boots was a thunderous drumbeat on the stone ground, and Tarn was surprised as he felt a tingle of martial frenzy.

But of course it was just a drill. Belicia halted her advancing shield wall at the very brink of the water's edge and then the recruits were dismissed to their barracks up on Level Three.

"You're making progress," he congratulated her when she took a seat beside him.

"I know, but it's a big wharf we've got to defend—all the way around the island. We still have nowhere near enough troops to hold the whole line."

"I'm sure it won't come to that," Tarn declared earnestly.

"Well, I hope your trip to Daerbardin can help keep the peace. Are you going soon?"

"I have a berth on the next lake boat, but I'm sure I can get a seat on the one after that. Tomorrow, if you can get a little time away." He took her hand, looked at her warmly. "We haven't had a chance lately . . . but maybe now . . . "

"Not now." Belicia surprised him with the sharpness of her tone. "I have important work to do. I'm teaching a hundred youngsters to shoot bows and arrows and these recruits have work to do on the city's defenses. And you, too, have a mission to accomplish."

"Yes, I do." He flushed and stood up. "I can see that's what matters!"

"Tarn, grow up! Of course it's what matters!" Belicia shook her head in exasperation. "But you might remember that you've been hanging around the docks for months, doing a whole lot of nothing. You had time then, and so did I! But it seemed to me you weren't ready to take advantage of it."

He hung his head. "I guess you're right," he said stiffly, stung because so much of what she said was true. He remembered weeks, months of lethargy when nothing seemed important or urgent. Time had stretched away from him then, an apparently eternal stream of placid ease.

And now that lost time suddenly seemed precious.

"Do you think you'll be allowed to see the thane of the Daergar?" asked Belicia.

"I think so. First, I'll stop and see my mother. She's gone back to her family home near the port. With any luck, she'll be able to help me get a proper interview."

"I wish you good luck with your mission," Belicia said in obvious sincerity. "And . . . and I'll look forward to seeing you when you get back. All right?"

But he was still too stung and too proud to soften in the face of her pleasantries, so they parted with uncertainty lingering in the air between them.

He made his way to the east dock, where the passengers were boarding the chain ferry to Daerforge. Unlike the slender, sharp-prowed freeboats that plied the waters around all the dwarven cities, the ferry was wide and raft-like. This also insured that it was large and stately, offering comfortable booths and even sleeping accommodations to those who wished to nap over the six hour voyage. Now the craft was nearly full of passengers, mostly dark dwarves, though Tarn saw representatives from all the other clans—except the Aghar, of course.

This was perhaps his tenth voyage on such a ferry, but he still watched with fascination as the great hook lowered from the chain that was slowly clanking over the boat. The progress of the metal links slowed into an eerie silence and dwarf boatmen swiftly latched the steel prong onto the prow. Tarn braced his feet as the gears overhead resumed with a sturdy lurch and the broad ferry was pulled away from the dock. A small wash of water rippled away from the hull as the craft began its slow, steady progress across the lake.

He found his berth amidship, a comfortable couch in a

booth which he shared with three Daergar. The largest and most vocal quickly introduced the three as workmen who had helped to deliver the most recent shipment of raw steel. He was a black-bearded hulk with wide set eyes, now squinting against the Hybardin dock lights. He cheerily offered the half-breed a bottle, and Tarn swilled down a fiery draught of fungus wine.

"We've got a spot of pay. Plannin' to pass the time with a few throws of the dice. Join us, if you've the cost of a game," he suggested with a look of appraisal at Tarn's silk jacket and elegant, polished boots.

"It would be a pleasure," the half-breed agreed readily, producing a few steel coins without putting any real dent in his purse.

They passed the bottle and the hours, gambling with an assortment of pegs and spikes cast in various patterns onto the deck. The lights of Hybardin soon faded into an agreeable wash in the background as the clinking chain pulled their craft farther across the silent sea. Even from a great distance the Life-Tree stood outlined in its funnel shape, marked by thousands of twinkling lights that gradually merged into a general glow.

Tarn enjoyed the crude, easy sociability of the dark dwarves. He liked the way his comrades insulted each other without taking offense. It was an interesting contrast, he thought, to the way things were managed among the Hylar. Even saying farewell to Belicia had seemed to him like walking through a maze of verbal traps.

And at least one of those traps had been sprung, he reflected ruefully. Suddenly wishing that he'd been more sensitive and understanding during that conversation, he vowed to make it up to the dwarf woman as soon as he saw her again.

Finally, with his head swimming slightly and his purse poorer by a score of steel pieces, Tarn felt the darkness that was the true underworld settle all around him. Daerforge rose from the black distance, and his keen eyes made out the terraces and balconies, the bulwarks and towers that jutted from the steep cliffs surrounding the dark dwarf harbor. There, near the top of the crest, just before the wall curved outward to form the lofty roof over the underground sea, he saw the proud bastion of House Bellowsmoke, his mother's great manor.

The surroundings were fully black, with no sign of lantern or fire, but as the boat pulled into a stone-walled slip carved into the bedrock of the waterfront, Tarn was struck less by the darkness of this city than by its strange silence. There was activity all over the place—cargoes loaded onto other boats nearby, here a hundred passengers debarking from the chain ferry, there crowded into a narrow plaza arcing between the sea and the cliff, a thriving market bustling with sellers and buyers alike. Yet everywhere the Daergar went about their business stealthily. They spoke no louder than a hushed whisper, and even the scuffing of the steel-hulled boat against the stone wharf was but a muted scrape. Only when the doors of a waterfront inn burst open did the true and raucous nature of the dark dwarves echo across the docks for a few minutes.

Weaving slightly as he bid farewell to his traveling companions, Tarn realized that the fiery wine had been surprisingly potent. Still, he was able to climb out of the boat and make his way through the dockside plaza to the base of a long, curving path. He started uphill, and was soon out of breath. This was a grade that really could have used a flight of stairs, he thought with a ragged gasp—and he was only just now coming to the second level of the city!

Daerforge had three different elevations. On this second one he paused to catch his breath and to take a look over the lake. Below him was a sprawling slope that looked like a garbage dump or the refuse of an ancient landslide. He remembered that this was Agharbardin, the home of many thousands of gully dwarves, though from this height he couldn't see any signs of activity in the ravines and troughs among the great rocks.

Moving up again, Tarn passed great manors, each a blocky structure more than half-buried in the bedrock of the steep mountainside. Some were guarded by spiked towers, others by lofty walls with many twists and turns. The pathway skirted the base of some houses and overlooked more of them as it climbed. Tarn saw that the stone houses were well fortified from above as well. Chutes had been excavated between many of the structures, insuring that any large band of attackers could be swept into a trap that would send the whole company cascading downhill. He had visited here many times since his earliest years, but had never before noticed this defense. Indeed, as he looked around, it occurred to him that the Daergar seemed quite a bit better prepared for war than were the Hylar.

Finally he stood before the lofty gate, a steel ramp upraised between two tall towers of black marble. A ditch, dark and full of pungent muck, blocked his path. He recognized the stone drum beside the moat. He pounded on the hollow boulder with the hilt of his sword, three long raps followed by a trio of staccato taps.

At the signal that identified him as one of the family, chains immediately clanked through their gears and the steel ramp slowly and quietly began to descend. By the time it provided him with a walkway, Tarn could see servants and a gateman waiting to receive him.

"Master Tarn," declared Karc, a grizzled footman Tarn had known since his earliest years, "It is an honor to have you among us again."

He allowed the attendants to remove his cape and satchel and was shown into a parlor while Karc went to find his mother. Garimeth materialized shortly thereafter, just as he was uncorking the carafe of mead that had been presented to him by a bowing servant.

"I was expecting you," Garimeth Bellowsmoke said, "though I didn't think you would get here quite so soon."

"I am here on business, I'm afraid," Tarn replied, pouring a couple of glasses and passing one to his mother. "Duty calls. I am on a mission for the thane."

He couldn't keep an element of self-mockery out of his voice, and Garimeth laughed. "I shouldn't think it would take much of an excuse to get you out of Hybardin, although it's good and timely that you've done so. You should stay here with me. You'll have a whole wing to yourself. This is a good time to be a Bellowsmoke in Daerforge."

"I am a Bellowgranite, remember?" he said, half sarcastically.

She sniffed. "Pay attention. Your dear uncle has just attained the throne of the Two Cities and he has great plans afoot. You will be able to play an important role, whatever you happen to think of your heritage."

"Your brother Darkend?" Tarn was impressed. "Good. My mission is to seek the thane himself and give him a message from my father. All the easier if it's Uncle Darkend."

"What message?" Garimeth queried, her brows knitting thoughtfully.

"You heard about the letter from Thane Hornfel, didn't you? And the 'Storm of Chaos, a danger that hangs over all Krynn like a blade of fire'? Well, I convinced father that the news should be shared with the other clans—that we should all make preparations in case of danger in Thorbardin."

"Indeed. Well, there's no hurry. Darkend is in Daerbardin and it will take you half a day to get there from Daerforge. Why don't you wait for a cycle? I'm expecting him here tomorrow and you can give him your message in person here."

The change in his worlds seemed to be catching up to Tarn and the notion of resting here, relaxing for a brief while, had a strong appeal. He helped himself to another glass of mead. "This is an excellent brew. Shall I fill yours up as well?"

Garimeth held out her glass and regarded her son through narrowed eyes. "Do you understand what kind of power I'm talking about?" she asked, leaning back to sip from her dark beverage. "It's rather unprecedented."

"To have our family on the Daergar throne. I'd say it's extraordinary."

"Not just that," Gari said impatiently. "But Darkend has been in conference with the thanes of the Theiwar, and the Klar . . . and it went rather well."

"Really? Remarkable! All three clans?" Tarn asked eagerly. "That *is* unprecedented. Are they still here? Perhaps I could see them—"

"No. They departed a cycle ago. But surely your mission doesn't concern them?"

"Not in so many words, but I know my father, the thane, was going to send emissaries to them as well. It's actually a rather ambitious plan that he has. I think it might work."

"Karc." Garimeth raised her voice slightly, and the attendant appeared immediately. "Bring us another bottle—the special batch from the back cellar if you please."

"Very well, my lady."

"Now, this plan you speak of?" She turned her attention back to Tarn as soon as the servant withdrew. "You say that Baker is informing the Klar and the Theiwar of the danger and trying to make some kind of an alliance?"

"Yes! And with the Daergar, too. That's where I'm going to try and be some . . . help." Tarn was aware that his mind felt very sharp, but for some reason his tongue was growing thick in his mouth. He probably should slow down with the mead, but then, it had been a long journey and the beverage was really quite refreshing. Taking another sip, he confirmed more detail for his mother.

Tarn continued to talk as the new bottle was brought and tapped. His mother declined with a gentle wave of her hand over the top of her glass, so the younger dwarf swilled and spoke contentedly. He had a brief recollection of his father's rude accusation that his mother had stolen the Helm of Tongues. Tarn felt a momentary inclination to ask her about it. But not now—the time wasn't right—and besides, the mead was so delicious.

Tarn was taken quite by surprise when the room began to spin. He reached for the table . . . his chair . . . anything . . . but his fingers were numb, his hands like useless clubs. His blurring vision gave way to darkness, and he didn't feel the thud as his limp body collapsed to the floor.

Interlude of Chaos

The stuff of Chaos tore at the fabric of countless worlds. War raged across the planes. The Queen of Darkness was pulled from the realm of her dark Abyss, summoned like all her pantheon by a transcendent need, forced into battle with the Father of all Gods. For the first time in her eons of existence she fought in the same cause as her nemesis, Paladine—yet even with the aid of that great platinum dragon and all the other deities in Krynn's cosmos, they were sorely pressed.

For Father Chaos was a wild and untamed enemy, rapacious and unstoppable now that he had finally gained release. In the places where immortals dwelled, toward the already battle-scarred face of Krynn, the blight of wild death and destruction swelled unchecked. Takhisis was compelled farther and farther from her own domain and had no attention to spare the Abyss.

And so from that place of nothing and everything they came, by wing and claw, by darkness and from hunger, a horde that served a single goal and followed but one master: The daemon warrior Zarak Thuul. Astride his mighty fire dragon, he gath-

ered his legion from all the corners of the Dark Queen's realm.

In the vanguard came a host of shadow-wights from the vileness of never-life, casting an eerie dark blanket through a vast swath of existence. These were beings whose presence evoked horror and dismay, for they were the cruelest of killers. Not only did they claim the lives of their victims, but in so doing they obliterated any memory, any lasting impact or continuing influence created by the hapless one's existence.

Other serpentine things also answered the summons of the mighty one. Primus was but one of the fire dragons—the greatest and most terrible to be sure—amongst a great host of blazing monsters that swept into the daemon warrior's wake. They swarmed into the sky like flaming spears, wings pulsing, great necks extending. Their fires were the beacons, pennants, and martial banners of the daemon warrior's army.

Following the blazing meteor that was Primus, the creatures of Chaos swarmed to the light and the fire and the promise of destruction. They flew through the thick murk that spills into the gaps between the planes as they followed the beacon, advancing to the command and the pleasure of the mighty daemon warrior.

And Zarak Thuul, feeling the unstoppable rush of combined power, threw back his massive head and howled with laughter.

Dark Chambers

Chapter Ten

His tongue was thick and terribly dry, like a dead, dusty corpse that had somehow come to rest in his mouth. When he tried to open his eyes his head was wracked with pain. He immediately twisted on some flat, yielding surface. He choked and gagged, mindlessly sick.

For a long time he held his head in his hands, groaning feebly and trying to squeeze out the agony that throbbed with such violence between his ears. Finally he rolled back onto what he now realized was a mattress. Still his mouth was dry and foul, and he gasped for air.

"By Reorx. Water. I need water!" He choked out the sounds, scarcely aware that he was speaking aloud.

"Here. Drink." A gourd was placed against his hand and he instinctively pulled it to his lips, quaffing greedily—and then spitting out a great mouthful of something really vile.

"What is this?" he demanded, "Dragon piss?"

The force of his voice brought a further throbbing to his aching head. Trying to ignore the pain, he blinked, but saw only vague shadows in the utter darkness of the room.

"No!" The stranger's tone was indignant. "This fine gully grog! You no like, you no drink!"

Tarn groaned again, closing his eyes and sinking onto the mattress in utter despair. Gully grog? And that accent . . . the petulant tone of wounded pride—not to mention the words spoken. This fellow beside him was clearly a gully dwarf.

But how had he come to be here? Indeed, where was he?

For a long time the throbbing in his head was too violent, too painful, for Tarn to think at all. Instead he merely lay in utter misery, unconscious of anything except for the awful pain and the horrid feeling in his mouth. He might have slept again or faded from awareness—he couldn't tell for sure—but when he finally forced his gummy eyelids apart he again saw the figure, squat and rotund, sitting beside his bed.

This time he could make out details: a pair of bright eyes, close set and sparkling, stared at him with unblinking attention. The rest of the room was large and well-chiseled. He could see a brass latch on the door, and gradually became aware that the covering of his mattress was a fine bearskin, a pelt very rare and treasured in Thorbardin. From these facts he deduced that he wasn't in some squalid gully dwarf hovel. He took this fact as no small relief.

But it still didn't answer the rest of his questions. He forced himself to reach backward in his mind, trying to reconstruct events. He saw Belicia, frowning at him, then turning her back. She was displeased. Why?

Because he was going away! The answer came like a stab of light, even though he realized that he had not defined the exact reason for Belicia Felixia's displeasure. But part of it was true—he had been going away. He remembered now. The lake, the crossing from light into darkness.

His mother's house. That was the last memory he had and it came to him with full and vivid recollection. The discussion in her parlor, the mead—the mead, by Reorx! Especially the second bottle, the special brew she had asked Karc to bring. Had Garimeth taken any drink from that bottle? He hadn't been paying careful attention, but he was pretty sure that she hadn't.

Of course—his mother had drugged him! His own mother! And now he was no doubt in some chamber of her house.

How could she do such a thing? And why? Why?

For a time he berated himself for his own stupidity. Certainly no self-respecting Daergar would accept a drink from one who refused to partake of the same beverage! How could he have been so careless, so disregarding of the most basic precautions?

The answer was clear: he had spent so much time among the Hylar where trust and goodwill were widespread. He had lost the edge needed to make one's way through dark dwarf society.

He thought of the Helm of Tongues, how he had argued with his father over the possibility of his mother's having stolen the artifact. Of course Baker Whiegranite must have been right. He remembered his mother regarding him through narrowed eyes, subtly encouraging him to drink. What had they been talking about? Had he given away any of the thane's secrets?

"Why? Why did you do it, mother?" he croaked the question aloud, through the painful splitting of his dry lips.

"I not your mother, silly. You say thirsty, I give drink. You say 'dragon piss,' and I no give you more drink. That why."

In spite of everything, Tarn uttered a harsh bark of

104

laughter. He had entirely forgotten his odd companion. After all, once he had realized that he was in his mother's house, it had seemed more likely than anything that the gully dwarf was a figment of his fevered imagination. Certainly Aghar-bashing was considered fine sport among the Daergar. Even the lowliest of his mother's servants would have had free rein to strangle or crush the little wretch if his presence were discovered.

"Who are you? And where are we?" His voice rasped painfully. He craved a draught of any liquid, no matter how vile. With a groan he forced himself into a sitting position, swinging his sturdy legs over the edge of the bed. He realized that his boots had been removed from his feet.

"Regal Wise-Always. That my name. We in the Big House."

Tarn regarded the Aghar, observing the sparse beard straggling from a rounded chin, the small, rotund figure, and a face dominated by a pair of bright, curious eyes. "What 'Big House'? Is this Daerforge, the manor of Garimeth Bellowsmoke?"

"Big Big House. And you in Agharhome, buddy. Best next best place in all Thorbardin!"

"No! I've seen Agharbardin. Nobody but a gully dwarf would go there, and I can tell you that it's not like this."

Tarn made the denial with a great deal of conviction. He could tell that this was a fine sleeping chamber, with a bed fit for nobility. Now that he was upright, he also noticed a settee, garment wardrobes, and a dressing table. It all looked vaguely familiar. This was not his usual room, but he was almost certain that he was somewhere within his mother's house in the port city of the dark dwarves.

"Well, you come to Agharhome here. You right by dark dwarves—they take you boots and plop into bed."

Forcing himself to think, Tarn reviewed his memory of Thorbardin, including the large gully dwarf slum called Agharbardin—or Agharhome, as the wretched inhabitants called it. He remembered that the gully dwarf city was a sprawling wasteland adjacent to Daerforge, but the two cities were distinct entities and clearly unalike. As a youngster during his visits to his mother's home city, he had joined Daergar youths in pitching rocks from the balconies and plazas of their city, hooting with derision as the missiles had tumbled through the crowded Aghar hovels that lined the lower elevations of the cliff. Come to think of it, he had thrown some of those rocks from the ramparts of this very manor. The squalid lairs of the gully dwarves had not been terribly far away.

"Regal. That's a good name, I have to say. How did you get here?"

"I walk. Me good walker, for sure."

"I'm sure you are." Tarn winced, knowing he could be in for a long conversation. "I mean, where did you go to come to this part of . . . er, Agharhome?"

"Over there . . . where I go now!" Suddenly the sturdy little fellow bounced to his feet and dashed with startling alacrity across the sleeping chamber, disappearing into one of the wardrobes that had been standing open. The door shut with a loud clunk, but then he realized that the noise had come from the large door to his room.

His mother stood in the portal now, staring at him with a pinched, thoughful expression. "I see that you're awake. Actually, one of the guards thought he heard you talking to yourself." She looked around suspiciously.

"Yes," he stated in a controlled angry voice, "I make better company than most people."

Garimeth sniffed as she came into the room followed by a pair of armed guards. "You could do with a bath," she declared acidly.

Vaguely Tarn smelled the lingering aftermath of Regal Wise-Always.

"I didn't sleep very well," he complained. "Something got hold of my stomach. Maybe you can tell me what it was?"

"It was Aminus Hybrythia." She gave the name of a rare fungus, widely known for its soporific effects. "It served its purpose, I have to admit."

"And what purpose was that?" demanded Tarn, rising to his feet and staggering in spite of his determination to show no weakness. He clamped his jaws against a swelling wave of nausea. "Why did you knock me out? My orders were to speak to Uncle Darkend, the new thane, and I must do so right away."

His mother's expression remained stoic, though the two guards who held small but lethal crossbows raised their weapons fractionally. Finally the truth dawned on Tarn.

"What day is it?" he asked dully.

"You've slept for the last three cycles. Poor thing, you seemed to be terribly tired."

"Then he's visited Daerforge and gone back to his palace already?"

"Yes, of course."

"Then I must go to Daerbardin and talk to him!"

"You'll do no such thing." Now the guards stepped forward to flank his mother as she moved closer to him. "For two reasons—one of which is for your own good—though you're probably too thick-headed to see it."

He waited, saying nothing, numb even to the retching of his stomach and the aching in his head.

"First, you're on a fool's errand. Darkend Bellowsmoke has no more intention of listening to Hylar counsel than he does of taking a goat for his wife."

"You can't know that!" Tarn protested.

"See—too thick, like I said. But it's true. In fact, after hearing you out, your uncle would have to kill you before letting you run back to Hybardin."

"That is why you knocked me out for three days?" he asked sarcastically.

"Don't tempt me to make it longer," she warned.

"How long do you plan to hold me here?"

"I can't have you talking to Darkend. This is not a good

time for such a family reunion. And believe it or not, this is the only place you'll be safe."

"Why can't I talk to Darkend? And why are you making it your business to see that I don't?"

"He's my brother, dearie. I've looked after his best interests ever since we were children together. Listen to me. What do you think Darkend has been doing since he took the throne? And why do you think he was meeting with the thanes of the Klar and Theiwar?"

"What do you mean?" Tarn's voice was dull.

"Perhaps you'd like to have a look."

Garimeth indicated the door. Sensing the alertness of the two guards and the arrows pointed at his back, Tarn followed her outside. They stood on one of the wide plazas of the great manor, a place with a view of the crescent of Daerforge's waterfront and the broad swath of the sea beyond. There was a lot of activity there, columns of dark dwarves forming on the docks and collecting in the streets beyond the waterfront.

The bay, Tarn saw immediately, was thick with boats. A great, metal-hulled flotilla was in the process of boarding and gathering at the dockside of Daerforge. The scene bristled with armed Daergar. This was the embarkation of an army that could only have one goal, one destination.

Tarn's eyes rose to the spire of illuminated rock in the middle of the subterranean sea. Hybardin stood out like a beacon from the murk of the underworld, torches and lanterns and bonfires lighting the pillar like an outline of distant stars. Specks of illumination reflected in the black stillness of the water. It was his imagination to be sure, but Tarn heard the banter of the dockyard markets, the tapping of kegs, and the searing of grilled meats—all against the backdrop of cheerful Hylar society. He suddenly realized that he missed home very much.

And he wondered if he would ever see it again.

"The Klar? The Theiwar, too? It's a general attack?" he asked, masking his rising panic by the cool disinterest of his voice. He was terribly afraid. All he could think about was Belicia Felixia and her newly-trained company of novices.

"Yes. The Theiwar shall come by boat from the other side of the sea and the Klar are taking the tunnels of the high route. With any luck, they'll be charging into that nest of grand dames and doddering old fools on Level Twenty-eight before the Hylar even know the attack is underway."

Tarn knew the passages she meant. The great homes of the nobles were on the highest of Hybardin's levels. Many of these had access to passages bored through the great dome of rock that arched over the sea. During the thousands of years Thorbardin had been inhabited, these tunnels had been expanded into a network of passages that could be used to connect Hybardin to virtually any other part of the great dwarf kingdom. Since they granted no access to the outside world, however, they had only peripherally been considered by those who planned for the Life-Tree's defense.

Level Twenty-eight was where Baker Whitegranite's house was, where his mother had lived for decades. The people who lived there now had been his mother's neighbors, her peers, and her companions since before Tarn had been born. He felt a wave of revulsion now at the thought that she could discuss their impending doom with such coldness. At the same time, he sensed that it was important not to let her see his true reaction.

"And Darkend organized this whole attack in the last few days?" he pressed.

"Actually, he's been planning it for some months. Since before he became thane, actually. My brother's a very good planner—not a dull, plodding scholar like your father. Darkend was waiting for a certain piece of news. When he got it, he was ready to move."

"Word about Thane Hornfel and the Hylar army!" Tarn's eyes tightened on his mother's face. He spoke heatedly in spite of his earlier resolve for discretion. "And you brought word from your own husband. You betrayed my father, the thane, the whole city."

"If you don't think the Hylar deserve it, then you've been sleepwalking through life," she retorted sharply. "For too many centuries the smug Hylar have been lords of Thorbardin, and the time for their arrogant rule has passed."

But Tarn's mind was following other paths. "Planned for months, while Darkend was waiting for word. . . . Then you have been part of this conspiracy all that time. And your divorcing my father had nothing to do with him?"

"It had everything to do with him. But I learned of my brother's ambitions and bided my time until my departure could serve a dual purpose."

"And the Helm of Tongues—did you take it just as father claims?"

"Of course," his mother snapped in exasperation. "The artifact has use to me. Indeed, I have in mind far more practical applications than your father's esoteric research. You might say that it is a key to part of my own little plan."

Tarn wanted to ask other questions, to probe farther into his mother's schemes. For a moment he considered challenging her, but he lacked the will. He was surprised to realize that Garimeth actually frightened him a little. Instinctively he took a step backward.

"What do you intend to do with me?" he asked. Once again he was suddenly very aware of his dry mouth, of the ache that had settled from his skull to permeate his entire body. His stomach was unsteady, but he now knew it was hunger. "Can I have something to eat and drink?"

"Of course. I have no wish to punish you. After all, you're my son. But of course, I can't let you go just yet. You're also your father's son, and that part of you will be in a hurry to get back to Hybardin. And as I have said, I cannot allow that."

The guards ushered him back to his room, where Tarn

was relieved to note that the wardrobe door was shut. The two bowmen stood watch until, a few minutes later, Karc brought a pitcher of cold water, another pitcher of beer, and a variety of bread, cheeses, and fungi.

"Thanks, old dwarf," Tarn said affectionately. "I don't suppose this beer came from that special batch, did it?"

"I really must apologize for the deception, Master Tarn," the venerable attendant said with apparent sincerity. "And no, you will find this repast quite untainted. As long as you must be detained, I shall do what I can to make the time pass pleasantly."

Karc and the guards departed. Tarn heard the door locked securely after it had closed behind them. He stood and listened carefully for several moments, certain that he heard three pairs of footsteps walk away.

Only after another full minute had passed did he cross to the wardrobe and pull open the thin door. He was determined to vigorously question Regal Wise-Always. Instead, he was startled to find himself staring into a small, empty closet. The back wall was the stone of the room's outer wall, and when he knocked on the surface there was none of the resonance that might have indicated a concealed passage.

Unsettled, he closed the door, then checked the other wardrobes. He was certain this was the one Regal had used for his escape. At first Tarn had assumed the gully dwarf knew a hiding place, but now he was certain that the Aghar used some secret path into his mother's house. And not just her house, but the very room where he was imprisoned.

And, Tarn figured, any way into the house was likely to work equally well as a way out.

Unless he had imagined the whole encounter. After all, his mind was still clouded by toxic fungus, and hadn't the guards said they heard him talking to himself?

He settled down to eat and drink, and for a time he was able to forget about everything except sating his hunger and thirst. He gulped down the whole pitcher of water, and half the beer. After many slices of thick, flavored bread, he began to feel better.

That was when his mind starting asking questions and making insinuations—even accusations. First of all, he saw that Axel Slateshoulders had been right and that he, Tarn, had been wrong. It was a mistake to want to inform the dark dwarves of the Hylar misfortune. Indeed, the matter of Hornfel's predicament and the threat of the Chaos storms had seemed utterly irrelevant to his mother, except insofar as it kept the Hylar army away and opened up the possibility of dark dwarf treachery.

This led him to his next thought: his own gullibility had led him to remove himself from any place where he could do any good. He couldn't help his father, and worst of all, the Daegar plot put Belicia Felixia Slateshoulders in grave danger.

Tarn leaped to his feet and stomped across the room to the door. He pulled at it, straining his shoulders in a futile attempt to bend the heavy bar. He fiddled with the latch, but he could see immediately that it was a steel lock that would only answer to the proper key. Finally he banged on the panel with his bare fist, demanding that someone come and let him out. Soon enough, growling in frustration, he ceased his clamor. He wasn't naïve enough to think such a disturbance would have any chance of aiding in his release. It might, on the other hand, bring about some treatment that was sure to be punitive.

He sat down on the edge of his bed and dropped his head into his hands. Never had he felt such loathing for himself. He told himself if he had possessed a weapon he would have been sorely tempted to drive it into his own breast.

"Great Reorx!" he moaned, turning and smashing his fist into the stone wall. "Why are you doing this to me?"

"Reorx doin' nuthin, far as I can see."

Tarn leaped to his feet and whirled around, astonished to see the gully dwarf standing on the other side of his bed. "Regal! You're back!"

"Regal Everwise, in person," he said with a little bow.

"Wasn't your name Wise-Always?" Tarn asked, delighted beyond reason at the little fellow's return.

"What difference? Got some beer left?" The Aghar wandered over to the table and began to snatch up Tarn's leftovers. Many bits of bread and mushroom were popped into his mouth and pockets in random order.

"Help yourself," said Tarn, indicating the pitcher.

But Regal was already drinking. Equal amounts of beer seemed to be going down the Aghar's throat and dripping down his sparsely bearded chin onto his clothing.

Meanwhile, Tarn looked at the wardrobe and saw that the door he had left closed now stood ajar. He felt a giddy measure of relief at this sight and grinned at Regal as the gully dwarf smacked his lips and began to lick off the platter upon which Tarn had been served his meal.

"I though you told me this was Agharhome," he declared genially. "But I happen to know for a fact that it's one of the finest houses in Daerforge."

"Yep." Regal barely looked up as he finished the platter and set to licking off the table. "Dark dwarves built lots of houses in Agharhome. 'Course, we Aghar gotta hide lotsa times, or they bash us."

Tarn felt a flush of shame at his own childhood memories. At the same time he couldn't help wondering, "You mean you live in these same houses and we—that is, the Daergar—don't even know it?"

"This part of Agharhome kinda nice, but we gotta be quiet. Sometimes hide."

"I guess so." Remembering childhood stories of fairies and other spirits that were often blamed for strange occurrences in his mother's house, Tarn suddenly had no doubt of the truth of Regal's assertions. "But then why did you let me see you?"

"You not smell like wunna them dark dwarves. You different."

Tarn was startled, and a little embarassed at the notion that there was a difference between Hylar and Daergar that a crude creature like this could actually smell.

"But tell me, Regal, how do you get to other parts of Agharbardin from here? And where did you go when those other dwarves came in?"

With Tarn following, the gully dwarf crossed to the wardrobe. He reached down and pushed on a corner of the flagstone forming the closet floor. Tarn was amazed to see the whole surface pivot easily to the side. He reached down, found the trapdoor to be plaster instead of stone. Beneath the door was a narrow shaft in the floor with a single-post ladder leaning against the rim. Tarn wondered if the ladder would hold him, but also knew he really didn't care. He was determined to get out.

"Did gully dwarves build this?" he wondered.

"We get some help sometimes. But you be surprised, you see what one clever fella like Regal Allatimesmart can do."

"Will you give me a tour, show me some of the rest of your city?" Tarn asked, picking up his boots and quickly lacing them onto his feet.

Regal looked around the room and shrugged. "No food left. No beer either. Sure, we take a walk."

Tarn went first, finding that the ladder could hold his weight. In another moment Regal was closing the concealed trapdoor over their heads.

Chapter Eleven

The Hylar thane stiffened in his chair, his entire body quivering with excitement. However, Baker Whitegranite avoided touching the ancient parchment that was so carefully laid upon his desk. He knew that the slightest disturbance might be enough to crumble the sheet into dust—a crime of cosmic proportions. He had finally begun to understand that here, at last, he had stumbled upon the treasure he had been seeking his entire life.

He took the time to carefully polish his spectacles, drawing a deep breath and telling his heart to be still. Without the helm it had taken him a whole hour to translate a brief passage, but he had just checked his work and felt certain he was right.

Turning back to the passage scribed in Chisel Loremaster's precise and unmistakeable hand, Baker read it again:

At first the young serpents emerged from the Grotto hesitantly, two or three at a time. They would perch at the edge of the precipice and stare into the eternal blackness over the distant sea, wings buzzing with an audible hum. And it was a vast space before them, for we were near the "summit" of the great, inverted mountain. The water was a long way down. Also, the mouth of the cavern faced in the precise direction where the cavern wall lay at its farthest extent from the pillar.

It was the most concrete evidence yet that the ancient lair of the good dragons had lain high on the southwest wall—actually, just west of southwest. Baker's earlier investigations included a detailed survey of the area. In fact, he had been so certain of his hypothesis that he had chosen to have his own house located here, in this quarter of Level Twenty-eight. But now he had real confirmation!

If only he could afford the time for further study. He looked at the scrolls piled at the edge of his desk, and knew that each one might yield a revelation as encouraging as the last one. But even now he knew these moments of scholarly inquiry were a luxury he could not afford.

In truth, he probably should have been in the Thane's Atrium right now. With a sigh, he pushed back his chair and rose. Clumping wearily over to the table, he tried to focus on some materials and information related to his duties as thane.

A messenger, his words duly conveyed to the palace scribe, had come from Belicia Felixia Slateshoulders. Her report told of mercantile interests on the waterfront that were resisting her efforts to make preparations. Next she had presented a plan for defense of the dockside in the event of a waterborne attack by some fractious clan of dark dwarves. Hence, Baker saw the merchants' objection. Belicia had stated that her small company could not hold the docks against any major attack. They would inevitably be outflanked and destroyed after a short and futile fight.

As an alternative she proposed to form a line of defense at the bottlenecks connecting the waterfront on Level One with the great trading plaza of Level Two. Four stout shield-walls could hold the broad stairways leading up from the dockside to the interior of the Life-Tree. With these steps blocked, Belicia was confidant that she could hold out for a long time against a force much larger than her own.

Beside the military report was a stack of letters from those same merchants. The diatribe from Hoist Backwrench, a prominent shipper, was typical. He complained that this young Hylar captain of the guard had ordered him to move the bulk of his stock up to the second level. He protested that such a demand far exceeded Belicia's authority and that, furthermore, it placed an intolerable burden on his ability to compete with his rivals.

Vale interrupted the Thane to announce that another messenger had arrived from the Thane's Atrium.

A young scribe, his beard short but bristling outward well beyond his ears, hurried in with a parchment. Baker felt a guilty sense of relief that the youngster had caught him here at his worktable instead of perusing musty scrolls at his desk.

"My Lord Thane," he said breathlessly, "this request from the Mercenaries Guild asks you to release weapons from the royal armory. They pledge to bring you two hundred sword arms."

"A good offer to be sure, but I thought all the guildhands went with Thane Hornfel," Baker inquired, perplexedly. He was unwilling to put too much hope into the prospect of additional forces from this unlikely source. "I know he put out a summons to all the mercenary companies."

"Er . . ." The scribe hesitated awkwardly. "I had a word with the guildman who delivered the note. It seems that these two hundred were unable to meet the requirements. The fact is, many of them are lame. Others are blind, or have lost an arm or a tongue. Still, the man said they were all willing to fight on behalf of the Life-Tree if needed."

"And what of this man who brought the word from the guild? Did he have a name? What was he like?"

"He seemed hale enough—if perhaps a bit on the gray side of middle age. His name was Broadaxe, as I recall."

"Very well." Baker signed the request, authorizing the Hylar armory—which doubled as the royal treasury—to issue enough swords, shields, and assorted elements of armor to outfit a company of as many Mercenary Guild recruits as would present themselves.

"Can you send word about this to Axel Slateshoulders?" he asked the scribe.

"Of course, my Lord Thane."

The young dwarf left. Baker wasn't yet ready to turn to the next paper, a requisition for some new dirtmoss that was needed to augment the water gardens on Level Twenty-two. He was suddenly startled by the sounds of a large crash. The thunder of rock and gravel suggested a cave in. Running from his study, he found Vale throwing open the door to the garden. The normally moist, cool air was thick with dust. Baker was stunned to see that a small section of the ceiling had tumbled down to reveal a dark passageway leading into the mountain.

"Here, you—stop that!" Vale darted into the garden, accosting a dwarf who had apparently dropped from the newly-created opening.

Baker caught a glimpse of wild eyes and a bristling, wiry beard. Then the newcomer whooped and thrust with a short sword. Vale gasped and tumbled backward into Baker's arms, as more dwarves dropped from the tunnel into the garden.

The thane pulled his loyal servant back through the door and slammed the portal shut, dropping the heavy bar. He saw that Vale's chest was covered with blood as he vaguely heard the strange dwarves shouting to each other in a bizarre sing-song. In seconds the sounds faded, and he knew they had charged out the garden gate onto the street.

"Klar!" he realized, appalled by the sudden, violent incursion. He looked down at Vale, felt the fading of his faithful servant's pulse, heard the last bubbling of his breath, and knew that the crazed attackers had come with murderous intentions.

The clamor of panic-stricken voices outside of his house drew his attention. He ran to the front door and burst onto the street to discover a young Hylar, a youth still beardless, covered with blood.

"Help! Please, help me!" The young dwarf suddenly pressed his hands to his eyes and began to weep.

"What is it? Speak!" Baker demanded, surprising himself with the sharpness of his voice.

"The Klar! They attacked my house, killed my family! They came out of the ventilation shaft in the ceiling, dropping down with swords and axes! My mother! By Reorx, my mother!" The lad drew a ragged breath, but when he finally fixed his eyes upon Baker they were clear and cogent. "My family is House Ferrust."

Baker nodded. He knew the house just around the corner from his own.

He heard more noise—commotion and violence—down the streets. Gradually the truth began to sink in. The Klar were attacking all across Level Twenty-eight, dropping onto the top of the Hylar city from the ancient passages that honeycombed the interior of this whole mountain range. But why?

"Come to the lift! We'll have to gather there!"

They joined a great mass of citizens running through the streets, instinctively converging where the King's Wall surrounded the great lift station. Here Baker was relieved to find that Axel Slateshoulders was arriving with the upward cage.

"What's going on?" Axel roared from within the shaft. Moments later the veteran warrior clumped into the lift station, accompanied by dozens of armed Hylar.

"We're being attacked," Baker summarized. "Small bands of Klar are coming through the ceiling of Level Twenty-eight. There's lots of fighting in the blocks, but survivors are making their way to the lift."

"Good. We'll start by holding our positions here, then."

Axel was already shouting orders. He wore a heavy broadsword at his belt, a weapon Baker recognized from the Wall of Honor in the Thane's Atrium. Hastily more armed dwarves spilled off the lift that had been filled to capacity. From the surrounding streets, others shouted incoherent details about "bloody Klar." Sounds of battle came from everywhere and many of them were the cries of wailing and anguish far more suggestive of a massacre.

A wild-eyed Klar dwarf, his sword and hands red with blood, rushed from a nearby house and was soon followed by several of his fellows. Wild eyes lighting up at the sight of the Hylar, the mad dwarf uttered a shriek of delight followed by a shrill, keening howl that was like a noise from the Abyss.

Axel Slateshoulders whipped his broadsword downward in a lightning-quick slash, cutting the first Klar down in an instant. Limping on his bad foot, the veteran Hylar stepped forward to meet the next attacker with the point of the blade. Other dwarves of Hybardin rushed forward, swarming down the street while more reinforcements came on the next shift of the lift. Other citizens of the Life-Tree continued to emerge from the long stairways and cargo tunnels that connected to Level Twenty-seven.

"My lord, stay back," cried a Hylar. Baker recognized him as his bushy-bearded scribe. The scribe brandished a sword he had grabbed from somewhere.

Now the young dwarf used the blade to pierce an axe-wielding Klar who had burst from a gap between two house façades. The scribe cut the maddened invader deeply, but the Klar seemed unaffected by the wound. He brushed the scribe out of the way and roared at the stunned and immobile Baker.

More Hylar appeared, rushing to protect the thane, and knocked the Klar with a barrage of blows. Still, the crazed dwarf did not so much as stagger until several fatal wounds marred his heaving torso. The gleeful look of triumph on the corpse's face sent a chill through Baker Whitegranite's shoulders.

The bold young scribe had dashed off before Baker could say anything. Axel returned, limping awkwardly, then leaned against a stone pillar as he tried to catch his breath. The elder's face was flushed, but his eyes were alive with a martial gleam that Baker found strangely exhilarating.

"There were seven of the bastards in there. They fought to the death, naturally."

"Naturally," Baker agreed, though in fact he was shocked by the thought of such brutal warfare. "And the Hylar family and servants?"

"All dead. Looked like six and twelve in the house."

Everywhere reports came from similar dwellings. Small bands of Klar were visible darting along the streets, but were quickly killed by the vengeful Hylar.

Baker looked around, took stock of the teeming mob of dwarves gathered and the others that continued to pour out of the lift. He saw many Hylar from his own palace, including all the cooks, many of whom had armed themselves with an impressive array of cleavers. Many of the maids were there, from local houses as well as royal, and they had gained steel from kitchen and shed.

Young females and males, as well as some venerable white-beards who nevertheless carried weapons, marched along the street with every evidence of spry good health. An impressive proportion were armed with honest-to-Reorx weapons of war. After all, even the meanest Hylar hearth generally boasted some such martial implement displayed in a place of honor. True, some of the broadswords seemed heavier than the wielders who trailed their scabbards across the floor. One frail veteran—probably of the Dwarfgate War—was hard pressed to keep his shield from dragging on the ground.

But they were Hylar defending their city, their clan, their homes. Grimly, purposefully, the dwarves set about reclaiming the massive blocks of Level Twenty-eight. In many places, they found that the houses had suffered no incursion. In others the occupants had closed and locked their doors against the bands of Klar that roamed the streets.

In the worst cases, the Klar had burst into the homes of Hylar families, emerging from ventilation ducts and private passages that led into the upper surface of the Urkhan Vault. They had wreaked havoc, with many families suffering total annihilation. The Klar, who rarely numbered more than a dozen or more in a single band, inevitably fought to the death when the enraged Hylar cornered them.

By the time most of the skirmishes had run their course, Baker found himself in front of his own house. Accompanied by several sturdy dwarves, he ventured inside his place. Other than Vale's cold body there were no signs of battle here. But the sight of his faithful servant nearly brought Baker to tears. Ignoring the flaring ache in his belly, he helped the others carry Vale back to the lift station where he could be taken down for entombment.

There, he found Axel and several burly helpers dispatching another band of suicidal attackers. Here, again, a few of the Klar hurled themselves on the weapons of the more numerous and disciplined Hylar.

"Why do they scatter so much, attacking with just a few here and there?" Baker asked, wincing as he watched the last of the attackers writhing on a blade of Hylar steel.

"Actually, that's pretty well coordinated for Klar," Axel replied. "We'd do just as well to wonder what has brought them here now with so many of them attacking at the same time."

That was a question with disturbing implications, the

thane quickly realized. "I need to get word to the water-front."

"Let's go," Axel declared.

As they approached the lift, Baker was startled to see the young scribe from his quarters. The Hylar's right arm ended in a bandaged stump, but nevertheless he approached the thane deferentially. Baker was aghast at the wound. It was a horror that struck home, even in the midst of this nightmare.

"My lord, I am glad you are safe."

"With thanks to you. But what happened? Your hand . . ." He was suddenly aware that he didn't even know who the young dwarf's name. "Please, tell me your name!"

"It's Sandhour, my lord. They call me Squinter Sandhour."

"Well Squinter Sandhour, I owe you my life."

"It was an honor to defend you, my lord. But all these Klar! What does it mean?"

"I have a feeling it means trouble, my good son. Terrible trouble. But come with me. Let's get you down to the healer."

By the time the lift clunked downward, the sounds of fighting had faded away and Level Twenty-eight was securely in the hands of the Hylar once again. Yet all the rest of Hybardin seemed alive with unusual noise. The echoes of panic and terror resonated deep into Baker Whitegranite's heart.

Chapter Twelve

Belicia looked out over the water, unable to ignore a rising feeling of disquiet. For one thing, the chain boats from both Daerforge and Theibardin were long overdue. Both the pulley and the gear systems had become disabled within a few hours of each other, each crippled by an unknown and therefore undiagnosable problem. Breakdowns in the chain ferry system were routine enough, but she didn't like this unusual coincidence. And then there had been the news from Level Twenty-eight. So far, they were nothing more than a series of wild rumors, but she was steadily growing more concerned.

Belicia climbed the wide stairway that led directly from the dockside to the great trading plaza on the second level of Hybardin. At the center of this wide space was the lowest terminal for Hybardin's main transport, the Great

Lift which led from the market plaza all the way up to Level Twenty-eight. The next higher lift station, at Level Three, was more than a hundred feet above and could also be reached from the waterfront by a long climb up several stairways or by one of the smaller lifts.

The stairs connecting the plaza to the docks were oriented to the four points of the compass and each was flanked by a pair of ramparts guarded by a low wall. Belicia took the time to walk around the perimeter of one such bulwark, observing that her archers would have a clear field of fire over any attacker. Because of the height and the crenelated defensive wall, the youngsters who made up the bulk of her missile troops would be well protected from direct contact with the attackers. As long as the shield wall held across the width of the stairs, the Hylar up above would be able to create a deadly distraction to the enemy trapped on the approach.

After a great deal of thought, she had decided to divide her shield company into five sections and place one group at each of the four stairways. The fifth group would include many of her best warriors and would form a reserve to garrison the trading plaza and also be ready to rush to the defense of any threatened quadrant. She had broken her archers into four bands, each with standing orders to garrison the ramparts of the stairways in the event of an attack. From here they would be able to direct a harassing fire onto boats approaching the docks, and Belicia was convinced that she could make an enemy's efforts to land prove very costly indeed. Furthermore, she had stockpiled a huge amount of arrows at each archery station.

She took a few moments to inspect the final cornerstone of her defense. One of the heavy ballistae rested on a swivel mount just above the stairway rampart. A pair of these overlooked each set of stairs, and she nodded in greeting to the three grizzled veterans who operated this particular weapon. The ballista was like a giant crossbow, powered by a massive spring and shooting a steel-headed missile whose shaft was made from the trunk of a medium-sized tree. Though even a veteran crew could shoot only one shaft every few minutes, each great arrow weighed hundreds of pounds and was quite capable of puncturing or capsizing all but the largest of lake boats.

But if she made her stand at the stairs, that meant abandoning the waterfront in the face of the first wave of attacks. The announcement of that decision had stirred up a hornet's nest. Now she turned to await the approach of a delegation of merchants and ship-owners, all of whom had spent most of the last two days demanding that Belicia's defensive arrangements be overruled.

"My good captain," declared Hoist Backwrench, a ship-builder who did a significant amount of business along the Hybardin docks, "You must reconsider your plan! We can't simply hand over the dockyards to our enemies, no matter how numerous their swords!"

"My plan is the only chance that gives an undersized force a fighting chance against a more numerous foe. Why can't you understand that?"

"We understand perfectly!" retorted Sootmaker Darkfern, a prominent importer of coal. "You're willing to throw us to the dragons so you can keep your own troops alive!"

Belicia flushed, infuriated by the words. Before she could snap out a reply that would have done nothing to soothe the merchants' fears, she bit her tongue and forced herself to take a deep breath. "You've heard the news from above?" she asked, knowing the whole city had been abuzz with news of the Klar attack.

"A few lunatics with more ale than sense, I'll wager," Hoist said. "No doubt we'll find out that most of the stories are nothing but exaggerations."

"Or it could be the start of an attack that's bigger than anything we've ever considered," Belicia said. Ever since she heard about the raid against the Level Twenty-eight, she had grown increasingly apprehensive about the vulnerability of the Life-Tree. "We have suspicious reports from three clans and clear signs of trouble afoot."

"Bah! There could be a thousand reasons why the boats have stopped!" insisted Hoist Backwrench.

"And one of them is that the thanes of the Theiwar and Daergar wanted to cut us off from any chance of warning. When you've heard that the Klar are already making mischief, didn't you think we would have to take this seriously?"

Before the argument could proceed any further, a pair of gray-bearded dwarves and their escort of palace guards approached the party. Despite her firm stance and utter self-assurance, Belicia was relieved to recognize her father and the thane.

"Ah, there you are," said Axel Slateshoulders, giving his daughter a wide grin. "Why don't you explain to these gentlemen what you told the thane yesterday? I'm sure they'll see that your plan makes sense."

"What makes sense is to hold the whole dock!" insisted Hoist as he crossed his arms over his broad chest.

"I'm surprised at you, Hoist," said Baker Whitegranite. "You know better than that."

The acting thane blinked at the dozen or so merchants who formed a glowering ring around them. His glasses were smudged, and Belicia wondered if he was having a little difficulty seeing.

"This is not about cowardice," the thane continued, "or throwing anyone to the dragons. It's about holding and protecting Hybardin if the worse comes to worst."

"And what's the news from above?" demanded a Hylar Belicia didn't recognize. "There are tales of Klar run wild!"

"I'm afraid that's true," Baker replied, turning his attention to Belicia. "Several bands of armed Klar burst into manors on the highest level. The Ferrust family was killed to the last dwarf and several others took casualties before their house guards were able to prevail."

"Then the attack was more than just an isolated raid?"

"Of course it was," Axel answered. "Perhaps a hundred or more different routes into Hybardin were used, and the attacks were as carefully timed as you could expect from the Klar."

"What about the King's Wall?" Belicia asked.

"We held at all four gates," replied Axel. "The fact is, they made a good barrier to hold the bastards away from the lift station."

"And your father had them cleaned out in a few hours," Baker added.

"Did you get my message about the halting of the chain boats?"

"Yes," Baker said. "That's what brought us down here."

Now Belicia spoke decisively. "Then I believe we have to treat the situation as though we could be attacked here at any time."

"I agree," Baker said firmly. He addressed his young captain again. "What else do you need to make ready for an attack?"

"We need to close and block the short lifts that lead from the docks up to the Second Level."

"You might as well close the markets!" wailed Fortus Silkseller, Hybardin's most esteemed fabric dealer.

"We can't use the stairs for cargo!" Hoist Backwrench added insistently.

"I have a feeling that the dark dwarves are going to be closing the markets for you," Belicia replied, "but there must be two score lifts connecting these two levels. We must block them all. Otherwise, even though we might hold these stairways, it will just be a matter of minutes before they've got us outflanked."

"And on the stairs you have four relatively narrow routes to hold," Axel interjected, speaking sternly. "You know she's right."

Baker quickly ruled in Belicia's favor, and Axel took on the role of insuring that the orders were followed. Each of the merchants was asked to provide materials—bales, barrels, crates, and coal—that would be used to fill the elevator shafts.

Though the merchants were still grumbling, Belicia got their attention before they clumped off to do as they had been told. "We all hope I'm wrong about this. All of us hope that nothing will happen. If so, in a few days the chain ferries will be running again and we can all be back to our regular tasks. But please listen to me. If the worst happens and we're attacked, Hybardin needs the help of all of you."

"What do you want of us?" growled Hoist Backwrench, who despite his surly expression seemed to be listening to her.

"I need you and all your workers. Take up whatever arms you have and join us atop these four stairways. There are places on the ramparts where those who are unable to wield a sword can join my archers. Or they can throw down oil, torches, even blocks of steel could do some damage. And the rest of you can help us make a stand that will make all of our descendants proud."

"Aye. We'll do that," Hoist grunted. "For if yer right, and if we fail, then we might not have any children left to hear the tale."

* * * * *

The Daergar came first, their boats appearing in a vast wave at the very fringe of Hybardin's ring of lights. Immediately the shouts of alarm came down from Levels Three and Four where people could see farther out over the water.

The Hylar on the waterfront made a well-ordered retreat to the four stairways. Only Belicia and the few of her troops skilled with the heavy crossbow waited, concealed among the debris near the edge of the water. The Hylar captain noted with suprise that Hoist Backwrench bore one of the shiny steel weapons and had a quiver of lethal looking darts slung on his back.

"Glad to see you," she said quietly, as the two of them crouched beside a crate that had just been emptied of its cargo of steel.

"Looks like you were right," the shipper said grimly, squinting at the line of hulls that edged forward out of the darkness of the Urkhan Sea. "Can't say I'm glad, but I'd like to think I'm big enough to admit when I've been a fool."

Belicia smiled grimly. "Not a fool. And I'm grateful for your crossbow."

"You've got my strong right arm, too," Hoist said, closing his fist around the hilt of a broad-bladed shortsword. "Don't fergit, this is my dock those bastards are trying to take away from us!"

She looked closely and was surprised to see tears in the corner of the burly Hylar's eyes.

The white wakes curling ahead of the Daergar prows were now visible. These were long-hulled lake boats, each of them with a sharp prow, and propelled by a dozen or more oars. Beyond the leering figureheads Belicia could make out fully armored dark dwarves, tightly packed in the hulls and staring grimly toward the land.

A rank of archers hid behind the rampart above and behind Belicia. The veteran crews at the ballistae were waiting for her sign. She took out her flint and used her dagger to scrape a spark into the small, oil-soaked torch she had prepared for this moment. Instantly the wick flared into yellow flame, a bright flash shining all across the waterfront. In less than a second she heard the loud crack and thrum of the two nearest ballistae as they cast their missiles.

The first arrow clanged off the prow of a Daergar boat, knocking the vessel sideways so that it collided with a neighboring craft in a tangle of curses and splintering oars. For a moment the advance was delayed by confusion, but Belicia grimaced when she saw the two prows quickly swing shoreward again. The great shaft from the second ballista had flown over the bow of a long, narrow-hulled craft, directly into the tightly packed crew. A chorus of screams vanished under the cheer that rose from the shore as that boat veered to the side and slowed to a halt, oars akimbo.

By the time the great weapons were loaded again, at least a hundred assault boats were visible, pulling up to the docks and to the broken rock of the shore. Two more ballista missiles rocketed out and downward at a steep angle. Each pierced the hull of a boat, sinking the metal-hulled vessels immediately. Shrieking Daergar splashed and floundered in the black water.

Belicia knew these dwarves were doomed. Although the boat sank but a stone's throw from shore, not one of the dwarves would be able to swim that distance. The dark dwarves hated the water every bit as much as the Hylar and their heavy armor drug them thrashing and burbling to the bottom of the sea. This time there was no cheering. Even for an enemy, death by drowning was a fate as cruel as any known to Thorbardin's dwarvenkind.

More boats swept closer, and now Belicia stood up. "Shoot!" she cried. "Give them a full volley!"

Arrows and darts hissed through the air, a deadly barrage that found targets in many of the crowded hulls. But the missiles couldn't stop the relentless onslaught, and in moments dozens of the longboats were pulling alongside the stone fingers of Hybardin's docks. Reloading once, Belicia took another shot, dropping the captain of one of the lead boats. Despite the barrage of arrows, the Daergar were swarming ashore in great numbers.

"Fall back!" she shouted, the command echoing among the dwarf archers still on the docks of Level One.

More arrows, light but lethal missiles which arced outward and down from the ramparts above, began to shower the gathering phalanxes of invaders. Belicia and

131

her advance guard fell back in orderly fashion. The line of the shield wall at the base of the stairs parted to allow their captain through.

"You were right about this, too," Hoist said, indicating the Daergar that were swarming across the dock. "We'd have been surrounded before half of us could have made it back to the stairs."

She nodded curtly. It had been obvious to her all along, but she was glad that he had finally seen the truth.

"Are you ready here, Farran?" she asked the young dwarf responsible for commanding this detachment.

"Aye, captain," replied the warrior. Just a short time earlier, Farran had been learning the rudiments of a shield wall while Belicia had banged his shins with a stout staff. "Bring 'em on!"

"That's the spirit!" She clapped him on the shoulder and offered a silent prayer to Reorx. She wanted to stay here on the front line, but with her company dispersed into five detachments she had to maintain her own freedom so that she could move around and observe.

"Reckon I'll stay here, too," Hoist said, with a casual salute to the female captain. She saw that he had picked up a shield from somewhere. It relieved her somewhat to have the capable old Hylar standing in the shield wall. "At least I can keep an eye on my shipyard," he added with a growl, as the dark dwarves began to spread across the waterfront.

The Daergar wore black armor adorned with spikes, blades, and images of bestial faces. Full helmets protected their heads, each with faceplate down and locked. The dark dwarves swarmed across the dockyard by the hundreds, scattering among the barrels and bales of what had once been a prosperous waterfront. Now they howled in outrage as they saw that virtually everything of value had been cleared away. From their positions on the stairways and ramparts the Hylar hooted jeers and derision, and a small group of infuriated Daergar rushed impetuously at the shield wall which blocked their passage up the stairs.

"Steady there, wait!" roared Farran, in the voice of a natural sergeant. The Hylar line had formed across the sixth stair so that the enemy would have to climb to reach them. The rank was three dwarves thick and now Belicia could only hope that it would hold. It had to hold.

The first of the dark dwarves scrambled up the steps, many of the attackers stumbling before they even reached their enemy. The others were quickly cut down, their bodies left to bleed on the stairs and create an additional obstacle for the much larger number following.

On the docks, the bulk of the Daergar were now forming into companies. Still harassed by the arrows showering them, they cursed and howled at the defenders, promising slow deaths and worse when they had won the fight. Bristling with axe and spear and sword, the teeming mass charged the stairway, scrambling over the corpses of their comrades. Scores of fanatical dark dwarves smashed with full force into the desperate Hylar's thin line.

"You archers, shoot double time," bellowed Belicia. "Let them have it!"

The young dwarves along the parapet showered their missiles down from the ramparts. Nearly every arrow found a target in the tight-packed army of dark dwarves, though many of the well-armored attackers were protected from serious wounds by their shoulder plates and steel helms. Still, the darts caused many wounds and added to the general confusion of the infuriated, battle-crazed Daergar.

No matter how many of the enemy rushed forward, only a small number of them could reach the shield wall of Hylar. The clash of sword and shield rang across the waterfront as the charging mob funneled onto the stairway and met the firmly standing line. Anchored by the rear ranks of their comrades and benefitting from holding the higher position, the Hylar shield wall did not waver from the shock of the first clash. From her position still higher above, Belicia saw that Hoist had taken on the role of anchoring the right end of the line while Farran displayed the poise and confidence of a veteran as he shouted encouragement to his troops.

Quickly the attack bogged down. Some dark dwarves at the foot of the stairway hacked at the backs of their own comrades out of sheer frustration. Despite the attackers' best efforts, the shield wall held. The enraged Daergar fanned out across the wide dockyard, large companies spreading to the right and left as they sought another route up to the plaza from where the archers continued their barrage. Roaring with fury, the Daergar hastened along the waterfront and Belicia knew it would only be a matter of minutes before they pressed the attack against the other stairways.

The Hylar captain stopped long enough to take stock of the archers who had been posted on the ramparts all along the market. Arrows still showered upon the attackers. Fortus Silkseller had taken command of one of these detachments and stopped shooting long enough to answer her questions. She urged the troops keep shooting, but to make sure that the archers were taking careful aim.

"Make each shot count!" she shouted, and the wielders of the dwarven short bows nodded in understanding.

The roar of battle filled the air, rising to the upper levels of the Life-Tree. From the balconies of the Third Level which overhung the waterfront by a significant distance, a shower of garbage, stones, and occasionally a flask or two of fiery oil fell upon the attackers. Small blazes sprang up here and there, and the Daergar howled, infuriated as much by the flaring brightness as they were by the heat and flame.

Belicia checked her reserve detachment, sixty dwarves under the command of a one-eyed veteran named Tenor Ironwood. He was anxious to bring his dwarves into the fray, but growled in grudging acquiescence when she explained the need to keep his warriors ready for the crisis that would inevitably come.

Finally Belicia hurried to the western staircase and saw that the shield wall was standing firm. She cautioned them that the Daergar were on the way, then headed back to the east to find the battle already joined. Here, too, the Hylar on the stairway held firm and the dark dwarves suffered under the arrows from the ramparts. The crowding forced their vast numbers into a narrow and deadly channel. A peg-legged mercenary captain called Broadaxe was profanely exhorting the Hylar of his shield wall into a killing frenzy.

The sounds of battle echoed throughout Hybardin and carried far across the Urkhan Sea. The main thrust still came at the southern stairway. Belicia was proud to see that Farran's line had only backed up five or six steps and each foot of ground gained was costing the Daergar dozens upon dozens of warriors. The lines at the east and west stairs, facing less pressure from the attack, had not been forced to give any ground, and the Daergar made no effort to circle all the way around the island to attack from the north.

Belicia was pretty certain why they were leaving the last route alone and her suspicions were confirmed an hour later by the shouts of lookouts posted on Level Three. She raced across the plaza to see that the lake was obscured by an unnatural bank of fog. The mist seethed across the black waters like a living thing, rolling steadily closer to the Hybardin waterfront. She was not surprised to see the Theiwar fleet appear. A long rank of slender hulls slid forward from the fog to the north and west.

The boats emerged from a barrier of mist far thicker than the shadows of the underground sea. She shivered at this first evidence of Theiwar magic. The vaporous barrier had concealed their approach until the dark dwarves were already well within bow range, and now the defenders had time for only a single, lashing volley. Still, a hundred crossbows snapped and a barrage of silvery arrows darted into the Theiwar mass.

135

But most of the missiles fizzled into ashes before they reached their targets as Theiwar magic again shimmered in the air, robbing the volley of most of its strength. The attackers hooted and jeered as the harmless dust fizzled into the sea, and the boats swept forward quickly. Belicia had no choice but to order her defenders onto the stairs, the Hylar abandoning the docks to make their defense at the bottleneck of the approach to Level Two.

She heard strange words, weird chants that seemed to writhe and twist across the waterfront, and then a barrage of flaming balls sparked outward from the boats. The dots of flame drifted easily across the docks, settling among the crates and barrels abandoned by the archers. In another second the entire area was obscured by fire, crackling sheets of flame that erupted from the deceptively gentle balls to seethe among the wooden obstacles.

Theiwar warriors, staring horridly with their wide, milky eyes, quickly swarmed the waterfront and rushed to the base of the north stairway where Belicia's last detachment soon had carved a bloody battle line.

The dark dwarves cast more spells. Hissing, sparking arrows suddenly began to shower into the Hylar. Some of the magic missiles were deflected by shields and armor, but others seared into skin and flesh. Dwarves screamed, but there was more anger than pain in the sounds as the vengeful defenders wielded their axes and swords with fury and skill. Even a magical cloud of stinking gas didn't break the line. When the vapors seemed to choke as many Theiwar as Hylar, the attackers finally set about the onslaught with the physical tools of war. Swords clanged against shields, and the Theiwar invaders hurled simple, brute strength against resolute Hylar stubbornness.

More Theiwar swarmed to the west and the Hylar captain watched with grim amusement as these newcomers set upon the Daergar, driving their fellow dark dwarves away from the base of the stairs. The defending Hylar took the chance to catch their breath, until the Theiwar rushed to take the place of the attackers they had just dislodged.

The battles raged at each of the four stairways, and each step of advance was purchased at a heavy toll in blood. Belicia held her reserve detachment at the ready, wondering how long her brave defenders could hold out.

More and more attackers swarmed from the darkness to all sides. Even if the battle waned, there was no denying the ultimate truth. The Hylar were surrounded by enemies and any hope of survival would have to be found within the hearts of those who were ready to give their lives in defense.

Interlude of Chaos

The fire dragons were joined by shadows of purest darkness. All around the cosmos, from every place where the beings of wildness and destruction had been held, the creatures of Father Chaos arose and heeded the call. They swarmed through the stuff of worlds, howled in the vast silences of space, and rushed toward the poor vault of dirt and stone and sea.

But Krynn itself could not even acknowledge the presence of danger. A mere piece of ground in the cosmos, that place of men and dwarves and dragons could only whirl in its appointed place and allow the dwellers upon and within it to face the host of horrors that swept in with the tide Chaos.

Already many of the realms under the sun had felt the sweep of undoing, for the creatures of Chaos had begun their war against the rulers of Ansalon. But soon the attackers and their waves of destruction swelled beyond the visible world, moved past the places that could be seen. Some of the horde soared through the skies and others moved into the bedrock of the world.

And these last flew through the rock and stone as if it was wispy smoke. They followed the beacon of Primus, who in turn was guided by his dark master. They flew, climbed, and swam in the world until the shell of that planet fell away to reveal a great underground sea, teeming cities—some bright with light and others inky black. They also found peoples of blood and flesh, victims for the coming of Chaos.

Zarak Thuul led, and the horde of Chaos followed.

Coming of Chaos

Chapter Thirteen

Though the lesson was painful, Tarn learned it quickly enough. The best thing to do was to try to breathe through his mouth. The air in the escape shaft had been tolerable, but when Regal had led him to an adjoining tunnel the stench had become fetid, the air almost unbreathable. By Tarn's best guess, their current passage was one of the sewage drainage tunnels underneath Daerforge. When he took a careless breath, this supposition was vividly confirmed.

"This Street Number One," Regal proclaimed proudly as he strolled down the great pipeway with no apparent discomfort.

"Street? Of what?" wondered Tarn, looking for anything that might distinguish the dark shaft as anything other than a big drainage pipe.

"Of Agharhome!" The gully dwarf seemed perplexed at

his thickness. "This Number One Main Street of city!"

"Does it smell this bad everywhere?" Tarn asked, still breathing through his mouth.

"What smell?" Regal took a loud, wet sniff, and shook his head in mystification. "I smell no smell. Maybe you smell?" He fastened a look of calculated appraisal on his companion, but then shrugged forgivingly. "Oh, well. You not smell too bad."

Regal continued to lead him down the long, damp tunnel. He finally turned into a different shaft, then crawled into a narrower pipe that forced the reluctant Tarn onto his hands and knees as well.

"This Main Street Number Two," the Aghar informed him.

Despite his resolve not to breathe through his nose, Tarn periodically found himself accidentally catching a tiny whiff of Agharhome. Each time he gagged on the stench, and they were forced to halt while Tarn drew desperate, rasping mouthfuls of air.

At first each assault of tainted vapor seemed like a toxin powerful enough to blacken his vision. But he was surprised to note that, very gradually, the hideous stench seemed to become somewhat less offensive. It was not that the smell was any less vile or any less intense. Instead, it was more like his nostrils had become desensitized, so that the occasional waft that passed through the guard of his closed palate ultimately brought no more than a sensation of mild distaste.

Regal Everwise—or was it Wise-Always?—continued to lead the way as the two of them moved through a series of tight passages that sometimes descended and sometimes proceeded in a more or less lateral direction. The passages were narrow and smoothly made, but nothing like a city in Tarn's mind.

"What's that?" the half-breed asked as they passed a wider passage and heard sounds of laughter and sociable conversation.

'That Main Street Number Two," declared Regal.

"I thought this was . . . never mind." Tarn decided it was best to follow along with as few questions as possible.

They finally emerged from the base of a cliff. Looking over his shoulder and upward, Tarn saw the sweep of stone wall rising to the uppermost of Daerforge's levels. He recognized the twin towers at the gatehouse of his mother's manor and realized he was really not that far from the dwelling of his maternal ancestors.

But as he looked around he also felt transported to another world. A slope before him led steeply downward. It was a surface of huge rocks teetering dangerously at unbalanced angles. The slope was scored by paths and gullies that twisted around the huge outcrops. Beneath and around the rocks Tarn could see countless niches and darkened alcoves. He guessed that these dens must serve as the Aghars' houses and other buildings—well, shelters anyway since they didn't seem to have actually been "built."

While he was watching, he noticed several small figures dashing from one of these entrances to another with every appearance of great urgency. They dove into the burrows under the rocks, vanishing as quickly as they had appeared. Agharhome covered a broad, steep slope that led from the base of the cliff to the shore of the Urkhan Sea. At a casual glance the gully dwarf city was indistinguishable from a field of strewn boulders. The network of ravines and channels served as roads, just as the crude niches between the rocks served as buildings.

"Here we find my friends," Regal said, his conversational voice sounding like a shout to Tarn after the long, silent crawl. As soon as he got over his surprise, he realized that the whole area was abuzz with noise: laughter, argument, snoring, all kinds of sounds—though there were still no Aghar immediately in view.

"Sure. Regal?"

"What?" The gully dwarf stopped and looked up at Tarn, scowling suspiciously.

"I just wanted to say, um, thanks . . . thank you for getting me out of there."

"Beer was gone anyway," Regal replied with a shrug. "My friends got more, but different kind. You will see. Gully grog got some real kick."

Tarn suppressed his misgivings, remembering the rather startling taste when Regal had shared his flask. "Well, I might have to take your word for it. The last time somebody showed their hospitality to me with a bottle, it didn't work out too well."

"Head hurts?" wondered the gully dwarf.

"Yeah, for starters," Tarn replied, still feeling the cottony thickness in his mouth and the queasiness in his stomach.

Regal sniffed, somewhat contemptuously. Any further critique was prevented by the sudden appearance of two more Aghar, who seemed to crawl out from beneath a nearby boulder. One was chubby and short even for a gully dwarf, while the other was taller with a red face framed by a bristling mane of frizzy hair.

"Regal Way-Too-Smart!" the short one declared, beaming. "You got home in time for . . . what? We gonna do something, I know." He turned to his companion while scratching his bushy head. "Why he come home?"

The second dwarf with an entirely hairless, egg-shaped face scowled. A seared and frazzled fringe of hair was visible at the back of the Aghar's head. The skin of his face was blistered. Even his eyebrows had apparently been burned away.

Regal cleared his throat with great formality. "This Poof Firemaker," he declared, pointing at the singed gully dwarf. "And Duck Bigdwarf."

Duck was undoubtedly one of the shortest Aghar Tarn had ever met. Even after he rose from his sweeping bow— a gesture which dropped him onto his face for a disconcerting moment—his head came barely to the level of Tarn's chest. Looking down, Tarn saw that the tangle of

Duck's hair was alive with fleas. Stepping quickly backward, Tarn tried not to let his distaste show.

Poof also bowed, and Tarn saw that the burn line neatly intersected his skull into fore and rear halves. It seemed obvious to Tarn that the Aghar Firemaker had held his face a little too close to some incendiary project. This suspicion was reinforced by the sight of a small tinderbox that the gully dwarf proudly held up for the half-breed's inspection.

"Come and have some grog, now?" asked Regal, showing every intention of crawling under the boulder where the pair of gully dwarves had been. It appeared to be no more than a small and dingy niche. "Plenty even for big thirsty guy like you."

"Thanks a lot," the half-breed tried to explain, "but I've got to be going. I want to look around a bit."

His reluctance was only partly out of distaste. In fact, his thought processes had finally begun to grapple with the next question. Where should he go? The answer was obvious: back to Hybardin, back to his father, and especially back to Belicia. He would have to travel by boat, but his hopes were dampened by the sight of the Agharhome waterfront. There were a series of small jetties made from tumbled rock, but these looked like precarious places even for walking, much less docking a boat. And there were no watercraft anywhere in evidence, which, he realized with another glance at the trio of Aghar, was probably very sensible.

Across the harbor, mostly hidden by the curling shoulder of the sea's steep shoreline, lay the crowded and busy waterfront of Daerforge. He saw the cables of the chain boats far out over the water followed their pylons to the distant, illuminated height of the Life-Tree. Could he get there, somehow sneaking aboard some dark dwarf boat without being noticed? He didn't care for his chances.

And then, before his disbelieving eyes, flaming balls of winged fire burst upward from the Urkhan Sea and soared high into the air.

* * * * *

"How is your ammunition holding out?" Belicia had located Fortus Silkseller on the rampart over the southern stairway and now she shouted over the din of howling dark dwarves. Just below them—despite having suffered hundreds of casualties—the Daergar still pressed against against Farran's shield wall. In several hours of battle the doughty Hylar had given up no more than six or eight steps on the wide stairway.

"We've used half our arrows," replied the grim merchant. "A while ago I told 'em to start taking their time, to make each shot count."

"It looks like they paid attention."

Looking over the mass of bodies sprawled across the dockside below, Belicia saw that many of the dark dwarves had been felled by the missiles sent down by the Hylar archers. Just below the wall several ladders lay scattered and broken, and the dead Daergar bristled with so many arrows that they looked like pincushions.

"They thought they could bypass the stairs," Fortus said with a loud spit, followed by a hearty chuckle. "Wanted to take us by surprise with a sudden rush and a few ladders. Guess we made 'em think otherwise."

"Good job," Belicia said. She pointed toward the center of the line where a dozen or so Daergar carried on with an attack that seemed to finally be losing some of its relentless ferocity. "Good timing, too."

Farran shouted hoarsely, and his shield wall pressed forward. In a few seconds they had regained all the steps they had lost since the attack began. Fortus laughed with real pleasure, and Belicia nodded in satisfaction. "It seems like the attack on the stairs is starting to slacken a little bit."

"About time." Despite his gruff manner, the merchant-turned-warrior looked immensely pleased. "What about the other three sides?"

"Every one of them has held. It seems like none of them

got hit as hard as you did here. We're all grateful. I know you've paid the price."

"Your boy there . . . Farran . . . " Fortus cleared his throat, "he's doing a yeoman's job, by Reorx. I was in the Lance War you know, and I've never seen a shield wall hold against such a press. The fellow looks young, but I'm here to tell you that he fights like a seasoned veteran."

"Yes . . . he does well," Belicia replied softly, her eyes misting at the memory of her young sergeant mere weeks earlier, stumbling over each foot as he was among the rawest of recruits. "I guess war has a way of maturing you quickly." A thought jarred her, as she recalled one of the hundreds of reports she had received today. "Is there any word on your friend?"

"Hoist Backwrench, you mean?"

"Yes. I know he was standing in the forefront of the shield wall. I heard he went down in the fight. How does he fare?"

"He'll live," Fortus said, trying unsuccessfully to contain his emotions. "I don't think they'll be able to save his eyes, though."

"I'm sorry." Belicia said no more, but she was touched by the obvious depth of the grizzled dwarf's feeling, and by the heavy toll this day was taking on the brave Hylar all along the waterfront.

" 'Just have yer warriors keep holdin' the line, here'— that was what Hoist told me, when I saw him a little while ago."

"I will. And you save those arrows, all right? I have a feeling we're going to need them pretty soon."

"It's a promise, my lady!" Fortus threw her a rigid salute, a true honorific. "You know, if the Daergar pull back a bit, we can even send a quick sortie down there and bring back some we've already shot."

"Good. Look for a chance, and then go," Belicia agreed, heartened.

She went to a small tower that rose from the rampart

over the stairs. From here, she had a wide view of Hybardin's waterfront. Her earlier observation was borne out as the exhausted dark dwarves, who had gained only a small foothold on the steep stairway, finally withdrew entirely to catch their breath on the docks and reorder their decimated companies. From her vantage, the captain could see that many more boats were gathering near the shore, oars stirring the water as they advanced in neat ranks. Apparently, reinforcements were coming from Daerforge—and no doubt from Theibardin as well.

Belicia was about to make another round of her defensive positions when the ground underfoot was rocked by an unnatural tremor. Explosions split the air, thundering and ringing with a dire, ground-shaking force. Spots of unnatural brightness began to glow across the black water. One after another these patches swelled into flaming eruptions like fiery rockets which shot into the air, trailing sparks and leaving hissing trails of steam in their wake.

Battling dwarves on both sides halted their violence, staring in awe, silent and stunned. Beacons blazed through the air overhead, and more forms moved along the docks—shadowy figures that emerged from the water. She had not seen them swimming and dimly realized that the forms were not even dripping.

They slithered along the shore like a silent wave of darkness—touching and surrounding dwarves. And then those dwarves disappeared! The rippling shades moved on, leaving only armor and weapons scattered across the dockside.

"What in Reorx is happening?!" gasped Belicia.

But the wave of darkness only swept closer.

* * * * *

"Hold steady there! Damn you, grab that rope!"

Darkend pitched to the side as a sudden surge in the

lake's surface rocked his command boat violently. One gunwale dipped below the surface, and a great gush of water poured into the hull.

Crashing onto a bench, the thane of the Daergar struck blindly at the nearest of his oarsmen. That dark dwarf took no notice of the blow as he tried to scramble away from the water sloshing along the keel. Darkend nearly gagged in revulsion as his hands, knees, and feet were all soaked by the chilly stuff.

"Who did that?" he sputtered, climbing to his feet and glaring about. "Who dared to unbalance his thane?"

Immediately he saw that the rocking of the boat was not the result of any careless sailor. In fact, the whole surface of the sea was pitching and surging, lifting the boat and sending Darkend tumbling once more. He heard the terrified shrieking of Daergar all about him. Even as the thane tried to recover his balance, he spat vile curses in all directions.

Grabbing the gunwale with both hands, Darkend pulled himself up, glaring in impotent fury at the scene along the waterfront. There were random explosions and flaming things in the sky. Dark, shadowy creatures were everywhere, feeding on his troops.

His warriors should have been reordering themselves, preparing for a new attack, but instead they seemed to be racing in all directions at once. He barely noticed that the Hylar also seemed to have been thrown into confusion by the strange events. Sputtering in helpless rage, he saw that dwarves of both clans were haplessly trying to defend themselves against the fire and shadow creatures.

A flare of brightness crackled across Darkend's field of view, searing his eyes with furious light. For a time the thane could see nothing of what was happening on shore. He felt the heat of the nearby flames and instinctively threw his arms over his head. At the same moment, a crash of thunder shook the great cavern, the echoes ringing in his ears so loudly that he could hear nothing else.

Blinking and shaking his head, Darkend tried to restore his senses. When he had done so, he saw a great, fiery dragon rising up from the water in a hissing cloud of steam. It tore free from the sea and trailed a cloud of vapor in the air behind it. The thane could see the broad wings and feel the heat of unnatural fire on his face. Against the brightness of the wyrm he vaguely saw a figure, coal black and liquidly supple, crouching between the shoulders of the massive creature. The rider was manlike in shape, apparently naked and unarmed. It raised both arms in an unmistakable gesture of exultant triumph.

A gout of water suddenly burst upward from the stern, pouring into the boat and sucking the metal hull down. Another dark dwarf tumbled against Darkend, jostling him rudely. The thane took the offending fellow by the scruff of the neck and pitched him over the side where his scream was quickly drowned by the cold, churning waters. Still clutching the gunwale of the boat, the ruler of the Daergar glared in mute terror at the chaotic onslaught that was throwing his carefully planned attack into confusion.

All around him dark dwarves shrieked in terror as the heavy craft heeled violently to the side, allowing a spill of black water to rush into the hull. In an instant the boat was filled. Just as quickly it plunged beneath the waves, carrying its crew into the depths of the Urkhan Sea.

* * * * *

Baker and Axel were on Level Twenty-eight inspecting the defenses that had been installed in the event of a further incursion by the Klar. Aside from the Ferrust house, the damage from the first attack already had been repaired. Baker could tell from the eyes of every dwarf he met that memories of the onslaught still lingered fresh and hurtful. As he accompanied the venerable warrior through the streets and gardens of Hybardin's highest places, he passed many clansmen who had lost family members. He found he easily could push his chronic gut-pain into the background when he considered the suffering of so many of his clan.

Bands of guards, each troop comprised of ten or twelve armed Hylar, patrolled the streets and checked vacant buildings. They moved uneasily down the lanes and streets, sending advance scouts into the darkest alleys and showing every indication of utmost vigilance. Baker was heartened to see that very few of these patrols had resorted to the characteristic dwarven garrison tactic of making sure every inn and tavern was well-defended while the rest of the city was left to take care of itself. Perhaps the suddenness and brutality of the Klar attack had provided a sobering lesson for all Hybardin.

"It seems damned solid, doesn't it?" Axel asked, lifting his eyebrows toward the ceiling that arched overhead. "You'd never know by looking that it's honeycombed with tunnels and caves."

Baker nodded, leaning back and seeing the vaulted roof as if for the first time. Stone arches and balustrades, excavated from the very bedrock of the mountain, formed supports where the mass of stone curved over the road. The walls of each house extended all the way to the ceiling, so that within each structure—which was typically a nest of apartments shared by dozens of dwarves—the natural ceiling of the mountain formed the upper boundary of the site.

"Nearly every house has some kind of route through the rock. And now all those secret tunnels are coming back to haunt us in a big way," Axel groused bitterly. "I should have thought of it, by Reorx! What kind of a warrior am I, that my mind has to wither faster than the rest of me?"

"It's not your fault," Baker counselled. "I could have thought of it, too—or anyone else could have, for that matter. What's important now is for us to come up with some kind of plan that offers long-term protection."

A shout of alarm from a nearby house interrupted Baker's next question. The clash of metal against metal punctuated loud cries of fear and anger. Instantly, several of the armed patrols that were posted in the street charged toward the structure. More blows echoed from inside. Hurrying along, Baker heard the sounds of clashing swords followed by the unmistakable keening of berserk Klar.

"They're hitting us again!" growled Axel, his broadsword held in both hands and raised for combat. "Let's get those bastards!"

More houses echoed with noise. In moments Level Twenty-eight was embroiled in battle once again. Tangles of Klar and Hylar tumbled from the buildings, taking their skirmishes into the streets. Patrols of armed Hylar quickly stormed in from all directions, responding to the alarm with swift counterattacks. Several formed a steel-edged escort around their thane.

Baker stood in the street, surrounded by guards and feeling terribly useless. A small sword dangled at his side, one of the ornaments from his audience chamber wall that he had decided he could probably carry around without cutting off his leg. Now, for the first time he drew the weapon. It felt awkward and ill-balanced in his hand.

The weapon was suddenly forgotten as his attention was drawn to a nearby wall where the rock surface seemed suddenly to shift and sag. It was moving. There was no other way to describe it. The rock melted before him, turning to thick sludge, then flowed away like cream.

And the strangeness, the darkness, the forms of chaos that emerged from that gap, were more terrifying than any onslaught of Klar.

* * * * *

"What do you mean 'escaped'?"

Garimeth's voice was low, but the rumbling menace in her tone was enough to whiten Karc's already pallid features.

"J-just that, my lady. He's gone! The door was still locked, but somehow your son found a way out."

"How?"

"I don't know," the servant's voice was shrill and filled with panic. "By your order we put him in a room with no windows, and the door was securely bolted and locked. It was never opened, I swear!"

"Did he walk through the walls, then?" demanded the matriarch, her tone loaded with sarcasm.

"They're solid stone, lady! And the floor and ceiling as well!"

"You idiot!" screamed Garimeth. "They can't all be solid or he wouldn't have found a way out! I should have you killed right now for your carelessness!"

Karc cringed. This was not the first time he had heard this threat, but he knew from experience that it was no mere empty phrase.

"Go back and look, you miserable wretch! Search on your hands and knees! Use that pathetic brain that Reorx gave you, or I swear it will cost you your head! And know this: if you fail to find him, your death will not come quickly."

Before Garimeth could continue her threats, the house was rocked by an earthquake of violent and wrenching force. She screamed as she was thrown headlong on to the hard stones of her floor. Looking up, the dwarf-woman gaped in stunned silence as the rock that formed the ceiling of her house began to ooze downward. It dropped with heavy, liquid plops onto the floor, nearly crushing her before she scrambled out of the way.

Karc was not so lucky. He groaned in pain as a gelatinous mass of rock struck him on the shoulder and knocked him face first to the floor. He reached desperately toward Garimeth, his mouth working on a silent plea for help.

But the matriarch was busy scrambling away. Finally she felt a wall at her back and crouched in the corner of the large room, watching in silent horror as the hole in her ceiling expanded. In moments the liquid rock had solidified, leaving a series of drooping tendrils, like smooth stalactites, dangling down into the room. The blobs on the floor had hardened as well, and now as the servant struggled to move he was anchored by a collar of stone that had clasped his upper body in a granite embrace.

When Garimeth saw the creatures that dropped through the irregular opening, her breath caught in her throat and she shrank into the shadows. Realizing that she was pressed against a large trunk, she quickly scooted behind the obstacle. There she crouched in darkness, peering with one cautious eye around the side of her shelter. Despite her ragged breathing, she forced herself to grow calm, sensing that she could give herself away as easily by sound as by sight.

She saw a gaunt, utterly dark shape, crouching over the squirming Karc. The creature reached down to touch the servant with a cold, clawlike hand and immediately Karc's struggles ceased . . . and more. There was no body, nothing but a pathetic bundle of clothes beneath the shadowy attacker.

And then, as more of the creatures dropped from the hole and started to glide through her house, she was startled by the knowledge that she could not remember who had been in the middle of the floor.

But her thoughts immediately turned to more direct concerns as one of the shadows, oozing like liquid through the air, soundlessly advanced toward Garimeth. There was no substance, no real shape to the bizarre attacker. It seemed to be nothing but utter, consuming darkness. She was stunned as she chanced to look into the deep wells of its lightless eyes and felt a sense of utter, hopeless despair immediately drain the strength from her limbs.

All she could do was stumble backward, falling over the trunk in a nerveless, instinctive retreat. At least that tumble broke the spell of those horrid eyes, and her senses returned. Garimeth trembled in terror and pressed a hand to her mouth, trying unsuccessfully to stifle her fearful moans. Knowing that to look back at the shadow was to die, she scrambled around the barrier, then threw up the lid of the trunk to give her another moment's protection from soundless, lightless death.

And her eyes fell upon the Helm of Tongues.

The bronze artifact lay in the trunk where it had rested since her arrival. In desperation, she snatched it up and set it firmly on her head. She barely noticed the keen, sensory tingle of its magical presence. There was no weapon nearby, nothing she could use to fight, so she fell back another step. Then she was in the corner and saw the murky form of the shadow as it seemed to reach out with tendrils of darkness to enwrap the big trunk in a chilling, lethal cloak.

With nowhere else to look, Garimeth's vision again passed across the front of the thing, but this time she felt no menace in the bottomless eyes. Instead, she sensed that the shadow paused in its approach, hesitant . . . even confused.

The helm's power focused her thoughts and with those keen senses she reached out, tried to peer inside the mind of the shadow. She recoiled instantly, horrified by the mangled morass of its chaotic being. But at the same time she saw that the formless beast had moved back. Now it writhed in torment, and with sudden perception she saw that it feared her.

"Go away!" she declared, her tone surprising even herself with its firm quality. "Leave me!"

To her utter astonishment, the shadowy attacker slithered backward, then turned and wisped silently out the door.

Gullywasher

Chapter Fourteen

"Golly. That some hot water." Regal admired the blazing vista of the Urkhan Sea, which continued to toss and churn and spume. Periodically another cometlike gout of soaring flame shot forth from the black water. The Aghar shook his head in awe, though he sounded more impressed than frightened.

Tarn couldn't speak, could only stare, struck dumb by a much deeper sense of wrongness. He felt as though he was watching what must certainly be the end of Thorbardin. The feeling of impending doom had gripped him at the very first onslaught when tremors had shaken the ground and magical fire had burst into view from countless sources. Rockslides had rumbled down the slopes for several minutes. Although that initial violence had subsided somewhat, the lingering effects were everywhere, a frightening and bizarre assault against nature and reality.

Tarn had a vague notion about taking cover, but in his heart he knew there could be no shelter from this apocalyptic storm.

Great meteors of fire, finally recognizable as dragons of flame, roared through the sky over the lake. From over the miles of water the sounds of terror and pain and death shrieked of distant woe. Closer, the waters of the underground sea pitched and rose, surging onto the shore to spatter between the long fingers of Daerforge's solid stone docks. Dark dwarves teemed there in great numbers, some aboard boats, others scrambling to get to higher ground. Many of the watercraft were hurled ashore like matchsticks. The clutching tendrils of churning waves sucked hundreds of Daergar off the docks and into the bay, and then the tide rose to hammer once more against the unyielding terrain of the wharf.

Tarn watched in horror as other waves surged into the lower reaches of Agharhome, roaring through the tight streets and bowling helpless gully dwarves along, many of whom were carried back to certain death in the deep and churning maelstrom of the Urkhan Sea. More water spilled into the hollows, no doubt inundating countless Aghar who had sought the illusory shelter of the underground burrows.

"Wow!" Duck Bigdwarf gaped as a sinkhole formed in the ground near them, rocks and ravines turning to sand and spilling into a widening pit.

"Quick! Get back!" Tarn urged as the street fell away before them. Scrambling desperately, he and the small group of Aghar pulled themselves to higher ground.

One of the fiery projectiles soared closer, veering to pass directly overhead. Tarn saw widespread wings, outlined in living flame and unmistakably draconic in nature. He watched in disbelief as the mighty creature swept close to the cliff wall above the dwarven city. Surely the wyrm would have to turn or dive before impact! Instead the terrifying dragon flew with unwavering speed, striking the smooth, dark rock and sweeping onward as if the barrier was no more than a film of gauze. The creature vanished into the solid stone, and in the monster's wake Tarn saw a gaping hole leading into the cliff face, a tunnel that glowed like a furnace.

That illumination slowly faded as the blazing dragon tunneled deeper into the rock. Finally the unnatural cave was quite dark. And then the beast abruptly reappeared, bursting out of the cliff face in a different place and demolishing a couple of Daergar apartments as it emerged. The dragon glided overhead for a moment before soaring over the water again and winging powerfully toward the Life-Tree of the Hylar.

"How they do that?" Poof Firemaker's tone was admiring. Duck Bigdwarf merely stared, awestruck.

"Just flies everywhere," Regal observed. "Not only in air. Maybe it's swimmin' in the rock?"

Of the gathered watchers, only Tarn reacted with deep unease. The Hylar part of his mind reached beyond the spectacle of raw destruction to confront the deep and fundamental questions. How could this happen? And what did it mean for the future?

He had guesses for both questions, but his hypotheses were even more disturbing than the original queries. Tarn tried to deny the growing evidence, to consider any number of logical causes for this bizarre phenomenon. But as he watched the shifting images of light and darkness on the lake, he knew that only one explanation was possible.

"Chaos." He muttered the word softly, to himself. "Father was right. Chaos has come to Thorbardin."

"Poor guys," said Regal, watching as a great shelf of Daerforge's second level gave way, tumbling in a crushing landslide, burying a corner of the waterfront below. Rocks tumbled through the streets and a cloud of dust rose to obscure the panic-stricken dwarves—though it did not mask the shrill screams of the injured and dying.

The collapse swept away the front wall of several crowded dwellings, and Tarn was startled to see directly inside these structures. He spotted some Daergar clinging to the suddenly created precipice, watched in horror as, one after another, they slipped free to plunge onto the broken rubble below. Snatching a quick look up the slope, he felt a surprising rush of relief as he saw that his mother's house remained intact—at least, on the outside.

"Awful bad stuff," Poof Firemaker declared, shaking his head sadly as more dark dwarves tumbled into the maelstrom of chaos. Even now, Tarn was amazed that the gully dwarves were expressing sympathy for the dark dwarves who tormented them so relentlessly.

For a brief time fire glowed amid the wreckage, apparently feeding on the bare stone. But soon the blazes faded and died or were masked by the billowing and still-growing dust cloud. Fewer Daergar were visible now. Those who survived had taken cover deep in the bowels of their dwellings. The thunder that had rumbled through this end of Thorbardin also seemed to be fading, although when Tarn looked across the water he saw the Life-Tree racked by blazing convulsions. He clenched his teeth, furious at himself for his absence from home and utterly frustrated by his inability to get back there. Even if it only meant that he would die beside Belicia and his father, it was suddenly very important from him to be in Hybardin.

"All done for now," Regal declared, looking at the debris settling in the ruined swath of Daerforge. His expression turned hopeful. "Go get some beer?"

"Wow," Poof said, his tone strangely subdued. "Real bad happening."

"All killed? All?" wondered Duck. He sniffled loudly.

"Agharhome was badly hit. I'm sorry to say," Tarn felt obliged to observe.

"Not hit like that!" insisted Poof, pointing at the ruined swath of Daerforge.

"Don't you sometimes think that the other clans

deserve the worst that happens to them?" Tarn wondered. "After all, it seems like you Aghar get treated pretty unfairly anywhere in Thorbardin you try to go."

Regal Everwise squinted, even rubbing his forehead in the effort of his cogitation. "What you mean?" he asked, clearly mystified.

"Well, just . . ." Tarn tried to organize his thoughts. He knew what it was like to be an outsider, to feel scorned and rejected by fellow dwarves. Yet never in his life had he been subjected to the level of abuse that was any gully dwarf's daily lot. "I would think it would bother you. In the rest of Thorbardin there's plenty to eat and drink, lots of gardens and fresh water. There are laws, even, to protect dwarves from other dwarves who don't like them. Yet we all seem to think nothing of kicking a gully dwarf, or keeping you in your own little slum here."

"Slum?" Regal bristled. "Agharhome fine excellent city! Got friendlier people even than Life-Tree!"

Tarn laughed in spite of the rising sense of his own indignation—an emotion inspired on the Aghars' behalf, but apparently not shared by those whom he felt had been wronged.

"Friendly people . . . you're right about that," he agreed, ashamed by his own pettiness.

"Come to our inn. We got some good food there. And beer," Regal promised with an expansive wave of his hand.

Reluctantly, Tarn followed the small dwarves through the ravines and gullies of their rock-strewn home. This far from the sea it seemed that the Chaos storm had done little damage, though in fact it was kind of hard to tell, given the generally crumbled nature of the gully dwarf city. He could see, though, that the waves had swept some of the lower portions of the place quite cleanly, even washing away some of the large rocks that had jutted so characteristically upward. Plodding along, the half-breed periodically stopped and stared, allowing his mind to once again wrestle with his one overriding problem. How was he going to get home?

They finally ducked under a low entrance, and after a moment's hesitation, Tarn stooped low and followed the creatures into a dingy and lightless hole. Despite the rank smells of unwashed bodies pressed into too tight of a space, the place was alive with cheerful conversation and even giggling bursts of laughter that erupted into a cacophony of hysterical amusement when Tarn stood up and bumped his head on a stone protruding downward from the ceiling.

"No beer for you!" one jeered. "You not even stand okay now!"

"Er, right," Tarn grunted, rubbing the tender spot on his skull. As he saw the dark and bubbling grog that filled the dirty communal mug, he was quite willing to forego the pleasure of a draught. The gully dwarves amiably passed the vessel around the group, chatting with apparent unconcern about food and beer. The half-breed tried to suppress a sense of utter disbelief. Didn't they understand what was happening to their world?

"Why you sulk?" Regal asked, eventually coming to sit beside the half-breed.

Tarn chuckled ruefully. "I didn't know I was sulking. The truth is, I was thinking about a problem."

"What problem? Regal Big-Time-Smart help you fix it!"

"I wish you could, my friend. I really do. But I've got to get to Hybardin, and I don't see how you can get me there any more than I can get there myself!" Tarn declared bitterly.

"Hybardin? That long way. Why not stay here? Got friends. Got grog. Here." Regal held out the filthy mug, which still contained a splash of mysterious looking dregs. Tarn politely declined. "Why in a hurry to go?" asked the Aghar again.

"I've got my father there, and a friend . . . a lady friend. You saw what happened over there, what's happening to all Thorbardin. I'm certain that they need my help," the half-breed declared urgently.

"You help to fight?"

"Yes, probably," Tarn agreed. Abruptly his hand went to his belt, where he usually carried his sword. Naturally, the loop was empty. He hadn't seen the blade since he had been drugged at his mother's house. "Although I have to admit I'm in sore need of a weapon."

"Here! This cutter too big for me," offered the tiny Duck Bigdwarf.

"Thanks, friend." Tarn took the proffered short sword, wondering how an Aghar had come to possess such a splendid weapon. Only then did he recognize the gem in the pommel, see the crest of white granite in the hilt, and realize that it was his own blade. He opened his mouth to say something, then shut it. What was the use?

Meanwhile, the gully dwarves had put their heads together in a murmured council, during which another mug of grog was passed around and several voices had risen in heated discussion. Just when the vile beverage was beginning to look almost palatable to Tarn, Regal Everwise lifted his head from the group and fixed him with a direct glare.

"Can we go to Hybardin too?" Regal asked bluntly. "We never go there before; wanna go now."

"I don't think this is the time for sightseeing," Tarn replied, his mind distracted. "And I really think you'd be safer here."

"Safer?" Duck declared indignantly. "We safe alla places. But how you get to Hybardin, you not have our help?"

"I don't know," Tarn declared with a rueful laugh. "But just for the sake of argument, how would I get to Hybardin if I did have your help?"

"Easy," declared Poof Firemaker, with a dismissive wave of his hand. "We could fly there, or swim!"

"Or we could ride that fire dragon. Big fun!" added

Duck Bigdwarf.

"Hmmph!" sniffed Regal. "This big dwarf not looking for fun. He gotta go see his pop and his lady love."

The other Aghar nodded pensively, clearly understanding this high motive.

"Thanks anyway," Tarn said. "But I don't think I can fly or swim that far. As for the fire dragon, I'd hate to be the one who had to ask him for a ride."

"No, no, no. Those stupid plans," declared the everwise Regal. "We go to Hybardin, we do it right!"

"And how do you do that?" Tarn couldn't refrain from asking.

"Easy. We go to Daerforge and steal a boat."

Dark Dwarf Decisions

Chapter Fifteen

"Help me, you fools!" Darkend thrashed in the water, clawing over the sinking bodies of his crew. He cursed his gauntlets as his fingers slipped from the metal hull of the swamped lake boat. Panic rose in his gorge, horror of death by water penetrating to the very core of his being. Feeling the cold liquid soak through his beard, rising to his chin, he shrieked desperately at any Daergar in earshot.

The thane could see nothing beyond the piercingly bright image of that fiery dragon that had been scarred into his mind. His feet were loosely touching the hull of the boat, but that tenuous support was completely submerged and sinking fast. Frigid waters rose past his face, spilling into his mouth, choking, gagging him. He felt himself sinking deeper and deeper.

164

And then the boat was gone from underneath him, and he was surrounded by a suffocating presence. His hands broke the surface momentarily, clawed futilely at the air, and then he was sinking faster into the vast and murderous nothingness of deep water.

Abruptly a hand reached down to sieze him by the wrist, and Darkend found himself being hauled roughly into the hull of another boat. He was tumbled onto the deck with an utter lack of ceremony, and for several minutes he could only cough and gasp at the feet of his rescuers. Shivering, retching, he clung mindlessly to life. Finally he caught his breath and sat up, glaring around him with eyes that had begun to regain some semblance of darksight. Each inhalation was still a horrible, bubbling effort.

He couldn't stand to face the brightness of Hybardin's docks, so he examined the dark dwarves in the boat with him. The Daergar crew that had rescued him was a veteran lot, many scarred from decades of battle. No doubt each of them had seen and worked considerable mayhem and bloodshed during those years. Yet now they glanced uneasily toward the shore, then looked at Darkend with expressions of pleading, of uneasiness . . . of fear.

His anger had settled somewhat, stifling his instincts of rebuke and rage with the realization that he was lucky to be alive. There was no sign of his original boat, nor of the dozens of dwarves who had served as their thane's loyal crew. Somehow the crew of this boat must have seen him go down and acted with desperate haste to grab him and save his life.

He forced himself to look at the shore, squinting against a much greater illumination than had existed when the attack began. Steam in great clouds wafted across the surface of Hybardin. In places the mist swirled away from the bedrock with a churning force and crimson glow. He sensed the raw heat that lay behind these eruptions. With another curl of moving air he saw that a great slab of the overhanging cliff was aglow with inner warmth.

"It's lava . . . melting rock," he breathed in awe.

"Aye, lord, and much has already flowed away." One of the nearby rowers spoke up, his own voice hushed. "Look there, if you please. Them was the docks where we first landed."

Darkend saw a smooth slab of stone, sweeping evenly to the edge of the water—an edge that was still bubbling and steaming as the liquid contacted superheated rock.

"A hundred dwarves was standin' there when the heat came. My thane, I swear by Reorx they were burned into ash as I watched!" declared another rower.

"What was that . . . that . . . flying monster?" asked the thane, addressing the gray-bearded coxswain at the rudder of his boat. "The living fire that came out of the water and took to the air like a dragon?"

"Never saw the like," declared the fellow. "But it sank a dozen boats in the blink of one eye. Then it touched the rock there—" He pointed at the hot surface of the cliff, which had poured away to reveal a shallow, black-walled cave. "—and just vanished. Like it was diving into water, it just flew into the cliff."

Another wave surged through the water, rocking the boat and reminding Darkend of the peril of his current position. Gusting winds, a strange and unnatural phenomenon in Thorbardin, whipped the water around him into spray. He saw some boats that had capsized and others that were half-swamped. And even with a quick count he guessed that at least a score of his vessels had already plunged to the bottom of the underground sea.

"You, there—and you!" He stood tall in the hull and pointed to two boats that still had full complements of warriors and were captained by seasoned leaders. "Get to shore and pass the word. I want the docks held! There is to be no retreat!"

"Aye, Lord Thane!" chorused the pair of warriors, immediately urging their men to press oars.

Before they got very far, however, the loudest explosion Darkend had ever heard rocked through Thorbardin. A great section at the bottom of the Life-Tree gave way. Massive slabs of rock tumbled downward and smashed across the waterfront and plaza. A cloud of dust swept outward, thick and choking, followed quickly by a surging wave raised by the debris that crashed into the water. Echoes rocked the air, mingled with the screams of crushed, dying dwarves and the exultant braying of the fire dragons that still circled and dove through the fringes of destruction.

The thane couldn't see the base of the city, but he was certain that hundreds, maybe thousands, of dwarves on both sides had been crushed to death in the collapse. Dark dwarves and Hylar had been locked in battle directly under the massive rockfall, but all sounds of combat had been overwhelmed by the thunder of crashing stone.

As the dust slowly settled, the watchers on the sea saw that the landscape of Hybardin's waterfront had been drastically changed. What had once been a region of warehouses and docks was now buried under mounds of rubble that jutted like hills and mountains across a landscape of utter destruction. Here and there antlike dwarves scrambled across the wreckage, but these seemed dazed and hesitant, no longer vigorous warriors in the midst of a campaign.

"Get me back to Daerforge immediately." Darkend didn't recognize his own voice as he directed orders at the coxswain of his own boat. His face was pale with shock and uncertainty.

"As you command, lord." The dwarf immediately set his crew to rowing. If any of them wondered about the propriety of their leader deserting his army on the crumbling shore of Hybardin, they were smart enough to keep such thoughts to themselves. A temporary retreat made sense to everybody.

The sea was smoother once they pulled away from the

Life-Tree, though high waves rolled past at measured intervals. Such waves were heretofore virtually unknown on the Urkhan Sea, and their surging rhythm added to the growing sense of fear. Fortunately, the crew was skilled and seasoned enough to keep their bearings, and very little water spilled over the gunwales as the boat pitched and churned across the surface. The rowers drove hard, but it was a long voyage, made eerily longer by the group's silence and the flashes of light that regularly pierced the comforting darkness.

At last they neared Daerforge, and the thane saw with dismay that parts of his own realm had suffered destruction, though not on the scale that had struck Hybardin. There were no longer any signs of the creatures who had caused the damage, and repairs were already under way here and there. As they drew closer he looked up at the cliff, saw that the twin towers of his sister's manor still stood watch, and wondered about his own palace. Had the creatures struck Daerbardin too or just the cities on the lake? He would have to wait to find out.

As the thane peered at a small section of waterfront buildings, he realized that they had been knocked down by forces of amazing strength and violence. Walls had been flattened and iron beams twisted into knots. He shivered, strangely exhilarated by evidence of such overwhelming power. Who, or what, had invaded Thorbardin?

He would have to confer with others and ponder his next move before regrouping and returning to Hybardin. In the meantime it was important that he show no signs of indecision or weakness. He was still the thane of the Daegar, after all, and still determined to conquer the city of the Hylar.

Regaining his composure, Darkend accepted no help as they pulled ashore at the wharf. Instead he scrambled ahead and began to issuing orders.

"Get back to the Hylarhome. See that our positions are

held and the attack pressed while I collect further reinforcements!"

"Aye, lord," the coxswain assented, but he couldn't help but looking disappointed at his orders. He cast off in haste with a longing look at the shore of his homeland. The other dark dwarf faces were likewise forlorn.

Once on the dock, Darkend had to wait only a short time before a shadowy figure in a black robe emerged from a pile of rubble and debris. At first Darkend tensed, not recognizing the newcomer and was suddenly aware that he was without his usual phalanx of guards.

"You should take better care of yourself, my lord." Slickblade's voice was an unmistakable hiss, though Darkend could not recognize the face of the speaker within the deep-hooded robe. "There are known ruffians about."

"Indeed," the thane replied dryly. "But tell me, what news of events in my cities? Tell me of this mysterious scourge. How was it manifested in Daerforge? And did it strike Daerbardin as well?"

"Your city here fares well enough. A few houses were taken down, and there is wreckage such as this throughout the city. As to things inland, there has been no word of occurrences there. Aside from the fiery dragons you no doubt observed, the attackers were strange creatures, cold and dark as our own shadows. They killed some, but no one seems to remember much about the fallen. It is as though the killing takes all thoughts, all memories of the slain when their life essence is destroyed."

"But the monsters did not stay in our city?"

"No. It seems that they move through air and water with equal ease. Those that struck Daerforge soon moved into the lake. They seem to be gathering in the direction of the Life-Tree."

"And what of the fiery dragons?"

"We saw some over the sea," replied Slickblade. "One of them came to Daerforge, bored a tunnel that destroyed a few smithies and apartments, then emerged into the air again and—I am happy to say—flew away."

"This may yet become a matter we can turn to our own ends," Darkend speculated. "But I must know more about these strange beasts. What are their origins, their nature, and their ultimate intentions?"

"I am not privy to these facts, but there may be one in Daerforge who could answer your questions."

"Speak."

"Ironically enough, he is your own nephew, come here upon the orders of his father, the Hylar thane. He was sent to carry word to you about this mysterious threat. A 'Storm of Chaos,' so he said."

"Where is he?"

"It seems that he went to his mother's house. Garimeth Bellowsmoke drugged him and imprisoned him there, ensuring that he could not bring his message to you."

"What?" The thane's pulse raced with the news, the familiar sensation of betrayal rising to create a red film over his vision. His sister would be tortured and executed according to an excruciating method.

Yet at the same time he had to admire her deviousness. Garimeth had made herself invaluable to him, had presented him with real intelligence about the Hylar defenses, and had assured him that the Hylar army was absent for an extended interval. For some reason she must have decided to conceal the true reason for that absence. Darkend was impressed by her ruthless tactics. She even betrayed her own offspring! If the opportunity arose, she wouldn't think twice about betraying a brother. What was her ultimate goal?

"Your information is good?" he asked Slickblade.

Slickblade sniffed disdainfully. "You don't need to ask that. But yes, drawn from a source within her very house. And there is more, as well."

"More?" Darkend was truly curious.

"I have learned within the past hours that your sister's

plan has miscarried. Her son, held prisoner in the house of his mother, has escaped."

"No!" The thane forced a chuckle, but the sound was dry and menacing, utterly devoid of any humor. "That is not good news. Especially for my sister. She will have much to explain, much to account for."

Darkend took a deep breath, bringing his raging emotions under control only with great difficulty. He trusted no one, expecting duplicity and betrayal at every turn, and yet the fierce urge for vengeance was almost overwhelming.

But finally he calmed himself.

Across the water he could see the inverted mountain of the Life-Tree, crackling with spots of flame, dripping and glowing and shimmering. More boats were making their way back to Daerforge, some of them pretty banged up. All were filled with cowed and bedraggled Daergar. Darkend was certain that the survivors among his landing force were holding on to their position in Hybardin. But how many had survived? How many had avoided being crushed by the massive rockfall?

These cowards currently arriving would be sent back to the fray, packed into boats, and he would lead them toward the foe, toward ultimate victory.

But first he had a personal matter to take care of.

"Come, Slickblade," he said in a voice that was a lethal whisper. "Let us pay a call to the house of Garimeth Bellowsmoke."

The Weight of a Throne

Chapter Sixteen

Somehow in the chaos of the battle Baker Whitegranite had lost his glasses. He crouched next to the garden wall of a fine Hylar manor, feeling along the ground, trying to find the place he'd fallen when the bizarre shadows had first attacked. It was then that his spectacles had been knocked off of his face, though in the grip of confusion and terror he hadn't noticed the loss immediately. Still frightened, he tried to stay low as he scooted along the ground, hearing screams and shouts and clashing weapons nearby.

Finally the sounds faded, and Baker crept back to the place where he had first fallen. Through his blurred vision he saw a hint of crystalline gleam and finally put his hands over the familiar golden frame. Touching the twin lenses, he breathed a sigh of relief as he discovered that they were unbroken.

Baker quickly wiped his spectacles on a corner of his stained tunic, then put them back onto his face. His sight was still bleary, and one of the lenses seemed to have been permanently scuffed, but they were clear enough to confirm that things on Level Twenty-eight looked as bad as they sounded.

And that was very bad indeed.

The fight had moved on from here, though the echoes, smells, and gore still lingered heavily in the air and on the ground. He saw dead dwarves who had been locked in combat with each other, Hylar and Klar intermingled, mouths gaping and eyes bulging in mute testimony to the horror of their last moments. In other places he saw empty lumps of armor and clothing, weapons lying nearby. There was no sign at all of the dwarven flesh that had worn the pathetic remnants only minutes—or was it hours?—before. These were the places where the horrifying chill shadows had slithered past.

Baker heard shouts and screams and the occasional clash of a sword or shield coming from down the street. Looking up, he saw a hint of the shadowy attackers, manlike beings of pure darkness that moved steadily away from him.

He tried to reconstruct the last few minutes since the wall had melted and the wave of horror had surged into Thorbardin. But details were curiously vague in his mind. He recalled dark and shadowy beings, intangible but very deadly nevertheless. They had emerged in countless numbers, breaking right through the stone walls to sweep into the ranks of the battling dwarves.

One thing was certain. The shadowy invaders were no friends of the Klar. The crazed dwarves, already frenzied from battling the Hylar, had turned with fresh fury to fight the dark forms. The dwarves had been swept aside, eradicated like a nest of pesky rats. Although the mere touch of the shadow beings proved instantly fatal, this did not prevent the maddened Klar from pressing home their suicidal attacks.

Hylar had also fallen victim to the horrific onslaught, and Baker had seen many of his countrymen slain before his eyes. At least he thought he had—though when he tried to recall the battle, to put faces on those brave fighters, everything was terribly confusing. He looked at the wrecked Ferrust house. He clearly remembered old Blackbeard Ferrust, the prominent coal seller. Beside that ruin had stood another once-great house, emptied without visible damage by the shadow attack. It was a mighty edifice, and Baker was pretty sure that a very influential clan of Hylar had lived there. Yet that family had been annihilated by the shadow warriors, and now the thane couldn't recall their names, their roles in the city, or anything else about them.

Slumping against the stone in weariness, he wondered about his son. Was Tarn dead too? Was he caught in the onslaught of Chaos? Or had he joined ranks with the dark dwarves? Angrily the thane shook his head at the last notion. He refused to believe that Tarn's loyalties would be so easily twisted. Closing his eyes, he breathed a silent prayer to Reorx, pleading that the young dwarf remained unhurt.

Leaning against the wall, feeling the familiar burning in his stomach, Baker felt like giving up. But instead he listened again to the growing silence and then again heard the hint of sounds. Groans came from beneath a section of the wall that had fallen flat into the street. Baker hurried to the place and tried to move the heavy slab. Though he tore off one of his fingernails in the attempt, he could not budge the heavy weight. Once more he heard a fading moan.

Standing up, he was able to spot an elder Hylar kicking through the rubble of a nearby building. From his silk vests, shiny leather boots, and the magnifying eyepiece he wore on a gold chain, the thane deduced that the fellow was a gem cutter.

"Help!" he called, and the other dwarf hastened over to lend a hand with the flat piece of stone. But after they had moved it, they could only look down helplessly at the blue-faced corpse of a young dwarfmaid.

"She suffocated before we could get her free," Baker said, feeling horribly guilty.

"There were more noises over there," reported the jeweler, pointing to the nearby rubble where Baker had first seen him.

The thane accompanied the gem cutter, and they were quickly joined by more Hylar, young and old, males and females, who seemed to appear from nowhere. In a few minutes they had freed a mother and two children who had been buried alive, saved from being crushed by an overhanging shelf of what had once been their ceiling.

"Let's get them down to safety," Baker suggested, wondering if in fact any place in Hybardin was free from danger right now. "Does the lift still work?" he asked the group.

"The chain was broken when I passed it an hour ago," said one of the rescuers, a burly smith by the look of him. "They was workin' to get it fixed, though."

"Then let's get the injured to the station and see what can be done."

Willing hands lifted those unable to walk, while others limped along with the group.

For the time being the battle had seemed to settle into a quiet stasis. Baker stopped to take a look around his beloved city's highest level. He could see some of the creatures he called shadow monsters, far down the street from him, slithering around the ruins of several structures. The shadows glided like cats or oozed along the ground.

Baker turned toward the lift, surprised to note that the big blacksmith and several other brawny Hylar were waiting for him.

"What's your name?" asked the thane, grateful for the company.

"Capper Whetstone, my lord thane, at your service. I would be grateful for the chance to stand at your side.

I say with all respect, lord, that you should not be walking around here without protection."

"Yes, thank you." He briefly wondered about his earlier bodyguards. He had met them and conversed with them, of course, but now he couldn't recall their names or anything about them.

"I'll stay here and keep watch, my lord thane," offered a new voice, and Baker was surprised to see the Hylar jeweler, his single-lens viewer still hanging from its golden chain. "I've got a good eye, and I'll keep it on those marauding shades down there. I'll give a holler if they start coming this way."

Baker was touched by the fellow's loyalty. "That would be a good service. Just make sure to run while you're hollering," he replied.

And then he was struck by a question that suddenly seemed very important. "What's your name?"

"I am called Emerald-Eye the Younger," said the Hylar, touching his neatly trimmed beard with his fingers as he performed a deep and formal bow.

By the time Baker and his escort of a half dozen Hylar had neared the lift station, the engineers had made their repairs, and the great cage was rattling up to its landing. Baker was relieved to see that Axel Slateshoulders was returning from his mission of inspection. The veteran captain seemed strangely dazed, failing to react until the thane called him twice.

"What's the word from below? How does Belicia fare on the dock?"

A closer look at Axel's face cut off Baker's question and confirmed that the news was bad—bad as could be.

"The bottom levels are lost," Axel began, forcing words out with an effort that brought the veins bulging from his forehead. "The whole bottom of the Life-Tree broke loose and fell onto the docks and plaza. It's all buried. And Belicia. By Reorx, it should have been me!" The veteran commander staggered with a groan of pure misery.

Baker caught Axel by his broad shoulders and felt that sturdy body heaving in a tide of grief. The thane searched without success for words to bring him comfort. He settled for the solace he could offer with his embrace, even as his own despair threatened to overwhelm him.

"What happened?" Baker asked, utterly drained, but knowing the answer might well be important—if anything could ever be important again.

The question seemed to bring Axel back to some measure of awareness. "No one knows. My lord, there were no survivors. The First and Second levels were cut off, buried under a million tons of rock. The Third is full of corpses or worse. They're all dead. The Lift can't go lower than Level Four. I did the last descent by one stairway that hasn't yet caved in."

Baker tried to absorb the loss. Axel's daughter, their beautiful city, perhaps even his son were all gone.

For the first time he took note of the forty or fifty dwarves who had accompanied Axel in the lift. Some of them bore fine weapons. A few carried only big sticks, but it was clear that all were ready to do battle for their realm. They stood around waiting, looking at the wreckage that marked every one of the four avenues leading away from the lift station.

Baker spotted several apprentices from the palace library. They were young dwarves, and now they held swords and knives in hands that had been trained to use writing utensils.

"You dwarves," he said quickly. "Do you have quill and parchment?"

"Aye, lord thane. We all have our writing tools."

"I want you all to take down the names of every dwarf here," Baker said. "And find the others, the groups of Hylar that are scattered all around this level. From now on I want a record—a written record—of everyone who fights against these shade creatures."

The young scholars quickly obeyed. Meanwhile, Axel

found several veteran warriors among the throng of Hylar and appointed them sergeants. In a short time they had sorted the volunteers into a semblance of units, their number growing as more of the scattered patrols returned to the lift and added their number to the group.

Still the Hylar were disorganized and unprepared for the shock of a fresh attack when Baker heard the unmistakable cries of battle-ready Klar. The sound rose like a roar and rumbled through the whole city quarter. Within seconds, bands of frenzied attackers swept down two of the wide streets and rushed toward the lift station. Spittle flying from their grinning lips, they thundered closer with whoops and shouts of insane glee.

"Back, my lord!" cried Capper Whetstone, taking the thane's arm with a powerful grip. "Into the lift!"

"Wait!" snapped Baker, his voice sharp enough to pierce the din. His mind whirled. The lift was too small to hold more than a fraction of the Hylar gathered at the station.

Before he could issue further orders, the warriors of the two clans clashed in a barrage of blows. Many Klar tumbled away or writhed on the ground, halted by the stout Hylar defense. But many more frantic attackers pushed through the melee, desperate to stab, to kill. Baker held his little sword ready, standing just behind the dwarves in the front line. A Hylar fell, gouged deeply in the leg, and a leering Klar rushed through the gap to charge the thane. Baker cut down the wild-eyed berserker, surprised at the satisfaction he found in the bone-crushing swing of his weapon. He stepped forward, bashing at another opponent, then tumbled to the floor as something sharp and hot smashed him in the face.

He heard the fight raging all around and feared that he had been blinded—a dread that suddenly struck him as far worse than death. He clasped a hand to his face, wiping away blood and the broken pieces of his spectacles.

And he could see light! Wiping again, he discovered that he could see, though his vision was clouded by the blood that spilled into his eyes. He stood, trying to shake off a feeling of utter helplessness. Squinting, he realized that the Hylar had formed a protective ring around him as more Klar poured around corners to join the fray.

"Axel!" Baker cried urgently. "Come here! I need your eyes!"

"My lord, I can do nothing. May Reorx strike me dead as I stand—"

"Come, damn it! Tell me what you see down those streets!" Baker pointed around the lift station, into the avenues that were ominously silent. Unfortunately, anything more than a short stone's throw away was a mere blur in his vision.

"Down that street I see a mass of those shades—two, maybe three blocks away. The other street is quiet. No sign of dwarf or darkness."

"Up the street toward the shades—can we get away from the Klar by falling back that way?"

Axel looked around in astonishment. "For now. They'll have that side cut off in another minute."

"What if we were to run toward the shadows?" Quickly he outlined his daring idea.

Axel hesitated for only a fraction of a heartbeat, then his teeth flashed in a warlike grin. "Aye, my lord." In another moment his voice was a commanding roar. "Hylar! Fall back on my point! Double time! Break!"

Instantly the defenders swept back from the attacking Klar and poured around the side of the lift station as the pursuers tangled into a mass. A few of the frenzied warriors tried to sweep around the flank, but Baker used his sword and began slashing at the Klar who stood out from the blur. He drove the few maddened dwarves back with cuts and stabs.

The Hylar moved in a mass, following Axel's clumping lead without question. Soon they were running down the street, hundreds of howling Klar in pursuit.

"How far?" the thane gasped to Axel as he strained to

breathe over the unfamiliar exertion of a full run.

"Two blocks," panted the venerable captain, keeping up remarkably well despite his gout. "Now one after this lane, here."

Baker spotted the gaps of a narrow alley connecting the right and left of the avenue. Just beyond he now saw the indistinct shapes of utter darkness and knew that the Chaos shades were hungrily awaiting the onrushing dwarves.

"You head right. I'm going left," Axel called.

The rushing Hylar reached the pair of narrow lanes that diverged from the main road. "Split up!" cried Baker, pointing to the right and left. "Half go each way!"

The retreating dwarves quickly veered off, and the Klar kept going straight ahead down the wide street. A few of the crazed attackers tried to turn into the narrow alleys, but their way was blocked by several burly Hylar. The rest of the Klar were happy to charge onward, rushing down the street with howls of bloodthirsty frenzy.

And the shadows met them in dark but exultant silence.

A Scheme and a Treaty

Chapter Seventeen

Accompanied by his assassin and a handful of warriors he had gathered from the returning boats, Darkend started up the long road that climbed toward his sister's house. One of his escort quickly hoisted the thane's banner, and he was startled when, as the pennant of the Smoking Forge passed, he heard hissing and jeers from behind the closed doors of several buildings. Darkend's mission was too urgent to allow him to take time to discipline these traitors, but he took note of the addresses. He would be certain to take appropriate actions later.

Slickblade took matters into his own hand when one citizen dared to hurl a clump of rotten fungus from an upper balcony. The assassin and three Daergar warriors broke down the door to a private inn and went upstairs to grab the young dwarf. They hauled the struggling, barely bearded youth into the street where he was cast to the ground before Darkend.

"Is this the respect you show to your thane?" demanded Slickblade, drawing his short sword and prodding the fellow hard enough to draw blood. "Now wretch, beg for your life!"

"Thane!" the rebellious Daergar said, angry enough to conquer his fear. "Thane of what? My house was destroyed by Chaos. My family, gone! And now I look into a room that shows a woman's hand, and I cannot even tell you the name of that woman!"

"Kill him," snapped Darkend, moving on as the assassin carried out his order with a quick stabbing movement.

He stalked onward with regal dignity but was far more concerned than he dared show. How quickly they had turned against him! Now every doorway seemed to offer an ambush, and each shuttered window concealed conspirators and rebels.

And what was the nature of this new supernatural enemy? How could they steal thoughts and memories, affect the very minds of the survivors? They attacked and destroyed on a level that was almost impossible to comprehend!

The thane's party passed the Second Level and moved steadily higher, toward the twin towers of House Bellowsmoke. One of the thane's bodyguards uttered a sharp gasp and fell forward, the steel dart of a crossbow missile jutting from his back. Others in the band immediately closed around the thane. There was no one who doubted that the arrow had been intended for Darkend himself.

Slickblade led a half dozen warriors off the road, climbing through steep alleys and lanes, searching for the would-be culprit while the rest of the party hastened onward. Soon Darkend heard shouts and a brief clatter of weapons. Shortly afterward, the men-at-arms brought a battered Daergar and cast him to the paving stones before the thane. This one, too, would not grovel or beg. Instead he spit a stream of bloody saliva that very nearly touched Darkend's boot.

"Kill this one, too," ordered the thane. "But make it slow, very painful."

A thrust by Slickblade's silver blade brought forth a long, lingering scream. That mournful wail trailed off into slow gurgling as Darkend and his henchman once more started climbing.

"A deep, twisting belly stab," Slickblade explained smugly. "Inevitably fatal, but terribly slow to finish the job. It will be a good lesson for anyone else who's contemplating another act of insolence."

"Are you sure you got the right dwarf?" asked the thane.

"Not at all," the assassin replied calmly. "But the same purpose is served in any event, don't you agree?"

"Indeed."

For just a moment the thane paused to look over the Urkhan Sea. From here he could see for miles. Explosive lights burst through the darkness in many places. Columns of steam rose from the water, hissing and boiling into the air. Fires still raged on Hybardin, and several of the meteoric dragons, trailing their clouds of smoke and sparks behind them, circled in the air a long way off.

Darkend banged on his sister's entry drum, the sound of his mailed fist pounding through the pillar of stone and echoing in the solid bedrock beneath. Within moments the bridge dropped, and the portal was opened by a servant, who bowed deeply and skipped out of the way as the thane stalked over the drawbridge into the manor's courtyard.

"My brother, what an unexpected pleasure," said Garimeth, emerging from her own dressing chambers. She was wearing a gown of Hylar design, shimmering silver foil embroidered with large diamonds. The gems winked and glittered almost as brightly as her eyes as she took in Darkend's scowl. Oddly, the thane noted, she was also wearing a helmet of bronze, an affectation of fashion that the thane decided he didn't care for. With a polite curtsy his sister waited for him to speak.

"Unexpected, to be sure. As for pleasure, we'll see what you say in a few minutes."

"It is always a pleasure to be in your presence and to hear your wishes, Brother."

"It is my wish that emissaries from the other thanes be shown directly to me, not imprisoned in the houses of my relatives. It is my wish that those who bring me important news are not impeded in the performance of those tasks."

If she was shocked by his knowledge, Garimeth was shrewd enough to give no sign. Instead she frowned slightly, the delicate and feminine pout that had been in her arsenal of expressions since girlhood.

"My dear Brother, I had every intention of arranging a meeting between you and my only son. Unfortunately events have conspired against me. This affliction of Chaos has struck my own house. Surely you noticed the debris in the courtyard, the wreckage of stone, the grieving of the servants?"

In fact, Darkend had been studying his sister too intently to pay attention to his surroundings. She had a point, but he would not be distracted.

"I understand that this emissary—your half-breed son!—could have provided us with warning of this threat, the very Chaos that you claim so afflicts you. Yet he was drugged and held here until it is too late. Why?"

Garimeth's eyes narrowed, and Darkend knew she was trying to decide how he could have gotten such detailed information. No other sign of discomfort disturbed her graceful features as she replied.

"Tarn was worn and shaken by the journey. I merely gave him something to help him sleep. Apparently he was confused when he awakened and fled away from here before I could give him an explanation. Indeed, my lord and Brother, if my actions have in any way caused you difficulty, I extend my most humble apologies."

"You may extend your neck under my executioner's blade, and that will still not recompense for the harm that has been done," declared Darkend.

He thought about telling her the rest of what he knew, that Tarn had been a prisoner here for several days, that his drugging had nothing to do with the rigors of the trip from Hybardin to Daerforge. But for now he decided to hold his tongue. After all, there might be future need for his spy in this house, and it would not do to endanger his sources of information.

"Tell me this: where is Tarn Bellowgranite now?"

"He departed abruptly," Garimeth said smoothly, impressing Darkend with the ease of her dissembling—no admission that he had been a prisoner or that he had escaped! "I believe he intended to seek you, though no doubt he expected to find you at the Life-Tree. In fact, it was this agent here who summoned him and told him to await your pleasure." She pointed at Slickblade.

"She lies, Sire!" cried the assassin, his eyes widening behind the slit of his robe.

"Why do you deny this?" asked Garimeth smoothly, blinking in what Darkend took to be a reasonable façade of surprise. "Could it be that you—? But no, I don't understand!"

"There is no truth in her words! I did not come for the half-breed. Why would I?" Slickblade's tone was shocked, his manner grim.

"Indeed, why would Slickblade do such a thing?" asked the thane.

"Who knows?" Garimeth shrugged. "Perhaps he wanted to make you believe that I was betraying you."

"Lies! Let me kill her now, my lord," said Slickblade, his voice dropping to a soft and deadly hiss.

Darkend seriously considered the request, then shook his head. "No. There is more here than I know, and I will have some answers. Do not kill her. Not yet, anyway."

185

"Of course I am worried about my son, too. Where did you take him?" Garimeth asked Slickblade innocently.

"What?" The assassin's rage exploded. "I beg you, Sire. Please let me put the blade to her! Or to her bastard son!"

"Perhaps you have an idea," Darkend replied dryly. "In light of the recent, unforeseen events, he is probably no longer useful to me. Yet if I could find him, he could still serve one purpose admirably."

He turned to Slickblade, who had moved to glower from the shadows near the door. "You must find the half-breed and kill him. When you are done, I command you to bring his head here, so that his mother may admire his likeness for as long as she desires. His head will serve as a reminder of the price of treachery against Darkend Bellowsmoke."

"With pleasure, lord." His eyes flashed with delight.

Garimeth's face whitened as she heard the death sentence, but she was obviously shrewd and selfish enough not to betray her feelings. Instead, she merely stared after the dark figure of the royal assassin as Slickblade nodded and glided smoothly out the door.

"You don't believe me?" she asked sadly. "I tell you, your killer dwarf was here and came here with—according to him—a message for my son."

Darkend shrugged, then chuckled cruelly. "If you speak the truth, he will have no trouble finding the lad."

"Perhaps. But Tarn is resourceful."

Suddenly they were interrupted by a distant rumble. Quickly, Garimeth led Darkend outside to the vast balcony that overlooked the sea and the lower city. Columns of steam curled and twisted through the air. They watched as one of the fiery serpents veered away from the center of the cavern and started winging closer and closer to the two Daergar.

A great missile of fire, like a blazing meteor, coursed through the air over the Urkhan Sea and angled downward toward the balcony and the two dark dwarves.

Darkend turned his eyes away, wincing against the blinding light. He was only vaguely aware of a stark black figure amid the brightness of the fire dragon.

The great dragon flexed its broad flaming wings and came to rest in a cloud of sparks and smoke. Darkend still held a hand before his eyes to shield against the painful glare, but even so he could discern the tall, regal creature, manlike in visage, with skin that was smooth and featureless. The black figure dismounted and stalked forward to loom over him. Fire hissed and crackled with excruciating brilliance, a burning heat that felt painful against Darkend's face.

The thane knew with certainty that he was about to die.

Interlude of Chaos

Zarak Thuul felt a profound attraction, a compulsion that drew him across the vault of space and sea. Thoughts beckoned to him. A presence reached inside his head and touched him like no being—not even Primus—ever had.

He was astounded to see before him a she-dwarf and to know that it was her will that had drawn him. He could tell she felt awe at his beautiful appearance and that she coveted his mighty power. These twin emotions were immensely pleasing to the daemon warrior.

Laughing aloud, the harbinger of Chaos seized the female and lifted her into an embrace. She became one with him in spirit, desire, and mind. This was a worthy being, he knew, so different from the pathetic insects that were the rest of these mortals.

He put her down again and fell on his face before her, overcome with wonder and keen, soaring delight.

Chapter Eighteen

"Just suppose I agree with you. How would we go about stealing a boat?"

Tarn decided to ask the question, though he was pretty certain he would regret following this gully dwarf plan. Perhaps the rank air, the sticky goo on the floor, and the odor of the pungent grog—which he had thus far avoided sampling—had combined to cloud his judgment. Even so, he admitted to himself that the notion was better than anything he had been able to come up with.

"We just goes there and takes it—a boat," Regal explained.

The others in the dark and smelly saloon agreed with a whole hearted chorus of nods and belches.

"Lotsa boats!" proclaimed one expansively.

"Get big one!" urged a comrade.

"No, a fast one!" insisted another.

"I like a boat with lotta legs," explained Duck Bigdwarf, giving Tarn a bleary but scrutinizing look.

"Legs?" Tarn was taken by surprise, until he thought for a moment. "Oh, you mean oars, I suppose. Yes, we have to get one with legs. Reorx knows the chain boats aren't going to get us there."

Accompanied by a boisterous mob of gully dwarves, Tarn rose and made his way outside of the dingy inn. He took care this time to avoid smashing his head on the outcrop of rock. Surrounded by a chorus of voices—"What boat that? Go see! Your boots make good boat!"—they climbed to the crest of a large rock where they could get a view of the Daerforge waterfront. Dozens of gully dwarves had appeared, and the whole party was gathered along the steeply sloping surface of Agharhome.

The docks of the dark dwarf port city were clearly visible along the curve of the shoreline. They all saw the wreckage created when a part of the second level had collapsed to spill across some of the waterfront. The farther expanse of the broad wharves behind the pile of rock and steel left in the wake of the collapse teemed with activity. There, dozens of boats freshly arrived from Hybardin jostled for position as their crews tried desperately to scramble ashore. Everywhere the place was teeming with agitated dark dwarves. Tarn didn't see any way he and the Aghar could even get close to—much less steal—one of the watercraft without being spotted.

"See! Comes a fireflier!" cried one gully dwarf.

Tarn stared in horror as the flaming outline of a massive dragon soared over their heads. He flinched unconsciously, though the mighty creature paid no attention to the insignificant specks on the ground so far below. Instead, as Tarn watched in astonishment, the beast soared toward the upper level of Daerforge, toward the twin towers high up on the cliff. With a flexing of those great wings the creature came to rest on the broad outer balcony of his mother's house.

Tarn saw the black creature dismount from the dragon's back. With a sense of utter disbelief he spotted two small figures coming into view. He could recognize neither at a distance, but the bronze helmet on the head of one of them might as well have been a beacon proclaiming his mother's presence. Garimeth was wearing the Helm of Tongues, and she was greeting—now she was being embraced!—by this harbinger of Chaos.

For a long time the monstrous warrior seemed to speak to the Daergar. It seemed to Tarn that his mother did a great deal of talking in return. And then he saw the strange being prostrate himself at the dwarfwoman's feet! Finally the black rider returned to its fiery mount and soared into the skies on a course for Hybardin. Tarn was certain of one thing: some kind of nefarious deal had been struck.

Stunned, he tried to consider the ramifications of this development. Soon after, as Tarn watched, a party of dark dwarves, including the still-helmeted Garimeth Bellowsmoke, emerged from the house and started down the road toward the waterfront.

"What now, Regal Wiseallatime?" asked Duck Bigdwarf patiently. He gestured at the expanse of stormy sea, blazing fireballs, and wracked Hybardin. "This boring!"

"Wait for him, I say," Regal retorted, skeptically regarding Tarn. "He our leader. That is, if he ever do something."

Angrily Tarn shook his head, thinking. Why was his mother heading to the boat dock and still wearing that helm? Looking out over the sea Tarn saw the inverted cone of the Life-Tree, now scarred by countless fires, pocked by the ravages of destructive Chaos. The fire dragon must have returned there. In an instant of clarity he knew where Garimeth would be going with the treasure she had stolen from his father.

"Okay, you've convinced me," he said and turned to the gully dwarves, who erupted in a spontaneous cheer. Scrutinizing the dark dwarf city again, Tarn suddenly saw a possibility—not really an opportunity, perhaps, but at least the ghost of a chance. "See there," he told Regal, "on the closest part of the waterfront?"

"Right. Where rocks spilled, dock not so big on this side."

"No, nor so crowded." He studied that part of Daerforge where the collapse had isolated a small section of the waterfront. There were some dark dwarves and a few boats along the edge but nothing like the crowds that thronged on the other side of the lakeshore. "It's cut off almost completely from the rest of the city," he explained, his pulse quickening.

"Not so many boats there," Regal demurred. "We wanta choose from lotsa boats."

"But not so many dark dwarves, either," the half-breed countered. "And believe me, once you've been in a few boats you realize that they're all pretty much the same."

"I dunno." Regal was still skeptical, but he and his fellow Aghar nevertheless followed Tarn as he filed through the channels and ravines of the gully dwarf city. "Main Street Number One," noted Regal, though Tarn could see no way that this path was an extension of the subterranean pipe that had also been labeled as "Main Street Number One."

Nearing the edge of Daerforge, Tarn started down a steep descent. Abruptly one of his boots slipped, and he skidded several feet down the tumbling ravine. Quickly he recovered his balance and, still muttering curses, climbed to his feet. Beside him was a motionless gully dwarf. For a moment he feared he had knocked and dragged the fellow down with his own clumsiness.

"Sorry, friend. Can I give you a hand?"

Then he saw the arrow. A steel shaft had punctured the Aghar's neck from behind. Tarn knew the gully dwarf was quite dead.

"An arrow, and poisoned too!" he hissed through clenched teeth, immediately turning to scour the heights.

He could see no sign of the mysterious attacker as the other gully dwarves gathered around.

"Poor Rocco," Regal said sadly. "At least he got to walk right in front of you. That what he wanted."

"And he was shot right after I stumbled," Tarn realized, the knowledge bringing a prickle of alarm.

He didn't speak the rest of the deduction aloud, but it was a certainty in his own mind. That deadly arrow had in fact been intended for Tarn Bellowsmoke, not the unfortunate Aghar named Rocco. But who had shot at him, and why? He wondered if his mother had sent an assassin after him after she had discovered the escape. But he couldn't believe that she would stoop to something so evil as killing her own son.

Again he studied the rising ground behind them, seeing no sign of the attacker. They started down again, but now Tarn led them through some of the deepest trenches and urged the group into a ragged trot when they had to cross the occasional stretches of open ground. They could see several boats along the nearer section of the shoreline, as well as a few more pulling this way as their crews strived to reach the dark dwarf city. The "Main Street" took a dramatic downhill turn, becoming indistinguishable from a natural ravine, and Tarn felt some relief as they were able to follow the deep cut steadily toward the lake shore.

Finally they reached a shelf of rock directly above the flat stretch of Daerforge's docks. The water of the Urkhan Sea, still roiling from the Chaos storm, smashed against the solid stone bulwark of the wharf a short stone's throw away. Several rock piers jutted like stubby fingers into the water, but there were no boats docked close by. However, this section of the waterfront was concealed from the view of the rest of the city by the sloping pile of rubble that had been spilled by the collapse.

"Look! Here comes a boat!" cried Regal, standing up and pointing until Tarn grabbed his shoulder and quickly pulled him back to cover.

But the Aghar's observation had been correct, and now Tarn saw a long-hulled lake boat, propelled only by a half dozen oars, fighting its way through the pitching waters. After its crew had time to observe the crowd and the tangle of watercraft at the main portion of the docks, this boat veered away, making landfall near the isolated and relatively empty section of wharf where Tarn and the gully dwarves lay in wait.

"I'm going to sneak over there and try to get as close as I can," the half-breed whispered softly.

"We sneak too!" cried a dozen Aghar, not softly at all. Fortunately, the sound seemed to be swallowed by the general noise of storm and activity.

Tarn wasn't at all confident of his companions' stealth, but he quickly realized that there would be no dissuading the excited gully dwarves.

"Be careful," he warned, exasperated.

"We good sneakers!" Regal proclaimed, and, sure enough, the Aghar all but disappeared as they followed Tarn down the steep slope. They were indeed good sneakers.

Crouching at the foot of the embankment, Tarn scrutinized the dock, watching as the longboat lurched slightly in the swell and then glided up to the side of the solid wharf.

One dark dwarf hopped out of the boat before it had come to rest. "You wait here," he called over his shoulder to the others. "I'll find out our orders."

There was some loud grumbling from the rest of the crew, but ultimately they remained at their benches, holding the boat in the swell next to the dock while their compatriot scrambled over broken stones and soon passed out of sight.

Tarn looked skeptically at the boat. There were at least a dozen battle-hardened fighters sitting at the oars, ready to row or to fight. With the half-breed were perhaps twice that many Aghar, but he had few illusions about the fighting capabilities of his motley band. It was far better, he decided, to wait for a chance to take an unoccupied boat or one with only one or two dwarves on guard.

Regal Everwise, however, had other plans.

"Get boat!" he cried, leaping to his feet. He hopped down to the dock while the other Aghar, gaping in stupefaction, watched.

"Hey, you! I want boat!" Strutting like a lord, Regal ambled toward the craft. Tarn held his breath, realizing that none of the rest of them had been spotted. Instead, all the dark dwarves' attention was fixed upon the small, rotund Regal, who spoke with such annoying arrogance.

All but spitting in their rage at such insolence, several Daergar dropped their oars and scrambled onto the dock, stumbling over themselves in their eagerness to teach this gully dwarf a permanent lesson. Regal stopped his sauntering advance but made no effort to retreat back to safety.

And Tarn saw only one thing he could possibly do.

"Charge!" he shouted, drawing his short sword and leaping down to the dock. He didn't stop to see whether the rest of the Aghar followed. Instead, he raced at full speed toward the foremost Daergar, a hulking one-eyed axeman who had been quick to lead his comrades onto the dock.

The scarred warrior halted in surprise when Tarn appeared, then raised his axe with a look of enthusiasm, ready to meet this new opponent. But the sprinting half-breed was too fast, and he stabbed first, dropping the Daergar with a fatal piercing into the heart. Tarn's momentum momentarily staggered the rest of the dark dwarves, who were close together at the edge of the dock. With another swift hack and shove, Tarn sent a shrieking dark dwarf tumbling into the deep water beside the dock.

Then he fell back as more enemy fighters moved to his right and left, eager to surround him and cut him down.

"You leave my pal alone!" demanded Regal, advancing to take a place at Tarn's right side. The gully dwarf's long dagger snicked out, the quick slash driving the first of the Daergar back.

Dark dwarves swerved the other way, but Tarn was elated to see Duck Bigdwarf and Poof Firemaker counter to his left. The bigger gully dwarf cheerily swung a torch he had somehow ignited, while Duck dropped low and stabbed upward with a sharp, long-bladed dagger.

More of the Aghar were racing around, and now it was the Daergar who were surrounded and harassed on all sides by darting, taunting enemies. Poof's torch flared at the dark dwarves, who cursed its brightness. Swords and clubs flailed, fists and feet pummeled, and the press of the charging gully dwarves was just enough to check the advance of the enemy crewmen. Some of the Daergar still scrambled to get out of the boat while others fought, precariously balanced at the edge of the dock and terrified of the black water surging against the wharf behind them.

Duck crawled between the legs of a burly Daergar, and when the gully dwarf stood up the sharpened crown of his helm propelled the dark dwarf right off the dock. The armored warrior sank like a stone in the dark water, his screams unheeded by his crewmates who were still trying to scramble ashore. Then the Aghar were swarming over the boat, picking up oars—dropping several overboard before Tarn could stop them—and punching, kicking, and biting the few hapless dark dwarves.

Tarn leaped into the boat and was immediately startled by a loud clang from the hull beside his head. A steel arrow had just missed him. He whirled around, seeking the shooter. Judging from the force of the shot—the arrowhead had left a sizeable dent in the boat—he knew that the deadly archer must be nearby. But there were only gully dwarves in the vicinity.

"Look out!" Duck Bigdwarf shouted the warning, pointing toward one of the dwarves in the boat behind Tarn.

The half-breed whirled, realizing that the huddled

figure beside him was no gully dwarf but instead a small-sized imposter who had rushed across the dock in the wake of the Aghar charge. The fellow moved with lightning speed, and the silver blade of a short sword darted from the shadows straight toward Tarn's throat.

"No you not!" Duck leaped from the dock, and the stab intended for Tarn instead caught the gully dwarf in the chest.

The attacker tried to pull back for another attack, but now Tarn reacted. His sword came down against the Daergar's weapon, knocking the blade out of the dark dwarf's hand. With a hiss of rage, the cutthroat scrambled to the dock and raced away.

Tarn had no time to pursue. The few surviving Daergar made a charge to retake their boat. His sword caught one fellow in the forehead, dropping him in the hull of the boat. The gully dwarves made a splendid game of seizing the others and riding them into the water. After a great splash, each of the Aghar popped to the surface, while the armored and water-hating dark dwarves were not seen again.

Reaching down, Tarn pulled the assassin's weapon free from Duck, dropped the blade into the hull of the boat, and laid the motionless gully dwarf on a bench. The short sword was clean and gleaming, an insubstantial fire flickering along the razor edge of the blade. The hapless Aghar who had been pierced by the weapon was already dead.

"That was Slickblade!" gasped Regal Everwise, pointing to the disappearing assassin and then to the glaring skull embossed upon the silver hilt of the weapon. "He kill loads of Aghar!"

"If not for Duck Bigdwarf, he would have killed me as well," Tarn said, with a pang of grief for the courageous gully dwarf.

"You one hot fighter! You knock Slickblade's sword down!" Regal declared, looking at Tarn with eyes wide as saucers.

197

Tarn pushed his way forward, using his sword to cleave the last of the Daergar crew members. The bodies were unceremoniously dumped over the side. Tarn assigned two gully dwarves to each rowing bench, knowing that they had to put to sea swiftly.

At the same time, a roar of alarm went up.

Chapter Nineteen

The lift rattled to a stop and the cage doors opened upon another of Hybardin's levels. Before the passengers could disembark, however, Baker Whitegranite slumped onto a bench and spoke weakly.

"Wait just a minute, now." Baker held up his hand. The band of Hylar who served as his bodyguard stood at attention while the thane hissed through clenched teeth and bent double, his hands clasped over his stomach. "It won't be long—just until the worst of the pain passes."

"Are you wounded, my lord?" asked Capper Whetstone in real concern.

"No. It's just a pain in the belly. All too familiar, I'm afraid. Just give me a minute and I'll be fine." He tried to smile into the blurred, concerned faces, but the agony was too acute.

For all his reassuring words, it was all Baker could do to

keep from falling down in utter collapse. The fire in his stomach had afflicted him with increasing frequency as the defense of embattled Hybardin had progressed.

He tried to think, to divert his mind from the physical pain, but every memory seemed instead only to enhance his suffering. He thought of Axel Slateshoulders, laid low by the news of his daughter's fate, and Baker couldn't help but wince at his own culpability. It had been he who had assigned her to the post of ultimate danger, he who had been unable to provide her with the reinforcements and recruits that she had so desperately needed.

And what of his son? Was he on the lake, in the midst of the army of dark dwarves? The more Baker thought about it, the more convinced he became that Tarn, like Belicia and so many others, must be dead. The thought grew into a wave of melancholy so powerful that it seemed to almost overwhelm him.

The thane of the Hylar pinched his eyes shut, fighting a most undwarven onslaught of tears. Finally he gave in, holdng his head in his hands and sobbing. All these deaths. So much of Hybardin destroyed—and destroyed by an enemy they couldn't even fathom! It was too much tragedy for one dwarf to bear. After his body was seemingly drained of all tears, he felt no better. His spirit was empty, and everything about the future seemed hopeless. How could any leader, any people, be expected to cope with such a relentless and deadly onslaught?

The dark dwarf attack had been treacherous and violent, but also predictable in light of the long, bloody history of Thorbardin. Baker reminded himself that he had tried to plan for it.

The Chaos horde was something that seemed impossible to defeat, or even to resist effectively. Instead, the Hylar could only flee or die. The parts of the city that had fallen to the creatures of shadow and destruction had been completely destroyed.

The only bright spot had been the diversionary tactic that

had pitted the large attack force of Klar against the soldiers of Chaos. But Baker was under no illusions. This was not a tactic they could repeat with any regularity, nor did it gain them any ground against the shadowy power that had claimed so much of the Hylar city.

Whole blocks of buildings were gone, gardens wilted, waters fouled. They were somewhere around the middle of the Life-Tree now, having stopped for a look and a report at each of the lift stations on the way down. Snatching at hope, he tried to formulate some kind of plan. At least his stomach pain had eased somewhat.

"All right. I think I can move again." With an effort he raised his head from his hands, embarrassed by his display of weakness. "Let's go."

"This is Level Ten, my lord. Our first reports were that it has not yet been attacked," explained Capper Whetstone, overseer of the thane's ten personal bodyguards. Now they formed two ranks, one to each side of the thane, while Capper himself walked at Baker's side.

The thane looked around, not really seeing much. The onetime blacksmith had long since noted his leader's visual problems. Now he described their surroundings without being prompted. "No damage visible so far, Sire. There's a couple of bridges linking the roads to the Kings Walls, both intact."

"Good." Baker tried to detect some cause for optimism in the report, but his despair was too great to be eased by this news or any other.

"Look out!" shouted one of the bodyguards.

The thane whirled to see a dark shape rearing above another of the Hylar warriors. The dwarf moaned in terror as the tendrils of darkness slammed together—and then he was gone, in a shocking instant. Empty armor tumbled to the floor like a useless shell.

Capper Whetstone lunged and swung his axe with crushing force, but the weapon passed right through the vaporous apparition. The captain of the guard stumbled back an instant before a lashing limb of darkness could reach him.

And then the shadow was coming straight at Baker. The thane had drawn his sword—he didn't remember when—and he stabbed ahead blindly, striking into the center of the shade and feeling the darkness part before the edge of his blade. He cut again, feeling a shivering sensation in the air around him.

The shadow creature was gone.

"My lord, are you all right?" asked one of his men.

Baker nodded.

"How did you do that?" asked Capper. "I struck the thing square to no effect at all!"

"It was this sword," Baker said, looking at the short sword he held in his hand, "this sword from the wall of my Atrium, blessed by Reorx in the old days of Thorbardin like all the rest of those weapons." He was struck by an inspiration. "There's more of them there, all of them likewise blessed and enchanted. Come, we'll take them and use them in this fight!"

They quickly made their way to the Thane's Atrium. Soon they had removed all of the treasured artifacts from the wall except for a huge, long-hafted axe that was simply too heavy to carry. His bodyguards and a number of other Hylar warriors were thus armed with short and broadswords, axes and hammers great and small. If Baker's assumption proved correct, these weapons might cause some harm to the lightless attackers.

By the time the inspection of the next few levels was completed, Baker's "gut fire" had settled into a dull ache, a discomfort he was able to conceal as he passed the hopeful throngs of his people who had gathered on word of the thane's arrival. They were strangely silent, these worried dwarves, but Baker could sense the trust in their shining eyes. He silently vowed to prove himself worthy of his role as their leader.

Finally the lift rumbled into Level Five, the lowest station still controlled by the Hylar. Baker was heartened to see that the forges were still burning, encouraged to hear the hammering of smiths and the shouts of foremen as the dwarves worked hard in defense of their city.

But his mood darkened quickly as he remembered that it was not far below here, on the broad marketplace of Level Two, that Belicia and her valiant company had made their last stand.

"My Lord Thane," declared a young but battle-scarred Hylar, his head and one arm wrapped in bandages, "I was with the company in the plaza, below. I was told that I should give you a full report."

"Yes. Please, sit down." Baker gestured to one of the streetside benches, and the two dwarves sank together onto its stone surface. "What's your name? Can you tell me what happened down there when the Chaos horde attacked?"

"Thornwhistle, my lord—Farran Thornwhistle is my name. At first we were holding the bastards, lord. Captain Slateshoulders's plan was a good one. We beat back every one of the Daergar attacks—and the Theiwar's when they came ashore a few hours later. I can't say how many we killed, but it was hundreds, maybe more than a thousand."

Baker encouraged him to continue, the thane trying without success to imagine the bloody horrors that this young Hylar had survived.

"I had been wounded once or twice, lord like all the fighters. But still we held! I heard the songs of our ancestors, felt the drums pounding in triumph, and knew that the dark dwarves would rue the day that they attacked us. We bled, but we slew many of them, and our shield wall held!"

Farran took a deep breath, and suddenly his eyes were wild, haunted with memories. "And then—" Farran Thornwhistle's voice caught, and he shook his head in disbelief. "It was like the sea caught fire. It spread to the bedrock. I saw the south dockside just melt away, running like sludge from heat. My lord, I wouldn't even expect you to believe me—but the rock was melting, I swear it!"

"Did it seem as though the fire was aiding the dark

dwarves, perhaps controlled by Theiwar magic-users?" This was one of his greatest fears.

Thornwhistle scowled, thinking deeply. "No, lord. I don't think so. I saw more than a few of their boats go down. Some were melted, some capsized by the waves. And even on shore, the dark ones were running for their lives—especially those fleeing that fire dragon and the black one who rode it."

Baker nodded, having heard many reports of this menacing but mysterious being. "What did he do? Was he the leader?"

"Aye, lord. He seemed to summon others, sending them against both Daergar and our own Hylar!"

"What 'others'? What kind of troops did you see?"

"They were like shadows, lord, but shadows with an insatiable hunger and a lethal touch. A whole rank of my comrades fell dead, falling like empty sacks of flesh, drained into nothingness by a touch from these beasts. I could see their armor there, their weapons—but by Reorx, they were gone! And I don't even remember who they were! Men and women I had trained with for weeks, had shared the battle line with all day!"

Thornwhistle lowered his head into his hands and sobbed. Awkwardly Baker patted him on the shoulder, though his own grief felt every bit as heavy.

"Yours is confirmation of other experiences, even my own."

"Captain Slateshoulders rallied us. We tried to stand. By Reorx, her courage was the stuff of song and legend—and we failed her!"

"No. There is no failure in fleeing from these creatures, my young warrior. But tell me of your captain, Belicia Felixia Slateshoulders. Did you see her fall?"

"No. The shadows were too thick." Wretched and miserable, Farran looked at his thane with an expression of utter despair. "They came up the stairs and through the rock. Everyone was running for their lives. I was afraid, my lord— I was a rank coward, and I deserve to be punished!"

"We're all afraid, son. There's no shame in that. Were you still down below when the bottom of the Life-Tree caved in?"

"No. We were climbing by then, fighting on the stairs leading up to Level Three. But those shadows were after us, coming from everywhere!"

"You get some rest now. And eat something." Baker was thoughtful, trying to seize on a tiny ray of hope that he had discerned in these reports. He felt profound admiration for this young warrior and deep pity for the dwarves who had faced this ungodly threat. "You'll have to fight again, Reorx knows, but not before you have a chance to recover."

The thane left the young warrior with several matrons who promised to look after him. Baker's step was strangely buoyant, however, as he returned to the lift station. If truth be told, he felt better, more hopeful, than he had since the Chaos horde had first attacked.

He found Axel at the station and he embraced his astonished friend firmly, fiercely holding him against his chest.

"Is there news? Did you hear how Belicia fell?" asked the grieving veteran.

"No news, except this: we still remember her, don't we? What she looked like? Who she was?"

"Aye. It's all we have now," Axel declared bitterly.

"No it isn't," Baker insisted. "It dawned on me while I was talking to a young survivor just now. The story is always the same. Those who fall to the Chaos creatures are not only killed, but their memories are blotted out from all who remain as if they never existed."

"I know that!" snapped Axel.

"And you just confirmed it—you and I both—even that young warrior! We all remember Belicia vividly, don't we?"

"Aye." Axel's eyes flashed, suddenly sharing the insight that had uplifted Baker.

"Exactly! And if we remember her, then there's a very good chance that she's still alive!"

Chapter Twenty

"Have any of you ever been on a boat before?" Tarn asked, trying to keep his tone casual as the vessel took a sudden lurch to starboard.

"First time, by guff!" Regal boasted, with a chorus of assent from the gully dwarves who were shifting and bickering on the rowing benches. Somehow, three or four of them—all on the portside posts—had managed to get their oars wet and move the boat away from the dock. Now, with a clatter of lumber, the boat was moving with surprising speed.

"And by the way," Tarn added, bracing himself and raising his voice over the din of a dozen arguments. "I think you're supposed to row on both sides at the same time!"

The craft twisted back to port as the starboard oarsmen

all dipped their boards into the water and pushed with something approaching unison.

"What fun that? We just go straight then," groused Regal.

Somehow, despite the best efforts of the gully dwarves, the boat continued to move away from the dock. Water heaved all around them, and the slender vessel rocked back and forth, but the Aghar seemed utterly unperturbed by the tumult. Tarn tried to take some inspiration from them, though he still clutched the tiller for security.

The half-breed looked to shore and saw a boat full of Daergar warriors. The deadly assassin called Slickblade, his eyes expressionless in the slit of his black mask, stood rigidly in the bow as the pursuing craft pulled away from shore. The bow was aimed straight toward the Aghar pirates, oars striking the water in precise cadence and churning white waves before the sharp prow.

"Row! Fast!" he urged.

A splashing froth rose along the port side, and their boat wheeled grandly to starboard. The valiant gully dwarves frowned, and their oars skipped over the water as their concentration was interrupted. Tarn, in the stern, tried to shout instructions and encouragement, which mainly had the effect of causing his voice to grow exceedingly hoarse.

The other boat drew closer, and Tarn saw that Slickblade had armed himself with a long spear. The assassin seemed focused on Tarn. Fueled by memories of the dead Rocco and Duck, Tarn felt more than ready to meet that challenge.

"Come on!" he murmured.

The Daergar craft drove closer, aiming to ram the stern of the Aghar craft.

"Turn!" cried Tarn, adding his weight to the tiller. The boat heeled slightly, lengthening the distance from the enemy, but still their pursuers dogged their heels.

A spear soared at them, and Tarn knocked the weapon

aside just before the two boats collided. Tarn straddled two benches, holding his balance in the lurching watercraft. Keeping his weight low, he lunged toward the gunwale, thrusting his sword and striking a solid blow against Slickblade's spear. The assassin hurled his weapon suddenly, but the rocking boat made his aim go wide. The Daergar boat pitched again as Slickblade snatched up another spear.

"You'll sink us both! You're mad!" one of the dark dwarf rowers shrieked, casting a wide-eyed glance over his shoulder.

That gave Tarn an idea. If he could tip the dark dwarves' boat, every armor-clad warrior would sink straight to the bottom of the lake. The half-breed lunged, landing on the edge of the enemy boat, which tilted sickeningly under his weight.

Both hulls rocked wildly. The gully dwarves whooped and grinned while the panic-stricken Daergar rowers tried to pull away. Tarn himself would have toppled into the sea had Regal not seized his belt and pulled him back.

Ignoring Slickblade's hysterical commands, the dark dwarf rowers pulled away, making for the shore with all possible haste. The curses of the infuriated assassin were quickly drowned out by the tumult.

The choppy waters of the sea began to rock the boat. The forces of Chaos were wreaking havoc on the normally placid waters of the lake. The harbors of Thorbardin had been constructed without the breakwaters that Tarn knew were common protection for ports of the surface world. After all, why should the dwarves build a barrier to stop waves that had never before existed?

Tarn heard screams and saw one of the Daergar lake boats pitching dangerously against the docks. Pushed by a surge of water, the metal hull crushed several of its passengers and dumped more of them into the frigid and surprisingly deep waters. The armored dwarves immediately disappeared beneath the surface. Their panic-stricken crewmates made no effort to rescue them.

The Aghar, however, seemed utterly oblivious to the prospect of real danger.

"Whee! Ride waves!"

"Faster! Higher! Bigger!"

"This real ride!"

The gully dwarves howled with glee as the boat moved into the full swell of the Urkhan Sea. Tarn was sickened by the lurching and uncontrolled motion of their boat, but the Aghar seemed to enjoy the rollicking ride. Perhaps it was good that none of them had been on a boat before. They didn't understand how unnatural this roiling swell was on the enclosed underground sea.

On the other hand, the gully dwarves would have probably whooped with delight if they'd been faced with a hurricane. Tarn felt his heart skip a beat every time another wave sloshed into the hull. He recognized the imminent danger: every wave brought more water spilling over the bow and sloshing down the length of the long keel.

"Bail!" cried Tarn, seizing a Daergar helmet and scooping the water that sloshed around his boats. Several gully dwarves immediately joined him in that game, though it took many pointed instructions to get them to pour the water out of the boat instead of over their comrades at the rowing benches.

After much shouting and yelling, most of the little dwarves had begun to bail vigorously while those at the rowing benches—except for two or three who had already dropped their oars overboard—maintained something like a rhythm in the strokes of their blades. True, the boat never maintained a direct heading toward Hybardin, sometimes bearing to port and otherwise to starboard of the Life-Tree, but Tarn figured that as long as they held to the general direction they could get close and worry about the finer points of navigation later.

Moving air gusted past them, and even in his numbed

state Tarn was startled by this bizarre phenomenon. He had heard of wind, had even experienced it when he had traveled on the surface of Krynn during the decades after the War of the Lance. Yet it was a bizarre and frightening occurrence here in the enclosed world of Thorbardin.

The air seemed to be gusting from the direction of Daerforge and propelled them toward Hybardin. Somehow the boat managed to stay afloat, aided by the frantically bailing dwarves. Tarn and Regal stood in the stern, taking turns holding the rudder—which at their limited speed was more of an ornament than a directional tool. Tarn tried to shout in a cadence that would enable the Aghar to row with some semblance of coordination.

"Pull!" chanted Tarn in slow rhythm. "Pull!"

After a while Regal took over, and he too shouted the beat to the rowers, "One, Two, One, Two," with real enthusiasm.

Poof Firemaker crouched in the bow, encouraging the rowers and often turning to look eagerly at the smoking, burning pillar of the Life-Tree.

When he wasn't urgently directing his crew, Tarn lifted his eyes and took a few moments to glance around. The dwarven kingdom, Tarn felt certain, would never be the same. Fires burned in many places, using nothing more than rock as fuel. Thunder echoed and steam wafted through the air in great clouds. Across the sea he saw a bizarre, funnel-shaped cloud, whirling along the far shore. Every so often it would pick up a lake boat and cast the vessel and its terrified passengers through the air. The mist was everywhere in Thorbardin. Tarn suddenly became aware that his skin was clammy and the temperature was preternaturally warm.

All of a sudden the half-breed heard a moan of terror coming from the bow of the boat. He saw a shadow crouching there, and even from this distance he could feel the chill of its presence. He watched as, impenetrable and shapeless, the form reached out with two black limbs and embraced the trembling form of Poof Firemaker.

And then the horrific creature held only a limp and bedraggled bundle in its shadowy arms. A little tinder box dangled from the belt of the ragged clothes. Tarn couldn't recall from where the bundle had come, but he had no time to ponder that mystery as the shadow-wight moved down the hull. Panicked gully dwarves tumbled over the rowing benches, pushing and kicking at each other in their haste to get away.

Tarn was already in motion. Drawing his sword, he pushed his way through the throng until he faced the shadow alone near the bow of the boat.

Waves rolled past and the hull shifted underfoot, but he held his balance easily as his battle instincts took over. But how to fight this thing? It had no weapon and was in fact so tenuous in appearace that Tarn wasn't even certain it had a physical being. It was as if the thing floated directly above the hull of the boat, not adding any weight to the watercraft.

But then he saw the eyes, and he was shocked at the depth of the return stare. He was looking at himself. His saw his mother and his father in those eyes, and the contrast of light and darkness made his brain hurt, numbed his senses and even loosened the grip of his sword hand.

"Don't look!"

With a loud thwack, Regal hit Tarn over the head with an oar. The blow broke whatever force that held the half-breed even as it sent a throbbing pain shooting through his skull. Remembering his enemy, Tarn raised his sword and held his vision below the level of those hypnotic eyes.

The creature was a totally lightless shape, though Tarn could make out a gaping mouth and two gaunt, clutching limbs. A clawlike tendril of pure black nothingness reached forward, and Tarn intuitively knew that he couldn't let the creature touch him. Sinew in both arms flexing, he swung the sword with all of his might.

The blade passed cleanly through the extended limb,

but the monster only lifted its head and laughed coldly. The hand that should have been severed reached around and siezed the blade of the sword. Immediately Tarn felt an icy pain in his hands, and he was forced to release the weapon before his arm froze.

The wight tossed the weapon contemptuously over the side and soundlessly drifted a step closer to the stunned half-breed. Tarn recoiled, nearly stumbling over a rowing bench in his haste to scramble beyond that lethal touch. With deliberate slowness the deadly monster moved after him.

Behind him the terrified moaning of a boatful of gully dwarves rose, interspersed with shouts of advice.

"Fight him!"

"Run!"

Tarn knew that he had to stop the creature or the entire crew was doomed.

Weaponless, Tarn looked frantically around, catching sight of a silver short sword lying in the hull of the boat—Slickblade's weapon, the blade that had killed Duck Bigdwarf. He hesitated as he noted the leering skull emblazoned on the metal hilt, but he had no other alternative.

Snatching up the sword, Tarn thrust the bright, flickering blade at the wight just as the monster lunged forward.

But this time Tarn felt resistance to the thrust of the blade. He pushed harder and the shadow-wight uttered a surreal scream—not so much pain as great anguish. Fiercely elated, the dwarf slashed with the weapon, hacking again and again. Abruptly the creature vanished in a cloud of rapidly dissipating mist.

"Yea!" Cheering Aghar instantly mobbed the half-breed, a move that sent the boat rocking precariously. The celebration ceased quickly as the gully dwarves remembered the empty clothes in the bow. One big nosed fellow sniffed loudly, the others were strangely silent.

"To your benches!" barked Tarn. "Row!"

"You kill that?" wondered Regal, his voice full of awe as the other gully dwarves reluctantly returned to their stations. "You one tough war guy!"

"It was this sword," Tarn said in wonder, holding the plain-looking weapon up for inspection. It was assassin's steel, cold and starkly reflective. And it was his own sword now.

Somehow he and Regal got the crew back to their stations without sinking the boat, despite the fact that the water in the hull had risen nearly to the level of his knees. He set the bailers went to work again, lending a hand himself. Few oars had been lost, and they were able to keep going at a steady pace. The busy Aghar bailers emptied gallons of water out of the hull.

They drew closer to the Life-Tree, and all of Tarn's thoughts focused on the looming horror before him. He could see more detail now, and the sight was another blow to his spirits. The First and Second Levels of the Hylar city where Belicia had been stationed were now a mass flaming rock. He groaned at the horrible sight, certain that no one could have survived such a wave of destruction. Other levels, higher above, dripped and melted and burned. Would they find anybody alive when they got there?

As they drew nearer to Hybardin, Tarn saw that many Daergar boats were floating in the water just off the Life-Tree docks. The watercraft bobbed here and there close to the shore but didn't seem to have any purpose or formation. The crews had vanished.

And then, as if to punctuate the sense of gloom and disaster settling over Tarn, from the fully enclosed skies of Thorbardin came a shower of cold rain. Never before in the half-breed's lifetime had this happened. It never would have been thought remotely possible.

Their boat pulled toward the bleak shore, rising and falling on steep-sided breakers. With each stroke the pitching sea churned all the more. Waves rose, pushing them higher. Then with a thunderous crash the hull tipped and all the dwarves found themselves in the water.

Tarn felt the cold waters closing over his head. Then strong hands had him by the hair. He felt himself yanked violently upward, and then the grip had him by the ears and beard. He was bashed against a rock, pulled and twisted this way and that, until finally he was yanked ashore to gasp for breath on a ruined travesty of what had once been the proud city of the Hylar.

A Council of Chaos

Chapter Twenty-one

Garimeth knew four reasons Darkend Bellowsmoke brought his sister with him when he boarded a boat to journey back to Hybardin for the next phase of attack. First, her knowledge of the Hylar city was better than any other Daergar's. Second, the Helm of Tongues made her an invaluable translator. Third, the respect shown her by the daemon warrior had impressed the thane, even as it still caused her to shiver with remembered delight.

And finally, he had decided that he couldn't trust her out of his sight.

In the paranoid and scheming mind of the thane, no one could be trusted absolutely. She knew it was that universal suspicion that for now would keep Garimeth Bellowsmoke alive.

The Helm of Tongues allowed her to perceive all of this

and more, though she was careful not to reveal the extent and depth of her awareness. She kept a safe distance from her brother, trailing to the rear of the party of warriors that marched back down from Daerforge's upper level to gather at the waterfront. There too she gave Darkend a wide berth, watching patiently as the thane's force made ready to depart.

"You ride in the bow," Darkend informed her curtly at dockside. "I'll be in the stern, and I'll be watching you."

"Of course, my lord brother thane," she replied, with no trace of irony in her voice or her eyes—even as she "listened" to Darkend speculate about the hatred and scheming that must be simmering in her purely Daergar brain. She carefully masked her smug perception of his thoughts and impulses, continuing to obey him quietly and meekly. Oh, the Helm of Tongues was a marvelous device! She would have left her husband and stolen it long ago if she had suspected the full extent of its hidden powers.

"And when we get to the city, I want you to summon Zarak Thuul to me. Trust me on this, Sister: Your life depends upon your success."

"Naturally. Now, may I take a seat for myself?"

He let her find a bench in the craft while he supervised the handpicked crew of experienced Daergar boatmen. None of them displayed apprehension about the imminent voyage onto the preternaturally choppy sea, but they would not have been mortal if they had not felt at least a small measure of fear. Indeed, a quick survey of their thoughts showed they were consumed by fright—fears that did little to amuse Garimeth, since by necessity she would be relying upon their prowess and sharing their experiences during the dangerous crossing.

Darkend had chosen for the voyage one of the longest and deepest hulls among the Daergar. This boat would be propelled by no less than four dozen oarsmen. The coxswain, a one-eyed dark dwarf named Bairn Knifekeel, seemed quite confident, almost cocky.

"We'll get there, my lord thane," he promised with grim certainty, though Garimeth frowned as the Helm of Tongues allowed her to perceive that even this bold dwarf was inwardly quailing.

As they gazed out over the water it was obvious that conditions on the sea had deteriorated. Garimeth's thoughts were vividly focused on the encounter that had taken place on her balcony. She still recalled the awe she had felt when she had beheld the daemon warrior's beauty, the desire and power he had kindled within her. She had learned his name, Zarak Thuul, and that of his mighty flaming steed, Primus. And even more, she had invited him to touch her soul, to know her mind, and to hear her innermost desires. They had connected with each other in a way that she could not have imagined, resulting in a bliss that had weakened her knees. In some way she felt as though she were a young dwarfmaiden again. Perhaps the arcane power residing in the Helm of Tongues had made this first contact happen, but she now believed that she and the daemon warrior had forged a deep lifebond, something that transcended the realm of magic.

And when she had spoken to the daemon warrior, the creature had seemed to understand her. She told him that the Hylar were the real enemy, the time-honored foe deserving of death and destruction. She had made Zarak Thuul clearly understand the special vileness of the sanctimonious clan, and agree that they ought to be subjugated.

And he had consented to lead the Daergar into that battle of glorious conquest. Now all that remained was for Darkend and Garimeth to join with the Chaos army and sweep to victory.

"Go!" cried Bairn Knifekeel, taking the tiller and guiding the longboat away from the dock. "Stroke, on my count!"

Though the boat rocked and lurched sickeningly, the rowers had little difficulty guiding it forward. The sharp prow cut the waves easily, and they plowed steadily away from Daerforge Bay and onto the greater body of the Urkhan Sea. Still, Garimeth soon felt her stomach rising, seasickness suddenly churning in her belly. The voyage quickly degenerated into a vile, hateful ordeal, and she desperately hung her head over the side.

When it began to rain, the dwarves on the benches muttered among themselves in superstitious fear, and Garimeth heard an occasional silent but fervent prayer to Reorx. Even more than wind, this unnatural precipitation seemed to be a dire omen in the underground realm. She concentrated on trying to mask her own discomfort. This soon proved impossible when she began to retch over the side. Still, in the more tolerable intervals she noted with grudging admiration that her brother somehow managed to look grim and majestic, standing boldly in the stern, eyes locked upon his goal. In his two hands he held the wickedly spiked mace that had served him so well in the Arena of Honor. True, he too was afraid, as the Helm of Tongues informed her, but he kept the poise of leadership.

The fiery scars of the Life-Tree glowed even through the rain and the mist, and the dwarves had no difficulty arrowing towards it. About halfway through the voyage, the inverted mountain emerged from the gloom and the murk, rising high above them, clearly damaged in many places by the unnatural onslaught. That was when Garimeth went back to the stern, sensing that her presence was desired by the thane. He brother had realized there was no place for treachery on this perilous crossing.

So fixed was his attention upon his objective that Darkend even sidled over to give her room beside him. The Life-Tree looked as though it was dying, with occasional explosions marring its surface. Great chunks of rubble broke free here and there to fall into the sea or onto the crowded waterfront. Despite the increasing size of the waves, the coxswain and crew negotiated the storm-tossed sea with skill and they continued to make steady progress.

Closer still to the Hylar home they observed numerous lake boats bobbing in the rough swell around the fringe of the waterfront. Most of these craft were offshore, rocking in the turbulent waters.

"I see my fleet waits for me," Darkend announced in triumph.

"Aye, lord," agreed Bairn. "Many boats, their crews no doubt prepared to answer your every command."

But as their boat drew nearer to the bobbing fleet, both Bellowsmokes could see that there was no pattern to the deployment, that these boats had no crews. Scrap evidence of once-proud dark dwarf lives littered the decks. Empty armor and helmets rattled through the boats, oars flopped loosely in their brackets. The thane groaned in dismay and fear, recoiling from the horrible omen.

"They're all gone!" gasped one rower, as he looked into the empty vessels that bobbed and drifted on all sides of them.

Darkend whacked the dwarf's head with his gauntlet, but not before all of the terrified crew also had seen that the other boats were eerily vacant.

"To shore, you oafs!" commanded the thane, and the rowers pressed ahead with grim urgency, finally bringing the big lake boat gliding up to one of the few surviving docks.

"See, Brother! Your best plans are half-baked, subject to failure!" hissed Garimeth, as Darkend glanced around in horror. "Without my help—and that of my daemon warrior—you will never succeed!"

Even before their boat landed they noticed that the shore teemed with dark dwarves—most thankfully alive. But the none of the troops were making any effort to press the attack. Several hurried forward to take the bow and stern lines or to help the thane climb up to the stone wharf.

"Who's in command here?" Darkend demanded. A captain rushed forward as Garimeth hastened after her brother. "Why aren't you attacking?"

"There are no Hylar within reach, lord. The rockfall has cut off our approach. It collapsed the bottom of the enemy's lift and wiped out the defenders on Level Two."

"What do you mean? What about the higher levels?" Darkend was full of fear, thinking that all of his plans were coming to nothing. There would be no triumph in capturing a ruined slag heap of molten stone!

"Don't know. But the Hylar are sealed off from above. The rock melted right down the transport shaft!" blubbered the terrified commander.

"Then get your men digging!"

"I have, lord. They're making progress, but it will take time!"

"What about our allies, the Theiwar?" asked Darkend quickly.

"Their thane is nearby, sire, mustering his troops just to the west of here."

Darkend turned to his sister. "Go find Pounce Quickspring and bring him to me."

"Aye, lord," she agreed, more than willing to remove herself from her brother's presence.

Garimeth soon located the Theiwar thane. Pounce Quickspring was shouting angrily at his troops, but his clan also had been stymied by the same solid stone obstacle that was blocking the Daergar advance. He greeted the dwarfwoman suspiciously, but finally agreed to accompany her to Darkend. They joined the Daergar reinforcements on a wide, clear section of the docks. Pounce Quickspring looked expectantly at the Daergar thane.

"Now is the time to reveal our new war partner. Garimeth, summon the Chaos beast!" the Daergar thane ordered his sister. His voice nearly caught in his throat, for he dreaded the humiliation that would result if she failed. Pounce Quickspring and many of the Daergar dubiously looked to the sky.

Garimeth turned her voice and her thoughts to the sky,

speaking once again in that strange language enabled by the Helm of Tongues. She called to Zarak Thuul for long minutes, sending forth a message of her own adoration and desire, unaware of the passage of time as her emotions grew and she reached out, pleading and beseeching and cajoling.

A spot of brightness appeared in the subterranean sky, curling around the shoulder of the Life-Tree. The glowing form quickly grew into a blazing ball of fire that spilled toward the Hybardin waterfront.

Primus spread his vast, flaming wings and dipped down, coming to rest before the astonished dark dwarves. The brightness of his fiery visage was exceedingly painful in the eyes of the assembled warriors.

Even dismounted, Zarak Thuul stood as tall as a large man and towered over the dwarves. His face was blank, stony, yet handsome in a perverse sort of way. His crimson eyes flamed, the light an eerie color against that perfect blackness. Making no sound nor showing any expression, the daemon warrior moved over to Garimeth. Then he dropped to his belly, and gently kissed her feet. Finally he rose again to stand tall and magnificent, master of chaos and lord of the underworld.

In that visage Garimeth discerned images of other shapes as well, a vision of unspeakable blackness, and then a great, undead serpent draped in tendrils of festering flesh. An awareness of his awesome power once again made her knees weak, and she was his to command. The Helm gave her the ability to share his consciousness, to thrill to the awareness of his being.

"Please, my daemon, please know me, and grant me the freedom to sail on your power."

She murmured the words as if they were a prayer, too quiet for any of the dwarves to hear. But the flaming eyes of Zarak Thuul flared more brightly than ever, and she knew that he had heard and he was pleased.

She realized the creature's presence greatly exalted her

stature in the eyes of Darkend and the other dark dwarves. This knowledge gave her a sudden, powerful thrill.

"All our pieces are in place," Darkend ventured to say, gesturing to the multitude of dwarves amassed along the waterfront to either side. "Let our great attack begin."

Garimeth translated his words into that wretched, profane tongue. The monstrous warrior stood and listened impassively. Then she repeated Darkend's statement, seeking some sign of acknowledgment, all the time feeling the twisting pleasure and longing desire course throughout her being.

"Ask him this," Darkend was saying. "Can he create a route through the stone whereby our legions can climb upward and strike at the very core of Hybardin?"

Garimeth asked the question, following her brother's exact wording. Though Zarak Thuul gave no outward sign that he heard or understood, she sensed his pleasure with the violent command and his intent to obey. She turned back to the thanes and explained. "He agrees."

"I didn't hear anything," Pounce Quickspring declared skeptically.

"He told me alone," Garimeth said, with a meaningful glance at her brother.

"My sister speaks the truth," said Darkend. "She can communicate with him via this magical device. Surely you can see that!"

"Very well. Let the attack begin!" barked the thane of the Theiwar as he turned to lead his troops.

Immediately the dark dwarf companies were mustered away from the waterfront and they began climbing one of the large piles of rubble that had been left when some of the upper portions of the Life-Tree had collapsed. That mound came into contact with a wall of the overhang, and it was there, Garimeth said, that Zarak Thuul would create a passageway.

A familiar figure, robed all in black, emerged from

among the Daergar gathered at the edge of the water, and Darkend and Garimeth were quick to recognize the assassin, Slickblade.

"Ah, Slickblade. I assume this means that Tarn Bellowgranite is dead?" The thane shot his sister a look of cruel triumph, pleased to see Garimeth's face tighten, her lips trembling slightly as she made an effort to control herself.

"Sadly, my lord, no."

"My son lives?" demanded Garimeth.

"Aye, for the time being." The assassin's voice was devoid of emotion. "I tried to follow him, and I believe he has come here, to the city of the Hylar."

"Then find him now and kill him!" screamed Darkend.

"I am making every effort, my thane. The half-breed stole a boat from Daerforge with gulley dwarf assistance, and used it to make his way here. I believe that he is somewhere in the vicinity, perhaps skulking around on this very shore.

"Wait." The thane turned to Garimeth. "Where would he go first? Would he come here to the waterfront?"

"I don't know," she lied, certain that Tarn would in fact move mountains to make his way back to the city of his birth at this time of crisis.

"Don't trust her, lord. She deceives you!"

"Be aware that your own trust may be misplaced," she retorted, with a meaningful look at Slickblade.

She could tell by a foray into her brother's mind that he didn't believe her about Tarn, but he couldn't see any way to prove that she was lying either. Slickblade melted away into the shadows, but by then Darkend was distracted by the upcoming battle plans, and Tarn was temporarily forgotten.

The fire dragon rose up on wings dripping flame and spark, scalding dozens of dark dwarves who were too slow to get out of the monster's path. With the daemon warrior riding between its shoulders, the dragon ascended, circled once, then flew into the side of

Hybardin's stony pillar. The fiery beast showed no hesitation as it swept against the solid rock.

Immediately some of that stone tumbled away, and Darkend cursed bitterly as dozens more of his force were crushed by the rockfall. Other remnants of the dark dwarf army scattered in confusion. Before they could reform the monstrous attacker was out of sight. Behind, however, it left a wide cave, remarkably smooth-floored, which curved at a gentle angle upward toward the high levels of Hybardin.

After reforming their scattered troops into ranks and companies, the two dark dwarf thanes and Garimeth led the army into the newly bored passage.

The final attack had begun.

Interlude of Chaos

Zarak Thuul rode Primus into the stone, and the bedrock of Hybardin parted before him like waters breaking before the prow of a sleek ship. Wings of fire seared through the layers of sediment, rock sizzled into dust, and smoke billowed in a great cloud as the mighty serpent forged ahead, digging, driving, boring upward into the great Hylar city.

Primus brayed into the bedrock, and the daemon warrior laughed, relishing the power and the destruction, all the while fondly thinking of the dwarven female who had sent him such relentless and powerful appeals. She was intriguing, that one, undeniably intriguing and tempting. What was it that made her so different, so appealing? He didn't know, but he realized keen pleasure in working her will. There was one who was worthy, who brandished the unusual power to motivate him. In her name gladly would he destroy.

Despite his glee, the daemon warrior took care to keep the grade of the ascending spiral shallow enough for the footbound creatures to follow, for this was as the dwarven female had wished it. Weapons held ready, cries of war echoing from a thousand throats, the horde of Daergar and Theiwar marched in Zarak Thuul's wake, led by that entrancing female. In other places the shadow-wights wafted upward in their own way, following the surface of broken rubble, clinging to pipes and shafts and debris as they slithered over faces of bare rock.

Soon the daemon warrior and his fire dragon burst from solid rock into an inhabited upper level of the Hylar city. Some of the more foolish dwarves stayed to fight, and they died in cinder and ash without putting a single blade to Zarak Thuul or his mighty mount. The others turned and fled, vanishing into the maze of their city's Level Three.

Now Zarak Thuul and Primus flew down the wide avenues, crashing through walls and buildings, igniting fires that burst from the rock itself and soon filled all this level with a thick, choking smoke. Back and forth they flew, scorching their way through the maze, exulting in the powers of raw destruction and pure, unadulterated chaos. The killings were plenty, the dwarves burning and dying in numbers gratifying to behold.

Sometimes, for the sheer pleasure of power, Zarak Thuul dismounted from his blazing steed and swelled his body into monstrous size, striding through the streets in the guise of a great, skeletal dragon. In this form, devoid of flesh but grinning with razor-sharp fangs, the daemon warrior brought death to any who opposed him.

Then the blazing dragon and his master continued on, boring again into the rock, climbing higher and higher in the Life-Tree. As a worm might bore through the rotten wood in the trunk of some forest giant, Zarak Thuul and his dragon ascended upward into the highest reaches of the Hylar city.

And like that worm, the fire dragon was an agent of weakness and decay, twin factors that in any tree must eventually bring about its fall.

Darkest Night

Chapter Twenty-two

Great gears squealed in protest as the lift lurched to a sudden stop. The massive links of the support chain stretched taut as their tempered steel groaned under a slowly increasing strain. The world itself seemed to shake in a series of rumbles and tremors that brought dust and pebbles cascading down the long tube of the transport shaft.

"It's jammed!" Axel snarled, kicking at the bars of the cage. He turned to shout into the darkness overhead. "Get this thing moving, by Reorx, or I'll come up there and do it myself!"

"Patience, my friend," Baker Whitegranite said quietly, laying his hand on the agitated dwarf's sturdy shoulder. The thane blinked, trying to focus his blurred vision on the face of his fellow Hylar.

"But what if she's up there—if she needs me?" demanded the venerable warrior. "Damn it all, we've got to keep moving!"

"I know. I'm worried too. I have a son somewhere in this mess," Baker said quietly.

"I'm sorry. You're right," said Axel in sudden chagrin.

Before Baker could reply, the scream of straining metal rose to a shriek around them as the lift jolted free, once more rumbling upward toward the darkness of Level Six. Capper Whetstone and the rest of the thane's bodyguards looked relieved. The loyal Hylar had been most uncomfortable when their leader insisted on being on the last transport lift leaving Level Five.

The respite lasted only a few seconds, however. Once again the cage screeched to a halt, pinned in the girders that had been gradually twisted by the wrenching forces of Chaos.

Apparently drained, Axel slumped onto a bench in the corner of the cage. He looked at Baker, his expression pleading, and the thane was deeply moved upon seeing the defeat and deep furrows of age so clearly etched into his friend's face.

"And how do we know she's alive?" Axel asked for the tenth time. "She could have been killed by Daergar or buried in a landslide. We'd still remember her. It's only the shadow-wights that sap the memory!"

Baker had already acknowledged these suppositions, but he refused to give in to despair. "We don't know she's dead, and until we do I'm going to believe she's still fighting somewhere, still down there—perhaps fighting a rearguard action or trying to move her company up higher into the Life-Tree."

He didn't speak further, but in the dark silence both of them keenly relived the frantic scene below. They had taken stairs down to Level Four in order to seek information on the enemy advance. In the stairwell they had met panicked survivors who had been racing upward. They had reported that Level Four had been overrun before they fled. Those survivors, some of whom were now huddled on the lift with them, had told of the fire dragon bursting onto the level and moving swiftly through the streets of smiths and forges, setting fires that seemed to burn the very stone itself. That flaming monster had eventually disappeared, but the survivors believed it was boring a hole farther upward, extending the assault route toward Level Five and beyond.

Even worse, the dragon's onslaught had been followed by hundreds upon hundreds of Daergar who had charged through the tunnel that the fiery serpent had left behind in the rock. This was the first clear sign that the dark dwarves and Chaos creatures were now working together. Both Baker and Axel understood how hopeless that alliance made the Hylar's chances of a successful defense.

Then, as the thane and his party had reached Level Five, the attack had begun anew. The fire dragon and its black rider had torn through an entire quarter of what had once been the finest silver smithies on all Krynn. The few Hylar remaining here had either died in flames and ash or fled in panic from the horrific wave of destruction.

And there had been another beast as well. Though Baker's guards had shuttled him away at its first appearance, he had a fleeting glimpse of a massive, skeletal body. His weak vision had not provided much detail, though he was forced to wonder if perhaps that was not a slight blessing. Like the fire dragon, this vision of undeath had stormed through the streets and alleys of Hybardin, feasting and slaying with frenzied abandon. Baker had cringed at the noises of the doomed and dying.

All the dwarves could do was fall back to the lift station on Level Five with as much haste as they could manage. Even Axel, despite his bad foot, had made the trip rapidly without flagging. But now, as they tried to ride the cage up to the next level, Baker was forced to wonder what they could really hope to accomplish if Chaos beasts were aligned with the enemy clans.

One passenger had gone over to the corner of the cage. This young, muscular Hylar leaned far over the rail to get a look at the support mechanism above them. Despite his youth, he had an air of competence that Baker found somehow heartening.

"Let's all shift our weight over here," suggested the young dwarf. He had a small hammer, and he chinked it against the girder of the lift track. "We might be able to rock it free."

"Do you know anything about how the lift functions?" demanded another Hylar skeptically. "How do we know you won't break us loose and send the whole thing falling down there?"

The young Hylar spoke to Baker instead of replying to the questioner. "I'm an engineer, my lord thane. I was a journeyman of some years and was being trained in lift repairs before . . . " He couldn't finish the sentence, but Baker could see the skill and determination shining in his eyes.

"Good man, let's follow your idea. Everyone, obey him!"

Smiling thankfully, the young Hylar began giving instructions. "Everyone get into this corner. Now jump, on my count . . . now."

The passengers did as the Hylar engineer suggested, jumping up and down in a coordinated effort to break the cage free. The lift lurched slightly with a shriek of protesting metal.

"Now again. And again!" urged the young mechanic, as the passengers continued their efforts.

A heavy rumble shook the cage and girders violently. From somewhere down below Baker heard crashing noises accompanied by screams of pain.

"Look!" cried the engineer, his voice rising with fear.

All of them saw the crack, a deep, horizontal gouge in the rock wall of the transport shaft. Before Baker's horrified eyes it spread, growing wider and wider. He saw the metal rails that guided the lift bend and twist from the force of great weight, and it seemed clear to him that the cage was now firmly wedged in a vise of steel.

"Trouble down below!" grunted Capper Whetstone in sudden alarm.

A few of the passengers moaned as they looked down through the screen mesh of the cage floor. Baker's own blood froze in his veins as he saw a dozen or more of the ink-black shadows creeping stealthily up the walls of the shaft, drawing steadily closer to the cage of the lift.

"We're trapped!" screamed one battered dwarf.

"By Reorx, at least we can die fighting!" Axel declared bravely, but his eyes were hollows of grief.

"No!" Baker's voice cut through the panic like a sharp blade. "We're not finished yet. If we're going to die fighting, it won't be here!"

He paused, aware of all the blurred faces staring at him expectantly, and realized that his voice, his words, could give these people hope. And with hope, one or more of them might survive to carry on the fight.

"I am the thane of the Hylar!" he barked. "And I say we must escape and survive. Our hope is to climb higher. Keep climbing!"

"Quick! Out the top!" Axel cried, pointing to the trapdoor on the upper side of the cage. He pushed it open with the tip of his broadsword and pointed to the ladder that led to that point of egress. He addressed the two dozen terrified Hylar in the lift, pulling one matron bodily toward the hole. "Climb! Climb for all you're worth!"

One by one the passengers scrambled up the ladder and through the trapdoor. Some climbed with ease, while others, wounded or paralyzed with fear, needed to be helped.

"My thane, it's your turn. You must escape!" Capper urged, taking Baker by the arm.

"No! Not yet!" insisted the leader of the Hylar. Baker

clutched his small sword, determined to set an example. He was sick and tired of flight, of running here and there and everywhere else in a frantic effort to stay alive.

He had work to do right here.

He gestured to his enchanted weapon, to the blades borne by the guards, and to Axel's ancient broadsword. "Our weapons have the best chance against these things. Let's stay back until all the others are safe and give these weapons a try!"

"But you can't even see very well!" stammered Axel, lending his voice in support of Capper Whetstone.

"I can see well enough when they're right in front of me!" retorted the thane. "Incidentally, how close are they?"

Axel growled in exasperation, but gave up on trying to get Baker to climb to safety. "Twoscore feet, closing fast."

The last of the Hylar scooted up to the trapdoor as the two old dwarves stood with drawn blades beside Capper Whetstone and a few volunteers from the royal bodyguard as they waited for the onslaught. The dark shapes shifted, and Baker found himself looking at sharply focused images from his own nightmares. Indeed, one of the shades resembled his former wife, wickedly grinning at him, taunting and jeering.

But this image was tightly focused, unblurred, and in a flash of insight Baker understood that without his glasses he couldn't really see such a thing. It was entirely in his mind! He laughed out loud as he stabbed at the nightmare that no longer had the power to frighten him. He felt the silver blade cut through the shadows, and he heard a howling maelstrom somewhere in the distance.

And the shadow went away. Another stretched forward a tendril of darkness, and that too vanished after a quick jab of his sword. Again and again he stabbed with the blade, shouted curses at the unfeeling shadows, dispatched them one after another. He heard cheers and knew that the other Hylar had escaped, that his leadership had saved them.

Another rumble shook the mountain, jarring the lift so harshly that Baker thought for a moment perhaps the chain had broken and they were falling. Instead, the latest tremor merely released a shower of pebbles and boulders. Then a bigger quake shook the mountain, and even to the thane's blurred vision the crack in the shaft wall grew wider. With a splitting, grinding noise, the lower part of the transport shaft fell away, leaving the lift cage dangling freely in the air. Massive slabs of rock collapsed, breaking away from the bulk of the Life-Tree to tumble below onto the remains of the waterfront.

Baker looked up, seeing the lowest rungs of the ladder still secured to the side of the upper transport shaft.

"This cage isn't going anywhere," said the young engineer who had stayed behind. "That last rockfall pinched it in here like cement."

"Come, my thane," urged Capper Whetstone. "It's time for us to get out of here."

And Baker Whitegranite climbed with strength, knowing that the hopes of the Hylar climbed with him.

Chaos Falling

Chapter Twenty-three

For long minutes Tarn lay on the smooth rock of the shore, struggling to draw air through the raw, constricted passage of his throat. He knew he was in dangerous surroundings. But even if a company of dark dwarves had come along screaming for his blood, the half-breed would have been unable to so much as look for a hiding place. The lingering horror of his immersion in water—the nearness of death—had drained him. The fight to survive had utterly exhausted him. And even when he found the strength to lift his head, there was nothing within his range of sight to encourage him.

Around him the gully dwarves chattered and explored, though there was an uncharacteristic hush to their voices. Regal sniffed something, then called some of his comrades to help him move a large boulder. The industrious Aghar toppled the large rock to the side, but after several minutes of rooting around in the muddy crater they trudged glumly back to Tarn.

"Nuthin!" groused one.

"No food, not a bite," said another.

"No beer," Regal added mournfully.

Finally able to sit up and look around, Tarn tried to get a fix on their surroundings. He was startled to realize he was totally lost. Though he knew the Hybardin waterfront like he knew the hilt of his sword, he was now unable to recognize a single landmark. A pile of broken rock rose like a mountain before him, and to either side he saw a splintered wreckage of slabs, beams, fabric, and other debris. Looking straight up, he could see the bottom of the great stalactite that was the Life-Tree suspended overhead, though whether they could reach it or not was another question entirely. And even so, could they somehow work their way into higher regions of the city? It was inconceivable that the lift still functioned.

From his low vantage he was able to see enough to make several assumptions with a fair level of confidence. It seemed that all of Level One and Level Two of Hybardin had been buried beneath rockfalls. Obviously the Chaos horde had struck far more savagely here than in Daerforge. It was impossible to imagine that anyone could have lived through such a horrific devastation. Belicia Felixia Slateshoulder had been here, and Tarn faced the reality that she must certainly be dead.

Despair dragged his head down onto his arms. For a while he lay like a corpse, unthinking, uncaring, aware only of the black wave of hopelessness that swept over him. Very gradually he became conscious of an insistent tugging, something that had him by the elbow and was trying to lift him from the ground.

"Leave me alone!" he growled.

"Come on! Look up!" replied a voice that he remembered as Regal's. "We try to get to Hybardin—not stop now!"

Tarn whirled on the Aghar, his face twisted into a snarl.

"What Hybardin?" he demanded. "Look around, you imbecile! Can't you see that my city doesn't even exist anymore? Now do what I told you: leave me alone!"

"No!" insisted Regal, with surprising stubbornness. "You look around! City's up there!" The gully dwarf pointed a blunt finger at the dangling massif overhead. "Let's go see, okay? Kinda boring down here."

"Not boring no more," noted another little Aghar, who was squatting just above. The fellow pointed to the side. "Here come some guys."

Fighting through his despair, Tarn wriggled around to follow the direction of the second gully dwarf's stare. His heart pounded at the sight of several dozen Daergar poking through the rubble along the shore of the lake. They were a long way away, but coming in his direction.

Instantly the half-breed's malaise vanished as he realized that the gully dwarves, who had risked so much to get him here, would be easy prey for the villainous dark dwarves. Cursing his selfish melancholy, he looked around for some avenue of escape. Immediately he saw a large, flat slab of rock tilted up against the steep slope of the rubble.

"Get behind that!" Tarn whispered urgently. "Stay low and quiet!"

He realized that his latter commands were superfluous as the Aghar once again demonstrated their natural instincts for stealth. The score or so of his shipmates were already out of sight as Tarn crawled behind them into the low shelter, fairly certain that the Daergar patrol had not spotted them.

"Now climb!" he urged. "Get as high as you can!"

The makeshift wall served as good cover, and Tarn found that he could stand upright behind it and crawl upward towards the top of a rubble-strewn slope. For minutes there was no sound except for the gasping and panting of scrambling dwarves. The incline was very steep, and in many places Tarn and the Aghar had to pull themselves up with their hands and scramble on their knees to negotiate the grade. As they climbed still higher, Tarn was able to see great companies of dark dwarves marching up a neighboring mound of stone. Groups of shadowy creatures visible just beyond. It did not seem to the half-breed as though the Chaos creatures were menacing the Daergar and Theiwar formations. Indeed, he saw with despair that the two forces were actually advancing in concert.

"Look, there!" hissed Regal.

Tarn witnessed the black daemon straddling its fiery mount as the dragon spread its wings and flared into the air. The half-breed watched in fascination as the monster flew directly into the side of the overhanging rock, boring a hole right into the bedrock.

"Let's keep going," Tarn said. "And try to stay out of sight!"

For once the infamously curious gully dwarves agreed with his warning, and the party continued its surreptitious climb.

By now the half-breed could see that this pile of rubble ended dozens of feet below the overhanging terminus of the Life-Tree. From the top they were high enough to see that the whole lower reach of Hybardin was nothing more than a wasteland. Everywhere the ruins were crowded with dark dwarves and Chaos shadows. In one place Tarn saw a great column of enemy dwarves moving into the wide tunnel the fire dragon had excavated on the bottom of the Life-Tree. He caught a glimpse of a bronze helm at the head of the file of black armor.

Looking around, Tarn saw that more of the dark dwarf companies were spreading out along the waterline. They were poking and probing through the rubble, undoubtedly searching for survivors or treasure. Once more he turned his attention above and saw a gaping black hole in the underside of smooth rock, perhaps thirty feet overhead. Probably that was the remains of some transport shaft to Level Three, but there was simply no way to reach it—even from the highest pinnacle of rock on their little summit.

"Look! Now they comin' up our hill!" snorted a gully dwarf indignantly.

Tarn saw that the Daergar had spotted them and at least a hundred of the dark dwarves were beginning to converge at the base of the mound. The Daergar took their time, spreading out to form a ring around the conical hill. Then they began a slow and methodical climb toward the dwarves trapped at the summit.

"What we do now?" wondered Regal, with what Tarn thought was an impressive lack of panic in his voice.

"We can start by rolling rocks down on them," the half-breed said, "while I try to think of something a little more long-term."

The Aghar pitched into this new game with enthusiasm, and soon great chunks of jagged stone were bouncing, rolling, and ricocheting down the steep slope. Several of these hit individual Daergar, and the overall effect was a dramatic slow down of the climbers. But Tarn could see that their position would become hopeless within a few minutes.

"Gotta big one!" cried Regal, as several of his mates helped him to tumble a great boulder down the slope. While the Aghar shrieked and jeered, cursing dark dwarves scrambled to the sides to get out of the way of the deadly missile. A few of them were too slow, but that only seemed to solidify the grim purpose of the survivors as they once again resumed their implacable ascent.

"Psst! Tarn! Up here!"

At first the half-breed attributed the words to his fevered imagination, for it sounded exactly like the voice of his Belicia Felixia.

"Tarn!"

When she called again, he forced himself to look.

Now he discerned movement in the base of the tunnel leading upward into Hybardin. He saw several dwarves squirreled away in the far corners, and dimly realized that they were clinging to the rungs of a ladder mounted directly into a stone. With a flash of hope he saw that they were lowering ropes, three or four lines that dropped among the Aghar atop the hill.

And finally he recognized her, eyes shining as she looked at him from the dimness of the shadowy tunnel.

Belicia Felixia Slateshoulders was not only alive, she was hovering overhead like a messenger from Reorx, a vision of hope, promise, and rescue.

An Army Unleashed

Chapter Twenty-four

"Get into that tunnel, you gully dwarf-spawned bastards!" shouted Darkend, waving his mace over his head and menacing the file of Daergar warriors. Most were already advancing into the confined assault route, but their thane still cursed and lashed, uncaring of complaints as his spiked weapon gouged into the back of his warriors.

Still fuming, he whirled upon his sister who had just emerged with him from the tunnel that led up to Hybardin's Level Four. All around him was a ruin of molten rock, rubble-strewn streets, and pulverized landscape. A whole sector of valuable smithies had been smashed into unrecognizable garbage and soot beneath the power of fiery wing and crushing talon.

"Why didn't he wait here? Isn't that what you told him to do?" the thane demanded.

"Yes, that is what I told him!" insisted the female dark dwarf. "But he clearly had ideas of his own!"

Even as she spoke, Darkend noticed that his sister looked fretful. The strain of the long climb and the frustration at finding events reaching beyond their control had tightened the nerves of both Bellowsmokes. For several moments the brother and sister glared at each other. Darkend's gaze shifted, and as he fixed his stare at the bronze helm that gave Garimeth the ability to understand beings even as strange as the daemon warrior, he finally understood.

He was tempted to swing his mace against Garimeth right now, but some deep vestige of self control prevented him from taking the dire action. And he still could not be sure. Besides, Garimeth still had uses—or she would, if they could ever catch up to the rampaging daemon warrior.

Herein was the crux of his problem. Zarak Thuul had apparently taken to the thane's orders with passion, using his great serpent to bore a wide hole through the bedrock of the Life-Tree. Already thousands of Daergar and Theiwar had advanced along that route. But these attacking dwarves had found the city already reduced to waste. There were no conquered Hylar to show him honor. All of them were either dead or had fled into the highest levels of the city. Even the vast silver smithies with their great vaults of precious metal had been burned so thoroughly that the stockpiles of the argent metal had melted like water and vanished into the porous rock. This had been one of the great treasures of Hybardin, and Darkend had planned to turn the minting process to his own uses. But now, like so much of this accursed city, it was nothing but ugly wreckage.

And, from the look of things, there was still no sign that the Chaos lord was planning to slow down his onslaught or that he had any intentions of cooperating with the dark dwarf assault. Instead, the daemon warrior continued to take matters into his own hands, forging upward and onward on his own. Though advancing companies of dark dwarves hastened in his wake, the stocky, short-legged warriors were climbing much more slowly than the fiery harbinger of Chaos. Now Darkend's greatest fear was that he would conquer this city of wonders, only to find that the entire place had been destroyed beyond salvage by the depredations of his unpredictable, uncontrollable ally.

Worst of all, Darkend could think of no way to counter the daemon warrior's power or his implacable will. He dared not take his frustrations out on Garimeth—at least not now, for he saw that his sister might be his only chance to somehow still rein in that capricious power.

"My lord thane! My lord!" cried a Daergar warrior in great excitement.

"What is it, man?"

"A royal armory, lord! And it's still intact!" The dwarf pointed along the street. "We've set a guard on it, but it hasn't been burned yet! And it looks like the Hylar cleared out too quickly to take any of their treasure."

"This is more like it," growled the thane, allowing himself to feel the first hint of conqueror's pleasure. Darkend followed the other dwarf down a wide avenue toward a vast structure with a colonnaded portico and doors of reinforced steel.

"There's a trove of coin in here!" shouted a captain of heavy infantry, clapping his fist in salute as Darkend strode up the steps. The thane stalked down a wide, marbled hall, past more saluting Daergar, all of whom grinned with anticipation.

"In here, my lord—feast your eyes!" declared the messenger, standing aside to allow his thane to proceed.

The great vault was encased in thick plates of solid steel, but the doors had been forced open; one of the great slabs lay on the floor while the other tilted awkwardly on its single remaining hinge. As Darkend reached the end of the hall and saw the great room opening beyond, he knew that here at last was one prize worthy of his conquering army.

The vault was as large as his own throne room and was crowded with neat rows of crates and boxes. Darkend beheld a wealth of riches, coin of steel, platinum, and gold. Several Daergar were already moving amongst the packages, prying off lids and shifting some of the heavier crates onto the floor. They snapped to attention as the thane arrived.

"See here, my lord," cried one, who wielded a small axe. "They're all like this!"

The dwarf smashed his blade into the side of a crate, breaking the boards and releasing a cascade of silvery coins.

"These are steel, lord—but there's all kinds of coinage, imprints from across the face of Krynn!" The speaker smiled crookedly. "We've even found a set minted in Palanthas, bearing the image of Gunthar Uth Wistan himself!"

"The Knights of Solamnia are making a contribution to my treasury," Darkend declared, chuckling at the irony. "Do you have a count of the worth yet?"

"No, lord. But look over here! These bins are full of gems—diamonds and rubies of incalculable worth! And over there, emeralds—some of them bigger than your eye!"

"Indeed!" The thane, very pleased, was about to step into the vault when he heard cries of alarm. A blow shook the floor under his feet, and the air reverberated.

"What's that?" he demanded, staring about.

There was another great smash, and this time the vault rang like the inside of a drum, a deafening resonance thrumming in the air. Darkend stared in disbelief as the steel wall at the far side of the great chamber bulged inward, then began to glow a dull red. The thane recoiled, feeling a blast of heat against his face. He watched in dumbstruck horror as the metallic barrier brightened to yellow, then to pure, hot white.

And then fire was everywhere, exploding into the vault, roaring in Darkend's ears. He threw himself flat on the floor, crawled toward the doorway, and finally hurtled into the comparative coolness of the outer hall.

A tail of crackling oily flame lashed across the treasures— his treasures! Walls of steel and stone dissolved, and Darkend groaned in abject misery as he saw piles of coins turn to ash. A fire dragon surged past in an ecstasy of destruction, crushing a king's ransom in gems to dust as its inferno of heat melted coins of steel and gold.

"Fight, you worms!" cried Darkend, sending more of his warriors into the path of that killing blaze. "Save my treasure!"

A few obeyed and died, burned to powder by the touch of wing or claw. Others threw themselves flat on the floor, cowering and miserable, risking the wrath of their thane rather than facing certain death from the infernal wyrm.

And then the monster was gone, leaving an eerie, smoking silence. A great cavern yawned in the wall, marking the passage of flaming Chaos.

"My thane, we must hurry!" hissed Garimeth. "Our only chance is to keep climbing, to find Zarak Thuul."

"But, my baubles, my coins, my gems!" moaned Darkend.

"She's right." Slickblade was suddenly back at his side, oddly speaking in agreement with Garimeth. "We must go!" he urged.

"Why? What's the point?" Darkend looked at the singed and soot-covered survivors of his troops. He wanted nothing more than to have them executed slowly, while he sat and watched.

"There will be other treasures, I promise you. And your life means everything, does it not?" asked the assassin.

Darkend looked back once to see the vault shrouded in the same red smoke that permeated so much of this city. "What of Tarn Bellowgranite?" he demanded. "Tell me: is he dead?"

"No!" spat the assassin. "He is lost in the maze of this dying city. I have not been able to find him."

"Then come with me as we climb," snarled the thane. "We must catch the daemon warrior and stop him!"

"How can you hope to do that?" Slickblade asked.

"How should I know?" demanded Darkend. He pointed at Garimeth. "You may as well ask her!"

"I don't know!" she screamed wildly, irrationally. "But he's right. We have to try. Can't you see that?"

"What does it matter? What does anything matter? We're conquering a mess here! By the time we do anything, all that will be left of Hybardin is rubble, dust, and smoke!"

"We will catch him, but not until we can get to a higher level in the city," Garimeth said, her tone growing calm and surprisingly soothing to the agitated thane. "If necessary we will climb to the top of this miserable Life-Tree and find him there. We must stop him before it is too late!"

Darkend cursed but knew he had no choice but to follow her.

"Let's go, then," Garimeth said, fixing him with a steady glare. "But my lord, first I have a demand."

"How dare you!" Darkend's temper flared again, but he forced himself to listen. "What is it?"

"I need your promise—a bonded word—that you will not kill me when this is over."

"Very well, as Reorx is my witness, you have my word." Darkend gave the oath reluctantly, knowing the strength of the god's name. He might still choose to renege upon his word, but if he did so his treachery would surely cost him. It galled him to admit that he still needed Garimeth, needed the power she possessed with her artifact, the power that gave them their only hope of arresting the insane havoc of Zarak Thuul.

Love and Chaos

Chapter Twenty-five

"By Reorx, I thought I'd never see you again," Tarn declared weakly, embracing Belicia with one arm while he held the rung of the ladder with the other.

Similarly suspended, she returned his hug without speaking. Tarn could feel her shuddering and could hear her soft sobs as they desperately clung together.

Above them the Aghar, all of whom had scampered up the ropes without difficulty, were making great progress climbing the shaft. Playing leapfrog, swinging by single hands, and otherwise acting in a fashion more like monkeys than dwarves, they moved steadily away from the ruins of lower Hybardin. Hooting and jeering, clambering over each others' backs and shoulders, they bounded quickly and eagerly upward—though at any moment it seemed to Tarn that at least half of them were a hiccup away from a fatal plunge.

"I think we'd better do some climbing ourselves," Belicia said, indicating the enraged dark dwarves swarming below. The two were still at the bottom of the shaft with the long transport tunnel extending straight above them. A thirty-foot drop to the crest of the rubble pile yawned beneath them. "We're out of sword range, but I wouldn't be surprised if one or two of them have crossbows."

"You go first," Tarn insisted, then followed as Belicia hastened up the ladder.

One missile knocked into the heel of his boot and several more clattered off of the walls nearby, but in moments the two dwarves were safely above the lower terminus. Looking around, Tarn realized that this must have been the route for a small cargo lift. The tunnel was only ten feet or so in diameter and was marked by rails in all four corners as well as these rungs that formed a permanent ladder.

"How high does it go?" he asked. "Are the Hylar making a stand on Level Three?"

"You're out of touch," she said sadly, looking down at him from the rungs immediately over his head. "And so am I, I'm afraid. I know we're going to have to climb at least as far as Level Five before we get off this ladder."

"You lead the way."

"Actually, your friends are leading the way. Those are your friends aren't they?" Belicia asked, pausing while several Aghar swung, apelike, from the rungs just above her.

"And good friends, too," Tarn confirmed.

Grimly the half-breed labored upward. They soon reached a small lift station leading to Level Three, but the terminal was masked from the area beyond by steel doors that had been bolted and barred shut from the inside. The air was thick with pungent smoke, and there were no distinguishable noises coming from beyond the heavy metal barrier.

They stopped here only long enough to rest and catch their breath. Tarn tried to find out what had happened to the dwarfwoman, but Belicia's descriptions were curt. Her company had retreated from the plaza when the Chaos horde had swept into Hybardin. Many dwarves on both sides had been killed when the bottom of the Life-Tree had collapsed and sent tons of rubble cascading onto Levels One and Two. The rest of the Hylar had tried to fight on Levels Three and Four but had been expelled with heavy losses. Breaking into this transport shaft, Belicia and a handful of survivors had been prepared to risk a climb to safety when a sharp-eyed scout had noted Tarn and his companions trapped below. The half-dozen Hylar remaining from her band had already made their way upward, she explained, preceding the Aghar in the ascent.

Level Four was another hundred feet, with the fifth a similar distance beyond. The gully dwarves continued to scamper merrily into the higher darkness, while Tarn needed all of his concentration to keep his grip and move his cramped hands and aching arms upward. Periodically he stopped, linking his elbows through the rung before him while he panted for breath. Even this restful position quickly became uncomfortable, so he followed Belicia higher and higher.

"Soon now. Close," Belicia finally said, the effort of the climb audible in the staccato delivery of her words.

Tarn saw a gleam of illumination up above, and he watched the gully dwarves scramble off the ladder and disappear from his view. Obviously they had reached another lift station, and he allowed himself to anticipate the blissful sensation of a solid floor under his feet.

"Hey! We good guys!" came one indignant cry, followed by a volley of Aghar insults and the deeper, stern tones of Hylar guards.

"Ouch! You stoppit!"

"Get outa here, you runts!"

Finally Tarn and Belicia reached Level Five to find Regal

Everwise locked in a furious argument with a burly Hylar who seemed quite ready to pitch the gully dwarf and his scruffy companions right back down the shaft.

"No, don't! They're on our side," Tarn explained hastily, climbing off the ladder to join the others on a small, crowded lift platform. He turned to Belicia, glad to have both his feet planted on solid stone. "Without them I never would have made it back from Daerforge."

"Then we owe them a lot," Belicia said. "Now, let's find your father and see how things stand. I'm sure he can use us somewhere."

"Wait. There's something else," Tarn said, blurting out the idea that had been taking shape in his mind ever since he had heard of that unholy war conference in Daerforge. "My mother took something from my father—an artifact that I think she's using somehow to control that daemon who's leading this whole attack. She brought it here to Hybardin."

"What can we do about it?"

"I saw her with the elite guard of the dark dwarves. Her brother is the thane, and no doubt he's leading the charge. I saw them with the attackers pouring into that dragon tunnel down below."

"You've come to the right spot," declared the Hylar guard. His grim tone was underscored by the bloody bandage on his right arm and the singed, sooty state of his beard. "That very fire dragon came through here not long ago, burning a big hole through the floor. Haven't seen any Daergar yet, but I'm pretty sure they won't be far behind."

"The dragon already got this far?" Belicia seemed stunned by the news.

"Level Five's all but gone—just a few places left, like this station. We're holding out 'til the last of us move up. Fact is, I was about to start the climb myself before your lot came along."

The dwarfwoman seemed immune to grief; she merely

shook her head in despair. "Do you want to try and waylay your mother?" she asked Tarn.

"We have little choice but to try. We've got to get that helm back for Father." He paused, then shifted his gaze to the guard. "Is my father—I mean, the thane—is he all right?"

"He's fine, young fellow, and what's more, he's proved himself a good thane too. Now if you want to find that dragon-tunnel I was talking about, head down First Granite Road. Though I don't know what you can accomplish with them helping!" He looked askance at the gully dwarves, but then added, "Good luck."

When they left the lift station, they couldn't help but stare in horror at the devastation of Level Five. The place was no long recognizable as a city. Instead, it was more like the ruins left in the wake of a volcanic eruption. Rocky edifices had puddled into slag while molten lava still trickled from the piles of several ruins. Steam and choking vapors swirled through the air, sometimes thick enough to reduce them to choking and gagging.

"Look out!" cried Regal as a dark shape suddenly moved near them.

The shadow-wight reared back, tendrils of darkness coveting Belicia, who stared transfixed at the lightless visage. Tarn struck quickly with his silver sword, slashing through the intangible shape and quickly reducing it to evaporating mist.

"Wh–what was that?" asked the shaken female.

"Pure chaos," Tarn answered, "and I sent it back to where it came from. Now, this must be what's left of First Granite Road."

The yawning cave was unmistakable, even from a block away, for every one of the nearby buildings had been utterly destroyed. They could see little through the swirling smoke, yet the cadence of marching dwarves was audible as they drew nearer to the dark hole. Flames still flickered along the rim, and it felt as though they were entering an oven.

"Those marchers are coming this way," Belicia said, after listening for a careful moment. "They'll be here soon."

"Take cover," Tarn suggested, pointing to a shadowy alcove a short distance back from the street.

He, Belicia, and the dozen or so gully dwarves slipped into the yawning doorway of a ruined inn. The building had been shattered, walls and ceiling collapsed, but they were able to find hiding places with good views of the dragon-excavated passage. Eyes on the mouth of the tunnel, the half-breed waited for the appearance of the first ranks of the ascending dark dwarves.

The first black-armored Daergar came forth in a skirmish line, many with crossbows ready or swords drawn. Right behind them was a robed figure that Tarn stared at, then recognized.

"Slickblade!" whispered the half-breed, feeling a rush of hatred. Beside Slickblade were two other familiar figures.

"And there she is—your mother!" hissed Belicia, her hand tightening on his arm.

"Also Darkend Bellowsmoke, the Daergar thane," Tarn added in a whisper. "My uncle."

More of the Daergar warriors moved past the trio to work their way through the ruined streets. Fortunately, none came to check the smoldering hole where Tarn and his companions were huddling. The half-breed hunched as low as possible, keeping an eye fixed to the narrow crack between two rocks.

The assassin, the thane, and the dwarfwoman were next out of the tunnel. Immediately behind them marched rank upon rank of armored Daergar.

"First company, take that road!" shouted Darkend Bellowsmoke, sending two hundred Daergar charging along the street toward the lift station. In quick fashion more dark dwarves were dispersed in all directions as they emerged onto Level Five. Tarn had to drop out of sight, then strained to hear as more and more of the enemy marched past. He dared to steal another glance when he recognized his mother's voice.

"Zarak Thuul must have gone that way!" Garimeth declared, pointing through a series of buildings that had been flattened by the wings of the fire dragon.

"By Reorx, there's no catching him!" wailed Darkend, obviously distraught.

"There might be, but we've got to move fast!" she urged.

"Hurry, then!" barked the thane of the Daergar. Accompanied by Slickblade and his sister, he started along the rubble-strewn path. They moved right past Tarn's hiding place. "Find him before he goes any higher!"

So frantic were the trio in their pursuit that they didn't notice the half-breed and his companions slinking through the wreckage of a nearby building. As soon as they were out of sight of the dark dwarf legions, Tarn and Belicia led the gully dwarves over a wall and around a pair of columns. They paused a moment only before swarming against the trio of Daergar from three sides. Several Aghar tackled the assassin while Tarn drew his silver sword and lunged at the thane.

"Tarn!" cried Garimeth, surprisingly glad to see her son—at least her voice sounded glad.

"Give me the helm, Mother!" he demanded, his sword poised at Darkend's throat.

The Daergar leader sputtered in fury. Slickblade squirmed nimbly, killing a gully dwarf with a blow from his long dagger and breaking free to stand next to the thane. Tarn aimed a stab at Slickblade, who frantically twisted out of reach, and the distraction gave Darkend a chance to break from the scene. The thane ran back through the rubble at full speed.

"Help us! Over here!" Darkend Bellowsmoke's panicked cries drew a phalanx of warriors scrambling to his aid. Tarn looked around wildly, realizing that his mother and the assassin had sprinted away.

"We've got to get out of here!" cried Belicia.

So Tarn and his companions ran, scuttling through the ruins, spinning down a side lane, and darting through partially ruined buildings until they had left the dark dwarves—and, unfortunately, several of the gully dwarves—behind.

"I must have been mad!" groaned the half-breed. "To think I could just snatch it away from her in the middle of her brother's army."

"We had to try," Belicia consoled. She put an arm around him.

"But I was doomed to fail!" Will I always fail? He wanted to ask that question of the gods, but he had neither the strength nor the time to rail against fate.

"Is this what you wanted?" asked Regal Everwise, swinging a leather satchel into Tarn's arms. "I hope so. You carry big heavy thing. Too much for me."

Pulling the drawstring to open it, the half-breed looked down into the bag to see the Helm of Tongues.

Reunion

Chapter Twenty-six

"Are we too late to do anything?" asked Tarn in dismay as they emerged onto the ruins of yet another level. They thought they were somewhere around Eight or Nine, though all familiar landmarks had been obscured by rubble, smoke, and soot. They passed through a place that might have once been a garden, but the fungus and ferns had been smashed into compost and spattered with a mix of muddy, ash-stained water. Nearby was the shaft of the Great Lift, filled with rubble from which jutted the twisted wreckage of girders and one of the transport cages.

Stunned and dismayed, the half-breed shambled through the remains of the city of his birth, his youth, and his home. Hybardin had been ravaged beyond recognition. Guilt tore at him; anger clouded his eyes. With a growl of fury he kicked at a broken beam and looked around for some enemy he could smite with steel. But there was no one, nothing but this seemingly endless devastation.

"We're losing the city from below as the dark dwarves advance into the levels that the dragon has already burned," Belicia said gently, bringing him back to his senses. "Our only hope is to get ahead of them and mount a concerted counterattack."

"What if the Klar are attacking Level Twenty-eight again?" groaned Tarn, who had learned of that incident from Belicia. "What if the top of the city has suffered as much as the lower levels?"

She didn't answer. There wasn't really any answer, the half-breed realized.

Smoke was thick in the air, and not the clean coal smoke of a roaring forge. Instead, it was a choking vapor of thick, reddish hue, like nothing the half-breed had ever experienced before. They found a few Hylar warriors picking through the rubble. These battered veterans looked up as the newcomers approached. They were dazed, though they showed no sign of fear. But neither did they have the air of dwarves who were ready for a fight. Tarn sensed that these Hylar had already admitted defeat.

One grizzled dwarf, a veteran who had a wooden peg in place of his left leg, stood with a large battle-axe near a hole in the floor. "The dragon went on upward an hour ago. No telling how many levels are bored straight through."

"And the dark dwarves?" Belicia asked.

"Haven't made it this far yet. I heard there was a young warrior called Farran Thornwhistle who somehow got a few Hylar dwarves into a shield wall across the mouth of the cave one level down. He held for a long time, but last I heard they'd been overrun and killed to the last dwarf. Now we're trying to get the rest of these Hylar up to safety."

Belicia drew a sharp gasp at the news, and Tarn remembered a young recruit, freshly knocked in the shins by his stern teacher.

"What word of the thane?" asked Tarn.

"Came through here before on the main lift shaft. He and Axel Slateshoulder were with the last group to take the lift." The dwarf cleared his throat, shaking his head in awe.

"What is it? What happened?" demanded Tarn.

"The lift jammed fifty feet below. There was a bunch of them shadows crawling up after it and then the whole tunnel collapsed. Cage was pinched tight, but Baker Whitegranite held off the shadows with his sword until everyone got off. They called him a hero, those survivors. Now you can see even the lift station is buried. They had to climb up like you did. Word was they barely got away!" he concluded.

"Let's get to the Thane's Atrium," Tarn said urgently.

"A lot of the stairways are still open," advised the axeman. "They'll be less crowded farther from the lift stations, I'm guessing."

"Hurry!" Tarn shouted for the attention of the gully dwarves, a few of whom had already wandered off. Together with about eight or ten of his original crew of Aghar, they ran along the street, dodging blocks of stone, broken timbers and beams, and a tragic number of bodies. Several stairwells were nearby, but each of these was thronged by dwarves seeking to flee upward, so they kept running, making their way into the emptier reaches on the periphery.

"Here's one!" Belicia cried, finally discovering an entrance to a servants' stair in an alley behind several great houses. Kicking stones out of the way, she got the Aghar to help move a heavy beam, and finally they cleared enough space to get into the constricted passageway.

They rushed upward, gasping for breath as they

emerged onto the street again at Level Ten and made their way toward the thane's headquarters. Even here, the avenues were filled with smoke and flame. Most were abandoned and empty. The few live Hylar they saw were running, stricken by panic, hastening to find escape still higher in the Life-Tree.

A great smoking cave gaped in the floor of a broad intersection, clear sign that the fire dragon had bored through here as well. There was no corresponding hole above them, Tarn pointed out. "That could mean the daemon warrior and the dragon are still around here somewhere."

There was no immediate sign of the horrific invaders, nor was there any indication that the dark dwarf vanguard had made it this far. Nevertheless, Tarn suspected the next phase of the invasion would only be a short time in coming. Trotting despite their fatigue, they hurried toward the Thane's Atrium which stood intact with several grim Hylar on guard outside the doors to the ceremonial chambers.

"Is my father the thane here?" asked Tarn.

"Aye. And he'll be glad to see you," replied the guard captain who stood aside to let them enter. The Aghar, meanwhile, willingly took up positions with the guards outside the atrium, though the Hylar sentries seemed less than thrilled at the these grubby reinforcements.

Belicia and Tarn started down the wide hall at a trot, not noticing at first that Regal Everwise had tagged along. They raced toward the large office where Baker had spent most of his time. Even before they got there, two elder dwarves emerged, shouting aloud in astonishment and relief.

"Father!" cried Belicia, stumbling into the welcoming embrace of Axel Slateshoulder. The old warrior's eyes were shut, but they leaked streams of tears.

"Tarn! My son, you're alive!" Baker's eyes were moist as well, but his features were chiseled, hardened in a way

Douglas Niles

Tarn had never seen. His father's glasses were missing, but he was alert and clearly overjoyed. "My son!" he repeated, as if he couldn't believe the evidence before him.

Tarn clasped his father in a warm hug. "By Reorx, Father, I'm glad to see you. And I'm sorry!"

"Me, too—but enough of that. There's been too much sorrow."

"But our city . . . it's dying!" Tarn declared despairingly as he broke free from his father's embrace. He halted, dimly realizing that only days before he had been ready to turn his back on the Life-Tree and all things Hylar. How long ago had it been? He didn't know, couldn't even begin to reckon. If anything, the recollections seemed like a memory from another epoch.

"I'm afraid you're right," the thane concurred sadly. "We're encouraging the survivors to move upward to the highest levels of the city, but I don't know what else we can do. We could fight the dark dwarves alone—but with the army of Chaos? I fear they are too much for us."

"But Father, listen. I have this!" Tarn declared, pulling the Helm of Tongues from the bag. "In Daerforge I watched Mother use it to control the creature who rides the fire dragon."

Baker's eyes lit up at the sight of the artifact, but then he shook his head as he looked at Tarn. "I don't think so, not with this. At most, the creature was toying with her, perhaps attracted by the magic of the artifact. No, no. She could perhaps communicate, but never control. But tell me, what did you see?"

Tarn described the scene he had observed on the balcony of Garimeth's Daerforge manor house. "I swear the daemon bowed to her! And after that he left them alone, unharmed, and then flew away when Mother gestured with her hand."

"I see why you would think it was influenced by Garimeth, but that story doesn't shake my certainty that such a daemon creature would never allow itself to be controlled by a mortal being. These dark and shadowy manifestations come from Chaos, we know that now. And Chaos cannot be commanded or disciplined. I'm afraid this daemon creature was merely having fun at Garimeth's expense and doing just what it intended all along."

"Then you can't use it to stop the attack?"

Sighing, Baker shook his head. "Certainly not." He brightened again almost immediately. "However, there is something that it might be able to do to help!"

"What?"

"Come here, my son. I have something to show you!" urged Baker, his tone surprisingly enthusiastic.

Inside the Thane's Atrium there was a litter of scroll tubes and parchment, scrolls that had been tossed and thrown everywhere around the large room. Tarn was startled, recognizing these as the treasures that his father had valued above all others. And now some of them were torn while others lay unnoticed on the floor.

Absently Tarn took note of the wall beyond that had once displayed an array of great artifacts and weaponry from Hylar history. Now that surface had been picked clean of all the blades except for a single, long-hafted battle axe; undoubtedly the other weapons had gone toward the city's desperate defense.

The great stone chair, the throne of the Hylar thane, sat like a useless weight next to the wall. The seat was buried in scrolls and parchments, documents piled haphazardly there as everywhere else in the room.

"Remember something I told you, Son? You know the legend, that some portion of the Graygem's power was imprisoned in a platinum dragon egg and left in the Grotto?"

"Yes." Tarn remembered something about that, though he had dismissed it as part of his father's impractical daydreaming.

"This is the next part!" Baker was saying, waving one of

the sheets of parchment. "These are the oldest of Chisel Loremaster's scrolls. And you can see there is arcane script right here!"

"Yes, but again I ask: what does that mean?" asked Tarn.

"The Grotto, my boy! The Grotto!" explained the thane as if it was the happiest discovery in the world. He indicated a small circle on the page, a roundel that was marked with a small dash at the bottom. "This is the symbol right here. I just translated it!"

Tarn felt as though he'd been kicked in the stomach. He physically forced down the urge to take his father by the shoulders, to shake some practical sense into him. Instead, the son merely nodded sadly, wondering what possible usefulness his father saw in the ancient cavern—especially now, in the midst of this historic crisis, even if it was true that finally he had found a way to locate it.

"I've been wrestling with the rest of the translation for too long; it's beyond my poor talents. Now, with the Helm, I'll be able to read it."

"I suppose you will," Tarn answered absently. He felt completely, utterly defeated. There would be no help from the artifact, no help from any source.

Baker pulled the Helm of Tongues over his head and picked up the ivory scroll tube. He squinted, then beamed excitedly.

"Yes! Yes! I was right! It's here—the key to the Grotto! I know what it means! And what's more, I know how to find it!"

Bloodcurdling shrieks pierced the air from outside the throne room. The thick stone of the floor shuddered underfoot, trembling repeatedly from the thud of great weight. The chamber was rocked by a savage roar, a sound of physical force that battered Tarn's eardrums and nearly drove him to his knees. The thunderous bellow was followed by the sound of a powerful crash. Dust and plaster broke from the ceiling to shower across the throne room.

Abruptly a crack shot through the great wall and pieces of stone tumbled free, toppling onto the sturdy floor. Another part of the wall started to lean inward, sending the dwarves scrambling toward the far side of the chamber. As more of the barrier broke down, Tarn caught sight of a black body, eyes of fiery crimson that transfixed him through the smoke and the dust. An obsidian fist pummeled the stones, smashing a wide opening. The figure of the daemon warrior, surprisingly manlike in its purposeful stride, advanced into the room. The black head tilted back, and the mouth uttered a roar of bizarre laughter.

Axel was already moving, broadsword raised in both of his hands. He swung the weapon at the daemon warrior's chest, but the fell creature grabbed the blade and, with a wrenching twist, snapped it like a toy. A casual backhand slap sent the venerable warrior tumbling across the floor. Again came that horribly incongruous laugh.

Then the figure changed, shifting and growing before the dwarves' astonished eyes. The daemon rose into a great shape, a huge shadowy form that writhed at the edge of the throne room. Two Hylar guards charged through the hole in the wall, trying to attack it from behind, but the creature merely leaned down and tore them apart as casually as if it had been rending a piece of parchment.

Now the beast of Chaos loomed above their heads, fleshless jaws gaping to reveal teeth the size of knife blades. Wings bare of skin or any other membrane spread wide, supported by bones of stark white. Skeletal ribs outlined a massive body, and strips of rotted flesh draped those bones in a gory bunting. The monster had massive talons, great fangs, and all these instruments of death were crimson with Hylar blood.

"Try the helm!" shouted Tarn, turning to see that Baker still wore the artifact. "At least see if you can make it respond!"

"Halt!" cried the thane, his tone bold and full of command.

But the monster took a few steps forward and reached for Baker Whitegranite with talons of sharp bone. The thane stood still, his face white, teeth clenched as if fending off an onslaught of great pain. Tarn grabbed his father and frantically pulled him behind the throne as the monster's claws slashed through the air where Baker had been standing.

Baker gasped in agony as he tore the bronze helmet off of his head. With a groan, he clapped a hand to his sweaty forehead. "That thing was in my mind searching, trying to destroy. It would have killed me!"

Tarn drew the silver sword he had taken from the assassin, feeling as though the weapon was no more than a toothpick in his hand.

"Get out of here! All of you, flee!" cried Axel, pushing Belicia out the door. He grabbed Baker, who was still clutching the scroll and the helmet, and shoved him too. "Use what you learned! You'll know what to do!"

The monster roared, fetid breath reeking like death through the vast chamber. The taloned foot set down heavily, and the floor shook as if under the compression of a monstrous weight.

Tarn, sword in his hand, ran to Axel's side as the older warrior pulled the huge axe down from the wall. The elder's face had a martial gleam, a gleeful battle-fury brightening his eyes. He pushed his horned helmet down tightly onto his scalp, raised the long weapon, and all but growled at the hideous creature.

"I'll try to distract it, draw its attention over here!" shouted the half-breed. "You can get after it from behind!"

With another roar, the monster advanced a step closer. Dust rose in clouds from the floor as the thunderous crash of its footstep caused cracks to shoot through the walls and spiderweb up the walls. The beast took another step and a beam across the ceiling cracked, bending downward with a piercing shriek.

"No!" cried Axel, staring at Tarn, his face crazily

distorted. The great axe, taller by far than the Hylar warrior, gleamed brightly in his hands. "You stay with my daughter and your father! They will need you!"

"But—"

"Do it!" snarled the elder in a voice that brooked no argument.

Tarn backed to the door, as Axel, with the massive axe in his hands, advanced to battle the beast of Chaos. Again it bellowed, darting forward, then pausing.

The axe swung through the air, a dazzling display of silvery light.

And then the roars of the beast rose to a stone-shaking crescendo, echoing in Tarn's ears as he urged Baker, Belicia, and Regal to go and go fast.

Chapter Twenty-seven

Belicia and Baker halted in horror as soon as they burst through the outer gates of the thane's quarters. Tarn and Regal, hurrying after, bumped into the pair and then they, too, froze in shock and grief.

Where they had left the guards outside they saw only a mess of blood and scattered lumps of debris. With a groan of horrified dismay, Tarn realized that these lumps were the remains of dwarves, torn and rent by a force almost beyond comprehension. He saw the upper half of the captain of the guard, the brave Hylar's eyes glazed but wide open, his teeth clenched and sword grasped in the lifeless fingers of his hands.

"This was Capper Whetstone," said Baker, kneeling and reverently closing the sightlessly staring eyes.

Even the Aghar had been mauled. Regal sniffed loudly

as he looked at the remains of his companions. All the gully dwarves who had stayed here with the Hylar guards had been reduced to ragged bundles, bloody and still.

A savage roar emanated from the throne room, and more crashes shook the air. Through the din they heard the battle cry of a charging Hylar and knew that Axel Slateshoulders still fought.

Belicia looked back toward the throne room. "You go ahead," she said quietly. "I'll catch up."

Tarn gently put his hand on her shoulder. "Come with us now," he said softly. "There's nothing more to be done for him and every second is precious. You know that's what he wanted."

Shaking her head, tears streaming from her eyes, Belicia nevertheless followed his suggestion. The four of them fled the carnage, jogging down the street. Now even the fleeing dwarves were gone, leaving Level Ten with the air of a long abandoned ruin. In fact, to all appearances the place was utterly deserted of living inhabitants. Limp corpses lay like rag dolls in the street. The route of the great fire dragon was a clear path of melted rock, shattered gardens, and gory pieces of bodies.

Tarn started toward one of the main stairwells connecting this level to those above and below, but a block away from the place they heard shouts of barking dark dwarf sergeants and the sounds of many tramping bootsteps.

"Daergar!" hissed the half-breed in warning. "They're coming this way!"

"The dark dwarves are this high already?" Belicia asked in despair.

The party scuttled around a corner, crouching in the shadows as they watched rank after rank of their enemies charge through the streets. Some of the Daergar moved into a nearby stairwell and continued the upward charge through the Life-Tree.

"We have to find a better route so we can go all the way up to Level Twenty-eight," Baker said. "That's where we have to go. It's what I learned from the writing on the scroll!"

"You think one more clue is going to lead you to the Grotto?" Tarn asked, trying to contain his exasperation.

"I know it will," his father replied.

"And then what?" The younger dwarf's patience was frayed beyond reason. "What will we do besides see it once before it is destroyed?"

"Trust me. There is hope, there. Our only hope."

Tarn bit his tongue. He didn't see how finding the ancient lair of the good dragons was going to have any practical effect. Still, his own instincts suggested that they needed to climb. If this faerie quest gave his father motivation to attempt an ascent involving thousands of steep steps, then that was good enough for Tarn.

They darted down a side street and ran along a darkened, narrow byway. The buildings to either side were empty, dark, and abandoned though they hadn't yet been ransacked or destroyed.

Still moving at a fast trot, Tarn found himself in a section that was unfamiliar to him. The roads were narrow and winding here, with tiny alleys connecting blocks of buildings in unpredictable ways. Houses were small, with entries that were low and rounded, almost like burrows.

"Look! Aghar tunnels!" Regal cried in sudden delight.

"Come to think of it, there always were a lot of gully dwarves in this part of town," Baker noted.

"Where are they now?" Tarn asked. The alleys and slumlike dwellings seemed as empty and abandoned as every other part of this level. He hoped that, like the Hylar, the gully dwarves had the good sense to keep on climbing.

"Who cares?" Regal asked. "They got lotsa tunnels. We find a way up."

"Where? Show us the way!" said Baker, with a surprising amount of eagerness.

"Smells like people go this way," Regal declared cheerily, dropping to his hands and knees and crawling into a low hole in the side of the wall. "Goes up, too!" he called back as his feet disappeared from sight.

"Do you think you can make it?" Tarn asked his father, noticing for the first time the signs of Baker's age, the bleary eyes, the lines of fatigue and grief etched into the elder dwarf's face. Tarn questioned the wisdom of taking a tunnel used by gully dwarves. He didn't know if there was any way that Baker Whitegranite would have the strength and endurance to get through a constricted, steeply climbing passage.

"We don't have any choice," Baker declared. The thane stood straight, and Tarn saw that his father's eyes were in fact glinting with determination, even if they lacked a little focus. "I have learned I might be a little stronger than I look."

No sooner had Tarn entered the tunnel than he heard the presence of marching dark dwarves, hundreds of them to judge by the sound, pillaging through the avenues and passages of Level Ten. These warriors were even ransacking the rude hovels of the Aghar, perhaps because the fire dragons had destroyed virtually everything else of value. He took some grim satisfaction as several Daergar, to judge from the sound of their screams, apparently stumbled onto one of the rampaging, flaming serpents. But when the smell of burned flesh reached him, he could find no solace even in the deaths of his enemies.

He crawled after, just behind Belicia's boots, moving as quickly as he could. Before too long he found the others gathered in a small, circular chamber regarding several narrow passages that offered different routes.

"We should take the biggest," Tarn suggested, pointing to a tunnel that actually had stairs carved into the rocks.

"Not there," Regal replied with a firm shake of his head. "Smells like dark dwarves up ahead."

"Thanks for the warning," Tarn answered. "Which one do you suggest?" Though he couldn't smell anything unusual, he remembered that Regal's nose had enabled him to differentiate between the half-breed and the Daergar. He was unwilling to counter the Aghar's conviction.

"This way," Regal said, indicating the passage veering sharply to the right. "This best way."

Once again they plunged into a narrow passage, crawling upward on hands and knees. Tarn and the Aghar had no difficulty seeing, but he felt sympathy for Baker and Belicia, knowing that the two pure-blood Hylar were all but blind in such utter blackness. Neither of them complained, however. Slowly, steadily, the little group made its way upward.

Remembering the long journeys that had brought them to this point, Tarn was deeply saddened to realize that only Regal, Belicia, and his father remained from all their original companions. The doughty gully dwarf proved himself helpful again and again, smelling their enemies—dark dwarf or Chaos creatures—at each juncture in the winding progress of their upward passage. Always they found a way through, steadily continuing higher and higher through the dying city. At each level they looked into the streets and the vista was relentlessly unchanging: destruction and fire were everywhere. Smoke even seeped into the tunnels, though the vapors were never thick enough to choke them.

Tarn speculated that these winding, concealed passages must have been used all along by Aghar to get around the Life-Tree. It amazed him to think that there was such a network of tunnels that had existed entirely unsuspected in the midst of the Hylar city. He saw more clearly than ever how the little gully dwarves had managed not only to survive but to thrive amid the nations of their larger and more powerful cousins. He regretted again the hatred and prejudice that drove so many of Thorbadin's dwarves to despise and abuse the hapless squatters.

Some time later they all collapsed from exhaustion, uncertain how many levels they had climbed, knowing that the rack and ruin of the Life-Tree continued all around them. Utterly drained, they lay in a dark passageway, drinking a little water from a pool. Slowly, their gasps faded to more normal breathing. Unspeaking, they lay in numb silence, trying to let some of their fatigue melt away.

Belicia whimpered suddenly, and Tarn realized that she had fallen asleep. Gently he touched her. She sat upward with a jerk, crying out with a despair so deep that it tore Tarn's heart just to hear it.

"Don't," he consoled. "You're safe here, for now at least. I'm with you."

She cried softly, and finally sniffled and looked at him, her eyes bright in the near total darkness. "It came crashing down: tons of rock, falling all around me. Why did I live? What right did I have to survive when so many died?" she demanded.

Tarn said nothing, just pulled her against him. Firmly she pushed herself away.

"I don't know why I wasn't killed," she said. "I should have been. All my dwarves—Farran, Raggat—all of them: they're dead! Why was I the one to live?"

"They will have a legacy somehow," Tarn suggested awkwardly. "And you have to stay alive to make that happen."

"Aye, girl," Baker said. "He's right."

She talked of the courage displayed by her young company—the way they had stood at the docks and the stairways, the disbelief that had seized them all when the forces of Chaos had erupted into Thorbardin. The others let her talk, knowing that she needed to explain to herself as much as to them. Finally she breathed more easily, and they knew that she slept again. Tarn let himself drift off for a short time as well. He awoke to an awareness of movement around him.

"Are you ready?" Belicia asked softly. He grunted his assent.

Stiffly the thane got to his feet nearby. "I guess we'd better get going again."

For hour after hour they made their plodding way upward, passing through innumerable bleak, ruined levels of the Hylar city. Virtually all the dwarves had gone, either fleeing farther upward or already dead. The effects of the Chaos horde were everywhere. Whenever they passed a long transport shaft or connecting tunnel they heard the chants and pounding cadence of dark dwarves on the march.

Then they could climb no further. The tunnel emerged into the mushroom yard of one of the city's grand gardens. Dimly, Tarn recognized that they had climbed to Level Twenty-eight and had emerged fairly near to the quarter where his father had his house.

But his attention was quickly drawn away by his father, who indicated the nearby street.

"Here! This way!" said the thane.

Regal, Belicia, and Tarn hastened to keep up as Baker Whitegranite led the way down the avenue. They met a few frightened Hylar who Baker urged to keep climbing—to take to the tunnels in the ceiling that the Klar had used.

"Father, wait," cried Tarn, at last determined to speak his mind. "The Grotto's not going to help us. Our best bet is to keep on climbing, to do what you're telling these others and find a way out of the city."

Belicia added her own arguments. "Those tunnels in the ceiling are a good idea. We should go!"

Baker turned and looked at his son and the brave dwarfwoman. "It will be your turn, soon," he said. "But first—please—come with me. See what it is I have been seeking for all these years."

"There's still hope that we can escape!" Tarn replied, struggling to understand his father's irrational behavior.

But as he looked at his father, Tarn realized that the elder's dwarf's fatigue had melted away, his mood seemed positively bouyant. Baker was tall, clear-eyed, and stern. Tarn wanted to grab him, to slap him into some awareness of their situation, but he didn't have the heart. Instead, he listened as his father tried to explain.

"The Grotto—and the platinum egg, if it's there—is the only hope for any kind of survival for our people, for all of clan Hylar," Baker Whitegranite said in all sincerity. "That egg comes from the stuff of Chaos. It was said, by Chisel Loremaster himself, that a true ruler of the dwarves could release that power.

"If we were to flee, our enemies would continue to chase us. The ending would be the same. But these are beings of Chaos that are destroying our city. Doesn't it seem that they might be matched, even driven away, by that same power?"

"So we let them kill us in an ancient dragon lair instead?" demanded Tarn.

"I don't have time to explain further." Baker now stopped, and Tarn realized that they were in front of their own house. "I have to find that egg!"

"Come in here with me," said Baker Whitegranite. "If I'm guessing right, we'll want to head right down into the cellar."

Unwilling to argue, but feeling even more hopeless than before, Tarn felt that he had no choice except to follow.

A Queen of the Dark Dwarves

Chapter Twenty-eight

Pounce Quickspring stared through the dusty smoke, trying to find some semblance of order in the teeming mass of Theiwar. Everywhere dark dwarves choked the crowded corridors, a mass of attackers that should have carried through every vestige of resistance. They had pushed and charged, followed the daemon warrior and killed the Hylar. By rights, the dark dwarves should have been approaching their moment of ultimate conquest.

But instead they were stuck here, pinned so tightly that the Theiwar had turned against each other, dwarf killing dwarf in an effort to make a little breathing room. The Daergar of Darkend Bellowsmoke had taken a different route, vanishing into the maze of this dying city. For once Pounce longed for word from his allies, for some sense of how the other dark dwarf clan fared. But there was nothing but this press of Theiwar, an attacking wedge that had somehow compressed itself into this narrow passageway.

The spellcasters among the Theiwar clan had exhausted their magic. A few of the arcane dwarves had vanished, using what spells they possessed in order to disappear. Others stared wildly around, eyes bright and mouths wide as they neared a state of frenzied panic. Weapons flashed here and there as the anxious warriors were quick to use violence against each other.

The blaze began at one end of the choked tunnel, a crimson wash of heat that blistered even from such a distance. The brightness was already painful, an assault against the dark-tuned eyes of the Theiwar. As it grew brighter, the light became heat, and the nervous fear grew to a mind-numbing terror.

When the dragon roared closer still, the intense heat seared through flesh and melted armor. Dark dwarves screamed and burned as they died, the stink of charred flesh spreading down the corridor and preceding the killing serpent by a mere fraction of a second. The monstrous, flaming creature flew down the narrow corridor over the heads of the Theiwar, rushing along like an explosive fireball that destroyed everything in its path.

Pounce Quickspring shrilled his cry of hatred, watching the death of his army until the flames embraced him.

In that grip of fire he perished.

* * * * *

"How many more of these stairs are we going to have to climb?" demanded Darkend as he slumped against the stone wall in an effort to draw several ragged gasps of breath. Behind him the legion of dark dwarves paused, taking advantage of their leader's fatigue to get some much needed rest for themselves.

"No more than five hundred; we're almost there," Garimeth said, infuriated with his all-too-visible fatigue.

Couldn't he see? Didn't he understand? "We've got to keep moving! We don't have any other choice!"

In truth, Garimeth was more than angry. She was utterly terrified. Would the daemon warrior even notice her, much less hear her, now that she had lost the bronze artifact? She almost wailed aloud at the memory, the image of the Helm of Tongues stolen by a gully dwarf who had somehow tripped her and snatched it off her head. The thought still caused her to tremble with deep, abiding fear.

What if she did find Zarak Thuul, only to discover that he no longer knew who she was? She refused to let herself consider that possibility. Perhaps the helmet had enabled her to attract his attention, but surely they had established a bond that would not be sundered merely by the absence of a piece of metal, however arcane!

"Just keep climbing if you want to see anything left of your conquest. We have to get above Zarak Thuul to meet him before he destroys everything."

"As if there's any chance of that!" muttered Darkend.

She agonized over the deeper questions that she dared not voice aloud, questions that nevertheless were constantly whispering in her mind. Would the daemon warrior want her, even speak to her now that she did not wear the artifact of House Whitegranite?

In their wake came Slickblade and dozens of armored Daergar warriors, the elite cadre of Darkend's palace guard. The assassin muttered something to the thane, and Garimeth whirled under an onslaught of fresh suspicion.

"What is it?" she demanded.

"Slickblade suggests again that you betrayed me, and that you now betray us all," Darkend said coolly. "I am wondering if he is right."

"He's a fool who's afraid for his own life," Garimeth retorted sharply. She allowed herself a hint of a smile, pleased with the self control that allowed her to mask her deepest doubts. The assassin was terrifyingly vague behind his mask, and she wanted nothing more than to kill him right now. "Remember, it was he who lied to you in Daerforge."

"Don't listen to her!" barked the assassin. "I tell you, lord, she is not to be trusted!"

"Thus speaks the failed killer, failed bodyguard!" she spat back, turning her back contemptuously to resume the climb.

After a few more steps she stopped and whirled back accusingly. "How could you let your master be attacked by a half-breed and a mob of Aghar?" She demanded scornfully, then fixed her purple eyes on Darkend. "And even then he let my son escape. I ask you, Brother: who is the traitor?"

"Enough! Keep going!" commanded the thane.

On one level they emerged from the stairs to seek water and rest their weary muscles. Here they found a whole rank of Daergar armor and weapons. The clutter of black metal had been cast across the street where the shadow-wights had claimed the flesh of the dark dwarf warriors. They saw movement, black and soundless forms slinking toward them from the alleys and streets of this level. The thane's party hastened back to the stairwell, preferring the interminable climb to battle with an apparently unstoppable foe.

"They've been everywhere. This is no conquest I am leading; we are merely the caretakers of disaster," Darkend moaned, utterly despairing.

Garimeth only kept climbing, step after endless step. Where was Zarak Thuul? Would he come? She didn't know, but understood that if he didn't, she would have no reason to continue living.

"This is it," she finally announced after an interminable interval.

The dark dwarves' legs were numb. The exhausted party all but stumbled as they emerged onto the wide avenue of Hybardin's Level Twenty-eight. Everywhere was silence and death.

"We're too late!" cried the female, looking up and down the street with a groan of despair. Where was he? Would he come to her? He must!

"My city! My splendid conquest! It's a ruin!" wailed Darkend, miserable at the knowledge of the lost riches, the treasures, the secrets, the potential slaves, all of it had vanished with the tide of Chaos.

Everywhere smoke swirled and broken rock littered the roadways and gardens. Dead dwarves—Hylar and Klar in equal numbers—were all over. An eerie silence filled the air with a sense of impending disaster. More and more frequently they found no bodies—only clothes, or armor and weapons scattered on the street where the owners had been sucked into nothingness. The shadows seemed to display no preference, sucking the lives of Hylar and dark dwarves with indiscriminate hunger.

"Follow me!" Garimeth somehow found the strength to run. She lurched weakly through the littered streets, turning down a side lane after she paused for a moment as if to make certain of where she was.

"Where is he? Zarak Thuul?" she cried.

Darkend stumbled along behind as they emerged into a large square where two wide streets came together.

"I used to live down there." Garimeth pointed down the street and frowned as she saw the front of Baker Whitegranite's house still standing.

"Never mind that. Where are we going? Where is Zarak Thuul?"

The Daergar gathered around the murky waters of a half-filled basin, looking, questioning, waiting for a decision.

"This was once a reflector pool," Garimeth said scornfully, though Darkend found it hard to imagine anything mirrored in the dark, sludgy liquid. "A watery trinket, kept for mere ornament."

"An utter waste!" declared the dark dwarf thane.

"And now it seems my husband hasn't tended to his

city in my absence," she added with a twisted grin. "He has failed without me. He needed me in ways that I never needed him!"

"Forget that! We have to find Zarak Thuul!" demanded Darkend.

"Sire, could it be that she doesn't want you find him?" suggested Slickblade.

"That's ridiculous!" Garimeth was strangely terrified of the notion that she would never see the daemon warrior again. "I—we have to find him!"

"Do we?" the assassin questioned, his eyes shining through the slit of his black cloak. "I say to you, my lord, that you have trusted her too much."

"Aye, perhaps I have let myself be fooled," Darkend Bellowsmoke declared, swinging his mace free from his belt. "Kneel, Sister."

"Allow me to strike the blow, my lord," declared Slickblade eagerly.

"No, she is my sister," the thane said solemnly. "I will do the killing!"

"But I did not betray you!" Garimeth moaned, sinking to her knees, looking up, pleading. "You saw with your own eyes. Zarak Thuul worked my will. I know he will help us again!"

Darkend raised his mace, his tusked helm stark and frightening as he stared down at his sister. With a sudden gesture, he whirled and brought the weapon down on Slickblade's head.

The assassin fell, killed instantly. The rest of the Daergar warriors gasped softly, astonished by the dire turnabout.

"Let that be the end of his whispering," the thane observed coolly. "He forgot that whispered words, like a snake held by the tail, can turn on the whisperer."

The dwarfwoman didn't pause to reflect on her miraculous survival. Instead, she rose and gestured to the house. "You have made the right decision as always, brother. I am grateful. Come with me."

In her mind was a thought. Perhaps Tarn had brought the helm here and delivered it to Baker. She could try to reason with her son. Surely Tarn would understand why she needed it so badly!

She went to the large wooden door, but found it locked. No one answered in response to her violent pounding, so Darkend ordered several of his warriors to smash in the portal. Soon the party entered the house, kicking through the debris left by the broken door and stalking through the hallways and rooms beyond.

"There's no one here," Garimeth said anxiously.

She started down a hallway but halted abruptly as they heard a deep growling outside the house. They hastened back to the doorway, looking out to see a haze of fire roaring through the street.

"Primus!" she cried, as the fire dragon halted before them, furling his flaming wings.

A tall, dark form stalked forward, emerging from the bright background to loom before the two Daergar. The daemon warrior's eyes glowed, sparks of impersonal fire that flickered from one dark dwarf to the other.

"Zarak Thuul! We have found you!" cried Darkend triumphantly. He turned importantly to his sister. "Tell our great servant—our friend—that the attack is finished and we are very grateful for his help. But tell him he must wait, must hold any further attack until my dwarves have had a chance to consolidate our occupation."

"Please accept our humble gratitude," she began, looking into those feral eyes of fire, seeking some hint of the previous pleasures that had flickered there before. "And please know me, remember me, hear me, all-powerful one."

"Of course I hear you. I have always heard you. But I see you now with different eyes, and I think that you no longer entertain me." The daemon warrior's reply had come in perfect mountain dwarven, right down to the tone of insolent contempt.

"Zarak Thuul, look at me, know me!" Garimeth protested, throwing herself on the ground before the monstrous black being and reaching out her hands. She dared to touch the massive, taloned feet. "Please, grant me your favor once more."

"I shall do one thing for you, dwarfwoman. Rise."

Slowly, tremulously, she lifted herself to her knees, then stood staring upward at the immaculate beauty of his dark form. She thrilled as those fiery eyes dropped to regard her, shivered as that consuming gaze once again washed over her flesh.

"I am yours, mighty lord!" she cried, throwing her arms wide, offering herself willingly to this creature of Chaos.

"It pleases me to touch you again, to give you the stroke of my greatness." Zarak Thuul flicked a great claw, slicing into Garimeth's neck.

"I don't understand!" she cried, stumbling back, recoiling more from disappointment than from the force of the blow. Her vision blurred, light swam before her eyes, and she looked down in disbelief, watching as her lifeblood spilled into the street before Baker Whitegranite's house.

Interlude of Chaos

What did I ever see in that insect? Zarak Thuul was angry at the dwarfwoman and angry at himself for allowing himself to be deceived, to think that she was something mightier than she really had been. Without that strange helmet, she was pathetic— a silly mortal like all the rest.

Then Zarak Thuul threw back his head and laughed, knowing the deception didn't matter, that nothing mattered. And now it was time to finish this dwarven city and proceed to all the other cities of Thorbardin, to reduce them to rubble.

In truth, the female had been an interesting diversion, nothing more. She had intrigued him for a time, and it had pleased him to do the work that she desired. Something about her had touched him briefly, but that was gone. Instead, she had been proved feeble, just as utterly useless as any other mortal.

And now his power would be truly unleashed. This realm of dwarves would suffer as it had never suffered before. There was much for him to do, and he would continue until all this realm of shadow was reduced to a place of death, horror, chaos.

The Grotto

Chapter 29

"It feels like solid rock." Tarn said, stepping back from the wall with the hilt of his sword still humming in his hand. "There's no hollow sound."

"Get a hammer," his father said without hesitation. "This is the place where the waters of the light garden are born. I ought to know that well enough!"

"What does that mean?" asked the son, still unsure of Baker Whitegranite's intentions.

"The words on the scroll told me to seek the Grotto where the waters of light were born! It's the fountain in my own garden! Don't you see?"

Tarn saw the connection, though he still wondered how they could break through such a thick wall of stone. Still, the half-breed went down to the cellar hallway and into his father's small smithy—a standard fixture in most dwarf homes. In seconds he returned with a large hammer.

A solid swing smashed into the stone wall and Tarn—who had braced himself for the recoil—nearly tumbled forward as the hammer punched right through. Pulling it back, he pounded several more times, quickly opening a hole big enough for a dwarf's head.

"Keep going," Baker urged quietly. "Make it big enough that we can crawl through and get in there."

In another minute Tarn had worked up a sheen of sweat and the hole leading into darkness was roughly three feet in diameter. Stale air wafted out, and he speculated that this was a chamber that hadn't been opened to the outside for many thousands of years.

Baker was eager to advance, ducking and pushing his way through the opening to land with an "oof." In moments Tarn, Belica, and Regal had followed. They found themselves perched atop a slope of rubble at the base of the wall in a suprisingly large chamber. They scrambled down to join the thane on the floor. Tarn looked up to see a ceiling, studded with jagged stalactites, that arched high over their heads.

"It was here that it began thousands and thousands of years ago."

Baker spoke softly, his eyes bright with emotion. The thane of the Hylar looked around slowly, reverently, as he paced the circumference of the circular cavern. Tarn was vaguely aware of soft light, and he realized that a glow was emanating from the top of a mound near the chamber's center.

"The good dragons were here in the Age of Dreams. Here they hatched and grew and learned from Chisel Loremaster."

"Wait," Tarn interrupted. "Chisel was a dwarf, you said. And there were no dwarves during the Age of Dreams, were there?"

But his father wasn't listening. Instead, he bustled

around exclaiming about this, whistling in amazement as he searched the chamber.

To Tarn, except for the gentle illumination, the cave looked unremarkable, an ordinary hollow in the limestone rock that probably had been forged by water. Once it had been slick with moisture. Perhaps this dusty rock had once been crystalline and bright, but now it was old and mummified—dead.

"It's odd to think that it was under your house all along," Belicia observed.

"Not really," Baker replied. "In fact, I've long deduced that it was somewhere around here. That's one reason I chose to live in this quarter of Level Twenty-eight. And yet we never would have suspected where exactly. I believe there is a reason Reorx has revealed this to me now."

"Why didn't the wall sound hollow?" Tarn wondered.

"I assume that's part of the ancient protection of this place: a magical enchantment. This was once the lair of wondrous dragons, you know—great beasts of powerful magic and even a scion. It was sealed so that it wouldn't be discovered until the right time—until now."

Tarn looked skeptical. He still wondered what use this place could be now, but his father was too moved for him to interrupt. For Baker Whitegranite, this was the culmination of a lifetime's searching.

Instead, it was Regal who spoke up. "What's this stuff about a scion?"

Baker smiled. "All wise, he was, the recorder of our dwarven lore. The records call him Chisel Loremaster. He wrote the greatest histories of our race. But I have a theory: I don't think he was a dwarf. No. I believe he was one of the ageless wise ones of the sort that have ever lurked around the fringes of Krynn's history."

"Uh-huh. No doubt," Regal replied modestly. "Though I prefer to think of him as 'Ever Wise.'"

"Wait. Regal?" Tarn asked, alerted to a sudden change in the gully dwarf's manner. All of a sudden the Aghar didn't look so filthy, so plump, nor so ill-mannered. All of a sudden, he looked solemn, and maybe even wise. "Hey, what's happening?"

"Huh?" Regal asked, picking his nose. "To me?"

"It's you! The chronicler of the dwarves!" gasped Baker. "You're Chisel Loremaster!"

"Again, correct," replied the diminutive Regal, who suddenly transformed into clothes that, if not fine, were at least well cut, nicely adorned, and neatly maintained.

"The honor of this moment . . . I can't explain." The thane tried to speak, but Regal made a deprecating gesture with his hand. Tarn looked on with mouth agape.

"However, there is a job to do, if you are ready," the gully dwarf scion said.

"Yes, of course. The egg. Now, let's see. This was the nest—it must have been," Baker said, suddenly animated as he moved toward the large mound in the center of the large cavern. The white light was rising from an unseen source atop this domed shape. Tarn and Belicia followed, a little dazed.

"The young dragons were born in there?" asked Tarn, his head still whirling. Scions were beings of legend. In fact, most inhabitants of Krynn had never heard of the ancient race.

"Yes. Darlantan, Aurican—all their nestmates," Regal—or Chisel—explained. "And I happen to know that they left behind a single, significant artifact."

Tarn, Baker, and Belicia scrambled up the sides of the nest. Tarn saw that, despite the coating of dust and dirt, the nest was actually woven of metal wire. He cut himself on a sharp rock that was embedded in the metallic surface and was startled to see the facets of a huge ruby. All over the nest was studded with these fine jewels. But he didn't stop to explore, instead he climbed higher until he could join the others in looking into the bowl-shaped basket from the top.

The object inside was spherical, larger than a dragon

egg. It glowed and was covered with a sheen of pale silver–platinum.

"The Platinum Egg," said Regal solemnly. "Or The Silver Dragon Sphere. Whichever. Very powerful. Very dangerous."

"Father, what do we do now?" Tarn asked nervously.

Baker turned to his son and there were tears in the elder dwarf's eyes, a curious mixture of elation and sadness pouring from his face.

"Now that we have located the Grotto, found the Platinum Egg? And now that you have seen it too? My son, it's time for you and Belicia to go. I will stay here, for there remains only one thing for me to do."

"We've all got to go!" Tarn insisted.

"No. I'm afraid there's no time to explain. Now, you and Belicia must find your way into the ceiling above Level Twenty-eight, find one of the tunnels the Klar used when they attacked us here."

"Yes, but you—"

"No!" The thane spoke sternly. "This is one time you must obey me!"

Helplessly, Tarn looked at Regal.

"Your father is right," declared his diminutive companion. "It is written: the power of the Grotto will awaken when a true ruler of the dwarves takes the Platinum Egg in hand. And Baker understands—he has proven himself a fine leader and warrior, but he is also a great scholar. This is the power of the Graygem, the power that gave birth to Chaos."

"The true ruler of dwarves is me!" declared Darkend Bellowsmoke as he emerged from the hole in the wall. Several Daergar followed close behind him. The thane wore his black armor with the tusks jutting from his face plate and held a wickedly spiked mace in his gloved hands. Fierce and warlike, he glared around the sacred chamber. "You made a lot of racket with your pounding," he sneered. "Don't you know there are enemies nearby?"

More Daergar spilled into the Grotto, and now they stood in a line along the far wall. Several had crossbows, and these were held unwaveringly upon the four dwarves in the center of the cavern.

"Take aim," said Darkend Bellowsmoke. The thane of the Daergar spoke to his victims calmly. "Now, do you wish to die quickly, or would you prefer to writhe in excess pain?"

He advanced toward the nest. "A platinum egg of great power for the true ruler of the dwarves?" Darkend all but cackled. "Perfect timing! I will take the egg, and my conquest shall be redeemed!"

War's End

Chapter Thirty

Tarn tensed, ready to make a leap at Darkend, but Belicia's hand on his arm restrained him. The thane of the dark dwarves scrambled into the nest while Baker and Regal stood helpless off to the side.

"This is a bauble of some size. But what are its hidden powers? Let me see."

Darkend siezed the egg and then screamed in such agony that the others fell back as a sudden light pulsed brightly from within his body. Darkend flopped and gasped, pulled and twisted, doing every thing he could to break his grip on the Platinum Egg, but he seemed glued to the stone. His hair stood on end; his mouth worked noiselessly. No sound emerged, but a beam of white, pure light suddenly flashed from the depths of his mortal coil.

The others could only watch as his skin began to burn.

He screamed in unspeakable agony for minutes.

The Daergar warriors didn't wait to see the end. Every one of them fled back through the hole in the wall of the Grotto, running without a backward glance. Finally Darkend simply shimmered and burst, his armor, mace, and body all vanishing without a trace.

"A false leader of dwarves, that one," Regal murmured dryly, after a long silence.

"Perhaps I should give it a try," Baker said, tentatively stepping around the residue of ashes that was all that was left of his rival.

"Father, don't! You saw what happened!" Tarn said.

"Listen to me, my son. I must try. And you must do as I commanded you. Right now. It is our only chance, the only chance to stop Chaos from destroying Thorbardin forever."

The half-breed was silent, miserably afraid but compelled to agree.

"Go! Take Belicia, the Hylar, and all the Aghar you can quickly find! But get out of here as fast as possible!"

"But—" began Tarn. He stepped closer to his father, spread his hands helplessly. "Come with us! Don't do this. You don't have to do this."

"But I must. I am the last thane. Son, it is time for our paths to part. You must understand this!"

"Your father is right," Regal, who was also Chisel Loremaster said calmly. "Now, go—and quickly! The power of the ancients will be released if your father is successful. And you must be gone!"

"Go upward, out of Thorbardin," Baker commanded his son. The thane turned his attention to Belicia. "Take care, my child, and know that your father was very brave and very proud of you."

"And I was . . . am proud of him," Belicia said through her tears.

"You!" She took Tarn by the arm. "Listen to your father!"

Dumbly he followed her as they climbed down from the nest, crossed the cavern, and climbed toward the hole in the wall of the Grotto.

Baker and Regal watched Tarn and his woman depart.

"You're doing the right thing," Regal said, patting the thane on the back.

"I know." The thane of the Hylar sighed. It seemed to Baker that his whole life had been building toward this moment.

"Tell me, how did you learn the last lesson?" asked the gully dwarf who was really a scion of the ages.

"It was in my readings, the scrolls left by Chisel Loremas—by yourself," Baker explained softly. He looked around at the Grotto and imagined the great stalactite outside. "The power of the Graygem in this egg is the raw power of Chaos."

"Aye, it is."

"And only that power can match the forces that beset our realm. Only Chaos can reach out to destroy Chaos."

Baker Whitegranite took the Platinum Egg, placed his hands carefully, lightly upon it, his eyes unwavering.

He pictured the great stalactite around him, the shaft of stone that had been suspended here for more than ten thousand years. Perhaps he should have been feeling fear or sadness, but he remained strangely peaceful. His thoughts tinged with melancholy as he remembered the deaths, the suffering, the killing that had been the legacy of his time in the thane's chair.

And he knew that the saga was not complete.

"Do you think they have reached safety?" asked Baker Whitegranite.

"I know they have," Regal replied.

"Reorx forgive me, it is the will of Paladine himself." He murmured a soft prayer and felt the peaceful presence of his god, of the god who watched over all dwarvenkind.

As his grip slowly tightened, he felt the egg of platinum rotate smoothly in its socket. Light welled up, a soothing and cool light that embraced Baker Whitegranite and spread through the Grotto, seeping into the solid stone beyond.

Then it began, first as a slight tremor, a wobbling in the floor, in the walls, in the very air. Cracks spiderwebbed through the walls, and pieces of stone began to break loose and topple from the ceiling.

Brilliant white light burst from the egg, shining from the rock, from Baker himself. Yet he felt somehow outside of the experience, watching proudly as if from a distance, cherishing this moment, this place, his people.

And he became the light, streaming outward, rushing through the rock of the Life-Tree.

Wherever that light touched, the shadows of Chaos ceased to exist, wisping back to the nothingness that was their origin. Fire dragons sizzled to ashes; slithering creatures spasmed and vanished.

Where dwarves lay wounded or cowering in terror the light caressed them, and as they died the folk of the undermountain felt the tender embrace of their god.

The light rained downward, streaming through all the levels of the great city, probing into each ruined chamber, seeking, finding the beings of Chaos wherever they tried to hide. It found the suffering dwarves as well and carried them away more gently.

In the air over the Urkhan Sea, Zarak Thuul was shocked by the first wave of light. He emitted a long, tortured wail, screaming his defiance. The power of the light seared his flesh and burned hotter even than the fires of his eyes. The daemon warrior writhed under the onslaught of that magical assault, shaking his fists, howling in fury as the power of Chaos tore at him and drove him down, surrounding him and quenching his power. Primus, too, cried in surreal pain. The white light embraced the fire dragon, drowning the brightness of his pure flame and tearing him into shreds of chaos that settled toward the lake waters in a flurry of dying sparks.

The daemon warrior tumbled through space, still howling, striking out against nothing and everything as the power of the platinum artifact swept him away. The dark waters of the lake were all around him. And then they were gone. Still the magic drove him, smashing and pounding, irresistible and overwhelming. The planes of darkness whirled past, and shreds of aether tore at his burning flesh until once more Zarak Thuul tumbled into the bleak prison of the Abyss.

All of Thorbardin was illuminated as if it had been opened to the sky on a sunny day. In their cities on the shores of the underground sea the surviving Daewar gazed in awe while the Theiwar and Daergar howled, clasping hands to blinded eyes. Baker Whitegranite, who was the light, continued to expand outward. Knowing he was the tool of the gods and the ancient dragons, he embraced his destiny, spreading across the cool, dark waters of the Urkhan Sea.

When those waters finally took him, Baker accepted his end. The darkness that closed over his head brought him a renewed sense of calm.

And at last, peace.

Epilogue

Tarn had expected that his first daylight in two decades would be painful or, at the very least, uncomfortable to his dark-tuned eyes. Instead, he and Belicia emerged into the Valley of Thanes during the ghostly blue of pre-dawn, with the sight of the sky overhead the most beautiful thing he had ever witnessed.

There were thousands of other dwarves here, Hylar and Aghar and even many Klar, all of whom had escaped the Life-Tree and found their way through the mountain to the surface. This was only a percentage of those who had lived and died in Hybardin, but these dwarves were safe—at least for now.

He and Belicia had walked and crawled for a long time. Sometimes they had been alone, other times with name-less others, all seeking refuge. They had followed instinct and guesswork as they sought escape out of the mountain. And finally they had come here, to the ancient burial grounds of the kingdom, the lofty valley cradled among vastly higher summits.

Tarn was startled as a wild-eyed Klar rose to his feet from behind a nearby rock. The half-breed's hand went to his weapon, but something in the other dwarf's manner held his hand from the instinctive attack.

"What do you want?" he growled, stepping protectively in front of Belicia.

"Here," said the fellow, his gaze flashing between the two refugees. He extended a small object, and Tarn heard the splashing of water. "Drink," suggested the Klar.

"Thank you." At once Tarn noticed that he was terribly thirsty. He uncapped the flask and sniffed the odor of sweet water before taking a small drink. He then passed the drink to Belicia. She took a sip, then he slaked his own thirst before handing it back. "Who are you?" he asked.

"Tufa Bloodeye, thane of the Klar," declared the bedraggled dwarf, allowing a hint of pride to creep into his voice.

Tarn noticed that his eyes were shot through with crimson, so stark and red that they might in fact have been filled with blood.

"We're at peace again, your clan and mine?" asked Tarn hesitantly.

"Peace with you. You Hylar, right?"

"Yes, we're Hylar," Tarn replied. For the first time in his life he felt he really belonged to his father's clan. He and Belicia left Tufa Bloodeye, continuing into the vast valley and looking at the dwarves who were huddled everywhere.

"Did any of the Daergar survive?" asked Belicia numbly. "What about your mother?"

Tarn shook his head sadly. "I doubt it."

"And Regal—or Chisel. What about him?"

Tarn forced a rueful smile. "Him I wouldn't be so sure about."

"What is left of Thorbardin? What do we do now?" asked Belicia, slipping her hand through the crook of his elbow and pulling him close. She was numb and grieving, but her eyes were dry and her chin strong, high, firm.

"The hill dwarves will help us," Tarn said, with more confidence than he felt. "The time for war between the clans has passed."

"And Hybardin—will we go back there some day?"

"Perhaps we shall; certainly our children will."

"Until then, we'll have each each other," his beloved concluded.

And from the sky, low on the horizon after sunset, there came the gleaming twinkle of a lone red star.

NOVELS

Legacy of Steel

An Excerpt

by Mary Herbert

Available November 1998

Sara eventually found Fewmet just outside a tavern. The grimy establishment crouched not far from the ramshackle huts of the little Aghar colony near the city dump. Although not auspicious for human business, most draconians and ogres did not seem to mind the constant stench or the occasional ox-stunning odor that drifted over the area when the wind was right.

The stumpy gully dwarf was sitting on a wooden sidewalk, humming softly to himself and gnawing on a bone. When he saw Sara, he bobbed his head and offered her a shy smile while attempting to stuff the bone into the rags of his shirt.

"I've been looking for you," she said as she squatted down beside the dwarf.

He gazed at her in amazement. "Was I lost?"

"No," she chuckled. "I just didn't know where to find you."

He clutched his bone and glared at her suspiciously.

"Why you look for Fewmet? No one look for gully dwarf."

"I just wanted to thank you for helping me the other night. That was very brave of you."

Fewmet's wrinkled face beamed. "Knight woman nice. Should not feed to horaxes."

Sara laughed. "I was very glad to get out of there."

The gully dwarf hunkered down and glanced both ways before he said, "I hear you fight mean knight who kicks gully dwarves."

"News certainly travels fast around here," Sara observed. "Yes, I challenged him."

"Good. I no like. You remember this: knight have bad knee. I see sometimes. He go to many taverns in city."

Sara's brow drew together in a frown. "I've never noticed that Massard has a limp."

"Not always. He try to walk straight. But knee is weak. Remember when you fight." He wagged a filthy finger at her.

Sara tucked that piece of information away. She expected Massard would choose swords for his weapons, which meant she would have little opportunity to exploit the gully dwarf's information. Still, one never knew when such a tidbit could come in handy.

Ignoring the nasty looks and rude remarks from the draconian customers, she went into the tavern and ordered a bowl of stew, a wedge of cheese, and a honey cake. The barman, when he heard what she was going to do with the food, insisted she pay for the utensils too. Sara shrugged nonchalantly and paid, then carried the food outside to the gully dwarf. The barman had refused to let him eat inside.

Fewmet was delighted. He had never eaten an entire hot meal all by himself. Sara stayed with him, her sword close to hand, just to ensure his safety. Other gully dwarves gathered close to watch enviously, but no one dared bother him while the quiet woman stayed beside him.

He shoveled his food with both hands, licked every utensil clean, and then ate the honey cake in three crumbly bites. Sara watched him, guessing he probably could have scavenged a second meal just by combing his beard. After the meal, she presented the bowl and plate to him as a gift.

Sara solemnly shook the little dwarf's hand before departing. Glancing back, she saw him busily stuffing his new dishes into his bag and humming the same tuneless song.

* * * * *

The appointed day of the duel dawned with the first clear day Neraka had seen in weeks. The sun climbed into a flawless sky and, for the first time in weeks, the cold eased into a bearable cool. By noon the weather was positively balmy for a Nerakan winter. The unexpected warmth brought the crowds to the Arena of Death in droves.

Lately, challenges among the knights had been rare due to the scarcity of officers. So a duel between two of the older knights was cause for much anticipation. The fact that one was a man and the other a woman just made it more interesting. Betting grew heavy, and by noon Massard was the favorite two to one.

In the tents of the Red Quarter, the members of the Sixth Talon hovered around their junior officer until Sara wanted to scream at them. She appreciated their solicitous efforts to feed her and advise her and prepare her for battle, but all she really wanted was a little distance and some quiet to settle her nervousness. Instead Derrick insisted he should polish and sharpen her sword. Saunder had found a mail shirt that fit her and was busy repairing a broken link. Marika fussed over her tea and toasted bread. Kelena polished her boots. And Jacson paced back and forth demonstrating defensive moves that she already knew.

Sara tried to smile graciously, but it soon became so difficult that she finally took her food and weapons into the tent, firmly fastening the flap behind her. The five knights in training exchanged mournful glances and counted the minutes until noon.

In her tent, Sara drank a cup of her tonic for headaches and lay down on her cot to rest.

Knight Officer Massard appeared shortly thereafter, blowing in like a thunderstorm. He stamped around the tents and shouted, "On your feet, you yellow-backed spawn of gully dwarves. You have work to do." He sneered as they jumped to attention. "Yaufre, put that thing down. Conby won't be needing it. Put out that fire! Clean up this mess! What do you think this is, a latrine?"

Sara, still in her tent, decided wisely to stay out of sight. Sometimes discretion was the better part of valor. From his loud voice and ugly behavior, she knew he was trying to lure her out into the open. But this was neither the time nor the place to pick a fight.

Massard charged around, snapping orders like bolts of lightning and punctuating each demand with furious insults. When he was satisfied with the order of the camp, he lined the recruits up before his tent.

"Now that you're finished putting this dump in order," he growled, relishing every word, "you will report to Knight Officer Darcan at the stables. He has some muck for you to rake."

"No! We can't—" Jacson inadvertently cried.

Massard took one step to the young squire. His eyes narrowed to mere slits and before anyone could move, he viciously backhanded the youth across the mouth.

The blow sent Jacson reeling. Cat like, he caught himself before he stumbled into the fire ring and crouched, his hand reaching for his dagger.

"Jacson, no!" Derrick hissed. The bigger youth grabbed his friend's arms and wrestled him back into line.

"Wise," Massard said, his voice full of venom. "Now

move!"

They knew all the pleading in the world would not help. For some reason Massard did not want them to go to the duel with Sara, and his rank prevented them from gainsaying him. They shifted in their places. Jacson's face glowed red with fury, and Marika hunched her shoulders and clenched her fists, ready to strike Massard's sneering face.

"Yes, sir," Derrick said stiffly, forcing his hand to salute his talon leader. He turned to the others and drooped his right eye in a slow wink. His gesture acted as a balm to the others. They understood and relaxed. Angry but resigned, they followed Derrick to the western edge of the tent ring where a large complex of paddocks and stables housed the knights' horses.

Massard watched them go before wrenching off his sword belt and stomping into his tent. Flinging open the flap, he tossed the sword on the rumpled blankets of his cot and was about to leave when something caught his eye. A bottle, a familiar clay bottle with the wax-sealed cork and the maker's mark of his favorite dwarf spirits, sat on the stool near his bed. His mouth went dry. He should not drink, not this close to a duel when he would have to fight for his rank and reputation. The drink always slowed his reflexes and did strange things to his vision.

But why should he worry? The woman he was to face was no knight. She had not trained for twenty years or fought with Lord Ariakan during the glorious summer when the Knights of Takhisis had conquered Ansalon. True, she could handle a sword, but he was certain she would not be able to survive what he had in mind.

His hand reached for the bottle. He pulled the cork and inhaled the earthy fumes with a sigh of pleasure. Without bothering to wonder why a bottle of dwarven spirits had been left in his tent, he tipped the bottle up and let the fiery liquid burn a trail to his stomach.

* * * * *

Sara woke with a start. A noise had disturbed her, a light scratching noise that sounded like nails on fabric. She sat up, dazed, and stared at the dim, yellowish light leaking through the tent walls. She had been doing this all too often since Red Eric's brigands cracked her head. Every time she sat or lay down, she fell asleep.

The scratching came again, louder this time, and the tent material jiggled under the pressure. Someone was at the door.

Sara rose and groggily opened the flap. A goblin face full of obsequious good will, General Abrena's messenger in a filthy tunic and bits of purloined armor peered up at her. She recognized the scent of steaming stew, loaves of bread, and butter.

Suddenly the height of the sun registered in Sara's mind, and she cried, "Oh, no! What time is it?"

The goblin peered upward, wondering what the fuss was about. "It's midday. High sun. General sent me to fetch you. She says almost time."

Rubbing her neck, Sara tried to calm down. She tied her hair back out of her way, picked up her new sword and dagger, and strapped them on. If Massard chose any other weapon, the general would supply one. Sara had no armor to wear—she'd never had more than the basic pieces worn during training, and those were long gone. She slipped on the heavy chain mail Saunder had given to her. It was better than nothing.

She strode outside into the bright sunshine, the goblin at her heels. The camp seemed strangely empty without the squires. Now that the time had come to leave, she missed their noisy support. It was just like Massard's vindictive pettiness to send them on some onerous task instead of letting them witness the duel.

"Has Knight Officer Massard already left?" she asked.

The goblin shrugged his knobby shoulders. "Not in

tent. Must have."

"Good." Sara pulled out her new thong decorated with dragon scale disks.

"You won't need that. I'm right here."

Sara twisted around at the sound of the deep voice and saw Cobalt's horned head lying lazily on the ground beside her tent. The dragon lifted himself off the ground and ambled around beside her. In the noon sun his deep blue scales glowed with a richness all their own.

The goblin yelped and hid behind Sara's legs.

"Would you like a ride to the arena?" Sara asked the goblin in an effort to be polite.

"No," said Cobalt and the goblin in one voice. The goblin scurried off before she could make any more dreadful suggestions.

Cobalt waited while Sara saddled him. The dragon extended his leg so she could climb up to his back. As soon as Sara was settled in the saddle, he thrust off with his powerful hind legs.

Sara was grateful that he did not question the wisdom of her challenge. All she wanted now was a few minutes of quiet. She ran her hand down his long sapphire neck, enjoying the smoothness of his scales beneath her palm. She could feel his life-force surging below the protective scales in a hidden current of power and energy. She was thankful more than she could say that he freely gave her his support and companionship.

The dragon winged over Neraka, past the main gate, the Queen's Way, and the temple ruin. He finally circled over the southeastern side of the city where the Arena of Death sat next to the ex-lord mayor's Playground.

The arena, a remnant of Queen Takhisis's days in the city, was an oval-shaped coliseum used for various bloody entertainments and killing sports. Its attractions were quite popular with Neraka's residents and quite lucrative for officials who charged a few coppers for admission, sold beverages and food, and ran a betting ring. Consequently the lord mayor and now General Abrena made a habit of sponsoring events whenever possible. A duel between two officers was not quite as exciting as watching a mass slaughter of captives by hungry tigers, but there would be enough interest to draw a crowd, especially since the news of Sara's brush with the horaxes had spread throughout the city.

Cobalt circled around to fly over the arena, giving his rider a chance to see it from above. It was no wonder there was talk of repairing the place. It was a wreck. Too many years had passed, too much blood had been spilled in the sands, too many over-enthusiastic fans had trampled the seats or hacked at the stone with their weapons. Broken awnings and railings littered the grounds both inside and out.

This day a fair-sized crowd had gathered in the dilapidated tiers of seats. They cheered when the large blue spread his wings wide and coasted to the sand-covered floor of the arena.

General Abrena, several of her commanding officers from the Order of the Lily, and a Nightlord from the Order of the Skull walked across the sand to meet Sara. Lord Knight Cadrel carried the scepter of the Adjudicator, the knighthood's judge in matters of contention.

Sara had seen duels often enough to know the procedure. She slid down from Cobalt's back, formally saluted the officers, and bowed to the gray-robed Nightlord.

"May Queen Takhisis walk with me this day and guide my efforts in her service," Sarah intoned formally.

"Fight with honor, Knight Warrior," replied the priestess.

Governor-General Abrena frowned over Sara's mail shirt. "You wear no armor," she observed critically.

Sara stood straighter under the heavy mail. "My armor was lost, General. I have not yet been able to replace it."

"And yet you willingly fight a duel in simple mail?" She shook her head at the stupidity of certain knights. "I would prefer to keep you alive, Conby. Knight Officer Massard has not appeared yet; we have time to find you something more suitable than that."

Cobalt suddenly growled deep in his throat. "He comes."

Another ragged cheer rose from the crowd as a lone figure entered the arena at the far end and began to swagger across the open floor to the group of officers. He tripped once but regained his balance and halted in front of Governor-General Abrena. Knight Officer Massard saluted rather crookedly. Abrena's eyes narrowed, her full lips tightening in disapproval as her nose wrinkled suspiciously.

Massard suddenly belched. The reek of spirits on his clothes and breath reached out to them all. The Adjudicator rolled his eyes. The others stifled mingled sounds of disgust and amusement.

"Knight Officer," snapped the general, giving him a withering glare. "You are a disgrace. Where is your pride? In the bottom of some latrine? How dare you show up here to fight a duel of honor in this condition?"

Massard planted his fists on his hips and bellowed belligerently, "What difference does it make? I can fight her on one leg."

"Do you wish to let the challenge stand?" the Adjudicator asked in a hard voice.

"Blast it, yes! What'd ya think I came here for?"

"What weapon do you chose?"

"None." Massard turned his black gaze on Sara. "I'm gonna kill her with my bare hands."

Shocked, the knights began talking among themselves in harsh whispers. Bare-knuckled fighting was not considered an honorable alternative in duels. That sort of brawling was usually relegated to the lowest ranks of mercenaries and draconians.

Sara leaned back against Cobalt and tried to mask her emotions. The thought of fighting a big hulk like Massard with nothing but her fists scared her silly. At least with a sword she would have a chance to wear him down and wound him. This way she wouldn't have a hope.

General Abrena obviously had the same thoughts. She turned her swift glance to Sara and said, "No. Weapons must be chosen. I will not allow the duel for rank to be turned into a street fight."

Massard curled his lip. "Daggers, then. And that dragon must leave. I do not want to be scorched by him when she dies."

"I wouldn't worry about the dragon if I were you," Sara said caustically. "I'd worry about breathing near open flames. Your breath alone could kill an ogre."

The Governor-General held up her hand to stem the gathering tide of insults. "Daggers are acceptable. Knight Warrior Conby, do you desire armor?"

Sara noticed that Massard wore his usual tunic and padded leather vest. "My opponent is not wearing any. I will abide as I am."

The Adjudicator held out his scepter for the crowd to see and shouted for quiet. As soon the audience settled down enough to hear, he continued, "The defender has chosen daggers. So be it. The fight is to the death. Let the dragon withdraw to the limits of the arena."

Whistles and cheers met his announcement. The knights withdrew to the walled seats above the arena floor.

"He may be drunk, but he is strong and wily," Cobalt warned in a soft hiss. "Be careful."

Cobalt gently nudged Sara's arm, and she patted his neck in reply. Sara hooked her sheathed sword to the saddle and lovingly slapped his leg. He leaped up into the stands, crushing a few more wooden rails as he went, and took a precarious perch on the uppermost level of the coliseum where he could see Sara but still be considered at the 'limits of the arena.'

All too quickly the expanse of the arena was empty

except for Massard and Sara. A hush of anticipation settled over the crowd.

The Adjudicator stood on a platform above the sands and shouted, "You may begin."

Massard pulled his lips back in a sneer. Deliberately, he drew his dagger and threw it into the sand. "I want to feel your death with my bare hands," he grunted to Sara.

Sara drew her own dagger, letting its blade shine in the sunlight. "You'll have to catch me first, you drunken lout," she taunted.

Like a bull, Massard roared in anger and charged forward. But the spirits were working deeper into his system and began to interfere with his vision. He suddenly saw two identical women laughing at him, but before he could clasp either one of them, they ducked out of his grasp and ran around behind him. He staggered, caught himself before he fell on his face, and turned clumsily.

Sara looked into his eyes and recognized that unfocused look. Disgusted, she yelled, "Massard, you're a fool!"

The officer charged her again, and once more she slipped out of his reach. She hoped she could exhaust him by taunting him into these thoughtless rushes. As long he could not see her very well, she could easily stay out of his reach. She knew he was strong and heavy and could kill her if he caught her.

They continued this deadly dance back and forth around the arena for some time. Massard's face began to grow flaming red and bathed in sweat. He breathed hard whenever he stopped, his hands clenched at his sides.

Sara was tiring, too. The chain mail felt like a shirt of lead on her chest and shoulders and was becoming very hot. Her bruised ankle ached from the constant turning and twisting; her head had begun to pound.

Massard came at her again, his head lowered, his powerful legs thrusting his weight forward to crush her. This time she waited a fraction of a second longer as he bore down on her and slashed outward with her dagger before turning aside. The blade slid along his leather vest and skittered into the flesh of his upper arm. Sara dropped and rolled away. Blood had been drawn.

The crowd had grown restless during the charge-and-dodge game. Now they roared their approval and stamped their feet, calling for more action.

Massard ignored the wound. It was only superficial, a mere scratch to him. He shook his head and mopped his face with his tunic sleeve. His vision seemed better for the moment. He could once again see one image of Sara.

He sprang for her again, but this time he slowed down and controlled his rush enough to see in which direction she intended to leap away. As she dodged, he pivoted in the same direction and caught her by surprise. His fist swung up and slammed into her midriff. She staggered, wheezing with pain.

Massard punched her again and felt the tremendous satisfaction of his fist connecting with her cheek. The crowd roared with delight.

The impact knocked Sara off her feet. She fell flat on her back, her head ringing and her face feeling as if something had shattered it. The flesh around her eye began to swell. Gasping for breath, she looked up and saw Massard flying through the air to land on top of her. Desperately, she wrenched her body sideways just as he crashed to the sand where she had lain. She managed to scramble upright and put some distance between herself and the knight.

Massard climbed slowly to his feet. Blood trickled down his arm and sand covered his clothes. "Almost," he sneered. "Just lie down—you're good at that. Lie down and I'll kill you quickly."

Sara laughed in spite of the pain in her face. "At least I am good at something. You never were, Massard. Isn't that why Lord Ariakan sent you away? Because you couldn't do anything worth an ogre's spit? Isn't that why you drink yourself into a stupor every day?" She snorted in contempt and finished with, "How did you ever become a knight?"

Massard's roared, his blood burning with fury. He lunged forward to catch her again, but this time instead of trying to punch her in passing, he grabbed for her clothing so he could hold her down. His right hand closed on her upper wrist, and his left caught a fistful of her chain mail. He forced her wrist back until she cried out in pain and dropped the dagger to the sand, dragged her close and pressed his lips to her mouth.

The audience in the seats laughed and cheered him on.

Sara spit in his face. She struggled wildly, trying to break his grip. Realizing that her panicked struggles were accomplishing nothing, she forced her fear back and tried to think. Her son, Steel, had spent hours teaching her methods of self-defense, but she had not practiced them in so long that she had forgotten much. Leverage was everything, he used to say to her. Leverage . . . sparks of memory fired in her mind. Images became clearer. Phrases and words came back to her.

Another little snippet of information swam back into clarity. The gully dwarf had said Massard had a bad knee. It was too bad he had not told her which one.

These thoughts passed rapidly through her mind. In the time it took for Massard to tighten his grip on her chain mail, let go of her wrist, and pull back his fist to punch her in the mouth, she had decided what to try.

She collapsed her knees and dropped to a crouch. Her move took him by surprise and forced his balance forward over his toes. Sara abruptly straightened her legs, driving her shoulder into his stomach. She grabbed his arm and using his forward balance to aid her momentum deftly flipped him over her back. The knight crashed to the ground and lay gasping in the sand.

"Kill him!" The words echoed from one side of the arena to the other. "Kill him!"

Sara groped in the sand for her knife. Massard rolled

over and staggered up. He pulled a second knife, a black stiletto, from his boot and reared back to stab her. Shifting her weight to her arms, Sara lashed out with a booted foot at Massard's left knee, the one she had noticed he favored in the past. Her hunch was right. The force of her blow slammed his knee sideways, and he fell like a stricken ox. His knife dropped to the sand.

But if Sara had hoped he would lie on the ground and groan or nurse his knee, she was disappointed. Massard slipped beyond reason and the limitations of pain. Bellowing with rage, he scrambled over the ground and grabbed her leg.

In that instant, Sara saw her dagger half-buried in the sand just beyond her fingertips. She tried to reach for it only to be wrenched back by a vicious yank to her leg. Her face banged into the arena floor; sand ground into her nose and mouth and tore into her swollen skin. She spat out the sand with a mingled cry of pain and fury.

She twisted around to her back and used her free foot to kick at Massard's head. Her first kick missed, but the second connected solidly with his chin and knocked him backward just enough for his hands to lose their grip on her leg. With all the strength she had left, Sara jerked her leg loose and shoved herself back over to her dagger.

The knight bellowed angrily. He threw himself forward over her, crushing her down into the sand with his greater weight. His hands grabbed for her neck.

She felt his fingers tighten around her throat like a noose. They dug into her skin, cutting off the flow of blood and air to her brain. Her face turned a sickly red, and her lungs burned from lack of air. The pain gripped her like a red-hot iron band around her neck and head. She wanted to scream but could not make a sound.

Terror welled up from the depths of her soul. Almost every fiber in her mind screamed at her to struggle, to fight back, to pry those killing hands off her throat. But a few strands in the cold, reasoning part of her brain held her terror at bay for just a few heartbeats, long enough to give her hand time to reach for the dagger. She felt it still under the small of her back. If she could just get her fingers on it and pull it out, she could get him off.

Massard screamed incoherent oaths at her as he squeezed the life out of her. He paid no attention to her drumming heels or the struggle of her left hand to claw at his face. Nor did he see her right hand worm its way under her back and laboriously pull out the dagger that Derrick had so carefully sharpened to a razor edge.

Somewhere in the far distance Sara heard the murmur of the crowd like the hum of insects. Even fainter, she caught the cry of a dragon. Cobalt she wanted to cry. Cobalt, wait. The noises faded away into the thundering cry of her struggling heart.

Her eyes bulged as the world grew dark. The dagger felt like a bar of lead in her hand. It was so heavy she could barely lift it. She did not waste time trying to aim for a killing stroke; all she wanted to do was get his hands off her neck so she could breathe again. With the last dregs of her failing strength, Sara drove the blade into his side just above his belt.

Massard screeched in pain and twisted around to grab at whatever jabbed his side.

Sara's chest heaved upward in a frantic effort to breathe through her constricted throat. She gasped and coughed as he struggled to pull out the dagger. The blessed air in her lungs brought back her vision and a trickle of energy. The black roar faded from her head.

Massard was weakening. She could feel his body sway. Her nose, free to breath again, caught the odors of sweat and liquor mingled with the metallic tang of blood. He thrashed around so violently that she could not reach her dagger. But she could reach his. The black-handled stiletto lay just an arm's length away.

Her fingers groped for the handle. At that moment, Massard wrenched her dagger free from his side and raised it triumphantly above her, the bloody point aiming for her bruised throat.

Sara gathered the last vestiges of her strength. She closed her fingers around the black stiletto and brought it around and up. The slender blade punctured deep into the knight's stomach and sliced upward behind his breastbone. A look of astonishment slid over his bearded face. He gazed down at the handle protruding from his abdomen as if he could not believe it was there. The dagger in his hand fell out of suddenly nerveless fingers. It clattered off her chain mail and dropped harmlessly to the sand.

Slowly Massard toppled forward on top of Sara. His weight was more than she had the strength to lift.

She sighed once and let the world go dark around her.

THE CROSSROADS SERIES

This thrilling new DRAGONLANCE® series visits famous places in Krynn
in the pivotal period of time after the Fifth Age and before the
War of Souls. New heroes and heroines, related by blood and deed
to the original Companions, struggle to live honorably in a world
without gods or magic, dominated by dark and mysterious evildoers.

THE CLANDESTINE CIRCLE
MARY H. HERBERT
Rose Knight Linsha Majere takes on a dangerous undercover mission for
the Solamnics' Clandestine Circle in the city of Sanction, run by
the powerful Hogan Bight.

THE THIEVES' GUILD
JEFF CROOK
A rogue elf, who may or may not be who he claims, steals a legendary
artifact, makes an enemy of the Dark Knights, and rises and falls inside
the Thieves' Guild in Palanthas.

DRAGON'S BLUFF
MARY H. HERBERT
Ulin Majere and his companion Lucy travel to Flotsam and battle against a
dragon terrorizing the local populace.

CLASSICS SERIES

THE INHERITANCE
Nancy Varian Berberick

The companions of Tanis Half-Elven knew of their friend's tragic heritage—how
his mother was ravaged by a human bandit and died from grief.
But there was more to the story than anyone knew.

Here at last is the story of the half-elf's heritage: the tale of a captive elven princess,
a merciless human outlaw, a proud elven prince, the power of love, and how
tragedy can change a life forever.

THE CITADEL
Richard A. Knaak

Against a darkened cloud it comes, soaring over the ravaged land: the flying citadel,
mightiest power in the arsenal of the dragon highlords. An evil wizard has
discovered a secret that may bring all of Ansalon under his control, and it's up
to a red-robed mage, a driven cleric, a kender, and a grizzled war veteran to
stop him before it's too late.

DALAMAR THE DARK
Nancy Varian Berberick

Magic runs like fire through the blood of Dalamar Argent, yet his heritage denies
him its use. But as war threatens his beloved Silvanesti, Dalamar will seize the
forbidden power and begin a quest that will lead him to a dark and uncertain future.

MURDER IN TARSIS
John Maddox Roberts

Who killed Ambassador Bloodarrow? In a city where everyone is a suspect, time
is running out for an unlikely trio of detectives. If they fail to solve the mystery,
their reward will be death.

New characters, strange magic, wondrous creatures.

**ADVENTURE THROUGH THE HISTORY OF KRYNN
WITH THESE THREE NEW SERIES!**

THE BARBARIANS

PAUL THOMPSON & TONYA CARTER COOK

Follow a divided brother and sister as they lead rival tribes of
plainsmen amidst the wonders and dangers of ancient Krynn.

Volume One: *Children of the Plains*
Volume Two: *Brother of the Dragon*
August 2001

THE ICEWALL TRILOGY

DOUGLAS NILES

Journey with an exiled elf to the harsh, legendary land known as Icereach,
where human tribes battle for life and ogres search to reclaim lost glories.

Volume One: *The Messenger*
February 2001

THE KINGPRIEST TRILOGY

CHRIS PIERSON

Discover for the first time the dynastic history of the Kingpriest
and how his religious-political rule of Istar influenced the world
of DRAGONLANCE® for generations to come.

Volume One: *Chosen of the Gods*
November 2001